Praise for *So*

"Buckle up, horror fans! *Soulless* is one
you-out, irresistible read, pitting fierce sp
unleashing ravenous zombies on their on
unlikely and imperfect heroes—running from and into the heart of the apocaypse—had me in its grasp from start to 2 a.m. finish. Then I checked outside my windows and left the lights on."

—Cynthia Leitich Smith, author of *Tantalize*

More praise for Christopher Golden and his chilling horror novels

"*Wildwood Road* is a brilliant novel of supernatural suspense that reminded me of the early classics by Ira Levin—think *Rosemary's Baby* and you won't be disappointed. There's no baby, but oh baby, there is one creepy little lost girl that kept me turning the pages long after I should have gone to bed. This one's a keeper."

—Stephen King

"Golden is one of the most hard-working, smartest, and talented writers of his generation . . . Everything he writes glows with imagination."

—Peter Straub

This title is also available as an eBook

"I love a good scary story, but scares alone are not enough to carry a book; a good horror novel needs to be a good novel first, with a strong plot, interesting characters, and vivid and evocative writing. Golden delivers all of that in spades in *Wildwood Road,* the best ghost story I have read since . . . well, since the last time Stephen King wrote one."

—George R. R. Martin

"Golden remains someone to watch."

—*Publishers Weekly*

SOULLESS

CHRISTOPHER GOLDEN

New York London Toronto Sydney

Pocket Books
A Division of Simon & Schuster, Inc.
1230 Avenue of the Americas
New York, NY 10020

This book is a work of fiction. Names, characters, places, and incidents either are products of the author's imagination or are used fictitiously. Any resemblance to actual events or locales or persons, living or dead, is entirely coincidental.

First MTV Books/Pocket Books trade paperback edition October 2008

POCKET and colophon are registered trademarks of Simon & Schuster, Inc.

For information about special discounts for bulk purchases, please contact Simon & Schuster Special Sales at 1-800-456-6798 or business@simonandschuster.com.

Designed by Jamie Kerner

Manufactured in the United States of America

10 9 8 7 6 5 4 3 2 1

Library of Congress Cataloging-in-Publication Data

Golden, Christopher.
Soulless / Christopher Golden.—1st MTV Books/Pocket Books trade paperback ed.
p. cm.
Summary: The attempt of three powerful mediums to open up communication between the living and the dead has disastrous consequences when every corpse within a three-hundred-mile radius of New York City is animated and begins to prey on the living.
[1. Spitualism—Fiction. 2. Supernatural—Fiction. 3. Fathers and daugthers—Fiction. 4. Horror stories.] I. Title.
PZ7.G5646So 2008
[Fic]—dc22 2008012695

ISBN-13: 978-1-4165-5135-5
ISBN-10: 1-4165-5135-2

For Steve Volk, who woke the ghosts.

ACKNOWLEDGMENTS

Massive thanks to my excellent editor, Jennifer Heddle, who kept it lean and mean. To Jennifer Echols and everyone at the MTV Books blog. To Alex McAulay for kind words and good vibes. As always, love and gratitude to my wife, Connie, and our children, and to the usual suspects, who know who they are. Finally, thanks to the amazing Allie Costa, for her support and enthusiasm and her Herculean efforts.

SOULLESS

1

Manhattan, New York City

Curtains of punishing rain fell upon the sea of dark umbrellas populating the Manhattan sidewalks, commuters hurrying to get to work on time. From the tenth-floor studio, Times Square looked like a massive, sprawling funeral. The sky above the city hung low and black, a shroud of storm.

"Perfect weather for talking to the dead," Phoenix whispered, staring out through the plate-glass window.

"What's that?"

She leaned her forehead against the glass. *Well done. Talking to yourself always helps.* For a second, she'd forgotten she wasn't alone in the room. Phoenix turned around and smiled at Katie Phelan, whose job, apparently, was to take care of whoever was in the Green Room waiting to go on the set of *Sunrise,* the network's morning news show.

"Why do you call it the Green Room?" she asked, ignoring Katie's question.

The woman—at most four years older than Phoenix's eighteen, though her shortish dark hair made her look younger—seemed perplexed. "Any time you're on a talk show, or in a play or something, the room where you wait before you go on is the Green Room."

Phoenix smiled. "Yeah, but *why* is it called the Green Room? The room's not even green."

The lower half of the walls was lavender, the upper half an off-white. There were a trio of love seats in muted colors, a quartet of armchairs that were too fancy for a dentist's waiting room but not quite plush enough for anyone to buy them for their living room, and an entire symphony of end tables, coffee tables, and floor lamps. Snack bowls dotted the tables and an oblong window opened into a tiny bar area, which was dark at the moment. Nobody was going to be mixing Phoenix a drink, but there was a tall, glass-front cooler full of sodas, juices, and flavored waters beside the bar, and one of those little machines that made the perfect single cup of whatever coffee, tea, or hot chocolate beverage you wanted.

Nothing at all green, unless you counted some of the M&M's in the bowl on a round table beside her chair.

Glancing around, entirely mystified, Katie gave her a small smile and a shrug. "I don't have a clue. Never thought about it, really. Anyway, look, your father and the others are getting settled. They'll be doing the intro in a couple of minutes. Do you want to take your seat in the audience now?"

Phoenix actually had to think about that. She had never been entirely comfortable with her father's work. Did she want to sit in the audience and experience it with a bunch of strangers or watch from backstage, where she didn't have to hide her skepticism?

"Are they believers out there?" she asked.

Katie glanced at the door as though she could see through it with Supergirl X-ray vision. *Sunrise* had just finished its first hour. Local affiliates would be doing their headlines and forecasts right now. The second hour of the morning news show was scheduled to be devoted entirely to the conversation about death and spiritualism and ghosts that the presence of her father and his colleagues always prompted.

"A lot of them," Katie replied. "And the rest are mostly folks who'd like to believe."

Phoenix hesitated, then nodded. "All right. Lead the way. Beats hanging around in the Lavender Room, I guess."

Katie gave a soft laugh, then opened the door, gesturing for Phoenix to precede her. Together they strode down a corridor busy with production assistants fetching coffees, and sound and camera people hurrying back from the bathroom. Phoenix played it off like none of it was a big deal, but found herself quietly fascinated. She'd watched enough behind-the-scenes stuff on television to know that making a movie or TV series could be total chaos. But the beehive buzz backstage at *Sunrise* made her head spin.

Her parents had intended this summer as an opportunity for Phoenix to get to know her father better. They had divorced seven years ago, and Phoenix had continued living with her mother in the Alexandria, Virginia, house she'd grown up in. But even before the divorce, her dad had never been around much. When he wasn't teaching at Georgetown University, he was doing research or writing articles and books. Phoenix had a lot of sweet childhood memories of playing with her toys on the floor of her father's home office while he worked, or climbing up into his big leather chair whenever he vacated it. But hindsight rendered those memories bitter. In truth, he'd rarely worked out of his home office, and when he did, it still meant that work ranked higher than his daughter on his priority list.

In high school, she'd had tons of friends whose parents were divorced, and a lot of those situations were seriously nasty. Booze and drugs, torrid affairs, and abuse were among the highlights. Kendra Parker's father had gone to prison for attempted murder after beating her mother so badly she was blind in one eye, and rumor had it Aaron Stack's mom had been having sex with members of the hockey team at her own son's school.

So Joe Cormier didn't pay enough attention to his wife and daughter—boo-hoo. Nobody would cry for Phoenix, and she didn't do a lot of crying for herself. But in the quiet places of her heart, she wished that he had been a different kind of man, and that he and her mother, Mary, had never fallen out of love. She wished that her father had never been a medium or started writing about his theories about ghosts, making it so easy for people to label him a fraud or a nut job.

In the years since the divorce, Phoenix had usually spent one weekend a month staying with her father—when he didn't forget and completely screw up the plans—but in that time she'd gotten to know his colleagues better than she did her dad. At the university, they loved him and thought him eccentric, and they always doted on Phoenix. And when they spent time with other mediums, as odd as some of them were, even those people didn't seem as distant as her father.

But this year something had shifted in him.

From the first time they'd spoken about it, he'd actually seemed happy with the idea of her spending the summer with him. Maybe Joe Cormier had finally woken up to the fact that his baby girl wouldn't be playing with her toys on the floor of his office anymore, that once she went off to Boston College, everything would be different. Phoenix wanted to think that he had realized how much he had taken for granted and how much time he had wasted over the years.

In the last couple of months, he'd talked to her more than he ever had before, telling her stories about his childhood and his life and his work. Not that her dad had completely changed. He still became lost in his thoughts, and when preparing for events on his book tour he was still totally focused on his work, but he seemed different now, as though he kept reminding himself to include her, surfacing long enough to talk.

Phoenix should have been happy. She knew that.

But eighteen years of resentment and disappointment could not be erased with the snap of a finger. And hard as it would be for him to accept—and much as it made her want to scream—he'd woken up too late. All that he had withheld from her could never be regained. Her childhood was over.

Whatever the future held, the best they could hope for would be to build a new relationship, father and adult daughter. Phoenix did not know if she would ever really forgive him. But this time together was a start, no matter how many ghost hunters and whack jobs and snide debunkers she had to watch her father debate along the way. So now they were trying to define what their relationship would be, right in the midst of her father's promotional tour for his new book.

Katie led her to an industrial-looking set of double doors with windows set into each and a green bulb glowing above them. The production assistant slid past Phoenix, pushed through the door, and held it open for her.

At first glance, the studio reminded her of some of the talk shows she'd seen, or some of the more intimate off-Broadway theaters where she'd attended performances. But instead of hardwood and cobwebs, this place was all tech and cables and bland modern design. There was only enough seating in the audience for 150 or so, all arranged with a view of several different sets, including a news desk, a platform with tall black bar stools on it, and a homey-looking interview area. The backgrounds of each set were as fake as the walls in a corporate cubicle, but the cameras would never pick up the edges, zeroing in only on what they wanted the home viewers to see.

A smile tweaked the edges of her lips. Wasn't that almost exactly what her father was always talking about? People only saw what they wanted to see. Perception was limited. But television made it simpler, limiting perceptions even before the human mind's natural inclination to edit its experiences kicked into gear. Most people didn't want to see what was beyond the frame of their perception.

That might be nothing but bullshit. Phoenix wasn't sure. But after hanging out with her father on a regular basis the past couple of months, she knew that he certainly believed it.

"You're in the third row," Katie said, leading her along behind the cameras toward the center aisle. "I hope that's all right."

Phoenix almost laughed. She'd flown first class only once, when she and her mom had been bumped from an earlier flight and been upgraded, but this felt similar to her. For the duration of the time her father would be in the studio as a guest on *Sunrise,* she'd be treated as though she was special. But she knew if she and her father came back tomorrow, they'd be handled no differently than the rest of the public.

"It's fine," she said.

Katie showed her to her place, the fourth seat from the aisle, and then rushed off to whatever other duties awaited her. People looked at Phoenix as she sat down and she felt herself blushing a bit at the attention. She didn't meet anyone's eyes, turning her focus entirely toward the set.

Soft music played on the speakers in the studio. The hosts were having their makeup touched up and a flurry of people moved around them, checking their hair and microphones. The woman was Amy Tjan, who'd been on the U.S. Olympic volleyball team once upon a time. From what Phoenix remembered of the gossip sites, Amy Tjan had grown up in Hawaii and gone to some Ivy League school. The blond guy with the perfect hair, on the other hand, she'd only vaguely heard of before today. His name was Steve Bell and he wore a serious expression, like he was actually on camera at the moment. She wondered if his face ever changed.

Phoenix glanced at her father, the picture of academic authority with his graying beard and glasses and the tan sport jacket—with a hint of green—she'd helped him pick from his closet the day before. He'd wanted to wear a tie, but Phoenix had vetoed the idea. Joe Cormier looked about as casual as he ever got, and handsome enough. He'd had dates, Phoenix knew, but never seemed to have time for romance. Big surprise. Her mother had dated as well, and been through several boyfriends over the years, but never found one she wanted to marry.

Her father had a very light complexion, but dark hair and dark eyes. Phoenix favored her mother, people always said, and as she got older she saw the resemblance more and more in the mirror. Her brown hair—which she experimented with regularly but currently wore shoulder-length—framed her round face, and she had her mother's green eyes. At forty-six, her mother looked at least a decade younger, and Phoenix hoped she'd inherit that as well.

Her father sat with his colleagues on a sofa on the interview set, which was apparently meant to look like someone's living room. The makeup and microphone people were hovering around them as well, along with a twentysomething guy who had one of those carefully groomed stubble-beards. It worked for some guys, but not for him. Stubble Boy had a clipboard and was deep in conversation with Annelise, a fifty-seven-year-old woman from Austria who just happened to be able to talk to the dead. Phoenix had met her several times over the years, but in the past few months they'd had more opportunities to get to know each other. The community of mediums who took one another's work seriously was quite small.

To Phoenix, ghosts had always been things in storybooks. Mediums were charlatans and TV heroines, or, even better, tabloid whores who claimed to talk to the spirits of Elvis and JFK. But Annelise had graying auburn hair and crinkly, smiling eyes, made the world's best hot chocolate, and had a filthy sense of humor. She barely talked about spirits unless someone else brought it up first. Phoenix had the impression that what others called her gift just made her sad.

If mediums were charlatans, then what was Annelise?

Aside from her "gift," she seemed so ordinary, just like Phoenix's father. God, was he ordinary. Though she'd never sat in on one of his lectures, if his talks about spiritualism were any indication, she figured they must be incredibly boring. How anyone could make a subject as controversial as life after death boring was beyond her, but her father had such a dry sincerity that he could make her eyes cross. Yet in private he had a wit just as dry and could make her laugh with his sarcasm, even when she didn't want to.

And most of the time, she *really* didn't want to.

They had issues, Phoenix and her dad. But that was what spending this time together was all about.

"Two minutes to air!" shouted a woman with a headset, holding up two fingers.

Nobody hurried, but Phoenix didn't think it was because they weren't listening to the woman, who must have been a producer or something. They all just seemed to know their jobs. Cameras were gliding into place. Lights went on, illuminating the living room interview set. The chairs for the two hosts were still empty, but all three mediums sat up a bit straighter under the bright lights.

Annelise and her father sat on the sofa together. In a chair to their left, Eric Honen took a breath, leaned back, and arranged himself to look like he was hanging out in his own home. Phoenix rolled her eyes, watching him lift his chin *just so*. The kid was her age and disgustingly good-looking, with olive skin, black hair, and Mediterranean features. It wouldn't have bothered her—after all, Phoenix had no objection to good-looking guys—if his arrogance wasn't so obvious. Her father and Annelise insisted that his gifts were as real as their own, but Eric didn't take their sober, academic approach to the work. He said he wanted to help people. Said all the right things, in fact. But the ambition simmered around him like heat from a roaring blaze. The kid wanted to be a star.

Scratch that. He wanted to be a celebrity. The two had become very different things. You didn't have to be a star of anything, or *at* anything, to be a celebrity. It was all about getting the camera on you and keeping it on you, no matter the cost. He might have been eighteen, but he had the temperament of a twelve-year-old.

Eric was about to get his biggest opportunity yet to fulfill that ambition. All three of the mediums had been on television before, but never together, and never with something as majorly audacious as what they had planned for today. An hour of America's second-favorite morning show devoted to the largest séance in the history of the world. Her father's agent had told Phoenix the network anticipated enormous ratings, even though no one expected the plan to actually work. Even the agent himself was on the fence. He believed in his commission and had total faith in anything that would pay him ten percent. As far as Phoenix knew, the only three people in the world who believed the séance would work were the mediums themselves.

For her part, she withheld judgment. Her father was an intelligent, rational man, but Phoenix held on to doubt because the alternative—that it was all true—scared the crap out of her.

"One minute to air!" the headset woman shouted, one finger raised.

At the signal, the house lights went down and the stage lights brightened. Stubble Boy smiled reassuringly at Annelise and gave Eric and Professor Cormier the thumbs-up before scurrying off camera.

Amy Tjan and Steve Bell strolled casually onto the faux living room set and took their seats, perching on the edge of the chairs so as not to rumple their expensive wardrobe.

Phoenix smiled, surprised to realize that she was excited. Her dad had been on television before, but she'd never gone along with him. Dry as he could be, he did love to have a willing audience.

Headset Woman—who Phoenix assumed was some kind of producer—called out the ten-second mark. But when the ten seconds had elapsed, instead of going straight to the hosts, all of the monitors began showing a prerecorded segment that included clips from old horror movies and documentaries about ghosts. The voice-over belonged to Amy Tjan, but the woman herself was adjusting her clip-on microphone and smoothing her skirt.

"Death haunts us all," the voice-over narration declared. "But it intrigues us as well. Medical science spends billions every year trying to keep us alive a little longer. We argue over the existence of ghosts, but polls show that most Americans believe in the spirit and in some form of life after death."

The thin, stylish, middle-aged woman to Phoenix's left leaned toward her. "Do you believe any of this stuff?"

Phoenix offered her a noncommittal smile, not daring to answer just in case she was overheard. If someone recognized her as Professor Joe Cormier's daughter and repeated what she said, it might embarrass her father. That was a hard lesson, one that she had first learned at the age of twelve, when she'd told a friend's mother that she thought the ghosts were all in her father's head. It hadn't been long before her comments had been spread to every parent in the school. As cool as her own mom felt toward her father in those days—a year after the divorce—she'd been the one to tell Phoenix that people were talking. Though her father's beliefs sometimes embarrassed her, she had been ashamed that she had humiliated him.

From then on, she had been careful with her words.

"We ask all of the questions, but no one wants to discover the answers firsthand," the voice-over continued. "We grieve for lost loved ones, but what really happens to those who cross over, the spirits who've gone on to the other side? For a proper farewell, for comfort, or seeking knowledge, most of us would give anything to talk to them again, just for a minute.

"What if you could?"

Headset Woman kept well behind the cameras as she raised a hand to cue the hosts, as if they needed cueing after that intro. Amy put on her TV smile, which was pretty convincing, but Steve Bell looked as grimly serious as ever, like this whole subject had him thinking profound thoughts.

"That's the question for the next hour, America," Amy said to the camera. "We'll be spending it with three of the country's most renowned mediums, talking about ghosts, spirits, life after death, and presenting the first-ever live interactive séance that you can participate in from home."

Phoenix winced. When she said it like that, it sounded like an infomercial.

Steve Bell nodded. "You never know what the new day's going to bring on *Sunrise*. Let's meet our guests."

2

One by one, Steve Bell introduced the mediums and they went into the usual TV happy chat about how the hosts were glad to have them on *Sunrise* and the guests were happy to be there. Everyone was so freakin' happy. Phoenix fought against the urge to roll her eyes. It was TV. People talked about Disney World being the place where everyone was happy, but morning news shows came in second. No matter how hideous the news of the day might be, the moment the last word of bad news had been delivered, the smiles always returned.

Except for Steve Bell. His job was to be the serious one.

"Professor Cormier, you've recently released a new book, *Soul Versus Spirit,*" said Serious Steve. "I've read it and I have to say, some of your theories are incredibly innovative. In the introduction, you talk about the twin essence of humanity. Could you explain that for the audience?"

Don't do it, Dad, Phoenix thought. *Not the glasses. Don't—*

Too late. Professor Cormier reached up and adjusted the way his glasses sat on the bridge of his nose. It gave him the brainy air of a scientist from some old movie; totally uncool. How many times had she reminded him? Hundreds, but old habits were hard to break.

"There are some ancient philosophers who posited a similar theory, but in layman's terms," the professor began, and Phoenix figured half the audience was asleep already, "I believe that humanity is made up of three components: flesh, soul, and spirit."

Amy Tjan seized on that. "Is that a reflection of the Christian belief in the Trinity of Father, Son, and Holy Spirit?"

The professor blinked. "Not at all. Though the theory is predicated on the existence of some kind of afterlife, let's put aside focusing on any one religion. The point is that we have our bodies, and we have the divine spark that some believe is eternal. The soul. I believe the third component, the spirit, is actually the energy generated by our thoughts and experiences, by personality and will. Energy cannot be destroyed, only changed. The body dies. The soul returns to its divine source—whatever that may be—but the spirit is separate. When we experience paranormal phenomena, whether it be sightings of ghosts or a medium's contact with the dead, I believe we are encountering not soul but spirit, that sometimes the persona of the deceased individual lingers in this world."

Serious Steve looked out at the audience, careful to take in the camera at the same time. "So you do believe in ghosts."

"After a fashion. They're more like echoes of who we are in life, like a spiritual skin our souls have molted before moving on. They have identity, and can communicate, but they are not the core of *us.*"

"Interesting," Amy said, leaning forward. "Eric, Ms. Hirsch, do you agree with Professor Cormier's theory?"

Annelise seemed about to reply, but Eric cut in. The kid had been antsy, waiting for the spotlight. Now he meant to grab it.

"To a point, I guess," the kid said. He unfolded himself from the chair and spread his arms, drawing all eyes to him. "It makes a lot of sense if you think about it. If the soul is pure, it's not going to go on to the afterlife burdened by ordinary human concerns."

He smiled and shrugged, doing his best to be self-deprecating. "I mean, okay, I know, I'm the kid here. I haven't been speaking about my gift publicly very long. But I've been talking to the dead since I can remember. Since I was born, maybe even before—"

"Before?" Amy Tjan asked, frowning.

Eric paused. He'd succeeded. Suddenly the interview was about him. "I had a twin who died while my mother was pregnant. She nearly lost both of us. I've often wondered if that had anything to do with my becoming a medium. It isn't something you choose, you know?"

Annelise's expression became grim. "No one would choose it."

"Why is that?" Steve Bell asked. He seemed to have seized on her words, enjoying the opportunity to jettison lighthearted chat for darker subjects.

Annelise arched an eyebrow. "Would you like to have the restless dead pestering you day and night, hoping to get messages through to their loved ones or simply to complain about the injustice of their deaths?"

"I see what you mean."

"And what about you, Ms. Hirsch?" Amy said. "Your thoughts on the professor's theory?"

The older woman glanced at the professor and gave a kind of half-smile. "To be honest, I didn't require much convincing. It set me at ease to be able to separate my own religious beliefs from my experiences with the dead. Spirits are often sad and lonely, though I've also known them to be joyful and supportive. But sometimes they are cruel and vindictive. If spirits are only our personalities—our minds, really—without any trace of a soul . . . well, I prefer to think of them that way."

Eric leaned forward and put his hand on the arm of the sofa. "You've heard of astral projection, where the mind supposedly leaves the body and travels psychically? Think of it like that. The mind isn't the physical brain. It's who we are inside. What Professor Cormier calls the spirit."

"So you do agree?" Steve asked, lasering in on Eric.

The kid blinked. For once, he seemed stumped. Then he smiled. "Like I said, I'm the kid in this game. To me they're ghosts. They need someone to listen, someone to help them make a connection to the world they left behind. I'll let someone else argue the science and the theology. I just want to be here for them."

He sat back in his chair, smugly satisfied with himself. Phoenix wanted to hit him.

"It isn't a game," her father said.

"What was that, Professor?" Amy Tjan asked.

He glanced at Annelise, who nodded. Then he narrowed his eyes and looked directly at the camera. "It isn't a game. That's a figure of speech. I don't want anyone thinking that any of us feel this is a game."

Nobody looked at Eric. To his credit, the kid imitated Steve Bell's serious face and just nodded.

"Absolutely," Amy Tjan said.

"So, with your differing backgrounds," Steve said, "how did the three of you end up getting together?"

The mediums discussed their initial introductions, explaining that they had known one another by reputation and then crossed paths at various events until, at a paranormal lecture series where all three were appearing, Annelise Hirsch had made an idle suggestion that had stopped Professor Cormier and Eric in their tracks.

"It's a shame we can't just help them all at once, just open up the lines of communication between the living and the dead for a few minutes. Then the spirits could rest, and maybe we could, just for a while."

Annelise recounted her suggestion to the hosts and audience and home viewers of *Sunrise.*

"A mass séance," Serious Steve said, trying to be helpful.

"Exactly," Phoenix's father said. "But more so."

"In a séance," Eric interrupted, "people want to speak to the spirit of someone they love who's died. Other times, the medium locates a living person at the request of a restless spirit. Sometimes the spirits speak through us, or else they'll communicate in other ways. On rare occasions, they're strong enough to make themselves heard, even to people who aren't sensitive to that kind of thing. What we're doing today throws all that out the window."

Annelise cleared her throat, silencing him. "My suggestion was not serious. But my colleagues took it quite seriously. We all have our guides, spirits who have taken an interest in us because of our gifts and who help to be *our* voices in the spirit world, just as we offer to be the voices of the dead in this one. Professor Cormier suggested that . . . well, you explain it, Joe."

Phoenix smiled. She didn't know what she believed, but she knew that if this crazy stunt actually worked, her father should get the credit.

"For the past two months," Joe Cormier told Amy and Serious Steve and the *Sunrise* audience, "all three of us have been working with our spirit guides, who in turn have been, well, traveling the hereafter, I suppose, and gathering up all of the restless spirits in the northeast, letting them know that this opportunity was going to come. Today, if things have gone as planned, they're organized, and they're waiting."

Amy Tjan visibly shuddered. So did the woman next to Phoenix who didn't believe in ghosts.

"Waiting for what?" Amy asked.

Professor Cormier smiled. "Why, waiting for this, of course. To talk to those they left behind."

"Exactly!" Eric said, excited. "See, the spirits who are strong enough can manifest visibly or can make their voices heard, even from the other side. But with the three of us working together, and with our guides, if the spirits help each other, lend each other strength, we think they can all make themselves heard so they can make amends or say good-bye."

Serious Steve grew more serious still. "Even to people who haven't asked to talk to the dead?"

"Even to people who don't believe in any of this," Annelise said.

Now even Phoenix shuddered. The whole studio seemed to have grown colder.

Amy Tjan looked out at the audience, and at the camera. "Well, what do you think? You can take our online poll during this break."

"And when we return," Steve Bell said, "the world's biggest séance begins. We'll be right back."

Headset Woman held up one hand, counted on her fingers from three down to zero, and then gave a signal to let them know they were off air. Phoenix saw Amy Tjan let out a breath and smile, shaking herself. She was definitely creeped out. Serious Steve looked like he could have been reporting on the stock market.

The audience didn't seem to exhale. A few snatches of conversation rippled around her, but they were strangely quiet, just waiting. They'd been promised the incredible, the secrets of the dead, answers to questions they all had but were almost always afraid to ask.

Nobody would be changing the channel now. If anything, people would be calling and texting their friends to turn on *Sunrise*.

Phoenix exhaled and glanced around. Most of the audience still stared at the three mediums on their cozy living room set, but a cute guy in the front row and a few seats to her right had other interests. Phoenix caught him looking at her. She smiled curiously. When he returned the smile, she looked away, a picture of him in her mind. Yep, cute guy. A wild thatch of brown hair and bright blue eyes. They might have been contact lenses, but she didn't think so. He was interesting-looking, so Phoenix risked another glance at him. He'd turned away but seemed to sense her attention and shot her a quick look. Again, she broke eye contact.

The silent flirt was always entertaining.

She focused on the set again. The hosts and mediums were standing and the stage crew was removing the chairs and sofa. Other guys lugged a round table onto the set and then set up chairs around it, the living room becoming a dining room. Stubble Boy waved his clipboard at them and then muttered toward Phoenix's father, Eric, and Annelise to take positions around the table. Amy Tjan sat down on Professor Cormier's right and Serious Steve on his left. Five chairs around the table, ready for the séance.

"We're back in thirty!" Headset Woman called.

Soon she was ticking off the final ten seconds with her fingers. The hosts faced the cameras. Amy Tjan gave a quick recap to let anyone just tuning in know what they were up to and then glanced at Serious Steve.

"You know what I love about this show, Amy?" he said. "We never know what the day will bring. If you'd told me a month ago I'd be taking part in a mass séance, I'd never have believed it. But here we are, and I admit I'm kind of excited."

He didn't sound excited. In fact, he sounded the same way he always sounded—serious and professional.

"Me, too," Amy said, glancing into the camera. "So let's get to it. No more delay. The spirits have been waiting long enough, according to Professor Cormier."

She tucked a lock of black silk hair behind one ear and glanced at Phoenix's father, expecting some kind of reply. He just looked impatient.

"They certainly have, Amy," Eric jumped in, saving the moment from awkwardness. "I guess it's time to get started."

Professor Cormier nodded. "All right. If everyone would join hands."

They did as asked, with Amy Tjan mugging a bit for the camera to show she was nervous and Serious Steve looking grimmer than ever. Phoenix felt her muscles tense.

"Annelise, if you'd begin," her father said.

The Austrian woman closed her eyes. "Close your eyes, my friends. And all of you in the audience, please be silent. Their voices should be loud today, but it's better we not be distracted."

Eyes closed, Phoenix's father chimed in. "What we're attempting to create here today is something different, a new way for the spirits to speak. Instead of being their voices, we'll work with our spirit guides, making a circuit that will become an amplifier, a way to broadcast the voices of the departed into the world they've left behind."

Eric's head tipped back. Phoenix felt sure that anyone studying his face would have seen the change in him. He wasn't *on* anymore. His whole body seemed to have gone slack.

"It's okay, Bonnie," the kid said, his voice soft and tender, totally unlike the person he put on for the audience. "I'm back. Are you there? Are they with you?"

Annelise's eyes fluttered open, rolled back to the whites. One of the cameramen focused on her. Headset Woman pointed, making sure that everyone saw. Annelise began speaking in German, the only recognizable word the name Sebastian.

Bonnie. Sebastian. Their spirit guides. Just as Mrs. LaVallee was Professor Cormier's guide. Phoenix's father had written quite a bit about the old woman and those writings had garnered a lot of attention. Most mediums had guides who were the ghosts of people who'd lived so long ago that no one could confirm their existence. But Mrs. LaVallee had been a teacher at the elementary school Joe Cormier had attended. She'd died in the 1950s, just a few years before Phoenix's father had been born. Those who'd spoken to Mrs. LaVallee through Joe Cormier had either been convinced of his claims, or so adamant in their rejection of them that it was hard not to assume they were simply too afraid to believe.

"Mrs. LaVallee," her father said now, his voice a reedy whisper. "Excellent. She's gathered as many as would come. The others have done the same. There are . . . oh . . ."

Annelise began to tremble, clutching the hands of those beside her. "There are so many."

"Son of a bitch," Eric rasped.

The audience should have reacted. Or the crew. Phoenix blinked. It wasn't the sort of language network morning shows approved of. But no one said a word. The whole building seemed to be holding its breath.

"What was that?" Steve Bell asked.

Amy Tjan frowned, eyes still closed. She seemed to be concentrating hard, as though she wanted the *cameras* to see how much focus she was putting into the moment. But Serious Steve opened his eyes and looked around, and though Phoenix could scarcely believe it, he looked afraid.

"Did anyone else feel something?" he asked.

When no one replied, he closed his eyes again. Seconds passed in silence. At home, Phoenix thought maybe some people would change the channel after all. On-screen, it must have looked as though nothing at all was happening. Would those people at home—the soccer moms folding laundry and the teenagers on summer break just getting up—would they see the way the muscles in Steve Bell's neck tensed? Would they notice the way Eric had started breathing in short bursts and shivering?

Phoenix swallowed. She glanced over at the cute guy in the first row, but he had no interest in her now. His attention was entirely on the séance. Phoenix wanted to go back to the Green Room. The Lavender Room. She wanted to tell her father enough was enough, but she stared at his face now and she thought, *Daddy's not here at the moment, try back later*. Because his face was slack. His glasses had slid down the bridge of his nose and despite his compulsion, he did not so much as reach a finger to push them up.

Someone coughed in the audience.

"Jesus, it's cold," muttered a woman to her husband a few rows back.

Cameramen and members of the stage crew looked around nervously at one another. Headset Woman seemed unsure what to do for the very first time. Stubble Boy started walking toward her for a quick conference, and even as he did, he unconsciously rubbed his hands together.

It *was* cold.

"Gotta be some kind of trick," the skeptic beside Phoenix whispered, but her tone made it clear she wanted, needed it to be a trick.

Professor Cormier exhaled and his breath plumed with cold mist.

Phoenix stared at her father. For the first time in her life, she felt a little spark of fear for him. What the hell was going on? If this was all some kind of setup that the producers of the show had arranged to engage viewers, she didn't know whether she'd be relieved or pissed.

The audience started muttering. They'd been mesmerized, but now they were starting to freak out a little. People complained about the temperature. Some were afraid and others were annoyed. But not everyone was talking. Some were shushing others, trying to pay attention to what was happening on set. On camera.

"Amy?" Headset Woman called.

Phoenix held her breath, a fist clenching inside her chest. That wasn't supposed to happen. Headset Woman wouldn't interrupt the show. The hosts had earpieces through which they would hear prompts from the producers. The only reason for Headset Woman to talk was if Amy wasn't replying to those prompts.

Headset Woman gestured to Stubble Boy, who threw up his hands and shook his head. Neither of them had a clue how to proceed. The show had to be going on three minutes of near silence by now. At least their hosts ought to have been talking, keeping the home audience in the loop.

But Amy Tjan's expression had changed. The look of studied concentration had vanished, replaced by what seemed like a terrible sadness. She looked as though at any moment she might begin to cry.

Then her features tightened, brows tightly knitted. The exotic beauty convulsed, and then she opened her mouth and spewed a torrent of vomit across the smooth oak table.

A woman screamed from the back of the audience. A chorus of disgust rose, people reacting with revulsion.

The mediums did not react. Lost in communication with their spirit guides, they did not even notice. Annelise began to speak in a stream of German, but almost to herself. Eric did not let go of the hands of those beside him, but drew closer to the table and seemed to shrink down, just a boy now.

"*Oh my God, it's working!*" he shouted. But the voice that came from Eric's throat was profoundly deep and full of gravel. It was not the voice of a teenage boy.

Serious Steve began to jitter in his chair, eyelids fluttering, as though he might be on the verge of some kind of seizure. His expression had at last changed, now one of despair.

Phoenix hugged herself close. The temperature dropped so quickly that her fingers and nose began to hurt. *It's happening,* she thought. All along she had told herself she was keeping an open mind, but that had been a lie. That this might all be true had never really been a consideration.

For just a moment, Annelise seemed to come awake. Her eyes opened wide, full of sorrow.

"I think we have made a terrible mistake," she said, before her head lolled forward, eyes fluttering closed.

The lights in the studio flickered.

"That's it! What the hell is this?" Headset Woman shouted, as if someone on staff might be behind it all.

But Phoenix knew that wasn't the case. She stared at her father and saw that his lips were moving. Soundlessly, he was in the midst of a conversation, no doubt with Mrs. LaVallee.

The dead were here with them.

Just the thought made her heart pound harder. A phrase loomed up in her mind, summoned from her unconscious. What was it from? *Dracula*? It must be. *The dead travel fast.*

"Alan?" Professor Cormier said, abruptly raising his voice. He didn't open his eyes, but his head swiveled toward the audience. "*Alan, you're here, aren't you?*" An unnatural smile twisted his face. "*I'm coming to you, Alan.*"

A man in the audience swore, loudly. Then he said, "Dad?"

"I can't wait to see you, son. I'll come for you."

"Oh my God, ohmigod, ohgod . . ." the woman beside Phoenix began to chant. At last, she believed.

Someone screamed in the audience. Others followed suit. An old man tumbled into the aisle, clutching his chest, and people shouted for help.

"Do you smell it? What is that smell?" said one man.

Phoenix did smell it, and she knew exactly what it was. Her gaze had kept returning to her father, terrified for him now, and so she'd seen the moment when Serious Steve Bell had gone rigid in his seat, his tremors pausing, and she'd seen the legs of his pants darken under the table as he pissed himself.

She shot up from her chair. The woman beside her grabbed her arm, demanded to know what she was doing, where she was going. But others had started to rise in the back, trying to work their way toward an exit. Frost glistened on cameras, on the table, and on the hair and clothes of the hosts and the mediums. Amy Tjan slumped back in her chair, one of the buttons on her shirt undone, revealing a bit of bra.

You wanted ratings, Phoenix thought, a little bit of crazy echoing around in her head. *Looks like you'll get them.*

In the aisle she paused to clear her head, bit her lip. The pain helped her focus. Fear crippled people. If she'd been alone there, she would've run, or still been in her seat. But no matter how much bitterness she'd built up toward her father over the years, she couldn't just sit and watch him like that. Everything felt wrong. The air itself was full of ugliness and otherness. Whatever the three mediums had expected to happen, this couldn't possibly be it.

"Dad!" she shouted.

Other people were shouting now. Her voice was one in a storm of questions and demands and terrors.

"Dad!"

The light over the door to the back corridors burned red, indicating they were still on the air, but she saw the door open and Katie stepped through. Phoenix thought maybe the girl from the Green Room could help her, but Katie only stared at the séance and hugged herself against the cold.

Phoenix ran for the set.

Headset Woman threw up both hands and spun around, shouting to the crew. "All right! We're off air. Somebody clean this mess up!"

Stubble Boy darted toward the dining room table and shook Amy Tjan, trying to get her to open her eyes. Her body moved as loose as a rag doll. She had vomit on her chin.

"Dad!" Phoenix said as she pushed past a crew member. She crouched down by her father's chair, grabbing his wrist. "Dad, it's me. Wake up. Dad!"

She tried to break the grip he had on Amy Tjan's hand. Her fingers bumped into Stubble Boy's as he tried to do the same thing from Amy's side.

"Separate them!" she shouted.

Stubble Boy shook his head, pulling at Amy's fingers, then he brushed Phoenix away and dropped to his knees. He took her father's wrist in one hand and Amy's in the other and tried to force them apart. They were unconscious, or catatonic, or something. It should've been easy.

Around the table, others were trying to pry apart the hands of the séance participants. But they could not be separated.

"*Thank you, Eric,*" a young girl's voice said, issuing from Eric's mouth. The voice of a ghost. The voice of the dead. "*I love you, Eric. Thank you.*"

"Dad?" Phoenix said, staring at his slack face. He was the one who would have the answers, but he couldn't help her now. Couldn't help himself.

Stubble Boy looked at Phoenix. "What do we do?"

She had no answer.

3

Amherst, Massachusetts

Matt Gaines fumbled with his necktie, swore, and went to the small mirror above the sink in his dorm room. He could never seem to manage tying his tie correctly unless he was looking in the mirror. Bizarre. The tie was red with a barely noticeable yellow pattern woven through it. Red hardly seemed appropriate for a funeral, but there wasn't a hell of a lot he could do about it. Red tie, cream-colored shirt, gray pants. Home was a little town called Pelham in Westchester County, New York, too far to drive just to pick up a suit—if his old suit would even still fit him.

He told himself he looked fine. He'd shaved and trimmed his goatee into a neat, sharp-edged stubble, and he kept his hair so short that it wasn't much longer than the hair on his chin. A lot of guys he knew kept it tight to the scalp because they liked the look, but Matt's motivation was simplicity. His friend Jamal had let his hair grow out hoping for an old-school Afro, but instead he'd gotten a tangled mess of frizz. It looked all right on Jamal—he worshipped at the altar of Bob Marley and it fit with his image—but Matt thought it must be a lot of work to look that laid-back.

Hal Gaines had raised a serious son. Matt couldn't help it. As far back as junior high, his friends had tried to get him to relax, but Matt always kept busy. He'd wanted his own money so he didn't have to ask his father, so he'd worked in a bookstore all through high school and volunteered in political offices whenever he could. With his friends, he was always poking his nose in other people's business, trying to help them solve their problems. He couldn't help himself, and they always forgave him.

Today, he had no choice but to slow down. Summer-session classes had concluded, and his work giving campus tours was over as well. But he'd have been happy with those distractions instead of the grim business of the day.

He glanced at the clock: 8:35. The funeral started at nine. If he hurried, he could still make it to the church without having to sneak in and skulk to a pew in the back. One more glance in the mirror, then. He smoothed out his tie, patted his pockets to make sure he had his keys, wallet, and cell phone, and then went for the door.

Out in the corridor, the dorm was quiet. The University of Massachusetts offered plenty of summer courses at the Amherst campus, but it didn't make any sense to keep all of the dorms open. This year, the lion's share of the summer students were housed in JFK and JQA, twin dormitory towers named after presidents John F. Kennedy and John Quincy Adams. Matt had dropped two classes during freshman year—one each semester—and he wanted to make up for those credits over the summer so he could start sophomore year on track. Falling behind this early in his college career seemed like a really bad idea.

So despite it being summer break, there were plenty of students living in JFK at the moment, but most of the residents of the fourth floor were still asleep. Apparently, they didn't have a funeral to attend.

He picked up his pace, steps echoing along the corridor. As he approached the stairs, a door up ahead opened and Noah Eisen stepped out. Matt couldn't help frowning in distaste. There'd been friction between the two since they'd met the previous fall. Politics were mostly to blame, but for Matt it wasn't just that Noah was a vocal member of the Young Republicans Club, it was the sort of Republican he was. A debate had started up in a dorm common room during freshman year, the week before Christmas, and Noah had made it clear he believed in guns and money and his own personal welfare. He seemed woefully ignorant of economics or international relations outside of wealth and war. His politics were the yell-louder-than-the-next-guy variety. But what had really troubled Matt the most had been the exchange that had ended the discussion.

"I vote my heart, and you vote your wallet," Matt had said.

Noah had smiled and thrown up his hands. "Exactly! Thank you. You've made my point perfectly. I couldn't have summed it up better. You vote your heart, buddy. I hope it earns you a lot of hugs and pats on the back. But I'll vote my wallet, because that is what's best for America."

Matt had stared at him. "You seriously believe that? Money first, and to hell with people?"

"Democrats want to comfort people while the world falls apart around us, Gaines. Republicans are for a strong military and decisive economic measures because, long-term, that will help everyone."

"Decisive doesn't mean making good decisions, man. You can't sacrifice the hope and health of people short-term just because you think you can help whoever manages to survive to benefit from your long-range goals. Besides, we both know the only people who benefit long-term are the people who are already well-off."

"The rich employ the middle class," Noah had said, so dismissive, rolling his eyes. "You're always talking about protecting our natural resources, right? Well, protect the financial resources as well, or nobody benefits."

"You're a couple of decades behind," Matt had said. "It isn't rich people now, it's corporations. The government protects the big corporations who can apply lobby pressure—oil, tobacco, guns, HMOs, drug companies—and the people who benefit are the CEOs and board members and major stockholders, who are already rich, and who get richer. And they treat employees like they're office supplies. People are paper clips to them."

Noah had shaken his head, as if in pity. "And that attitude is why you'll never be more than middle class, Gaines. I have other plans."

Matt had balled his fists then, and might have taken a swing at Noah if the guy hadn't walked away. He was an ROTC kid who looked at the military as his ticket to a better life. The perfect soldier, saluting to whatever crap the government fed him.

In the spring semester, they'd mostly managed to avoid each other. But this summer, with so few other students on the floor, they crossed paths frequently enough and were always courteous to each other, if nothing else. When the rest of the students started coming back to campus, they'd both be moving on to new dorm assignments, and Matt figured they could stay out of each other's way until then.

But not today, apparently.

Noah pulled the door closed and checked to make sure it was

locked. As he turned away from his room, he looked up and paused when he saw Matt.

"Gaines," he said.

Matt nodded. "Hey."

He'd wondered many times why Noah insisted on calling him by his last name, if it had to do with some kind of deep-seated racial bias or if it stemmed from Noah's enthusiastic embrace of the military culture his ROTC training had instilled in him. Maybe it was just that Noah was the resident advisor on the fourth floor, and he thought that gave him some kind of authority.

Whatever. Today wasn't the day for arguments.

Matt took a second look at Noah. The RA wore a dark suit and deep blue tie. With that perfect, military-cut blond hair, he seemed so at home in the garb that at first Matt had barely noticed. But now he realized that this early in the morning, another explanation was far more likely.

"You headed to Professor Wickstrom's funeral?"

"Yeah," Noah said, adjusting the cuffs of his shirt, which stuck out a bit too far from the jacket sleeves.

"I'm surprised you knew him."

Noah looked up, expressionless. "I'm an engineering major. Doesn't mean I've never taken a history class. Freshman year I had him for Colonial America. Great teacher. I never had to study because his lectures were so memorable. He liked to talk politics after class. He was a good guy."

He seemed to hesitate, waiting for Matt to start a debate. But Matt was busy digesting. When he thought of Noah Eisen, he had an image in his mind of who this guy was. A lot of that stemmed from the persona Noah seemed determined to create for himself, but Matt knew part of it grew from his own political prejudices.

For the first time, he thought he saw someone else under the RA's shallow surface.

"I'll see you there," Matt said.

With nearly anyone else in the world, it would've been awkward for him to just walk away when they shared the same destination. But it was obvious neither of them had any interest in making lighthearted conversation while walking down three flights of stairs. Noah made a show of checking his pocket for keys and making sure his door was locked, and Matt took the opportunity to get a head start. On his way down the stairs, Matt could hear Noah's steps above him, but neither of them wanted him to catch up.

Outside, the sky was dark with storm clouds. Any moment the heavens would open and the rain would pour down. Did he still have that umbrella in his trunk? Matt wondered. He thought he did.

Matt picked up his pace, jogging along a concrete path between buildings. Beyond them was the parking lot where his car and umbrella waited. He glanced at the sky again and moved even faster, hoping to beat the rain.

The Bronx, New York City

Oak Park Cemetery sprawled over acres of land at the heart of the Bronx, high-rise condos, smaller office buildings, and billboards visible in every direction. An oasis of death in the midst of urban life. Big Boy had always found it peaceful. He didn't know anyone buried here—didn't know if his family was dead or alive and didn't care. But he felt at ease around the dead in a way that most people never seemed to be. Big Boy didn't believe in ghosts. The guys in his gang,

Smoke Dragons, they were all superstitious. Big Boy worried about bullets and blades, the real things that could hurt him.

He sat astride his motorcycle, a Suzuki GSX-R—blue and silver, built like a rocket, made him look like some anime badass come to life—and let the rain patter on his helmet. The sound seemed to come from inside his skull. Rivulets of rainwater ran down his arms and along the small of his back. Even his jeans were getting soaked.

Big Boy didn't care. He just waited in the graveyard, the low-slung gray sky stretching out across the city. He waited because Jack would've done the same for him. They weren't brothers, but they might as well have been.

But the guy better show up soon, or he'd be out of there. Way too early in the morning and way too shitty a day to be sitting out on his bike in the pouring rain. Had to be eight thirty already—probably past that. Big Boy liked chocolate-frosted donuts and there was a place down in Riverdale that made them like nobody else in the world. His stomach rumbled when he thought about it.

Big Boy wasn't actually that big; the name had come from his auntie Haneul. She'd begun calling him that while he was still in the cradle and it had caught on. Auntie Haneul had told him later that his nickname had been the first words his grandparents had ever learned in English aside from hello and good-bye. Big Boy, they'd called him, and Big Boy he'd stayed, at least around the neighborhood. Ironic, considering he stood five foot six and weighed about one forty. He could eat as many chocolate-frosted donuts from Do-Nirvana as he liked and not gain an ounce.

His stomach rumbled again. Big Boy needed coffee and sugar and sleep. The rain was starting to piss him off. He reached down and patted his right hip pocket, felt the outline of his cell phone there, and thought about calling Jack again. Either that, or he was about to kick the Suzuki to life and tear out of there. He took a deep breath, looked around the cemetery through the visor of his helmet, and let the serenity of the place roll over him.

Five more minutes, he vowed.

Twenty seconds later he heard the roar of an engine and headlights turned in through the cemetery gates, cutting through the rain and the gloom. The Ford Mustang was brand-new, silver with blue racing stripes, but Jack had sweetened the ride with larger rear tires and a serious upgrade under the hood. In the rain it looked like a ghost and growled like a smoke dragon.

Big Boy climbed off the bike and removed his helmet, propping it on the seat. He strode over to the Mustang as Jack dropped it into park and popped the door open. Not even nine o'clock and the storm made it seem like near dark. Rain swept down, spotlighted by the Mustang's headlamps.

Jack stepped out of the car and shut the door, leaving it running. He swept his long hair away from his face. Big Boy had often said they could've been twins if not for the fact that Jack was disgustingly good-looking. Both of his parents were Korean, but he had to have some other blood mixed in somewhere because he had the sort of exotic looks common to people of mixed ancestry. Jack's trouble was that he was *too* good-looking. It had been a problem every day of his teenaged years. All the girls loved him and all the guys wanted to stomp him ugly.

Now, two weeks before his birthday, the problem had gotten out of control.

The two Smoke Dragons met halfway between their rides and embraced. Big Boy hugged him tight.

"BB," Jack said. "What's up? You drag my ass outta bed this early, it's got to be bad."

Big Boy reached into his pocket for his cigarettes. The pack was damp but he managed to put one between his lips and light it with the brass-plated Zippo he'd carried since his first cigarette at the age of ten.

"Gaesomun," Big Boy said.

Jack wiped rain from his face and studied him more closely. "Now I know it's bad. You never call me by that name."

It was his real name, of course. The Kims weren't about to name their son Jack. Gaesomun Kim. But outside of a handful of Smoke Dragons and his parents, nobody even knew Jack's real name.

"What is it, Big Boy?"

"Those clothes clean?"

"What the hell? Yeah, they're clean. I took a shower, too. Brushed my teeth, if you're concerned."

Big Boy nodded. He gestured for Jack to follow him back to the Suzuki. When they got there, he grabbed a small waterproof backpack he'd brought along and tossed it to him.

"What's this?" Jack asked.

"Five thousand in there. One of those pay-as-you-go cell phones. A jacket. I would've packed you a lunch, but the bread was stale. You're going on a little field trip."

Now Jack only stared, any trace of a smile gone. He hefted the backpack, then reached out and took Big Boy's cigarette from his mouth, took a drag, and handed it back.

"This about Marta?"

"You know it is."

Jack shook his head, his jaw set in a grim line. "That was over months ago."

Big Boy took a drag on his cigarette. The tip burned orange in the gloom of the storm and hissed in the rain. Then he let it dangle at his side.

"Hector Velez only just found out about it. Guess that means it's still kinda fresh to him. If you discovered one of the D-Kings had been banging your girlfriend, I'm guessing you wouldn't get over it real quick either. Smoke Dragons would have to do something about it, too."

Jack had no reply to that. What could he say? He'd been sleeping with the girlfriend of the boss of a Dominican gang that the Smoke Dragons had a very tenuous peace with. They'd drawn a line through their Bronx neighborhoods, separating the drug trade. Share and share alike, just to keep from going to war.

"What'd Tak say?"

Big Boy shook his head. "Tak doesn't know. Not yet. But he'll find out, and soon. Today. Bet your ass the D-Kings are gonna make it known. There'll be bloodshed over this, Jackie. There's only one path open to Tak, and only one path open to you."

He waited for the realization to set in. Jack frowned at first, kind of cocked his head, trying to figure it out. When the moment came, Big Boy thought he saw a spark go out in Jack's eyes. Tak had to protect the Smoke Dragons and their business interests. Jack had risked the whole gang for some high school girl from the Dominican Republic. Tak's only choice was to hand him over, or at least look the other way while the D-Kings tore him up and put him down. Jack had signed his own death warrant.

He had one way out.

A look of terrible sadness came over him. He looked around at the buildings in the distance, at the only home he'd ever known.

"I've gotta go," he said, discovering the answer even as he spoke the words.

Big Boy nodded. "And now, Jackie. Right now. They could come for you anytime. I wish I could've done more than five thousand, but in a hurry it was all I could come up with."

He pointed his cigarette at the backpack. "There's a gun in the bag, though. Five clips."

For a few seconds Jack glanced around, looking lost. Then he nodded, almost to himself. He offered his hand and Big Boy took it. They shook. As kids they had talked plenty of times about the bond between them, that each was the brother the other had never had. But they weren't kids anymore. Big Boy was eighteen, Jack nineteen. Lucky to live that long in the Bronx in a gang like Smoke Dragons.

"Thanks," Jack said. "Do what you can for my mother."

Big Boy nodded. He didn't speak, not because he was tough but because his throat had closed up tight with emotion he could not bring himself to show. Instead, he took a drag on his cigarette and reached for his helmet. He wouldn't be able to do a damn thing for Jack's parents. They'd think their son had just vanished. If Big Boy tried to tell them their son was still alive, the Dragons would hear about it eventually, and they'd know he had something to do with Jack taking off.

Jack clutched the backpack in one hand and ran for the Mustang. He climbed in, reversed it, and the tires spun as he backed up all the way to the cemetery gates. The car shot backward into the street, hesitated a moment, Jack invisible behind the tinted glass, then shot forward into the rain and out of sight.

Big Boy flicked his cigarette away and slid on his helmet.

As he did, he noticed movement out of the corner of his eye. He turned, peering through the visor and the rain. Beyond a pair of huge, old oaks, something lay on the ground in the midst of the rows of gravestones. He figured maybe a homeless guy had gotten in through the gates and hidden out, but if he'd been lying there unconscious, Big Boy would've seen him before now.

He looked at the trees. Could the old guy have been sleeping up there and fallen? He'd seen homeless people sleeping in stranger places. Wherever the guy had come from, he was in rough shape.

Not your problem. Take off.

The guy might even be dead already, in which case he was right where he belonged.

But then he moved. One hand out in front of him, he started dragging himself along the ground but still couldn't even lift his head.

"Damn it," Big Boy whispered, his voice muffled inside his helmet.

Striding toward the guy, he slid a hand into his pocket and pulled out his cell phone. Not that he'd be able to make the call wearing his helmet. With his free hand he reached up to unsnap the chinstrap.

"I don't need this shit. Not today."

Through the visor and the rain he couldn't see very well. It started to pour down harder. Lightning flashed. In that instant of illumination he saw something else moving in his peripheral vision. Someone else, maybe. He spun around and saw someone coming toward him through the maze of gravestones. For a second, he felt relieved. Must be some caretaker or something; Big Boy could let him worry about getting the homeless guy some help.

But the way this guy moved, quick and determined, made him blink and rethink. Had the D-Kings been following Jack already? Had somebody seen Big Boy give him the news and the backpack? Smoke Dragons were his brothers, but with Jack gone, if they had to give up Big Boy to keep the peace and keep business running smoothly, they'd do it. He'd gone behind Tak's back. Nobody would speak up for him.

And he'd given Jack his gun.

Big Boy shoved his cell phone back into his pocket. The rain drummed his helmet so he couldn't hear much and could see even less now. He reached up and pulled the helmet off, felt its comforting weight in his hand, thinking how easy it would be to crush a skull with the helmet if he swung it right.

Then he frowned, helmet clutched in his hand. This guy wasn't Dominican, but tall and thin, dressed in a decent suit and tie, and as white as anyone could be. Too white. In the storm, he looked almost gray. Walked funny, too, which made Big Boy look at his feet. Why the hell wasn't the guy wearing shoes?

Not that he cared. The guy came on quick, obviously full of dark intentions. That was all right. His hands were empty, no weapons, and he wasn't a 'banger. Big Boy would wreck him, maybe introduce him to granite and marble tombstones. It was a little early in the morning for it, but Big Boy never minded giving trouble to someone stupid enough to come looking for it.

"You got a problem?" he said, issuing the challenge only because the guy hadn't said a word and it was creeping him out.

It surprised him when the guy nodded, face slack. "Empty," he said, voice like a grunt. "I'm empty."

Something was wrong with his face, skin pulled tight over the bones. On one cheek, it looked like it had split, but there was no blood. Just the rain slicking back his hair.

Big Boy took a step back and his heel landed on something that snapped under his weight. He looked down and saw the homeless guy, who'd crawled closer while Big Boy's attention was elsewhere.

Big Boy blinked.

The homeless guy had no legs. His clothes were moldy and rotten, his skin like the papery inside of a wasp's nest. Pale bone jutted from his torso where his legs ought to have been.

The rain let up a little, as though the storm were taking a breath.

A breeze blew across the cemetery and with it came a chorus of moans.

"I'm empty!" the tall man shouted furiously.

The legless man grabbed hold of Big Boy's ankle and looked up as though pleading with him. There were no eyes in that decayed face.

Big Boy shouted and tore his foot from the thing's grasp. With a cry of disgust and fear he drove his heel down on that hideous face. The skull gave way and something squelched underfoot.

Those few seconds cost him. Big Boy turned just as the tall man lunged for him. All he could do was stagger back and put his left arm up to defend himself. The man grabbed his arm in both hands, opened his jaws, and darted his head forward, ready to bite into muscle and flesh.

Big Boy swung his helmet. It struck the side of the tall man's skull. The tall man—the dead man, no denying that now. His head split and something dribbled out, blood and brain matter, and ran down his cheek to be washed immediately away by the rain.

For good measure, Big Boy hit him again.

Even as he did he heard that moaning again, above the wind, and he knew what it had to be. He spun around and saw them. Nearby, the dead were dragging themselves up from their graves, some just hands, digging themselves out, and others beginning to stand. All across the cemetery they were rising up.

"No, no, no, no!" Big Boy shouted.

He bolted toward the Suzuki, running for his life. Some of them—the older corpses, he thought—moved slowly, some even crawling. But others looked more recently dead and they were nearly running now. He leaped over a crawler. One of the upright, moldering dead got in his way but Big Boy darted around a gravestone to avoid her, this woman in her rotting dress with her rotting flesh. How could she see him without eyes? How could that be?

He didn't let himself think anymore.

Out by the paved road, one of the quick dead lunged for him. Big Boy hit him with the helmet, knocking him down, then hammered his skull twice more to make sure he wouldn't get up again. The motorcycle stood just a few yards away. He ran to it, threw one leg over, and started it up. The engine roared to life.

Lightning flashed in the sky and thunder rolled out across the cemetery like the world was splitting open. And maybe it was.

Big Boy hurled the helmet at the nearest corpse and gave the accelerator a twist. The tires spun, rubber squealing, and the Suzuki shot toward the gates of the cemetery like a bullet. He had to swerve and dart, weaving among the dead. One of them lunged in front of the bike and Big Boy nearly fishtailed on the rain-slick pavement. He could feel the bike about to go out from under him and his heart pounded in his ears as he got it under control.

They swarmed toward him now, and toward the gate.

But he was going to make it.

The rain pelting his face, soaked to the skin, he smiled.

The red Cadillac turned in through the gates at a crawl, but Big Boy was flying on the Suzuki. The car jerked to a halt, blocking the narrow archway. Big Boy had no choice but to ditch the bike. He cut left into a skid. The motorcycle went out from under him, scraping pavement. He hit the ground and bounced. His right arm dragged beneath him, shredding skin, and then he rolled. Bones snapped inside him and he felt his left arm twist wrong and give way with a crack. Somehow he managed to keep his head safe.

His eyes closed for a second and when they opened he lay in the rain on his back, the agony of torn flesh and broken bones firing through him. He heard a car door open and managed to roll his head over to see a fortyish woman coming out of the Cadillac. Through the window he saw she wasn't alone. The old woman in the passenger seat looked very small and scared.

Coming to talk to her dead husband, Big Boy thought. *Visiting the cemetery because she can't let go.*

"Oh my God, I'm sorry. Are you all—" the younger woman, maybe the other one's daughter, started to say.

And then she started to scream. Stunned by nearly killing Big Boy, and with the rain, she hadn't paid enough attention to the people walking through the cemetery, hadn't wondered at how many of them there were. Hadn't gotten a good look.

The dead had her then. A husk of a man, strings of hair plastered to his skull by the rain, snatched at her left arm and jerked it toward his mouth. His teeth sank into the flesh and muscle and tore, blood spurting onto the dead man's forehead. The woman screamed and tried to pull free, but then other hands grabbed her, holding her other arm. A staggering dead thing stumbled into her, throwing its arms around her in an embrace, and began to chew her face. Others bit and tore. Blood showered to the pavement to mix with the rain.

The old woman in the car shrieked louder and louder. They attacked the Cadillac, shattering the windows, and then they were hauling her out through the broken passenger window, dragging her over jagged glass. They fell on her, moaning.

"Empty," he heard one of them say. "So empty."

Hands grabbed hold of him. Big Boy looked up into the hungry, lost faces of the dead. He felt numb, up until the moment when the corpse of a young girl thrust her hands into his belly—long fingernails puncturing his abdomen—and bent down with her mouth eager and open, a smile on her face.

Manhattan, New York City

The studio was in chaos. Once *Sunrise* had gone off the air, people in security shirts and others wearing ID tags from the network started ushering the audience out. Someone shouted about calling 911, but already a couple of medical personnel—network staff, apparently—had appeared and were looking over the five people who still sat around the faux dining room table in a catatonic stupor.

Ray Creedon didn't move. He stood in front of his seat and stared at the bizarre tableau unfolding in front of him. The three mediums were clearly unconscious, but their mouths kept moving in silent whispers. The hosts of *Sunrise* hadn't fared so well. Amy Tjan had puked again and now sat back in her seat, head drooping to her chest. Steve Bell had pissed his pants and the place stank of urine.

Staff buzzed around the table. At first they tried to separate the mediums but gave it up pretty fast when the medics—or whatever they were—barked at them to back off. Ray had seen enough, though. Whatever had happened to the people at that table, no one was breaking their grip on each other. The circuit couldn't be broken without hurting them even worse.

Someone tried to shoo away a girl—maybe nineteen or twenty—who screamed at the producers to tell her what had happened to her father. Only then did Ray realize that she must be Phoenix Cormier, the professor's daughter. He'd caught himself staring at her during the warm-up to the séance. Or, more accurately, she'd caught him. It wasn't her beauty that had drawn his attention. There were far more beautiful women. But with her shoulder-length brown hair and green eyes and the gentle curves of her face, there was something ethereal about her that made her looks striking in a way that beauty didn't quite explain.

"Sir?" a woman's voice said. "Excuse me, sir, you'll have to leave."

The security guard looked steadily at Ray, expression grim.

"What?" he said, glancing around.

There were dozens of people in the studio but all of them seemed to be staff now, except for four or five who were on their cell phones. From the snippets of conversation he heard, he gathered that they were print or online journalists who were calling stories into their employers. One woman had taken her seat and was typing furiously on a laptop.

"Sir, right now, please," the guard said, taking him by the arm.

He shook her off. "I don't think so."

Her eyes darkened and she started to call to some of the other security people.

"Listen, Annelise invited me to be here. I run mediumsrare.com. It's a website. It's painfully obvious that nobody knows what the hell just happened to these people. I'm not claiming to be an expert, but since I don't see anyone else around here who knows anything about channeling spirits or psychic phenomena, I think making me leave right now would be a really bad idea. I can help."

The woman scowled. "What're you, seventeen?"

Ray gave a small sigh. "Twenty. But Eric, the kid up there on the stage? He's eighteen and you've got him on your show talking about dead people. Just let me talk to the producer of the show. If I can't help, I'm sure they'll have you dragging my ass out of here in thirty seconds."

She hesitated.

Ray glanced at Phoenix again. She knelt by her father's chair, stroking his arm and talking quietly to him as tears ran down her cheeks, maybe asking him to wake up. To open his eyes.

"What's your name?"

"Ray Creedon."

"Stay right here," the guard said. "Let me see if anyone will talk to you." She softened. "They're obviously pretty freaked-out right now."

"I don't blame them. What are they showing?"

The guard frowned and looked at him. "Huh?"

"Broadcasting? They had to cut away from this show. What did they put on instead?"

She shrugged. "Not sure. Look, sit tight. I'll be right back."

The security guard walked off and Ray glanced around. The woman sitting at her laptop looked up. "Hey."

Ray nodded.

"You wanted to know what they're broadcasting instead of this?"

Curious, Ray moved into the aisle and walked up her row. "Why, do you have something?"

"Are you kidding?" the woman asked. "It's been nearly twenty minutes since the weirdness went down. First they put on commercials. By the time they came back from that, they had switched to the main network news studio upstairs. Andy Schmidt—guy who does the news desk for *Sunrise*—hadn't left the building. They put him on to anchor, mentioned that illness had interrupted the interview; they didn't even call it a séance. No comments at all about what we all saw, the voices we heard. No rerun of the live footage. Then they went into the news, like nothing had happened."

Ray laughed. "Seriously? They're just going to pretend everything's okay?"

"They tried," the woman said. "But CNN and FOX News picked it up immediately. FOX is already calling it a hoax. CNN claims they're waiting for word from within the studio as to whether anyone's injured. Nobody here is saying anything. You can bet their publicity department is trying to spin something right now, but they'll do it on their own air, not in a comment to a competitor."

A chill went through Ray. "What'll they say? None of them know what just happened. They're sure not going to tell the truth."

"Chances are they're hoping to get these people conscious or at least separated before they say anything. I'm Leah, by the way."

"Ray." He put out his hand and shook, then nodded at the laptop. "You've got live news on there?"

"Wi-Fi, streaming video. Something you want to watch?"

Leah grinned at her own joke. Ray smiled back but knew it was a weak effort. He glanced again at the five people whose hands locked them in a chain around the table.

"Mr. Creedon."

He turned and found himself face-to-face with a rumpled-looking man in rumpled-looking clothes. His pants and shirt—rolled up at the sleeves, barely tucked in—desperately needed an iron. He kept his head smoothly shaved and wore wire-rimmed glasses. Behind him stood the security guard.

"That's me," Ray said.

"I'm John Volk. I produce this show. There are a lot of people in this building who outrank me, but I'm the closest you're going to come to talking to the boss. You'd have to be blind not to see I've got a crisis on my hands. Apparently, you claim to be able to help. Are you gonna waste my time?"

Ray took a deep breath. "I hope not."

"So, what's happening here?"

"Do you believe in this sort of thing, Mr. Volk? Spirits, mediums?"

Volk scowled. "Never have before. But what we just saw was pretty crazy, so I'll keep an open mind for about thirty seconds. What've you got?"

Ray glanced at Leah, who seemed to be half listening even as she frowned at something on her laptop. When he looked back, Volk's impatience was clear on his face.

Beyond Volk, though, he saw Phoenix Cormier. She'd stood up and was watching them with those distractingly green eyes. With all the people working around her, cleaning up puke and checking heartbeats, doors opening and closing, she'd zeroed in on them. Now she rose and stepped away from her unconscious father, starting toward them.

"You understand what Annelise and Professor Cormier and Eric were trying to do here, Mr. Volk?"

"Didn't I just say I was the producer of the show? Don't be an idiot. Talk."

Ray slid his hands into the pockets of his jeans. Volk's stare was intense but he didn't look away.

"I think they succeeded. If you go and look at the playback of the séance, you'll see what I mean. You're broadcasting a television signal. They were trying to do some broadcasting of their own, opening a channel for spirits to travel out into the world and talk to the people they've left behind. I'll bet your phones are ringing off the hook—not just yours, but every police station and news outlet—with people talking about seeing ghosts and hearing the voices of their long-lost family and friends."

Volk's expression closed down. "Thanks for your opinion, Ray. But so much for your expertise. We've gotten plenty of calls, wondering what just happened, but nobody who's seen a ghost."

Phoenix had come up behind Volk now and was listening to every word. Ray looked at her a moment too long, gaze locked on her eyes, and he realized she was thinking the same thing he was.

"Not one?" Phoenix asked.

Volk stepped back to include her in the conversation. "Not that I've heard. And if Ray here was right, I'm guessing we'd have heard plenty. Let's just take care of our people, all right? We've got ambulances on the way. We'll get them to a hospital and then we'll see what the official word is. Last thing any of us needs is bad publicity."

Ray didn't smile. Neither did Phoenix. Even the security guard had the sense to look away, disgusted by the way Volk tried to spin the situation even while they were still in the room. All he cared about right now was how the story would play in the media.

"Actually, I'm sure this will do wonders for the sales of Professor Cormier's book," Ray said. "But something tells me he doesn't care much at the moment about his royalties."

Phoenix's eyes narrowed and she gave a tiny nod, a silent thanks, and Ray felt a bit flush. Something about the girl's attention on him made him want to do anything he could to help. He wasn't the type who usually responded to the whole damsel-in-distress thing, and she didn't seem like a girl who'd do anything but laugh or punch him if she knew what he was thinking, but he couldn't fight the instinct she brought out in him.

"What the hell?" Leah said, causing them all to turn toward her. She looked up. "Hey. I hate to interrupt, but you'll all want to see this."

She took a small plastic bud from her right ear—Ray hadn't noticed it before—and unplugged it from the computer. With two clicks, she had the sound on and she turned the laptop so that they could all see the screen. Others began to gather around for a look as well.

"Excuse me," Phoenix said, obviously getting pissed off, "but we sort of have our own crisis going on here."

Ray nodded, about to agree, but Leah spoke up again.

"I know. But you'll all want to see this."

Volk and the others gathered around the laptop. Ray stepped up beside Volk to get his attention, but faltered as he caught sight of the action on the screen.

The local ABC affiliate's logo was at the bottom of the screen. The reporter was Carlos Diaz, whom Ray had been watching on this channel most of his life. He stood in the pouring rain, without even an umbrella, which spoke to the speed of his team's response. They must have been in the area when the call came in. Or maybe they had a Jersey office. Whatever, the scene was a mess.

Beyond Diaz, the camera picked up a pair of police cars and an ambulance, all with lights flashing. The rain made it hard to tell the difference between police and EMTs, but several people in uniform milled around in the background. Screaming could be heard in the distance. It sounded like a war zone.

"What the hell?" Volk said.

"—riot seems to have broken out in this Hoboken neighborhood. Police say that it began near St. James cemetery, prompting dozens of calls from local residents and passing motorists in the space of just a few minutes. Already a cordon has been set up as police attempt to calm the crowd. What sparked this riot has yet to be determined, and authorities say restoring peace to the neighborhood is their first step—"

The reporter was cut off by the sound of gunfire. Carlos Diaz was a veteran television journalist. That didn't stop him from swearing on a live broadcast, flinching, and turning to his cameraman.

"You getting this?" Diaz asked as they all watched.

A voice mumbled something Ray couldn't make out.

More gunfire followed, and screams and shouts of fear that were louder than before.

"Mr. Volk, please!" Phoenix said as she came up next to Ray. "Do something. What the hell's wrong with you people? My father's—Oh my God."

The camera fixed on a bunch of police officers who crouched behind their vehicles, guns leveled over the tops at figures rushing toward the cordon in the rain. The cops shouted to one another but the words were impossible to make out.

"Rioters are attacking the police officers now," Diaz said, voice low. He stood just to one side of the televised image, half crouched. "I just saw two men carrying a wounded woman toward an ambulance. Others are running away from the rioters. Jimmy, get that shot!"

The camera swiveled and locked on the image of a boy about twelve years old carrying a younger girl, perhaps his little sister. His eyes were wide with terror and his face streaked with blood that ran like mascara in the rain. The shot was framed by the backs of police cars as the boy tried to get the girl to safety.

"Come on, kid," one of the cops shouted, loud and clear.

A figure darted through the rain, so much faster than the boy. He drove the kid down on the street, slammed his head on the pavement, and the child didn't move again. Then the attacker picked up the injured girl as though he meant to carry her himself—at least, that was Ray's thought, until the man drove his mouth down and tore into her.

"Oh, Jesus God, cut away!" Carlos Diaz cried.

The camera angle swept to one side just in time to see Diaz bend over, vomiting into the little river of rainwater that ran in the gutter. More gunshots sounded.

Again the cameraman swung back. Ray had always thought these guys were either madmen or heroes, standing in the midst of natural disasters and battlegrounds. How could he not just turn and run? Screw the camera.

But the image closed in on the cops again, who were firing at some of the figures moving in the rain. A woman jumped up onto the trunk of a police car. One of the cops backed up, took aim, and shot her three times in the chest. She staggered backward and fell, landing on the trunk of the other police car, cracking the rear windshield.

Then she got up again.

"Let's go," Carlos Diaz said, his terrified face appearing in sudden close-up. "Let's get out of here."

The image shook and jumbled as the cameraman started to run with Diaz. But a moment later, still in motion, the view swung back toward the police cordon. Rioters were swarming up and over the cop cars now, attacking the officers. Gunshots echoed in the wet air.

A cry of pain came from off camera, then a scream of terror. The image shifted again, turning to focus on two women who had latched onto Diaz like lampreys, their jaws clamped to his flesh, blood running over their chins and cheeks. Looming up behind them was a withered man who rushed toward the camera, his skin pitted with rot, eye sockets hollow.

The camera fell.

The view was of a curb, grass growing up from the cracks.

Screams, gunshots, and the picture went black, then the image changed back to the news desk at the ABC affiliate. The young black woman with perfect hair and designer clothes who sat behind the desk stared blankly at the camera, in shock.

"Dianne!" someone in the studio snapped.

The woman put a hand over her mouth and shook her head slowly, back and forth.

The station went to commercial.

"That . . ." Leah said quietly. "That can't be real."

Ray felt a chill spider-walk up his spine. "What, you think it's a hoax? Like people are saying this was?" He gestured to the catatonic mediums. "I don't think so."

"But it's impossible," Volk said, almost sneering.

Ray laughed, feeling sick. "Keep telling yourself that."

"No, no, no, no," Phoenix said, shaking her head, backing away from all of them. Tears slid from the corners of her eyes, and she'd gone pale, as though little pieces of her were breaking apart inside.

"It wasn't supposed to be like this," she said, staring at each of them in turn.

"Wait, you mean you think . . ." Volk said, and then turned to stare at the set, where the three mediums and the show's hosts sat motionless in their chairs. "Christ, you think we started it?"

Ray saw the horror taking each of them in its grasp, felt it clutching at his own heart, and shook his head.

"We can't know that. We can't be sure," he said.

"But the timing—" Leah started.

"We can't know!" Ray snapped.

"What do we do?" whispered a member of the stage crew who still hovered by Leah, watching her laptop screen. "What are we going to do?"

"Wait and see," Leah said. "That's all we can do."

Phoenix looked at Ray again, and then over at her father. "It wasn't supposed to be like this," she said again, in a whisper.

Ray reached out to touch her shoulder. "Listen, there's so much we don't know about the other side, about spirits. Your father just scratched the surface in his research. When he wakes up, I'm sure he'll be able to tell us what went wrong."

"This wasn't the plan," Phoenix said.

Glancing again at the computer screen, Ray swallowed. His throat was tight with fear.

But it was Leah who replied, a sharp edge to her voice.

"Yeah. It looks like the dead have a different plan."

Trumbull, Connecticut

TANIA CAME AWAKE TO the gentle lull of the limousine's engine. One of the tires hit a pothole and jostled her a bit, and she opened her eyes. She could see the controls for the DVD player and the case for her laptop on the floor, and bottles of water and juice in the cup holders. The leather of the seats was soft, but she'd balled her sweatshirt up under her head. A thin line of drool had drizzled from her mouth and she reached up to wipe it away.

Through the glass partition she could see the back of Derek's enormous shaved head. There were rolls of flesh at the back of his neck, strangely lighter than the deep black of his skin. She'd never met anyone darker than Derek, and rarely encountered anyone bigger. He made most people nervous, mainly because he looked like he could eat them for breakfast and still have room for bacon, eggs, and French toast, but that was why Tania had hired him in the first place. His sweet nature, though, was the reason she couldn't imagine ever not having him in her life. Derek was her big teddy bear. He might be fifteen years older than her, but if she'd liked guys, she would have found it very difficult not to fall in love with him.

She could hear muffled music through the glass, something jazzy. Tania liked that. Derek hated pop, which made her happy beyond reason. He had no interest in her music or her celebrity.

Stretching, she let out a little groan and then sat up, adjusting her seat belt. She'd slipped the shoulder strap off in order to lie down. The air conditioner was on, but she saw droplets on the windshield and the swish of the wipers. It had begun to rain.

With a yawn, she hit the button to lower the partition.

"Where are we?"

Derek glanced in the rearview, smiling. "Hey, sleepyhead. You nap all right? Tried to keep the music down."

"Perfect." She reached through and put a hand on his shoulder. He grabbed her fingers and held them gently a moment, then put both hands back on the wheel.

"This is the Merritt Parkway. Not long now till we cross into New York."

Tania leaned forward, face in her hands. Getting to New York might be necessary, but her stomach fluttered at the thought. She reached back and took the clip from her long, curly blond hair, then pushed her fingers through it.

"Now don't be like that, darlin'," Derek said, alternating between watching her in the mirror and watching the road. "It's all gonna be all right."

She took a deep, cleansing breath and let it out. "What, you don't think they'll ask me?"

"'Course they're gonna ask you," Derek said, shaking his head. "But you don't have to answer, do you? Seriously, now. You're seventeen. You ain't supposed to be having sex with anybody, boy or girl, as far as the moms and dads of America are concerned. Not like you're one of those party girls, is it?"

Just tell the truth, her father had said. Tania had considered it, but the truth just wasn't that easy. Derek knew better than anyone that she had nothing in common with the girls who created a frenzy over themselves through bad behavior. She didn't like to go clubbing. Even if she liked coke—which she didn't; she'd totally freaked out the one time she'd tried it—she wasn't going to be doing rails off the sink in the bathroom someplace where the young and beautiful gathered. And sure, she'd gone commando plenty of times, but never while wearing a miniskirt, and never since the cadre of Hollywood pop tarts had decided flashing their goods to paparazzi would be their newest attention-sucking strategy. Drunk driving. Fabricated feuds.

It all made her sick.

Tania had started her career as a Nickelodeon child star and now she had a megaselling CD to her name and two tiny supporting roles in independent films. She wanted to be appreciated for her work, not become some kind of carnival sideshow. Since the age of ten she had been so careful. So very careful.

But all it took was a whiff of scandal, of sex and heartbreak.

Heartbreak.

She bit her lip. Unable to help herself, she glanced at her tiny purse where it lay on the floor, picturing the cell phone that lay inside, ringtone turned off.

Tomorrow morning, she'd be performing on *Sunrise,* and then Amy Tjan would interview her. It ought to have been a major score for Tania—certainly her publicist had called it that. But that had been before TMZ had snapped pictures of her last Friday night leaving Touché, a restaurant in West Hollywood. The images were burned into her mind. The photog had snapped her coming out the door with one hand over her mouth, tears streaming from her eyes, mascara running. She looked like some Hollywood hooker, blond hair all crazy, gym-perfected body stooped in sorrow. Other pictures showed her running toward her waiting car . . . and then raven-haired Emma following her, so apologetic, dragging Tania into her arms, the embrace as they wept together, and finally that single, tender kiss before Tania pushed Emma away and got into the limo.

The kiss had been chaste, just at the edge of Emma's lips, and girls kissed all the time. But for anyone willing to entertain for an instant the possibility that America's latest sweetheart might be a lesbian, the photos told the whole story. Love and heartbreak.

Emma had been part of Tania's life since the earliest days of her career. They auditioned for all of the same parts and became friends. To the public, they had been best friends for years. But Tania had been in love with Emma since the age of thirteen. She'd never loved anyone else. Emma, though . . . apparently she'd found someone else to love.

She squeezed her eyes shut, but couldn't escape the memory in her mind, the way Emma had looked at her from underneath the veil of her stylishly jagged, short black hair and told her they couldn't be together anymore.

Tania opened her eyes.

"If they ask me about her during the interview, I'll probably cry."

Derek shot her a hard look in the mirror. "Darlin', you cry and you're screwed. You know that. You just gotta suck it up, make it through. Nancy told you she wasn't gonna set up any more interviews for a week or so, but you cancel on this, you might as well just tell the truth, 'cause the world's gonna believe it anyway."

Tania smiled. How to explain to Derek that they already believed it? His job was to protect her and it had been grinding at him that he hadn't been able to protect her from *this.*

They rode in silence for a few miles, the radio playing low.

"D?"

"Yeah?"

"If she comes right out and asks me if I'm a lesbian, I can't lie. I can't just say 'No, there's no truth to that.' Someday, it's going to come out and when it does, everyone will say 'And she lied about it, too.'"

Derek grew quiet, eyes narrowed. He took a deep breath and nodded. "All right. We just hope they don't ask it flat out like that. And if the question does get asked, you just say your personal life is your personal life. You value your privacy, and why should it matter who you love?"

Tania let out a breath, tension easing. "I can do that. As long as Amy Tjan doesn't mention Emma's name, I even might be able to do it without crying."

Derek chuckled, nodding, and reached out to turn up the music. He had satellite radio in the limo and had found some seventies funk song she had never heard before. Tania felt it down inside of her and closed her eyes, letting the music thump in her chest.

Abruptly, Derek turned the radio down.

"Hey, T, you hungry?"

Tania thought about that. She was always hungry, of course. Not that she was some bulimic nut job, but she ate very little and worked out nearly every day. You didn't get abs and a belly like she had, even at seventeen, without sweating.

But there was hungry and then there was hungry. Chicken Caesar salad was, like, two whole food groups. With all the crying she'd been doing, her publicist—Nancy—had gently inquired as to whether she was drowning her sorrows in ice cream and fast food. Emma had torn her heart out, but that didn't make Tania stupid. All right, she'd had a single Ben & Jerry's binge with some friends, but she wasn't eating donuts and cheeseburgers at every meal. Still . . .

"I could eat."

"That's my girl," Derek said. Big D could always eat.

Over the purr of the engine, and the patter of the rain, and the swish of the wipers, and the quiet funk on the radio, she barely heard the low, grinding buzz from her purse. Her phone was set on vibrate, and the zipper on her bag shook from the tiny tremor inside.

Snatching the phone from her bag, she saw it was Nancy calling. A smile touched her lips. Not the kind of smile she shared with Derek, though. This was Tania's business smile. She liked Nancy, but the woman wasn't her friend. She watched out for Tania because that's what Tania paid her to do.

Tania flipped the phone open. "Hey, we were just talking about you. Are your ears burning?"

"Oh, thank God, where are you?"

"What?" Tania flinched. She'd never heard this tone from Nancy before.

"Where *are* you? Right now, where are you?"

"We're on the Merritt Parkway. Not far from the city, I guess."

"Pull over."

Tania clutched the phone. "What? Nancy, what's wrong?"

"Listen to me, honey, pull over *right now*. Don't go another foot."

Fear rippled through Tania. "Derek, pull over."

He gave her a dubious look.

"Seriously. Right now. Something's wrong."

"Damn, T, I can't pull over. Nowhere to pull over here. You want me to get off?"

"Yes, yes, next exit," she said. Then, to Nancy, "There's like, no breakdown lane here. We're getting off at the next exit. What the hell's going on?"

In her mind she spun nightmare scenarios in which paparazzi camped out in front of her hotel and grilled her with questions about Emma. But she'd been through that, learned to avoid reporters and photographers a long time ago. This had to be something else.

"You're not listening to the radio?"

"Satellite radio. Just music. Nancy, talk. You're scaring me."

"The whole city's gone crazy. Not Manhattan so much, but Brooklyn, the Bronx, Queens. There are riots everywhere. Riots and . . . I don't even know how to describe it. They're not showing the worst footage on TV, but online it's just . . . it's insane."

Nancy—rock-solid, always-in-control Nancy—was totally losing her shit.

"It's in Jersey, too. It's spreading."

Tania felt the car slowing and looked up to see that they were turning off the Merritt Parkway.

"What's spreading?"

"They're—" Nancy began. And then she stopped. It wasn't the sort of hesitation people make if they're confused about how to continue. Tania knew that right off. No, Nancy had cut herself off because she had been about to speak words she then decided not to utter.

Tania heard her heart beat a few times.

Then Nancy went on. "It's some kind of sickness. They're violent. Lunatics. Attacking the police and anybody else that gets near them. I think a lot of people have been killed."

They passed a gas station and a Ninety Nine Restaurant. Up ahead was a small strip mall and then a stretch of nothing, just a couple of homes on the main road.

"Jesus," Tania whispered. "So where are you?"

"In my office, honey. And I'm not going anywhere until this all blows over. I don't think it's safe out there. If it really is spreading, it might not even be safe up where you are. You've got to turn around, head back north until you know it's all right."

Tania frowned. She peered through the windshield. In the distance she could see the white steeple of a church that must have been the town center. Derek had been planning to get off anyway, she remembered, looking for somewhere to eat.

"D," she said, "I think maybe we should get back on the road. We need to go back the way we came."

"You're off the Merritt?" Nancy said. "What are you doing?"

"You said to get off!" Tania snapped, fraying at the edges.

"Are you even listening to me? Turn on the radio! You'll hear it for yourself. I don't think you've got any time to waste. It's spreading, Tania. If it's in Jersey already—"

The limo began to slow. "Something going on up ahead," Derek said, peering through the gentle rain now. "An accident or something."

"Better turn around," Tania said.

He nodded. "I'll fill the tank back at that Mobil and we're out of here."

But even as he spoke, he bent over the steering wheel, trying to make out the cause of the commotion ahead of them. The limo slowed further. Along the left side of the street there stretched a long black iron fence that ran the perimeter of an enormous cemetery. A police car sat at an angle, blocking the entrance to the graveyard. Half a dozen cars were stopped in the middle of the road, halting travel in either direction. Most were damaged, metal torn and crumpled, having collided with one another.

People crawled on the cars, pounding on the glass and on the hoods and roofs. Some seemed to be trying to get at the people inside the cars.

"Derek?"

"Holy shit," he whispered.

"Tania?" Nancy demanded on the phone. "What's going on?"

She barely heard her publicist's voice. Snapping the phone shut, she let it fall to the seat and stared out the window at the figures walking and running and crawling across the cemetery, climbing that black iron fence, spilling into the road.

For a few long seconds—dangerous seconds—neither Tania nor Derek said a word, able only to stare. And suddenly she understood what Nancy had been about to say, the words the woman could not force herself to speak. This wasn't some plague. These people weren't sick. They were dead.

"Oh no. Uh-uh. You have got to be messin' with me now," Derek said to himself, or perhaps to God. "I am not seeing this."

"Turn around, D," Tania said, ice flowing through her veins, fear clutching at her heart. "Damn it, Derek! Drive!"

"Hello? Seriously, girl. Do you *see* the zombies? Is this shit for real?"

"Of course I see them!" Tania shouted, shaking. "Why do you think I'm telling you to turn the goddamn car around and drive? Get us the hell out of here!"

Some of them had taken note of the limo now, and were leaving the damaged cars to the others and coming along the road.

"Derek!"

Under his breath he had started to pray. He dropped the limousine in reverse and floored it. Tania held on. The car jetted backward twenty, forty, eighty yards and then Derek cut the wheel. In that moment when they were stopped, the dead rushed toward them, some unnaturally swift.

Derek hit the gas and the limo rocked hard to the side as he pulled away from the cemetery, gunning it back toward the Merritt.

"Where do we go?" he asked.

"I don't know," Tania said, her voice barely a whisper. "I don't know. Nancy said it's spreading. Just drive away from the city as far and as fast as you can."

Her cell phone buzzed.

Tania screamed.

Then she snatched up the phone and stared at the name of the caller. *Emma.*

Tania held the phone to her chest and wiped at her eyes, trying desperately not to cry. Derek pulled the limousine back onto the Merritt. Already the traffic had thickened going north. Pretty soon the roads would be jammed. Anarchy. She prayed they would be able to stay ahead of it.

The phone stopped buzzing.

If Emma tried calling again, she promised herself she would answer it. She just needed to catch her breath, figure out what all of this meant.

A small laugh caught in her throat.

"Damn, T, what's funny?" Derek demanded, staring horrified at her in the rearview.

Tania took a breath. She bit her lip. It didn't seem funny anymore. She wondered if she might be in shock.

"I was so afraid of that interview, like it was the scariest thing in the world," she said, feeling hollow. Sounding, to her own ears, hollow. "But I'm old news now, D. This changes everything.

"Nothing else is going to matter anymore."

5

Amherst, Massachusetts

Fans turned lazily in the church rafters. Though it was still early—just after nine thirty—someone had turned the lights on inside All Saints. A light rain pattered the stained-glass windows and the wind had picked up, rattling them in their frames. Matt Gaines could have come up with a dozen metaphors about the sky crying for the deceased, but he didn't have to make the effort—the priest had used them all.

He sat a dozen rows from the altar, close enough to see Professor Wickstrom's family huddled together in the first two pews. His wife was there, along with people Matt could only assume were Don Wickstrom's grown children and their spouses, a couple of grandchildren, one or two older people who looked like siblings. They were quiet, reassuring one another with sad smiles, sharing their loss bravely.

Out of respect for the family, Matt forced himself not to fall asleep. Church had always had that effect on him, but today his father wasn't there to tell him to sit up straight, and his little sister, Sara, wouldn't be able to pinch him if he started to nod off. The sadness of the day had him missing them more than usual.

The rain had brought with it terrible humidity, and despite the slowly turning fans the church had become stifling. The late Don Wickstrom wouldn't have cared if Matt nodded off. It wasn't one of his lectures, after all. But Matt felt he owed it to the man.

Two rows up and on the opposite side of the center aisle, Noah Eisen sat beside another familiar face. Amanda Littrell taught American literature at UMass. A huge chunk of the student body—or, at least, the liberal arts majors—took their turn in her class at some point during their time on campus. Professor Littrell was in her late thirties, athletic and thin, and wore her dark hair short. Her hair was dyed an impossible ochre-red, a color possibly found in nature, but not in humans. In many ways, she reminded Matt of Sister Rita, who'd been the principal of St. Bridget's, the elementary school he'd attended in Pelham Manor.

Professor Littrell was funny and attractive and very popular with her students. Today her smile was not in evidence. Today she cried.

The university president sat toward the front with a number of other members of the faculty, but only a handful of them looked at all familiar.

Matt sat up straighter, the hard wood of the pew helping him to stay awake. He focused on the priest, waiting for the moment when he would begin the communion blessing, signifying the mass had reached its final act. He wondered how many of the people in the church would follow the funeral procession to the cemetery and stand in the rain while Father Ryan said a few words over the casket. Not many, he thought.

We're all pretenders. This truth was not new to him, but it struck home harder than ever there in the church. He would go to the graveside and stand in the rain under his tiny umbrella because he wanted the family to know that the man they'd lost had been well loved and would be missed by many. He would go not because he wanted to, but because he felt he should, and because inside his heart he hoped that one day others would do the same for him, that people would gather to bid him farewell, that he would be remembered.

Someone coughed and he glanced over to see it was Noah. For some reason he did not feel the usual ripple of disdain the RA usually brought out in him. They were opposite in so many ways, their beliefs and convictions impossibly at odds. But at the funeral of a man they had both respected, it was hard not to see that they were fundamentally the same. Matt had heard death referred to as the great equalizer, and he felt that truth keenly today.

The congregation stood. Matt hurried to follow suit, trying to figure out where in the liturgy they were. He saw that the gifts—the communion wine and wafer—had been brought to the altar, and he felt relief. Soon they would be out of the stifling church. Humid as it was, at least the rain and wind would be cool.

He ran a hand over his goatee to hide a yawn.

"When supper was ended he took the cup—" Father Ryan said.

A heavy thump resounded in the church, making the priest blink. One of the kids in that front pew, Matt figured.

"—again he gave You thanks and praise. He gave the cup to his disciples and said, 'Take this, all of you, and drink from it. This is the cup of my blood—'"

Thump, thump!

Matt frowned. What the hell was that? The people in the front few rows had started to whisper. Father Ryan faltered, glancing down at the family and then at Don Wickstrom's casket. The priest cleared his throat.

"'—the blood of a new and everlasting covenant. It will be shed for you and for all, so that your sins may be forgiven. Do this in memory of me.'"

The thump came again, followed by a loud crack like the splintering of wood. This time, Matt was staring at the casket where it sat on a dais at the front of the church, and he saw it *jump*. Saw it *shift*.

The church fell silent.

Father Ryan stared, wide-eyed, at the casket, communion chalice still held aloft as though he'd forgotten it was in his hands. There was a whimper and a whisper at the front, where Professor Wickstrom's wife had turned to one of her grown sons and clutched him in fear and confusion.

Something inside the casket rocked. It shifted. Then it rocked again and the coffin tumbled from the dais, struck the marble floor, and cracked open with terrible splintering. The body of Don Wickstrom spilled out onto the marble floor of the church, pale and pasty with funeral parlor makeup.

People screamed. Others cursed and swore. Father Ryan dropped the chalice from his hands and spilled purple wine down his cassock and across the altar.

And then the corpse began to move.

For a second—amid the shocked collective intake of breath and then the screams—Matt could only blink and stare at the impossible as his mind searched for some rationalization. When he struck upon the obvious answer, that the professor had only been mistaken for dead, it made utter sense to him for five or six seconds. Precious seconds, in which it became clear that he was not the only one to whom this had occurred.

"Don?" Mrs. Wickstrom said in a quavering, hopeful voice. "Oh my God, Don?"

She struggled to extricate herself from her family, pulled herself out of the pew. Staggering, she went to him, fell down on her knees beside her husband and the jutting, awkward ruin of his coffin.

Matt shook his head. Mistakes might have been made in another age, but this was the twenty-first century, not to mention the Catholic Church. Cadavers were embalmed.

He had already been on his feet and now he stepped out into the center aisle, into a maelstrom of people, some trying to flee this horrid thing they could not understand and others trying to move up for a better look at this miracle.

"No," he said as Mrs. Wickstrom reached for her husband. But the cacophony of the congregation drowned out his voice.

Don Wickstrom sat up, lolled his head back as though he was having trouble holding it up, and would undoubtedly have been staring at his wife if it weren't for the thread that had been used to sew his eyes shut. His face was slack with what could only be sadness, and he tried to mumble something but his lips had also been sewn together.

The widow's tears had streaked her face black with mascara. Her hands trembled as she reached out to touch her husband's hair. A moan escaped him that could be heard throughout the church in spite of the anarchy within.

The professor opened his mouth, mortician's thread shredding his lips. He clamped his hands on either side of his wife's head and drew her toward him as though for a kiss. Instead, his jaws closed on her cheek, teeth ripping skin, and he tossed his head back in a single motion that tore a huge gobbet of flesh and muscle from her face as he choked it down without chewing.

The shrieks shook the rafters. A stampede began, nearly everyone heading in the same direction now. At the altar, Father Ryan clutched his stomach and then stumbled toward the sacristy. Mrs. Wickstrom's sons rushed to her aid, pulling her back, one of them stripping off his coat and holding it to his mother's face. The other tried to grab hold of the thing that had once been his father, but the dead man snatched at his son's hand and buried his teeth into the meaty forearm.

Matt went against the tide. He shoved several people out of his path, focusing only on the abomination unfolding in front of the altar. Someone called his name and he glanced over to see Noah hustling Amanda Littrell along with the exodus.

"Move!" Matt shouted. "Out of the way!"

Like frightened animals they turned their eyes upon him before shuffling aside. Wickstrom's son was roaring in pain, punching his father in the head again and again, but like some guard dog, the dead man would not unclench his jaws. Others went to help now, trying to pull him away.

Bone crunched and the dead man's teeth tore loose. He spun on an older man, some relative or friend, and lunged at the gray-haired man, driving him to the floor and burying his face in the man's belly with ugly strength and terrible speed. His jaws gnashed as he drove his face against the man's abdomen, trying to bite through his shirt and flesh to get to the soft organs inside.

If Matt had given himself a moment to react—if the screams had not made it impossible for him to think rationally—he would have joined in the shrieking and run the other way. But others were pulling at Wickstrom's arms now and the old man on the floor might be torn open any moment.

"Get out of the way!" he roared at a well-dressed man who'd been just standing and staring in disgust and fear, doing nothing to help.

Matt tore himself loose from the last of the crowd. He stood only feet from the bloody melee in the shadow of the altar and knew that whatever unnatural thing had been set loose this morning had to be stopped immediately.

Without another thought he reached out and grabbed the tall, heavy brass candle stand, lifted it over his shoulder like a baseball bat, and swung it.

"Move!"

They moved.

Despite his sewn-shut eyes, Don Wickstrom began to turn as though to look at him. Matt put all his strength into his swing. The weighted base of the candle stand struck Wickstrom in the temple and caved in his skull with a wet pop.

The corpse fell to the ground, head split open, and did not move again.

The screaming continued.

Someone tried to grab Matt—though whether to thank him or somehow blame him he would never know—and he shook the grip off and started down the aisle. The church had nearly emptied now and he stumbled, dazed, away from the altar and out the massive arched doors.

The wind whipped cold rain into his face and he blinked as though coming awake. Nearby, ambulance and police sirens wailed. Down on the road in front of the church parking lot, cars bulleted along at insane speed, far too fast for a quiet street in Amherst.

Some of the congregation had umbrellas but most had left them inside the church. Their eyes were wide with shock and rain ran down their faces, slicking their hair. Matt saw at least half a dozen people with cell phones out, probably calling the police.

Then he spotted Noah and Professor Littrell. They were standing together, Noah on his cell, looking more like a secret service agent than a college kid, and the professor glancing around with wild eyes. She spotted Matt coming toward her and her face crumpled a bit in relief at the sight of another familiar face.

"Are you all right, Professor?"

She nodded. "Fine. Just . . . just completely out of my mind."

"Only if we all are," Matt told her.

She put a hand over her mouth as though to stifle a cry, then ran a hand through her soaking red hair and gave him a grateful look.

Noah snapped his phone shut and looked at them both.

"This is . . ." he started, words trailing off. Noah glanced at the church and then down at the street. A Toyota drove by doing at least seventy, the driver laying on the horn and swerving on the wet road to go around one of the parked cars.

"This isn't just happening here," he said.

Matt stared at him. "What?"

"This!" Noah shouted, blue eyes flint-hard, a tinge of hysteria in his voice. He pointed to the church. "This! It's happening everywhere. I just talked to my girlfriend. It's all over the news now. It's happening all over the place down there—New York, Jersey, Connecticut. And now it's happening here! She was trying to call me during mass, but I didn't want to answer."

He laughed, eyes frantic. "Didn't want to be that guy, you know? The rude guy. And all the time, Mara's trying to call me because the dead are rising from their graves! It's the friggin' End Times and she wants to be with me if things are really ending, if it's the Rapture, which I don't even believe in!"

Professor Littrell stared at him. "Did you see what happened in there? Do you believe in *that*?"

For several heartbeats, the three of them only stared at one another. Matt broke the silence by patting his pocket to make sure he had his keys.

"Professor, I'm sorry, but I've got to go. You'll be all right with Noah. But my family's down in New York—my dad and my little sister—and if this is really happening, whatever it is, I've gotta get to them. Be with them."

Noah locked eyes with him. "Where in New York?"

"Pelham. In Westchester County."

"My girlfriend's in Scarsdale."

Matt hesitated. In the space of minutes the world had turned into a nightmare around him. It made him giddy with disbelief to even think the thoughts that were racing through his mind. The dead rising up, killing people. Trying to get to his family might get him killed. If he was going to die, he hated the idea that the last face he would see would belong to Noah Eisen. But he also didn't want to go alone.

"Ride with me," Matt said.

Noah frowned, wiping away raindrops that ran down his face from his rain-darkened hair. "What're you driving?"

"A Prius."

"You can ride with *me*. I'm in a Jeep Cherokee. If something comes at the car, I'd rather be in something higher up and a little more substantial."

Matt nodded. He couldn't disagree with the logic. People all around them were starting to hurry off toward their cars, wanting to get home to their loved ones or at least somewhere inside where they could lock out the world and watch it all unfold on television. Safe. Or so they hoped.

"Professor," Matt said, turning to her.

"Amanda," she said. "I think we're a little beyond formalities, Matt."

"Okay, Amanda. You going to be all right here?"

She thought about it, gaze shifting toward the parking lot, considering. Though Matt had always thought her attractive for a woman pretty much twice his age, Amanda looked ancient at that moment, the crinkles deepening at the edges of her gray eyes.

"I probably would be, yeah. But my mother lives by herself in a condo in Paramus, New Jersey. I need to get to her, but I don't want to try traveling alone. Can I ride with you as far as you're going, and figure it out from there?"

Before they could reply, a scream tore through the storm. Matt wiped rain from his eyes as he turned. Down on the street—hard to see through the gray wash of the day and the curtain of rain—someone staggered from the sidewalk, lunging after two women who cried out and ran into the road.

Brakes squealed and tires slid on the wet pavement, and with a sickening crump, a Volvo station wagon struck the man who was pursuing the women. The women kept running, but the driver got out, shouting apologies and prayers. He bent over the man in the street, calling for anyone with a cell phone to call 911, though it seemed obvious the man was dead.

Until the dead man grabbed the driver and pulled him down to the rain-swept road.

"We're out of here," Matt said.

They started running, following Noah toward his Jeep.

"We need to start thinking ahead," Noah said. "What happened to Professor Wickstrom?"

"I stopped him. Hit him . . . in the head." He didn't want to be any more explicit than that for Amanda's sake. The two teachers had been friends.

Noah pulled out his keys, unlocked his Jeep, and as they climbed in, he fired the engine up. He glanced at Amanda in the passenger seat, then looked back at Matt.

"We're gonna need weapons."

Manhattan, New York City

THE EMTs WEREN'T COMING. The police weren't coming. It had taken Phoenix a while to get used to the idea that nobody would be responding to the crisis in the *Sunrise* studio. Five people were catatonic, a couple of them clearly ill, all linked together in a circuit of held hands that could not be broken. Any other day and there would be paramedics there to help. Doctors. Cops. Experts working on figuring out what the hell had happened to these five people and how to fix it. How to wake them up.

How to wake her father.

But this wasn't any other day. The windows that overlooked Times Square showed chaos in the rain, a churning mob of people leaving their jobs, trying to get home to the people they loved—the ones who were still alive. With traffic locked in a standstill, others abandoned their vehicles to join the throng, only making the jam-up worse.

There weren't many cemeteries in Manhattan. Old, tiny ones mostly, with bits of ancient bone no longer able to maintain any cohesion at all. But up in Washington Heights there must be places where people were still buried, and in the outlying boroughs there would be thousands of graves—hundreds of thousands—millions.

God . . . millions?

And how many recent enough that the remains within could still be held together with whatever spiritual energy inhabited these corpses now? How many?

Phoenix didn't want to think about it. Especially after some of the reports they had seen on the news of people murdered, savaged by the walking dead, who had then risen from the dead themselves. They would multiply with hideous speed. However many there were now, by nightfall there would be three times as many, perhaps more.

Hugging herself, chilly with the air-conditioning, she walked over to a group that had gathered beneath one of the huge monitors that hung in the studio. Most of the staffers from *Sunrise* had gone upstairs to the regular news broadcasting center, lending their assistance where they could. The show's producer, John Volk, had stuck around, as had two of the security guards and the young guy she'd thought of as Stubble Boy, who turned out to be a production assistant named Peyton. He looked like a Peyton. Beyond them, the only people who remained were the network medic—a physician's assistant, really—the small handful of reporters, website journalists, other audience members who'd stayed behind, and the publicist for Eric Honen, who'd been crying steadily ever since they'd all watched the newscast from Jersey on Leah's laptop.

The medic hovered around the table checking the pulses of his catatonic patients every few minutes but seemed otherwise totally baffled. Phoenix wanted to scream at him to do something, to fix them, but supposed that as long as they didn't get worse there was little else he could do for now.

On the huge television monitor—set to the network's own news coverage—Andy Schmidt talked to reporters from as far south as Washington, D.C., and as far north as Boston and Albany. What they called a phenomenon—and what Andy himself seemed to have dubbed "the uprising," as though the dead were coming back to life to protest something—continued to worsen. Stories had begun to come in about people opening their doors to discover recently deceased loved ones on the front stoop. The dead were hungry, but there was more to it than that.

The dead were going *home.*

Phoenix had tried calling her mother a couple of dozen times. The phone lines were jammed. Sometimes she got a fast busy signal but other times that annoying recording came on, telling her to try back later. Eventually she gave up—at least for the time being—feeling the same sense of useless frustration that she felt while waiting for a slow-moving elevator. Even as a kid, shopping in department stores with her mom, she'd always pressed the elevator button over and over in impatience until her mother made her stop.

She'd try calling again later. Maybe she'd get lucky.

On the monitor now was an aerial view of a cemetery outside of Philadelphia. The earth on many of the graves had been disturbed and there were bits and pieces of long-interred bodies scattered in the cemetery like debris after a flood. Some were partially intact, withered things of bone and strips of skin or muscle, twitching and dragging themselves but getting nowhere.

The camera view widened and now a familiar scene unfolded of police and the undead engaged in a chilling skirmish. Suddenly the view altered, went out of focus, the camera swinging around as the helicopter maneuvered into a different flight path. Another helicopter could be seen approaching, but this enormous black flying beast was not a news chopper. The new arrival had to be a kind of military airship.

Phoenix squeezed her eyes closed and glanced away.

"This can't be," someone whispered nearby. "It's just not—"

"Possible?" Phoenix snapped, rounding on the man, a journalist from the New York *Daily News.* "If I hear one more person say this is impossible, I'm going to start swinging, I swear to God."

John Volk and Peyton looked up from their conversation with the medic, but watched for only a moment to make sure she wasn't actually going to assault anyone. Leah, the web journalist who'd been the first to find the hellish news, looked up from her laptop with sympathy in her eyes. Though Leah was short and pale and seemed to carry around a lot of baby fat, she had to be at least thirty, and had a quiet confidence that lent her an air of authority.

But Phoenix wasn't in the mood for authority. Leah started to say something, but Phoenix just shook her head and walked away. The others kept watching the monitor, but she'd seen enough. It was happening all over the northeast and spreading fast. They were probably safer in the middle of Times Square than in some suburb. It would take the dead time to get here—she hoped.

Still, she'd have to ask Volk if the network had sealed off the doors. Somebody had probably already thought of such things, but it would be best to be sure.

She felt a small laugh bubbling up inside herself and kept it from leaving her lips. Madness lay in that direction. She managed a strange calm, but she knew if she scratched the surface of that calm she'd find hysteria underneath.

Phoenix walked over to the table in the faux dining room set. The medic had dragged a chair up beside her father but then abandoned it, so she sat down next to him. His brow was furrowed. It might have been easier if he seemed peaceful, as though sleeping, but wherever his mind was now, Joe Cormier was troubled.

"It'll be all right, Dad," she whispered, face flushing with emotion. Tears threatened but she refused to shed them. "You'll wake up. And I'll be right here."

When Phoenix was in the fifth grade, her mother had brought a locksmith to the house and changed all the locks. It had taken her father three days to discover that his key no longer worked. His long hours at the university, both lecturing and advising students, and his work as a medium, had kept him away from home far too often. Mary Cormier had had enough of being ignored. She'd even accused him of infidelity, but Phoenix had never believed it. Her father was distracted, lost in his own world—lost, really, in the past, both in the study of history and in the spirits of the dead with whom he had always claimed to converse. He had spent far more time focused on the dead than the living.

For years after that, Phoenix rarely saw or spoke to her father. Once she'd gotten her own email address, though, that had changed. He seemed better able to express himself that way. They had begun a very tentative correspondence, and when he'd asked her to come along with him on the book tour for *Soul Versus Spirit*—to spend the summer with him—she'd agreed. Her only hesitation had been worrying about what her mother would think, but to her surprise, her mother had already known he planned to ask her, and she approved.

For years, her father had been so wrapped up in his work that he seemed almost to forget he even had a daughter. But living with him this summer, she'd found herself recalling mostly fond memories—days at the beach when she'd been a little girl, or helping her dad clean out the garage. He'd taught her how to ride a bike and how to throw a baseball so Jimmy Kelso would stop saying she threw like a girl, and he hadn't punished her when she'd whipped the ball at Kelso hard enough to raise a lump on his forehead.

Grudgingly, she'd admitted to herself that in those times, Joe Cormier had been in the moment with her, focused on his daughter. He wasn't incapable of surfacing from his work; he just couldn't stop his mind from drifting back there most of the time.

Just last week, after a book signing in Cambridge, Massachusetts, he'd taken her out for ice cream and astonished her by remembering her favorite was black raspberry. There'd been a moment of connection then that she held on to now.

Her father's disinterest had colored her entire life. If she wasn't careful, she knew that resentment could taint everything the future held for her. For her sake, if not for his, she had to find a way to forgive him. And over the past couple of months, she'd been working at that, and at convincing herself that he had always loved her but didn't know how to behave any differently. He hadn't been there for her drama club productions or her soccer games, hadn't worried the way fathers were supposed to about who she was dating and if she was having sex. Presents came when they'd occurred to him, often far too late for birthdays or Christmas, and she'd hated how happy it made her any time he remembered her.

But the time had come to put the past behind them, to define what their relationship would be in the future. "Forgive and forget," people had a habit of saying. But at eighteen, Phoenix had pretty much figured out that while she could manage the forgiveness, the forgetting didn't come so easily.

Still, they were starting to learn the new dynamic that existed between them now that she was older. Phoenix had actually begun to admit to herself that, despite it all, she actually liked her quirky workaholic father.

And the world had fallen apart around them.

You have to wake up, she thought, clutching his arm and staring intently at his closed eyes. Phoenix tried to will him awake, but he did not so much as stir. Her heart filled with terror as she considered the possibility that even once he was separated from the other members of the séance, he would remain catatonic. What if her father never woke up again?

She dragged her chair closer and laid her cheek against his shoulder, the rough fabric of his jacket against her skin.

Her father exhaled.

Startled, Phoenix pulled back and stared at his face, searching for any change, but his condition had not changed. Crestfallen, she reached up to brush his hair back.

"*. . . can't help it,*" he said.

Phoenix gave a sharp cry and pulled back, staring at him.

"Daddy?"

As she studied him, waiting for more words, wondering if she had imagined the whole thing—his lips hadn't moved, had they?—others ran over, gathering behind her.

"Is he coming around?" Volk asked.

"Professor?" someone said. "Professor Cormier?"

Phoenix glanced up and saw that it was Ray Creedon, one of the web journalists who'd been sitting in the front row.

The medic pushed between them and felt her father's pulse. Phoenix saw with dismay that his grip on Amy Tjan's hand seemed as tight as ever. The medic started calling his name again. Her father's expression didn't change, but she heard a kind of rasp.

"Quiet!" she snapped.

Everyone hushed and listened.

"*. . . want what they were promised,*" her father exhaled again.

"Did you see that?" Volk said. "His lips didn't even move."

"What is he talking about?" Leah asked, pushing up beside Phoenix. "Is he having a dream or something?"

Phoenix shook her head. The voice didn't belong to her father. It was too high, too thin and reedy. It was an old woman's voice, a soft, rasping whisper.

"They want to see the ones they left behind . . ."

"That's not Professor Cormier's voice," Ray said. "He's just a conduit."

"What the hell are you talking about?" Volk snapped, rubbing a hand over the stubble on his head.

Ray looked at her then—looked at her like he knew her, like they were old friends—and she wondered who this guy was really. Handsome in a scruffy sort of way, he seemed far too confident for his age. A connection crackled between them, an unseen, unspoken awareness that they were allies, and she almost reached for his hand to thank him for being on her side.

"Who is it, then?" Leah asked.

Phoenix turned to answer, but Ray beat her to it.

"It's got to be Mrs. LaVallee. She's his spirit guide."

They all stared at him. Phoenix had been about to say the very same thing.

"You're saying that's the voice of a ghost?" Volk scoffed.

Phoenix scowled at him. "Go look at your monitor, pal. Watch a few seconds of the news and tell me you have a hard time believing that."

Admonished, Volk nodded. "Fine. What's he—or she—talking about?"

A sigh escaped her father's slightly parted lips, a cold mist pluming from within. The cold that had descended on the studio during the séance, shorting out lights and freezing cameras, had quickly abated afterward. But inside her father, the chill remained.

Feeling foolish, Phoenix leaned forward. "Mrs. LaVallee? What do you mean? What were they promised?"

Her father's body shuddered. Where her hand touched his, her skin grew so cold she pulled her fingers away.

"Just want to talk, to see the ones they love. But the flesh is so heavy. So heavy.

And they are so empty inside. They can't help feeling empty, feeling hungry. They only wanted to talk."

Phoenix shuddered. Now she understood.

"But they're killing . . . some of them are killing the people they love, the ones they came back to see."

A tear ran down her father's cheek and she wondered if it was Joe Cormier or Mrs. LaVallee crying.

"They can't stop. They're only spirits. Memories and emotions, but nothing pure. They're soulless, and all they know now is hunger and the yearning for . . . for home."

Her father began to choke. His body twitched once, twice, and then a trickle of blood flowed from his nose.

"Check him!" Volk snapped.

The medic reached for one arm and Phoenix for the other. He still had a pulse, was still breathing. Still alive.

"Mrs. LaVallee?" Ray Creedon said.

This time, no reply came. She had withdrawn; whatever effort the spirit had needed to speak to them either weakened her or had done some kind of damage to her host.

Phoenix used her sleeve to wipe the blood from her father's nose, held on to his wrist, and said nothing more. The others broke up into small groups, whispering among themselves. Only Ray Creedon stayed with her, looking over her shoulder and then circling the table to check on the others again.

"Who are you, anyway? How did you know about Mrs. LaVallee?"

He shrugged. "Just a guy. Kind of an expert on mediums."

"Wait, you're, like, a fan?" She hadn't meant it to come out so dismissive, but most of her father's "fans" tended to be ethereal flakes or way-too-intense nut jobs.

Ray didn't seem to be like that. He might be a little intense, and the crazy hair marked him as odd, but she'd always had a thing for quirky guys.

Ray gave her a quick, sardonic smile. "He's your father. Aren't *you* a fan?"

The question brought her up short. Half of her was insulted at the comparison. She was Joe Cormier's daughter, part of his life, and Ray Creedon was just some guy who obsessed over life after death, or whatever. But the other half of her wondered how she would answer the question. He probably knew more about her father than she did, and it was obvious he hadn't meant any offense by it.

"Will they wake up, do you think?" she asked, turning to gaze at her father.

"They'd better," Ray said. "These three may have started all this, but they're also probably the only people in the country who'd have the first clue how to end it."

As he spoke, John Volk approached. He'd overheard Ray's comment, and he gave a shake of his head.

"I don't know about that," he said. "We were just talking, and it certainly stands to reason that if the séance started all this, putting an end to the séance may stop it. We've got to get these people separated."

Phoenix frowned. *We?*

"We've been trying to pull those people apart since they all went catatonic or whatever," Ray said. "They can't be separated."

Volk glanced over at the five unconscious people around the table on the faux dining room set. He scratched the back of his head. "It's been suggested that maybe we haven't tried hard enough."

Phoenix stared. The medic, Jim, and Stubble Boy Peyton were shifting the chairs in which her father and Steve Bell sat. The medic wrinkled his nose at the smell of dried urine that still wafted off of Bell. They muttered quietly among themselves, and then crouched and began to tug the two catatonic men's arms, trying to force them apart.

Jim gave up first. "Hold on."

He moved in close to the two men's joined hands, trying to force a gap between their clutched palms. Phoenix watched in trepidation, wishing that by some miracle those hands would come apart.

When Peyton stepped over with a letter opener and tried to slide it between the joined palms, Phoenix flinched.

"What the hell are you doing?" she asked, storming over to him.

Jim looked chagrined, but Peyton rolled his eyes.

"What does it look like we're doing?" he asked, as he bent again to try to push the letter opener between their palms.

Phoenix slapped his hands away. He looked up at her, blinking in surprise, and she put both hands on his chest and shoved him back.

"Stay away from my father."

Peyton looked to Jim and to John Volk for assistance, but the medic glanced away in frustration.

"Phoenix, something's got to be done. If they're responsible—"

"You don't know that," she snapped.

Volk turned to Ray Creedon. "Didn't you two just establish that?"

Phoenix held her breath, afraid of what Ray might say.

He nodded. "Yeah, all right, everything points that way. But there's no reason to think that separating them is going to stop anything. The door's open. The dead are coming in. It might as well be a forest fire. This might've been the match that started it, but it's beyond anyone's control now."

"You think?" Peyton snapped. "You don't know any more than we do. And if there's even a chance we could stop it here, we have to."

Jim cleared his throat. "Yeah, that'd be nice. But I can't see any way to separate these people. So the point is kind of moot."

Phoenix shot him a grateful look.

Peyton wasn't satisfied. "We have to find a way."

"Just stay away from my father," she told him.

He didn't reply, only walked off, talking quietly to John Volk. The medic gave her an apologetic shrug and followed after them.

A terrible, icy feeling coiled around Phoenix's heart.

"Thanks," she said to Ray.

"No problem," he replied. But he studied the five people around the table, and the junctions where their hands met, and she could see that he was weighing, considering, and the knowledge scared her.

Joe Cormier might have been a lame excuse for a father, but he was *her* father, and a good man. Right now he couldn't protect himself, so that left it up to Phoenix, and she refused to let any harm come to him.

At eighteen, she knew she was an adult. Hell, she'd felt like an adult since the first day of high school. But adult or not, she missed her mother. Soon, she'd try the phone again, but she knew that only a dead line or a busy signal awaited her.

Phoenix touched her father on the shoulder and glanced around the studio, on guard. Her father had a lot to make up for, and she wouldn't let anyone take away their future together.

6

Dobbs Ferry, New York

The town sat on a hill that sloped down to the Hudson River. The main street had changed very little in the past twenty or thirty years, a single street lined with pizza places, restaurants, and small shops. Spaced along the sidewalk were lampposts and trees that grew up from round patches of earth carved out of the concrete. It might have seemed odd if not for the acres of trees that loomed farther up the hill, a picturesque view from the quaint little downtown.

Tomko's Grille sat on a steep side street where the buildings rested against one another in a terraced row. A pair of minivans parked at the curb flanked a quartet of motorcycles, but Tomko's seemed the kind of place that would appeal to both minivan families and bikers alike. Neon beer signs gleamed in the window, but the pub was too well cared for to ever be called a dive.

"Here you go," the waitress said, and slid an oval plate across the table. "Get you anything else?"

Jack Kim glanced at the ham and cheese omelet, stomach growling, even as she set a smaller plate with wheat toast beside it. Once out of the Bronx he had purposely lost himself in Westchester County, stopping in Dobbs Ferry only because he needed to clear his head and think about his next move. Breakfast had been an afterthought, just something to do while he contemplated, but now that the omelet had arrived he discovered that he was starving.

"Actually, yeah. Some of those breakfast potatoes would be great."

The waitress smiled. "Somebody's hungry."

He laughed as he caught and held her gaze for a few seconds. Her name tag read KELLI. She had skin like caramel and eyes the color of new pennies, and her smile woke something up inside of him. Big Boy liked to say Jack had "girl trouble," but the trouble had always been too many girls. Jack couldn't help himself and, for better or worse, often the girls couldn't help themselves either.

"It's going to be a long day," he explained. "Don't know when I'll stop to eat again."

"Busy guy. Where are you headed?"

"I'm trying to figure that out. Any suggestions?"

She smiled. "Florida's too hot this time of year. Maybe Maine. It's peaceful up there. Quiet."

"Maine, huh?" He nodded. "Maybe."

Kelli narrowed her eyes, seeming unable to figure out what to make of him. A lot of waitresses Jack had met were detached from the world, just sleepwalking through their jobs until they could get home, but Kelli did not share that quality. She inhabited the moment instead of drifting toward the end of her shift in a trance.

Despite Kelli's preference, Florida sounded much better to Jack than Maine, no matter how hot it might be. Even here in this little pub, he felt like an outsider. He'd shed the colors that marked him as one of the Smoke Dragons, but a Korean guy from the Bronx whose arms were covered with tattoos wouldn't exactly fit in up in Maine. He'd feel a lot less out of place in Miami or Fort Lauderdale.

"Let me get you those potatoes," Kelli said.

Jack nodded. "Thanks." He felt a momentary temptation to flirt. Another day he might have asked her to ditch work, climb in the car with him, and just take off. But this wasn't another day. He had too much to think about. Big Boy had put his life on the line to help him, and Jack would never forget that, but it was only now beginning to sink in that he wasn't going to be able to go back to the Bronx for a long time. Maybe forever.

He smiled until Kelli walked away and then he rubbed at his temples. His stomach growled again. He shifted and his foot hit the backpack on the floor under the table—no way was he leaving all of that cash in the car—and it reminded him again that he'd been cast adrift. He'd need a job and a place to live, and it couldn't be anywhere he might run into someone he knew.

It's like pressing restart, he thought. He had to begin his life all over again.

Jack used his fork to cut off a section of omelet, loaded it on top of a slice of toast, and put it to his mouth as though he were eating a piece of pizza. Starving was a bad idea. He'd think better on a full stomach.

A few minutes later, Kelli reappeared with a plate of breakfast potatoes.

"There you go," she said.

As he glanced up at her, Jack noticed a group of people had gathered in front of the bar. Tomko's Grille served food all day long, but the bar couldn't possibly be open during breakfast unless they were serving some kind of fruity champagne brunch drink or something. And yet Jack spotted a couple of waiters, a busboy, and half a dozen patrons standing around and staring at the television mounted behind the bar. He couldn't see the screen from where he sat, but he was sure it hadn't been on when he came in. A couple of shaggy bikers stood beside a family who'd been eating their breakfast when Jack arrived. They had to have finished by now; maybe they'd been on their way out when their attention had been drawn by whatever was on the screen. As he watched, the mother clapped her hand over her preteen daughter's eyes.

"What's going on?" Jack asked.

Kelli arched an eyebrow, then turned to see what he was looking at. He glanced up in time to see her frown, a troubled expression on her face.

"No idea. That's not even supposed to be on."

Her words carried a certain weight, an acknowledgment of the thought Jack had already had and which she could not possibly avoid. *This is bad. Whatever's happening, it's big.*

Jack slid out of his chair. He and Kelli exchanged a glance and started for the bar.

A screech of tires burst into the relative quiet of Tomko's. Every head turned. Outside, a car skidded into view on the steep side street, fishtailing wildly. For an instant, Jack felt sure that it would plow right into the plate-glass windows at the front of the restaurant, but then the nose of the car swung back the other way as the driver tried to get control. The rusty old BMW struck a telephone pole with a loud crunch that shook the windows in their frames.

The two bikers at the bar ran for the door, swinging it open and rushing to help, if they could. As the door swung shut behind them, the father who'd been on the way out with his family started to follow.

"Russ, no," his wife said, grabbing him by the arm.

The father turned toward her and she gave him a meaningful glance, holding her daughter with one hand and her husband with the other. Holding her family together.

"We can't stay in here forever," he said.

She hesitated, then nodded. "All right. We should go, before it gets worse. Get home, I guess."

"We'll be safer there," Russ said.

"Safer from what?" Kelli asked.

Jack had been about to ask the same question. He went to the plate-glass window and watched the bikers looking in the window of the ruined BMW, trying to get the doors open. Then he hurried back toward Kelli and looked up at the television over the bar.

He shook his head. "What the hell are you all watching?"

The busboy glanced over at him. "It's CNN."

Jack almost laughed. Sure, it said CNN at the bottom of the screen, but what Jack saw were cops shooting at walking, rotting corpses. This had to be a horror flick showing a fake news report.

"It's not just CNN," said one of the waiters, an older guy with a sunburn, glasses crooked on his nose. "It's on every channel."

The busboy snorted. " 'Course it is. The apocalypse comes, that's pretty much the big news of the day."

Kelli hugged herself, shivering, and stared at the screen. She shook her head. "That can't be real."

Then they heard sirens in the distance, and they weren't coming from the television set. Jack and Kelli glanced at each other and then hurried to the front of the restaurant. Russ the Dad and his wife and daughter were already there, peering out through the glass. Jack noticed they hadn't actually left, despite the rush they'd been in moments before.

The girl couldn't have been more than eleven. Her blond hair had been pulled back in a ponytail and tied with a band of beads with a purple butterfly on it. It was the kind of thing girls stopped wearing when they reached a certain age, or when they started paying too much attention to the rest of the world.

"Mom, what's wrong with that man?" the girl asked.

Her blue eyes were narrowed and the scattering of freckles under her eyes and on the bridge of her nose crinkled up in a kind of childish revulsion. At first Jack thought she meant the poor bastard who'd been driving the ruined BMW. The bikers were now dragging the guy—who seemed conscious, though bleeding badly from a scalp wound—out of the car, helping him move toward Tomko's Grille.

Then the girl raised her hand and pointed up toward the intersection with the main street, where a figure staggered through the rain in tattered clothes, one arm missing and half his face obliterated. In the gloom of the storm it might have been nothing but shadow and illusion, but when the figure turned slightly, Jack could see the rain glistening on yellowed skull.

Jack bolted for the door, throwing it open, and called to the bikers, who were half dragging the injured BMW driver back toward the restaurant.

"Move it, man."

The two hulking bikers glared at him, but Jack pointed toward the dead man shambling along the rain-slicked pavement. They glanced that way and then doubled their speed, nearly lifting the bleeding motorist off his feet to get him through the door of Tomko's.

The blare of a car horn cut through the storm. Jack looked up in time to see a pickup hit the one-armed dead man with a dry snap. The car skidded on the wet road and came to a stop and the driver jumped out. Jack would have yelled to warn him, but the thing he'd hit with his truck wasn't moving at all.

"This is happening," one of the bikers—a redheaded Viking-looking guy—said to the other as they carried the barely conscious guy through the door.

"So what do we do?" Russ the Dad asked, pulling out a chair for the injured driver.

The bikers exchanged a look, then the Viking turned to Jack, who shrugged. He glanced over at Kelli before answering.

"I'm just passing through."

The Viking laughed derisively. "You see the TV?"

"Yeah," Jack said.

"How far you think you're gonna get?"

It was a damned good question.

Pelham, New York

A TERRIBLE QUIET ENVELOPED Sara's bedroom, disrupted only by the hissing white noise of the rain on her windows and the low hum of her computer. She sat at her computer desk, mouse frozen in her hand, and stared at her monitor. Zack stood behind her, one hand on her shoulder like he'd put it there to comfort her and then forgotten all about it.

Her father never liked her to have Zack in her bedroom, which amused Sara to no end. Okay, he was cute enough, and he'd given up on the saggy-jeans-and-knit-hat look he'd adopted for a while in favor of spiky gelled hair and tight T-shirts that looked a little silly on his skinny white-boy frame. But Daddy didn't have anything to worry about, because she thought of Zack as a brother. Sometimes she thought he had other things in mind, caught him looking at her the way guys looked at girls, but Sara never encouraged that sort of thing. They were already as intimate as she could ever imagine being with a guy, no sex required.

Just then, however, Sara barely registered the hand on her shoulder.

Not that it mattered. Her father had left for work that morning as always. When Zack showed up at her door, rousing her from bed with his knocking and then babbling about riots in the city, it hadn't occurred to her that the danger would spread north.

"My dad," she said, reaching for the phone. She dialed his office in White Plains.

"Harold Gaines's office."

"Hi. This is Sara. Is my dad there?"

The assistant hesitated. "I'm sorry, sweetie, he's not. He had a meeting off-site this morning. I've tried his cell, but I'm having a hard time getting through. Are you all right there?"

Sara frowned. "Are you watching the news?"

"No," the woman said. "There's no television here. But I hear it's pretty bad. Don't worry. I'm sure they'll have these people under control in no time."

Blinking, Sara looked at her computer monitor. Nothing would be under control anytime soon.

"If my dad calls in, can you ask him to come home, like, right away?"

"I will, honey. I'll make sure he calls you the instant he gets in touch and I'll tell him what you said."

Sara thanked her and ended the call, then immediately started dialing her father's cell. The sound that crackled in her ear was nothing she'd ever heard before, a signal that the emergency had overloaded the system and no service was available. Her own cell phone sat in the pocket of yesterday's jeans, which lay in a crumpled pile in front of her closet. She got up from her chair and retrieved it, then sat down again and turned it on, hoping there might be a message from her father.

Nothing. She told herself he must be having just as much trouble getting through to her. Quickly she tried her brother's cell phone. Matt had stayed at college for the summer and didn't bother with a land line. But she didn't have any more luck reaching him.

"When are your parents due back from Toronto?" Sara asked.

"Three days," Zack said. "And I tried them in their hotel before I came here. I left a message. Maybe they were at breakfast. I got through to my mom's cell, but her voice mail picked up."

Slowly, Sara forced herself to look at the computer monitor again.

"It can't be real," Zack said.

Sara clicked the volume off. The shouting and the wailing of police sirens was too much for her. She opened up a Breaking News story titled "Zombie Uprising in New York Spreading" and read the first few paragraphs. At the bottom of the article, in italics, the author had written *Developing . . .*

A small laugh escaped her lips. "There you go. Leave it to the online news people to use the word."

"What?"

"Zombie. All the live feeds from the networks and stuff keep talking about 'the dead.' Before they had proof of that they were all, 'Oh, it's terrorists, biological warfare, a virus turning people into homicidal lunatics.' It's happening right now. A hundred cameras are filming the end of the world but it takes computer hacks to actually start using the word everyone is already thinking."

"And that's funny to you?"

Sara swung in her chair and looked at him. Zack had paled and his blue eyes had lost their usual brightness.

She punched him in the arm. "You have to ask that? You think *I think* this is funny?"

He rubbed the spot where she'd hit him. " 'Course not."

"All right, then."

They focused again on the screen. Sara closed the window with the news story, bringing the live camera feed from Easton, Pennsylvania, back onto the monitor. The local station there was an ABC affiliate, and the network had locked onto the feed. The image shuddered as the camera operator ran from the chaos, making it nearly impossible to figure out what was being filmed.

"Turn the sound back up," Zack said.

Sara felt a sickening twist in her stomach and a chill rippled down the back of her neck. The rain seemed to grow louder on the roof and windows, but her monitor showed no rain at all in Pennsylvania. The sun shone down and glinted off the cars that the camera jostled past. At a certain angle she caught glimpses of blue sky, a perfect summer day.

She unmuted the computer. Voices came through the speakers.

"—stop, stop. We're clear. Put the camera on me. We've got to get this."

The view swung around to focus on a surprisingly momish-looking reporter. The terror in her eyes made Sara hold her breath. She hugged herself, rubbing her hands over the gooseflesh that had risen on her bare arms.

"This is Kate Schafer in Easton. My cameraman, Joe, and I are getting off the street as soon as this report is done and I advise all of you to do the same. Wherever you're watching this, barricade yourself in. If you have loved ones who aren't home, get them home, right now. There's no telling how far or how fast this is spreading, but it's real."

Her voice cracked on the last word and the microphone shook in her hand. "Some of you might think this is all a hoax. It's not. It's all real."

"She's crying," Zack whispered, his voice almost lost in the white noise of the rain.

Sara said nothing, only watched the tears slide down the reporter's face and wondered if she was indeed a mother, if her kids were somewhere watching this report.

"You still think this is some kind of stunt?"

Zack crouched beside her, staring at the screen. "I guess not. It's just so hard to believe."

"Not for me. I mean, okay, is this the apocalypse I was expecting? Hell, no. But seriously, every freakin' day some government moron comes on TV and tells us something awful is going to happen, a dirty bomb is going to take out a major American city, terrorists are coming, the environment is going to poison us, the world's going to flood. The media choke us on this crap. I listen to my dad and my brother and other adults talk and it's like ever since 9/11 they've just been waiting for something worse to come along, like it's inevitable. Well, here it is."

He turned to look at her. "But this? Nobody could have expected anything like this to ever *really* happen."

"But it is." Sara shuddered, the sick feeling in her stomach growing worse. The last thing she wanted was to cry in front of Zack, but she felt her eyes moistening and bit her lip. "It is, Zack. It really is."

"Hey," he said softly, and reached out for her.

A scream ripped from the computer speakers, the pitch so high they crackled with static. Sara tore herself from Zack and stared at the quaking image of the reporter standing paralyzed with fear, unable to run, frozen in the summer sunshine with her hands shaking out of control. For a second, Sara didn't understand why the woman had started screaming, why the image juddered that way.

Then she got it.

Something had grabbed hold of the cameraman. He still clutched the camera and it jerked in his grip. Other sounds lurked beneath the screaming. Wet, crunching sounds that made Sara put both hands over her mouth.

"Run, you dumb-ass!" Zack shouted.

But as her screams died, the woman only began to shake her head, muttering denials as she took a step backward. A bloodied hand passed in front of the lens, then the camera fell and struck the pavement, and the image went black and silent.

The feed returned to the ABC studio, the camera on a gray-haired anchorman wearing a stylish suit and a flashy tie. He stammered, staring straight ahead, and then fell silent. Several seconds passed and then the angle switched to a red-haired woman who normally did medical and health reports. She had started to stand and begun to unclip the microphone from the lapel of her suit when the camera caught her in motion.

"Heather!" someone hissed from behind the camera. A low chorus of voices could be heard in the studio chattering worriedly.

"We'll . . . we'll be right back," the redhead said. "I'm sorry."

She snaked the clip-on mic out from inside her blouse and dropped it on the desk and the network cut to a commercial for toothpaste.

From the crouch he'd been standing in, Zack sagged backward

and sat down hard. He put his head between his knees and wrapped his hands around the back of his neck, taking deep breaths.

Sara felt numb, staring at the computer screen. How could this be happening? How could it be real? The world didn't operate like this. School was real. Worrying about getting into a good college, and what she'd do for a living, and what condition the country and the world would be in when she had her own children someday . . . those things were real. Terrorists were real. But this?

"Oh no," she whispered to herself, barely aware that she'd started to rock in her chair, running her hands over the tight denim that wrapped her legs, taking some kind of subconscious solace in the texture of her jeans.

Sara shivered. It was August—she shouldn't be cold. She blamed the rain, and tried to remember where she'd left the UMass sweatshirt Matt had given her last Christmas.

They should go down to the living room, watch the television there. It would be quicker to switch channels, get a better idea of how widespread it all was. From what they'd seen so far online—starting with a single line about a riot in Hoboken—Connecticut, Jersey, Pennsylvania, and New York were all affected. The reports from Brooklyn had been the worst, up until just now.

"We should, I don't know, get some wood up over the windows. Like a hurricane's coming, maybe. Put the couch in front of the door," Zack said.

Sara jumped onto her bed and stared out the rain-spattered second-story window at the street below. Nothing moved outside except for trees bent by the wind.

"He'll come back," Zack said.

"Can I try your cell?"

He fished in his pocket and handed it to her. Sara dialed, thinking maybe it would make a difference having a different phone, a different service provider. But Zack's cell was worse and she had no tone at all, no message that she could not be connected. Not even the hiss of dead air, the way you got on a land line sometimes. Just nothing.

"All right." She handed his phone back. "Let's go downstairs and put the TV on. And maybe see what we can use to block the windows."

Sara thought her voice sounded calm. That was good. She didn't feel at all calm, but if they were going to try to protect the house—like they lived in Florida and there was a hurricane on the way—freaking out wouldn't be helpful. Inside, though, all she could think was *Come home, Dad. Come home, Dad. Come home, Dad,* as if that internal mantra could summon him up, like Aladdin rubbing the lamp to call the genie.

She went to her closet and dug out her hooded UMass sweatshirt, zipping it up. It smelled of laundry detergent, warm and soft, and it lent her some small comfort, making her think of Matt and Dad at the same time. As she closed the closet door she got a look at herself in the mirror and turned away quickly, hating the fear in her eyes. Her hair, which she usually worked hard to tame, was a bushy mess.

The house felt eerily empty.

"Sara."

As Zack said her name, another sound joined his voice—the roar of an engine. She spun, saw the way he'd bent to look back out the window, and ran to his side. Out in the storm, a silver Lexus tore along the street, rain sheeting off of the roof and windshield. One headlight illuminated the gray day; the other was destroyed. The front right quarter of the car had crumpled inward. Something dark flapped in the wind, attached to the nose of the Lexus.

Frozen, Sara watched her father's car spin out in front of the house, right itself, then bump over the lawn, only halfway on the driveway. The car mowed down the lamppost with the sound of shattering glass. Sara narrowed her eyes at the sight of the weird whiteness of the windshield, then realized the safety glass had been shattered, spider-webbed, but not collapsed.

"Daddy," she whispered.

The Lexus jerked to a halt in front of the house and the driver's door popped open. Her father, Hal, stumbled from the car toward the front steps, the engine still running, calling her name, and she said silent prayers of gratitude. They'd be all right now.

Sara bolted for the door, Zack hurtling along behind. She slid her hand along the railing as she hurtled down the stairs, then leaped the last five. In the foyer she could hear her father's key finding its way into the lock. Throwing the dead bolt, she hauled the door open and he staggered in. His eyes were desperate, his bald head beaded with rain.

Without a word, he wrapped his arms around her and held her close. She could feel his heart hammering in his chest. Her father trembled.

"Mr. Gaines?" Zack said. "What happened to your car?"

"Zack," he said, pulling back from his daughter. "I'm glad you're here. Saves us having to go and get you. With your parents still in Canada, no way was I leaving you home."

"Dad, what are you—"

"Pack a bag, sweet pea. We're out of here in two minutes. Some underpants, couple of shirts, couple of pairs of jeans or what have you. Go. Right now."

Sara stared at him. "But where are we going? On the news they're saying stay put, board the windows—"

"We stay here we're good as dead. They're just down the road now. Spreading out through the town."

Zack grabbed her arm. "I don't think we have two minutes."

He pointed. Sara and her father both turned to see several figures shambling through the rain. They didn't seem to have noticed the open door of the Gaines house yet, and Hal swung the door almost all the way shut, peeking out around it.

"All right. We go for the car. Engine's still running. As long as they haven't seen us . . ."

His words trailed off. Sara watched as her father hung his head.

"Janice," he said.

"Mrs. Goldschmidt? Did they get her?" Zack asked.

Sara forced her father to make room for her and she saw the figure, a woman in a housecoat, gray hair slicked on her face. Mrs. Goldschmidt stood by the open door of the Lexus and peered inside. As Sara watched, she swung her gaze toward the house.

Her eyes were wide, glistening white, and she bared her teeth like an animal. Her mouth was smeared with something dark and part of her lower lip hung in a ragged flap on her chin.

"Empty!" she howled in anguish. "I'm empty!"

With a bestial cry she hurled herself toward the front steps. Sara and Zack both began to scream. Mr. Gaines slammed the heavy wooden door and threw the deadbolt just before Mrs. Goldschmidt slammed into it with a wet cracking sound.

"Little pigs, little pigs," Mr. Gaines whispered.

"Daddy?" Sara said, afraid for his mind.

He turned grim eyes upon her. "Brick house, baby. We've got a brick house." Then he whacked Zack on the arm. "Move it, boy. Help with the windows. Janice may be the only quick one out there right now, but there'll be others along. God help us, there'll be others."

TRAFFIC CRAWLED ON THE Merritt Parkway. Tania perched on the edge of the limo's backseat, practically sticking her head through the open partition. The temptation to crawl through into the front seat with Derek was growing. Over his shoulder she could see the gas gauge.

"D, we've got to stop. We're gonna run out of gas."

Derek checked his mirror and slid the limo into the left lane. Horns blared.

"Next exit. I promise."

"That's what you said three exits ago."

Tania hated the whine in her own voice, but it wasn't petulance. She was terrified. At her request, Derek had shut off the car radio. She hadn't decided yet if she preferred ignorance to bad news. The silence felt almost worse. Not that they needed the radio to tell them the obvious. In the blink of an eye, the world had gone to hell. She told herself that as fast as it might be spreading, they could outrun it. The radio might tell her differently and, if so, she'd rather not hear.

"There were no signs for gas at those exits," Derek said. "We been over this."

They had tried to stop at a gas station before getting back on the Merritt, but there had been an abandoned car at the pumps and several dead people mulling about, so they'd been forced to drive on. Now, though, the needle had descended just below E. There couldn't be much more than fumes in the tank.

Tania stared out the tinted windows. She would've thought the southbound lane would be empty, but Derek had reminded her that lots of people had family and friends back there where it had all begun, where the worst of it was unfolding. Plus, they'd seen emergency vehicles and military caravans headed south.

Then there were the dead.

So far they'd seen just a few dozen—less than fifty—along the side of the highway. But at the exits they'd seen others coming down ramps at a walk or a stumble. They strayed close to cars that slowed, reaching out for them, but the only vehicle Tania had seen them pursue was a convertible, as if the vulnerability of the driver's exposure was too tempting to ignore.

The ones along the roadside weren't all going the same direction, but they did not appear to be wandering. Each one moved with an air of purpose. Wherever they were headed, these travelers were more intent on reaching their goals than they were on attacking passing motorists.

If she and Derek were on foot, though . . . that would be different.

"We've got to stop," Tania said, hating to tell him what he already knew.

"Do you see the cars, girl? I'm doin' the best I can." His huge head shook with frustration.

"I know, D. I'm sorry."

Tania tried to catch his eye in the rearview mirror but Derek was no longer paying any attention to her. He leaned forward.

"Son of a bitch," he snapped, jerking the steering wheel to the right.

A horn blared. A momentary screech of tires gave way to a loud crump as a van struck the passenger side of the limo. Tania cried out as she tumbled across the seat and struck her head on the door. Sprawled across the back of the limo, disoriented, she could just see the top of Derek's head as he shouted again and gunned the engine. Metal scraped on metal as the limo lurched forward.

"T, you okay?" he shouted, glancing into the backseat.

"I don't know," she said softly.

"Get up where I can see you. You all right?"

Slowly, braced for another impact, she did as he asked. She heard the furious blare of more horns.

"What happened?" she asked.

Derek nodded forward. "Traffic's at a dead stop up ahead. We get stuck in this, we'll be out of gas in a few minutes."

Tania stared past Derek at the road ahead. The Merritt Parkway curved slightly, but she could see a drifting tower of dark smoke rising in the distance.

"An accident, you think?"

"Maybe."

The word said everything neither of them wanted to say out loud. There would be a lot of accidents today, but there was equal chance that whatever caused the smoke ahead had been more attack than accident. Even now she saw several of the dead moving from the sides of the highway toward the cars that had come to a stop.

A battered old Jeep flew past them on the grass shoulder of the road, shaking as it hit every rut and stone.

"Go, Derek. Go right now!"

He glanced over his shoulder to see how many other cars were going to follow the Jeep's lead. "We bottom out, we'll be stuck."

"We're stuck anyway! Go before there's no room to get by!"

A PT Cruiser beeped over and over in warning as it went past them.

Derek swore and pulled onto the grass. Tania sat back and put her seat belt on even as the entire limousine began to shake. Derek leaned on the horn and swerved around a pickup trying to get onto the shoulder, but he didn't slow down. Instead, he sped up.

"Exit's not far," he said.

Tania could already see it, maybe a quarter of a mile away. Other cars had started to get off the Merritt as well, but only a trickle. Most people figured north was north. They were stuck in their cars, terrified of the things they tried not to see on the side of the road. All they wanted to do was get out of there, but Tania figured even if they didn't need gas, getting off the Merritt would've been the right move. The dead remembered the highway. They knew where they were going, somehow. Back roads might be better, and there'd sure as hell be less traffic.

"All right, all right," Derek said, nodding as they bumped back onto the pavement and he steered the limo along the long, curving exit ramp.

As they came to the end of the ramp and Derek began to turn left onto a rural two-lane road, Tania scanned the horizon. Just ahead was a short, squat building that had to be some kind of industrial manufacturer or something. The whole thing looked to be made from cinder blocks with a corrugated metal roof. But a mile or so farther, up a long, sloping hill, she saw a Burger King and a Mobil gas station, their signs battling for attention a hundred feet off the ground.

No dead men in sight.

The engine began to choke. The limo lurched once, twice, and then stalled, ticking with the heat under the hood as Derek pulled it onto the shoulder.

He hung his head and took a deep breath.

"No!" Tania shouted, slapping the seat with both hands.

"I'm sorry, girl. That's it."

For long moments they just sat and listened to the car cool. A motorcycle buzzed past them, and then a Toyota Corolla with a man and two wide-eyed kids inside, all headed away from the Merritt. Tania fixed her gaze on the Mobil sign at the top of the hill, then looked around for any sign of the dead.

"Pop the trunk," she said, opening her door.

"What? Where're you going?"

"We don't know how bad this is going to get, Derek. We can't just sit here in the car. Pop the damn trunk and let's get some gas."

He stared at her for a second, so she slammed her door. As she walked around to the back of the limo, the trunk opened. Tania said a silent prayer as she raised it to look inside and nearly wept with relief when she saw the black plastic gas can. She grabbed it and slammed the trunk.

Derek climbed out of the driver's seat and shut the door. The limo chirped as he pressed the button on his key ring to set the alarm. It seemed a ridiculous precaution somehow.

"Let's go," Tania said.

They started walking and immediately heard a car approaching from behind them. Tania turned and stuck out her thumb. The driver did not slow. If anything, the woman behind the wheel sped up.

Cursing, she quickened her pace up the hill.

"Keep watching the trees. Don't want any of those things coming up on us," Derek said.

But Tania focused mainly on the Mobil sign. "Just hope someone else comes by quick. Someone who watches television."

All her life, she'd wanted to be famous. Now she only prayed she was famous enough that someone would recognize her. All of her efforts to be successful as an entertainer meant little today, except that if she was very lucky, fame might save her life.

7

Route 91, South of Hartford, Connecticut

A rusty little Ford flew by going north on the southbound side of the highway, forcing them to swerve out of the way. But Noah couldn't blame the guy, what with the way traffic had stacked up northbound.

For the past half an hour, Amanda had been uncharacteristically quiet for a college professor, and Matt hadn't said a damn word. That was fine by Noah. Until they had some new information to go on, there seemed little point in talking. All three of them were busy worrying about the people they loved. They didn't have time to worry about one another and couldn't afford to care.

Noah thought about his sister in Philadelphia. Elaine was four years older, and though she'd always been good to him when they were children, once Noah had started high school and Elaine had gone off to college, they'd grown distant. Then, in the spring of Noah's junior year in high school, their mother had gone out to hang laundry on the line in the backyard and never come back in. Her heart had given out while nobody else was at home.

He'd found her in the backyard, flies buzzing around her. One alighted on her left eye, and it was the sight of that that had set him screaming. Noah had cried then, but not since.

Never since.

He'd called 911 first, and then Elaine, and only then had he bothered to phone his father at work. They'd never gotten along. Jerry Eisen was a doctor with no bedside manner, at work or at home. As far as Noah could tell, his mother, Suzette, had been the only person who ever really liked his father, and even then only some of the time. Dr. Jerry Eisen had been raised negative. Negativity was in his blood. For years, Noah had tried to mold himself to please his father, playing basketball, learning chess, taking an interest in biology, but his father found fault everywhere, so eventually Noah switched gears, making every choice based on how much it would piss his father off.

After his mother died, he gave up on that, too. It didn't seem to matter to his father either way. He'd bitch about whatever his children did. Noah realized that his sister had the right idea; he should do what he wanted, and not give his father another thought.

He rarely spoke to the man now. Since the first of the year, he had talked to his father perhaps twice, and not since May, at least. As a result of distancing himself from his father, though, he'd also distanced himself from Elaine. It was an unintended side effect. For a long time, he hadn't really cared, maybe because he'd worked so hard not to care about family at all. Now he worried about her.

But Elaine was in Philly. He couldn't do anything for her right now. And she had friends, and a boyfriend, to look after her. Right now, his only concern had to be Mara.

Mara first, he thought. Once he had Mara with him, could hold her close and protect her, then he would let himself start to fear for his sister and everyone else. Except his father. His father could go to hell.

In the first two years of high school, when he'd been trying to piss his father off, he'd gotten in more than his share of trouble. Teachers, cops, his mother, even his old friends had given him shit, and nobody had believed that he could turn his life around, that he'd be able to hack it in college. After his mother died, Noah had changed. Now, when he told people from home that he was in ROTC, they thought he was joking. Sometimes they laughed at him.

Mara never laughed. She was the only one who ever believed in him.

ROTC had taught him the discipline he'd been looking for, but without Mara, it would be for nothing.

The drive from Amherst to Hartford had taken about an hour, which was normal, even with the rain. They'd listened to the radio for a while, but the news reports were confusing, with conflicting information and some outlets talking about "outbreaks of violence," as if they couldn't admit what was actually happening. Eventually Amanda had pleaded with Noah to turn the radio off, an edge of hysteria in her voice.

Now they rode in silence.

From what he'd heard on the radio, and the traffic they'd encountered, Noah figured the worst of the hysteria had just begun. The exodus had started. Fortunately for them, most of the people who'd realized they needed to evacuate were headed the opposite direction. Whatever had caused this—a virus or biological weapon or something—it had started around New York City. People were running away from the epicenter instead of driving toward it, like Noah, Matt, and Amanda.

If he let himself think about it too long, it freaked him out, so he stayed focused on the road.

The only vehicles they'd seen driving *toward* New York were emergency and military, or people Noah assumed were like him and had someone they loved stuck in the dead zone—that's what they'd started calling it on the radio, congratulating themselves on their cleverness. There were more civilians driving south than Noah would have expected, more people willing to risk their lives for someone else than he'd have guessed, but then, he'd been cynical since birth.

When they hit Hartford, driving through the city on Route 91 had become impossible. The military had put a roadblock up, as though they thought they could contain what had already spread far beyond their reach. A little time and determination had been all it cost them to make their way around Hartford and hook up with 91 again on the south side. By then they had seen dozens, perhaps hundreds of the dead in ugly city neighborhoods and in quiet suburbs. All it had cost them was an extra forty-five minutes, the rear windshield of the Jeep, and an axe Noah had bought at Home Depot right after they'd left Amherst.

Now he drove south through the rain with a claw hammer at his side. Matt held a second axe in the passenger seat. In the rear seat, Amanda cradled a baseball bat on her lap as though it were made of glass. He worried about her. When she talked, the professor had an edge in her voice he didn't like, brittle and quiet at the same time, like she might start screaming any second.

In the back of the Jeep there were several other items they'd acquired in Hartford, including a sledgehammer and a shovel. Noah wished for guns, but the one store they'd passed had been locked up tight and Matt and Amanda had both insisted he not break in. *They'll learn,* he thought. *Before this is over, breaking and entering will be the least of our worries.* Survival was about improvising, and doing what needed to be done.

He slid the Jeep into the right lane and veered onto the exit for the Merritt Parkway.

"Wait, why are you going this way?" Matt said.

Noah glanced at him. *Gaines could be a problem.* The jury was still out. Back in Hartford, he'd surprised Noah by holding it together when things got ugly. The guy had backbone, which was good to an extent. But the friction between them hadn't evaporated just because they were in the middle of a crisis, and Matt didn't seem like the type to take orders. As long as they agreed on their course of action, things would be fine. But Noah couldn't let himself forget that Gaines was a bleeding-heart liberal, and if that was going to prevent them from stealing the guns or food they needed to make it through all of this, he'd have to cut the guy loose.

"Isn't it faster to take 91 down to 95?" Matt asked.

"You saw the fires back in Hartford. Heard all the sirens and stuff. We're gonna run into a lot more of that the farther south we go on the interstates. Plus, I'm betting that guy in the Ford isn't going to be the only one deciding that driving the wrong way on the highway will get him where he's going faster. The cops are a little too busy to worry about pulling people over right now."

"And you think this is going to be any better?"

"I'm gambling."

Matt looked into the backseat, but if he hoped that Amanda would agree with him, he must have been disappointed. She said nothing, only gazed out the windows, studying the cars and the road around and in front of them, and cradled her bat. In the rearview mirror, it almost looked like her lips were moving, like she was talking to herself. That didn't bode well.

Noah guided the car onto Route 15 South. Heavy traffic clogged the northbound side, moving at the same snail's pace as the exodus on Route 91. A ripple of unease went through Noah. It troubled him that it should be so much simpler to head toward the impossible instead of away from it. Every instinct screamed that they should never have started this trek and instead should have joined the herd in fleeing. But the girl he loved waited for him in Scarsdale. He had left Mara a message on her voice mail when they'd started out, but now all he got was the annoying little *x* on the screen of his cell that said "Emergency Service Only."

But he'd see Mara soon enough. He wouldn't allow himself to even consider other possibilities.

They made it three miles on Route 15 before they found the southbound side of the parkway blocked by a single police car, lights flashing in the rain. The Jeep shook, buffeted by gusts of storm wind that swept across the road.

"Not again," Amanda said.

"Take it easy, Professor. Let's see what's what."

Noah frowned. Matt's tone might have been condescending or comforting, he couldn't decide which. Either way, the comment was moronic. Beyond the Connecticut State Police car, Route 15's southbound lanes were empty of traffic. In the distance Noah could see a minivan parked on the ragged grass beside the road, hazard lights flashing.

"What's there to see? Looks like a roadblock to me."

Matt shot him a dark look, like he was some kind of villain for dashing Amanda's hopes. Noah ignored him. It hadn't been easy adjusting to the reality of what was happening, but pretending things were going to be all right was just stupid. Like they did in war, all the rules had changed. ROTC had taught Noah that once someone pulled the trigger, there was no looking back.

The trigger had been pulled.

"Pull up next to him," Amanda said. "Maybe he'll let us pass."

Noah doubted that, but figured they could probably learn something from the cop about how widespread the uprising had become, maybe determine whether some routes were less dangerous than others.

But as he tapped the brake and let the Jeep roll to a stop only a few feet from the police car, he frowned. They hadn't taken the exit. The cop had to have heard the engine. The police car's light bar flashed, colors refracting off of the rain, but no one got out of the car.

Noah put the Jeep in park and gripped the claw hammer. He glanced at Matt.

"You guys sit tight," Noah said.

To his credit, Matt did his best not to let the fear show. The goatee made him look like a tough bastard, and maybe he was, after all. Noah didn't bother making the effort to pretend. He was scared shitless and didn't care who knew it.

"I'm coming with you," Matt said, popping open his door.

"I'm not sitting in here by myself," Amanda announced. She unsnapped her seat belt and gripped the baseball bat in her hands.

"Fine." Noah wasn't about to waste time arguing their stupidity. If something bit his face off and they stayed in the car, they could drive away. But if they wanted to come with him and ended up dead, he'd be too dead himself to care.

He left the Jeep running, door open. When Amanda got out, she shut hers hard. The sound echoed off the road and the rain, but still nobody stirred in the police car. Noah thought all sorts of pithy, quippy things about donuts and naptime but didn't say any of them. If they found a state trooper asleep in the car, he'd laugh then, but the odds weren't good.

Matt led the way. Noah let him.

They moved hesitantly up to the driver's door, weapons brandished, bending down to try to get a better look inside. The storm made that impossible. Noah leaned forward, one hand on the rain-slicked hood, and put his face right up to the windshield.

Amanda touched his arm and he jumped.

"Damn it! Don't do that!"

"Sorry," she said, eyes wide. Her dyed red hair had mostly dried, but it stuck up in various places, curled into short ringlets, like she'd just gotten out of bed.

"What is it?" she said.

"Over there."

On the peninsula of grass that separated Route 15 from the exit road there stood a green and white sign identifying the exit as FOLEY STREET/CONGDON. Sprawled in the grass around the sign were two unmoving figures, one with its limbs twisted around like a marionette and the other tattered and ragged and thin.

"They're dead," Amanda said. "I mean actually dead."

She looked from Noah to Matt. "Maybe it's over. Do you think it's over?"

Noah couldn't help himself. As callous as he'd forced himself to become to be able to deal with the hell unfolding around him, a spark of hope rose. But when he strode over to the dead men, he realized he should have known better. It had begun in an instant and it might end the same way, but not yet.

"Bullet holes. Right through their heads," he said, glancing around for sign of any other walking dead. "I'm guessing our missing cop took them out."

"So the movies are right?" Matt said. "Destroy the brain and you make them dead again?"

Noah shrugged. "Looks like. Makes sense, doesn't it? Whatever's jump-started them, all the body's commands come from the brain. Destroy the brain, no signals are getting through to the muscles."

"This isn't just muscle," Amanda said.

She went to the corpses and crouched over them, studying them intently, like she was trying to make sense of the whole thing just by looking at them. Noah tensed, waiting for one of them to lunge, but neither so much as twitched. With one foot, she nudged the withered corpse, which looked like it had been buried for quite some time before rising.

"No way is there enough muscle and connective tissue left on a cadaver this old for it to get up and walk," she said, falling into a professorial tone, maybe escaping into habit.

"Then how did it get here?" Matt fingered the handle of his axe and glanced around nervously.

"There's got to be something holding it together still," Amanda said. "But whatever it is has to be supplemented by something outside the body. They're being animated by something."

Noah grunted. "Look, you can stand here and debate ectoplasm or radioactivity or comets all you want, but I've got Mara waiting for me. I'm not standing around in the rain."

"Sorry. Let's go." Amanda pushed her newly rain-flattened hair away from her face. They were getting soaked all over again.

"Hang on. What about the cop?" Matt said.

Noah nodded. He went back to the police car, wiped the rain from the rear driver's-side window, and bent to peer inside. With a frown, he tried to get a closer look. Something was moving in the backseat. For a second, he thought maybe this was a K-9 unit.

Then it lunged at the glass. He pinwheeled his arms, staggered backward. The window exploded outward. Shards of glass flew and long arms thrust from the police car and grabbed hold of Noah's shirt. He fell, dragging the thing after him over the jagged shards of remaining glass jutting up from the window frame.

The dead cop's mouth opened too wide, lips splitting as the corpse drove its jaws toward his throat. He'd expected hate or savagery or madness, but its eyes were full of despair.

Amanda screamed and swung the bat, which glanced off of the dead trooper's back with a thunk of meat and bone but had no effect at all. Noah cried out as he swung the claw hammer up, but the zombie moved too quickly, and instead of shattering its skull he had to use the hammer to block its attack. Teeth clacked on the head of the hammer and he shoved away, afraid to be bitten, afraid of what a bite might mean.

Headlights washed over them, but the car turned onto the exit, not noticing them in the midst of the storm. Noah bucked, trying to throw the dead cop off. He didn't see Matt coming, but then the axe flashed through the rain and sank into the corpse's shoulder. Its eyes widened and it twisted toward Matt, not in pain but pissed off. That arm hung at its side, useless.

Fear churned inside Noah, but he ignored the nausea and the way his throat closed up and the panic screaming in his head. He bucked again, swung his legs up, wrapped them around the dead thing's torso, and spun it off of him.

He rolled away and leaped to his feet, shot a look at Matt. "The head, you asshole."

"I was *aiming* for the head!"

Noah gripped his claw hammer and started for the zombie. The thing had already scrambled to its knees and was rising. Amanda readied her baseball bat but didn't attempt to go near it.

The dead thing gnashed its teeth and tried to grab him again, but Noah swung the hammer, caving in its skull. It shuddered, faltering, and he tore the tool out, breaking bone and squelching in gray matter. He swung it again, burying the metal claws into the trooper's brain.

He felt sick.

The zombie fell to the ground and did not move. Noah's breath caught in his throat and he had to get control of himself. The cop had already been dead. He hadn't actually killed someone. But he still felt sick, still needed a moment to breathe.

Then he went through the dead man's pockets, took his keys and handcuffs, then took the gun that had been in the holster at his hip all along.

Amanda glided past him and brought the bat down. She hit the dead thing over and over, pulping flesh and breaking bone. It twitched with each blow.

"No, no, no!" she shouted, punctuating each word with a blow.

Matt grabbed her, stopped her swinging. "Hey," he said gently as he restrained her. "It's dead, Amanda. It's not getting up again."

She let go of the bat, spun on him. "You don't know that!"

Matt hesitated, then offered the bat back to her. She stared at it, and then she whimpered, putting a hand over her eyes.

"Listen," Matt started.

Amanda shook her head. "She's dead."

"What?" Noah asked, standing up. "Who is?"

"My mother. I'm sure she is. She's not well anyway. This is . . . they're everywhere. I know what I'll find when I get there."

"No, you don't," Noah said.

"Fine, maybe not today. But we're fooling ourselves if we think once we get where we're going, everything will be all right."

Matt picked up her hand and closed her fingers around the bat. She took it with a sigh, deflating.

"We don't know anything yet. Not really. Me? I'm trying not to think what comes after. I just want to be with my family, to know they're all right, and then I'll worry about where to hide or what's next."

"Exactly," Noah said.

Matt shot him a surprised look. They didn't agree on much. But Amanda was having a hard time holding her shit together, and Noah knew this was something they should do together.

Amanda looked at him. "Are you all right?"

"Not at all." He held up the gun. "But this helps. If I can avoid Matt chopping my head off with that axe, I'll be even better."

Matt still held the axe in both hands and looked like he was still ready to use it. "I was trying to save your damned life."

"Yeah," Noah said. "Thanks for that. Maybe worry about yourself, though."

"From now on, I will."

The two glared at each other for several seconds, and then Noah turned his back and strode to the police car. He and Gaines had never been friendly and never would be. But Matt had bought him precious seconds. Might be the guy actually had saved his life, much as Noah hated to admit it.

He used the keys to pop the trunk and took out the shotgun stashed there. Noah handed it to Matt, who nodded in silent agreement. He located a strongbox that contained backup ammunition for the trooper's pistol and the shotgun and gave it to Amanda. Then

Noah got into the state police car and drove it up onto the grass. He turned off the flashing lights, killed the engine, and climbed out.

"No more roadblock."

Though it was not yet noon, the storm cast such darkness that it seemed night had arrived early. Noah hurried to the Jeep, but paused before getting in to glance over at Amanda and Matt. In the rain their faces were gray blotches, devoid of life. The storm blurred them into figures indistinguishable from the dead.

Noah shivered and slid into the Jeep. He wondered how far the effect had spread and thought about his mother's grave in Pennsylvania. Then he pushed the thought into a dark corner of his mind and built a wall there to hide it. Noah wouldn't let himself think about it again. The dead who were rising had to be put back into their graves. They had to be.

He clicked on the radio. Amanda could freak out all she wanted; they needed information. Voices babbled from the car speakers, panicked and strident but a comfort nevertheless. Matt and Amanda got in and closed their doors, but she said nothing about having the radio on. Noah figured reality was setting in for Amanda. For all of them. He dropped the Jeep into drive and hit the gas, headlights peering into the storm, seeing nothing.

Dobbs Ferry, New York

THE LITTLE GIRL AND her mother screamed as the plate-glass windows at the front of Tomko's Grille shattered and the dead stumbled and crawled and climbed over the jagged glass left in the frame. The biker Jack had thought of all morning as the Viking glanced at him and nodded. They each held a Molotov cocktail—a bottle of

150-proof rum with an alcohol-saturated rag hanging from its neck. Jack flicked the lighter in his other hand and ignited the rag, as the Viking did the same.

The screaming went on.

"Throw it, Jack! Burn them all!" Kelli shouted at him. Her eyes were wide with terror and fury. They'd become close in the past hour or two, trying to stay alive.

The Viking hesitated. Maybe because the quickest of the dead, the one right up front, had been on the inside of the restaurant with them until twenty minutes earlier. Jack had thought of him as Russ the Dad. Now he was Russ the Dead, who'd been so desperate to get his family out of there that he'd run for his car. They'd gotten hold of him and now he led the way.

"Lolly, come to Daddy," he said, knocking a chair out of his way, head hanging at a terrible angle on his broken neck. He sounded hollow, voice muffled. "Daddy's dead 'cause of you, pumpkin. Wouldn't have gone out there if I didn't have you to worry about. Come on to Daddy now."

Jack threw the Molotov cocktail and flaming liquor splashed all over Russ's face and hair and clothes. The dead man ignited, fire engulfing him. Some of the alcohol spattered other dead things and they, too, began to burn. Then the Viking tossed his, spreading flames across three figures that were still crawling through the shattered window.

For a moment, Jack hesitated.

Russ the Dead screamed at his daughter that she owed it to him, that they should be together now. Jack tried not to listen. He ran to the girl and clapped his hands over her ears.

"We've got to go!" he shouted to her mother.

Maybe she couldn't hear him over her own screaming or maybe

she was beyond hearing him. Either way, the woman shook her head wildly and screamed as her husband's burning corpse stalked toward her. One of the kitchen staff swung a knife at Russ, took him in the chest. The dead man grabbed the cook by the front of his shirt and fistfuls of cotton began to burn, spreading to the man's apron.

Kelli grabbed the mother's hand and tried to pull her toward the back of Tomko's Grille. The woman actually resisted for a moment, her mind lost. Kelli slapped her, bringing a stinging awareness to her eyes. The mom—whose name Jack had never learned—blinked and then looked at her daughter, Lolly.

The four of them ran together.

"I don't want to leave my dad!" the girl sobbed.

Russ's daughter must have been nine or ten. Jack put an arm behind her and hustled her around a table toward the kitchen, ignoring her cries. Nine was old enough to know the difference between dead and alive. The guy might be walking, but he was dead. And she had to live with the things that whatever remained of him had said to her.

"That's not him anymore. It's just trying to bring you in close so it can get at you. It'd say anything."

She cast him a doubtful glance and Jack made sure his expression remained neutral. Otherwise she might have seen that he didn't really believe his own words. Some part of Russ the Dad was missing now, more than just the spark of life. But hearing his voice, the thin gasp of death, Jack felt certain that other parts had been left behind. The cowardly parts. The desperate parts. The cruel parts.

"Jack, come on!" Kelli called as she pushed through the swinging door into the kitchen.

Screams echoed behind them. Jack felt growing heat against his back from the fire he and the Viking had just started. On fire, the dead had still managed to get hold of the cook and at least a couple of other people who'd been hiding out all this time in Tomko's. Jack didn't look back. He pushed Lolly ahead of him, watching as the girl reached out and caught her mother's hand, and then mother and daughter were together, hurrying through the kitchen; the door swung closed behind Jack.

One of the Viking's friends and a waitress named Gina had made a break for it through the back door around ten thirty. In front of the restaurant, they'd watched through the plate-glass windows for the biker to reach his motorcycle or to signal them somehow, the way he'd promised to do once he was clear. No signal came, and no sign of the guy. Arguments that had begun almost from the moment they had seen the first zombie had erupted again. Stay or go? Wait for rescue or try to escape? Jack hadn't wanted to stick around but according to the news reports, they'd have a long way to run to get out of the dead zone. Better to stay locked up tight, out of the way, and wait for something to change than to risk the kind of end they'd seen through the front window.

Until Russ the Dad had done a runner and the dead had heard the screaming inside. Until he'd led the charge against the plate-glass window, trying to get to his wife and daughter. To get *at* them.

Now the choice had been taken away.

But everyone in the kitchen had faltered, staring at the back door, hesitant to make the first move.

"Open the damn door!" Kelli shouted at the manager. "They're already inside!"

The Viking plowed the manager aside and grabbed the doorknob. He threw back the dead bolt. Jack braced a foot against the base of the swinging kitchen door, knowing they'd have company in seconds.

He heard rain against glass and looked up. Above the prep table in the middle of the kitchen was a raised skylight.

Out in the restaurant, the screaming stopped.

The Viking threw open the back door and charged out, followed by the manager, who carried a small cleaver from the kitchen as though it might frighten away the walking dead. Others followed. Lolly and her mom joined the rush. Kelli rushed them all ahead of her, making sure everyone was out, then turned toward Jack.

"What are you doing?" she said.

He grabbed a cast-iron skillet from a rack. "Watch out for the glass."

Something thumped against the kitchen door and for a second he thought the zombies were too stupid to know how it opened. Then he remembered the words of Russ the Dead and reminded himself that these things were not mindless. Not at all.

The door swung inward and the cook, face charred from fire, dragged himself through. Through the open door, Jack saw the upper torso of a withered corpse clinging to the cook's leg, holding on with both hands and gnawing flesh and bone.

Kelli screamed.

Jack hurled the skillet at the skylight and stepped back, shielding his eyes as it shattered and glass showered down with the rain. When he looked up he saw shards jutting from the frame and he scanned the kitchen, panicked.

"Lolly. Naughty thing. You can't run far," Russ said as he stepped over the legless dead thing and the dying cook.

Out of time, Jack thought.

He turned to shout at Kelli to run, but she was already in motion. The waitress had snatched up the heavy iron coat rack from the corner of the kitchen and now she stepped up and swung. Russ the Dead noticed her too late. He began to speak in that voice full of bitterness and despair, and then the black iron silenced him. The side of his head caved in and he fell, still burning in patches, on top of the crawling dead thing. The cook screamed and looked up at Jack, desperate eyes in a fire-blackened face.

"Give me that!" Jack said, reaching for the coat rack.

Breathing hard, hands shaking, Kelli gave it to him. Jack jumped onto the prep table, thrust the coat rack up into the frame of the skylight, and used it to break off the jagged pieces of glass that remained. Standing in the rain that came through the opening in the roof, he tossed the rack aside and reached for her hand.

"Let's go."

"But the others—"

"Are out with *them.* Let's get a look at what we're dealing with."

She took his hand and he hauled her up onto the prep table. Jack put his hands on her waist.

"Jump on three. One, two—"

On three, she leaped up and he lent his strength, propelling her upward. Kelli scrambled through the broken skylight, turned, and looked down, rain streaming down her face.

"I can't lift you."

Jack smiled. He only had a few inches on her in height, but he'd been breaking in and out of places his whole life.

"I got it," he said. Crouching, he jumped and grabbed the skylight frame, swung once, and as his legs came back he hauled himself up high enough to prop his elbows on the roof's edge. Cold rain ran down his back as he brought one knee up, a small shard of glass digging through his jeans to the skin.

Then he climbed out.

"Are you a gymnast or something?" she said.

"Or something. Do I look like a gymnast?"

Kelli studied him. She had to have seen the scar on the side of his neck, but that could've been anything. Even if he'd been wearing the colors of the Smoke Dragons, she wouldn't necessarily have known he was in a gang. Maybe she thought the tattoos were just for style.

"No, I guess you don't."

Down below, someone or something stomped into the kitchen. Jack didn't look back. He caught his breath and looked up to see Kelli, blue eyes wide, hair damp with rain.

"What about Dave?"

"Who the hell's Dave?"

"The cook."

Jack got up and walked toward the edge of the roof, looking down on the alley behind the restaurant. "You want to go back for him, be my guest. Either way he'll die. Question is, will you?"

Smoke rose at the front of the building, just where Jack figured the entrance to the restaurant would be. The fire they'd started inside wouldn't spread quickly thanks to the rain, but it would gut the place soon enough. The roof wouldn't be safe for very long, but a couple of minutes was all he wanted.

Sirens wailed in the distance. Someone screamed, far off, but he couldn't tell if it was anyone he knew. Down in the alley, a pair of dead teenaged girls in their best clothes—the clothes they were buried in—walked hand in hand. They looked rough, but recently dead. Jack figured a car accident, drunk high school kids wrapping a car around a tree. Now they were back, and still the closest of friends.

He shuddered and looked the other way. Down at the opposite end of the alley, rotted corpses dined on the Viking, driving their faces into his open chest cavity, his shattered ribs jutting up like broken spears.

"Shit."

Kelli stepped up beside him, took in the scene below, and turned away. She stared off toward the trees above Dobbs Ferry. Jack noticed smoke rising to the west, down by the Hudson River.

"The river," he said.

"What?"

"We could get out of here on the river. Find a boat down there, maybe. Hell, we could get all the way to Canada."

She didn't reply. Frowning, he turned to find her studying him.

"You'd do that? Just take off? What about your family and friends? There isn't anyone you need to check on?"

Jack gave her a hard look. "Nobody I'm willing to die for."

"My father's in a condo on the other side of town."

He wiped rain away from his eyes, then walked the perimeter of the roof, wary of the fire that must still be burning inside. He stared down at Chestnut Street. Smoke poured out of the shattered plate-glass window in the front of Tomko's Grille. Up on Main Street he saw a figure stagger by in the rain and then another silhouette wander along in the other direction. But the dead that had been down there had either gone in through the broken windows or scattered. They had an opening, and he didn't know how long it would last.

"See the Mustang right there?" he said, pointing at the car through the storm. "That's mine. We need to reach it."

The Mustang sat on the opposite curb, just down the block in front of a small market with cigarette ads plastered on the door.

"And go where? The river?"

Jack squeezed his eyes shut, thought about the Smoke Dragons—his brothers—and his parents and all the other people he'd ever walked away from just because it was the easy thing to do. His parents had all but disowned him because of the gang. There'd be no going back for them now. They might already be dead, and even if he found them, he doubted he'd be welcome. Hell, if he tracked down the Smoke Dragons, they'd feed him to the zombies.

"Yeah. The river. After we get your father."

Kelli grabbed his hand and squeezed it. Her eyes were filled with tears or rain, he couldn't be sure which.

"Thank you," she said. But he had a feeling she was holding on to him just to make sure he didn't change his mind. "So how do we get down from here?"

"Only one way down," he said, pulling his hand away.

Chestnut Street was steep. At the western end of Tomko's Grille, the roof was at least twenty feet from the sidewalk. But on the upper end it was more like twelve. Once more avoiding the middle, Jack led Kelli to the northeast corner of the roof, scanned the street again, and looked at her.

"When I go, you've gotta come right after me. No way to tell what's down there. Just run for the car."

Kelli pulled a face, wiping her eyes, and managed a tiny smile. "Duh."

Jack grinned. Girl was a little crazy. That was good, though. Might help keep them alive.

He got down on his knees and slid himself backward over the edge, dangled from the roof by his fingers for a second or two, then let himself drop. He hit hard and off balance on the steep sidewalk, tumbled into a roll that ended in the rushing torrent of rainwater that ran along the gutter. Soaked, he stood up just in time to see Kelli drop. Smoke billowed out around her in a cloud. She landed perfectly, adjusting for the incline, and then she was off and running.

Cursing loudly, Jack fell in beside her and they sprinted for the Mustang. All they had to do was climb in, drive a couple of blocks, and they'd be at the river. There'd be some kind of dock. Not everyone who had a boat would have thought of getting out onto the water, or made it down there if they had thought of it. Hot-wiring an engine would be easy enough for him. He'd done it to dozens of cars.

But they weren't headed to the river, because a girl with a pretty smile couldn't leave her father behind.

Idiot, Jack thought. *Gonna get yourself killed.*

8

Pelham, New York

Sara Gaines sat on the plush chair in her living room and let the cushions envelop her. It felt good, as though she could burrow down inside and hide from the world. She shifted, folding her legs beneath her. Not that she thought dead hands would reach out from under the chair, but every unknown frightened her right now. Every corner. Every shadow.

From the dining room came the sound of hammering. Her father had acted quickly, recruiting Sara and Zack to help him get the windows covered. Zack might be skinny, but it turned out he was stronger than Sara would have expected. Her father, on the other hand, had always seemed strong to her—all her memories of him sweeping her up in his arms and tossing her into the air or hanging her upside down while she giggled like a crazy kid had made him seem like Superman—but he'd needed their help, nevertheless. Hal Gaines hadn't hit fifty yet, but age had started to catch up to him, from his little potbelly to the bald spot that had grown so large he'd decided to shave his head entirely.

Still, he was strong enough.

Strong enough to hold up the wood to board up windows, and strong enough to keep them safe. They'd taken the doors off of the bedrooms, closets, and bathroom upstairs and nailed them across the windows in the living room and dining room, then snapped the legs off of two corner tables and nailed those over the small windows in the downstairs bathroom and above the kitchen sink. Zack had wanted to nail the back door closed, but her father had refused, just in case they had to go out that way. Instead, they'd dragged the dishwasher out from under the counter and put it against the door. Sara and Zack had managed to maneuver a heavy bookcase into the foyer to block the front door.

Now her father and Zack were adding nails to reinforce their work. There were only two hammers, leaving Sara on her own in the living room. With the windows covered, she had turned the lights on, and shadows gathered everywhere. The rain pelted the house, but otherwise she heard no noise from outside. Mrs. Goldschmidt had wandered off while they were boarding everything up. Last Sara had seen of her, the old woman—the dead woman—had been headed for Rolling Lane, where her niece and *her* family lived.

Now the only way to get a glimpse of what was going on outside was to go upstairs, and Sara didn't like the idea of being up there by herself. She grabbed the remote and submerged herself into the plush chair again, clicking on the television. Scanning channels, she found that a number of them had gone dark. MTV and VH1 were playing nothing but videos, which Sara remembered hearing had once been their format all the time. All of the networks and the cable news channels were covering only one story, and the end of the world was running commercial-free.

"National Guard troops from more than a dozen states have been called up," the CBS reporter said, in a tone that betrayed his own fear and uncertainty. "The Department of Homeland Security has stepped in to coordinate the federal response with local and state law enforcement. Rumors of executive orders giving extraordinary powers have not been confirmed, but no one we've spoken to has expressed any doubt that the governors of the affected states will have requested assistance. Thus far, we've confirmed that this phenomenon, what many are already calling 'the Uprising,' has affected an area including portions of New York, New Jersey, Connecticut, Pennsylvania, Massachusetts, Rhode Island, and Maryland. Conflicting reports have begun to come in suggesting that states as far away as New Hampshire and West Virginia may be affected, seemingly confirming New York City as the epicenter.

"White House spokesman Arthur Shaw has announced that, at this hour, army and Marine Corps units are being mobilized to take part in the overall effort both to implement cordons to contain the spread of the phenomenon and to enter the affected areas and put down the Uprising. Sources close to the department suggest the effort will begin at the outer edges of the affected areas and move inward, though that strategy leaves the worst- and longest-affected areas with little to no aid at this dire hour.

"Officials in New York and New Jersey have already decried this plan, but debate continues about how to best make use of available forces during what is inarguably the greatest domestic health crisis to hit America in modern times. Representatives of the Centers for Disease Control have released a statement saying, simply, 'The CDC is studying the situation, and we hope to determine the source of this contagion and the method of its transmission, so the spread can be stopped . . .'"

At that point, Sara couldn't listen anymore. Whatever was really happening, the government referring to it as a phenomenon and a health crisis, and the spread as contagion, was just their way of trying to reassure people they were going to be able to do something about it. Sara wondered how many people were buying that bullshit. She might only be in high school, but to her it sounded ridiculous. Contagion required viruses or bacteria or whatever. It affected living people. Even if something could get into the ground, maybe carried in the rain or something, it might taint dead flesh, but that wouldn't be a problem as long as nobody *ate* it. Some virus wasn't going to be able to put life back into a corpse. She'd gotten a B+ in biology this past spring, good enough to know cells divided and reproduced in some way that needed energy, or maybe created energy, or something like that. Life. A body needed life to move, and death was the absence of life.

Life wasn't a virus.

Sara believed in God. She believed in heaven and hell and in the immortal soul. She went to church and she sang with all her heart in the choir. That didn't make her perfect. There were lots of subjects on which she didn't agree with the church. She wasn't some virginal angel. But she believed in God.

Science couldn't explain this. God might, but he wasn't talking. What frightened her were thoughts of the Rapture. In the last days, when the worthy were drawn up to heaven, the dead were supposed to rise. Flipping through channels on TV, she had run across a few preachers talking about that very thing, and she'd kept going right past those channels.

She couldn't let herself think about it.

The CBS reporter, or anchor or whatever, did a short interview with some police chief in Connecticut. The old cop's eyes looked haunted as he talked about what his officers were doing to try to help, putting down those who'd risen and urging everyone else to stay in their homes, to find safe, secure places to wait for it to all be over.

Over, Sara thought. *There's more than one way for this to end.*

The anchor started in again with the main story. His perfect hair and teeth couldn't cover for the doom-filled resignation in his voice, like this was the end of the world.

Way to inspire hope in your viewers, Sara thought. But she couldn't even pretend to find humor in it.

"You really want to watch that?"

Sara glanced up to see Zack standing in the archway that led to the dining room.

"Not really."

She clicked off the TV and tossed the remote onto the sofa. The hammering in the other room slowed and then stopped. She stared at Zack, wishing he would say something. Wishing she hadn't always made it so clear to him that she could never see him as anything more than a friend. Sara badly needed to be held, and not the way her father would hold her. Not the way a friend would, either. He was a cute boy. Beautiful even, in his way, with those blue eyes and his high cheekbones. His few pimples didn't detract much from that. Zack got teased by the other guys at school—mostly by his friends, in that way guys gave one another crap. For a while, his skater-boy phase had been a reaction to that, she thought; he'd been trying to make himself less pretty. Sara had called him on it. Judging by the Disneyfied poster boys in the magazines her girlfriends read, Zack was exactly the kind of clean-cut, safe-looking guy they loved.

He'd *hated* being called safe.

"Zack . . ."

Her father walked up behind him, much taller, almost imposing. Zack looked at her expectantly, waiting for her to finish whatever she'd been about to say. But Sara burrowed further into the chair and focused on her father's broad features and the kind eyes that had always been able to soothe her.

"All done," Hal Gaines said, reaching up to scratch at the crown of his bald head, obviously trying to think if he'd missed anything.

"Good. So what now?" she asked.

Her dad shifted the hammer in his hand. "Now nothing. I'll make us some lunch. We sit tight and we stay alive."

"For how long?" Zack said. "I mean, how long will it last, do you think?"

Hal had never been one for bullshit. He met Zack's gaze without flinching. "As long as it takes. We're in for the duration. We watch the news, hope they'll tell us what we need to know. Even if it doesn't stop, maybe there's a limit to how far it'll spread, or a way to avoid them. If the power goes, I've got batteries for the radio. We just have to wait and see now."

"I don't know how long I can do that without going nuts," Zack said, shoving his hands into his pockets.

Sara's father frowned, knitting his brows. "As long as it takes."

Zack dropped his gaze. "Yes, sir."

"I don't think I'm hungry, Daddy."

"We've got to eat, baby. Keep up our strength. I'll get lunch going," Hal Gaines said, and he turned toward the kitchen.

And hesitated. "You kids hear that?"

"Hear what?" Zack asked.

But Sara paused. With the TV and the hammering silenced, she thought that she could hear something outside, over the hiss of the rain.

"It sounds like a baby crying," she said.

Her father took a step toward the door, seemed to realize he wouldn't be able to see anything without opening it, and then rushed for the stairs. Sara and Zack followed, feet pounding the steps. Hal's bedroom was at the back of the house, with the guest room and Sara's own room on either side of the corridor, windows facing the street. Her father went into the guest room, but Sara went into her own room by instinct. She and Zack stood in the very same spot where they had been when Hal had driven up in his damaged car.

The car remained parked in front, only partially on the driveway. The door hung open. The rain must have been doing terrible things to the upholstery of the driver's seat by now. Where the back left tire had torn up grass, a puddle had formed in the mud.

"Do you see anything?" her father called from the guest room.

"No."

Zack unlocked one of the two windows and slid it up. Rising over the hiss of the rain came the baby's cries. Sara opened her window as well and pressed her face to the screen.

"I can't see it," Zack said. "Hang on."

He left the room and Sara heard windows opening in the guest room.

"We can't see anything from in here either," her father called.

"Me either," Sara said.

But then she caught just a glimpse of pale flesh. Moving to the edge of the window, crouching down low, cocking her head at just the right angle, she saw a small fist waving in the air, and then a leg.

"Dad!"

Hal and Zack came running.

"Do you see it?" her father asked.

From her crouched position, Sara looked up at him. "It's in your car, right on the front seat."

"What? How the hell—"

"Someone must have been trying to get away," Zack said. "Maybe they knew they weren't going to make it, so they left the baby—"

"No one would do that." Sara shook her head. "No way anyone leaves their baby lying around."

But she saw the look that passed between her father and Zack. Her dad had paled considerably.

"Someone might," Hal said. "Zack is right. If they . . . if they knew the only way to save the baby was to lead the zombies away, sacrifice themselves, they might."

"Screw might. They did." Zack pointed toward the window. "The baby's out there. And that crying is going to get attention pretty quick."

He turned for the door.

"Zack, no!"

Sara started after him, but her father got to Zack first, grabbing him by the shoulder.

"Hang on," Hal said. "There's a right way and a wrong way to do this. Zack, you've got the door. Lock it behind me and be ready to open it when you hear Sara call down to you. Sara, you're staying at the window. When you give the all clear, I'll go out. You see anything while I'm out there, you can warn me."

A terrible dread settled in the pit of her stomach. "Daddy, please."

Hal walked back to her, reached out and caressed her face. "Honey, we can't leave that child out there. We don't do something, we'll all have to carry that on our souls the rest of our lives."

Sara stared at him. How could she argue that? But oh, how she wanted to. At last she nodded.

"Go fast."

Her father smiled. "Damn fast."

She forced herself to return his smile, but the moment he and Zack left the room, Sara's face went slack. Pressing her eyes closed, she bit her lip to keep from calling him back. Outside, the baby began to wail again and Sara opened her eyes. The crying helped. It tugged at her heart and reminded her that her father was right. They had no choice.

Taking a breath, she pressed her face to the screen again, but she couldn't get a decent view of the front yard at that angle.

"Sara, what do you see?" her father called from downstairs.

"Hang on!"

She unlatched the screen from the left-hand window and popped it out, barely hanging on, then slid it into her bedroom and propped it against the wall. Sara leaned out into the rain, bracing herself on the window frame, and surveyed the yard and the street as far as she could see. A couple of doors down a figure stood in the rain on the front walk. Other than that, the area seemed deserted.

"Sara, the baby!" Zack reminded her.

As if she needed reminding. Quickly, Sara raced into the guest room and checked the side window, darted to her father's bedroom, then back into her own.

"Anything?"

"One in front of the Baumans' house. Otherwise all clear!"

From below came the sound of wood scraping wood, her father and Zack sliding the bookcase away from the front door. Sara tensed, icy cold trickling down the back of her neck. Again she leaned out the window, but the warm rain could not dispel the chill of fear.

Her father ran from the house and she held her breath. The silhouette standing in the rain in front of the Baumans' did not move. The storm rustled the trees that lined the street. A police siren screamed not far off. But nothing else moved down there except for Hal Gaines. He glanced around frantically and ran around the car toward the open door. Sara saw her father's fear and it froze her.

He came around the open door and ducked his head out of the rain, reaching for the baby, whose pale arms still waved helplessly, hands tightened into fists.

"Hurry, Daddy," Sara whispered.

Hal staggered back out of the car, hands held up in front of him, but empty. He stared in through the open driver's door.

"What is it?" Sara shouted, feeling panic take hold. "Dad, what's wrong?"

Slowly, her father turned his face up to stare at her. His expression had gone slack, totally blank.

"It's blue," he said. Then louder, "The baby's blue."

Sara didn't understand him at first. Then it dawned on her. Blue. As though it had been asphyxiated. *Dead.* That's why the mother or father had abandoned the child. It had died and come back to life. *And, oh my God,* she thought, *that's what we've been hearing. A dead baby crying.*

Still, even then, why put the baby in the car?

The answer hit her hard enough to drive the air from her chest for a second. Then she hung out the window, barely holding on, and she screamed.

"Daddy! Get back inside, right now! Come back!"

Still stunned, her father took the time to cast one last regretful glance at the dead baby inside the car. Then he started for the house.

The thing underneath the car moved fast. It slithered out from its hiding place like a serpent, hands striking, grabbing her father by the ankles. Hal Gaines cried out and looked up at his daughter again, a terrible understanding in his eyes. Then he fell, shouting, trying to shake off the hands of the dead thing even as it scrambled back beneath the car, dragging him after it.

Sara caught enough of a glimpse to recognize Janice Goldschmidt. The old woman had gone off toward her niece's house but had come back. The niece had recently given birth, and the baby could only have belonged to her.

Now it was bait.

Her father tried to grab hold of the door frame, to keep himself from being pulled completely under the car, but the thing that had once been Mrs. Goldschmidt was too strong. Sara screamed for her father, screamed for Mrs. Goldschmidt to stop, even though she knew that the part of the woman who had waved to her in the neighborhood and always had the best candy at Halloween was no longer there.

Sara screamed.

Then she turned and ran from the windows, raindrops dripping down the back of her shirt. She careened from the room and hurtled down the stairs, running full out for the front door. Zack stood there staring at her, eyes huge with fear and confusion, up until the moment she grabbed for the doorknob. He slapped her hand away and she tried for it again. Zack took her by both wrists and pressed her against the wall, trapping her there, shouting at her, though she couldn't seem to hear him, couldn't hear anything but the crying of the baby outside and the scream of her father—abruptly cut off.

Sara froze, mouth open, eyes wide, staring at Zack as it sunk in. Zack shook his head as though trying to apologize, but no words came out. Then he pulled away and went to the bookcase, started trying to wrestle it back into place. Sara stared at him for a long moment, and then went to help him. As the bookcase scraped the floor, sliding into place in front of the door, her tears began to flow.

Putney, Connecticut

TANIA SAT IN A chair in the quality control office at Coville Machine, keeping to herself. The place reeked of oil and burning metal, though all of the massive machines out on the work floor had gone silent. The building was concrete and steel wrapped in aluminum siding on the exterior, like some kind of military bunker.

The dead had emerged from the woods and come after them, just as she'd feared. She'd screamed and frozen, locked in hysteria. Seeing them outside the windows of the limo had been one thing, but that close, and not protected, all she'd been able to think about was their teeth on her, the pain and the blood. Derek had snapped her out of it, gotten her running. They'd had a head start, but for the long seconds they'd spent banging on the metal door of the machine shop, she'd been sure the dead would catch up.

Then the door had opened, and they'd practically fallen through, screaming at the young guy who'd let them in. Tania couldn't even remember now which one he'd been. In her panic, all she'd really focused on were the oil stains on his hands.

For the moment, they were safe.

Somewhere around here she still had the gas can she'd been carrying, for all the good it would do. They weren't going to make it as far as the gas station. They weren't going anywhere.

Coville Machine had been the only building nearby when the

dead gave chase, but Tania figured she and Derek were lucky. It seemed like a safe place to hide. And yet, as grateful as she was that the workers had let them in, all she wanted to do now was get the hell out.

The machine shop managers and some of their employees were up in the conference room watching the news. Derek had gone up to see what he could learn. In the quality control office, a couple of guys sat with their shirtsleeves rolled up, glued to their computer screens and rattling off to each other the hideous stories they were finding. All over the northeast United States the dead were rising up and eating people, and the more recently deceased were showing up on the doorsteps of their still breathing family, friends, and lovers.

After a while, Tania couldn't listen to them talk anymore. Not without screaming. Instead, she tuned them out, but she couldn't ignore the glances she got every few minutes from the younger of the two, an olive-skinned Italian guy.

She shifted in her chair, wishing Derek would come back downstairs. He had gone up to check out the news, but promised to get her something to eat in the meantime. D always took care of her and she loved him for it.

Maybe it's time you started taking care of yourself, she thought.

Tania closed her eyes. Wasn't that the truth? Her fans had seen her grow up on television. The producers and her manager had always stressed that she was a role model, which meant she had to be as smart and cute and wise beyond her years as the character she played. But she'd never been any of those things. Not that she wanted to be some kind of celebu-whore, out clubbing every night, doing jail time for DUIs and possession, flashing her goods to the paparazzi.

But image could be suffocating, and though all she'd wanted her whole life was to act and sing and be famous, at seventeen she had now begun to understand what fame cost, and it terrified her.

Now, all of that had come to an end. There'd be no *Sunrise* interview for her tomorrow. Maybe not ever. Cataclysm had shattered her carefully constructed world. How could celebrity matter to anyone anymore? Tania knew that hundreds of people were dying, that the world was in turmoil over both the horror of what had begun to happen and what it might mean for those who wanted to kill one another over faith and worship.

Churches and temples would be full today.

The door to the quality control office stood open. Every few minutes one or two workers would appear in the doorway and get an eyeful of her, then move on. Some just walked by and glanced in. There were older men who worked with the machines as well—she'd seen them out there when she'd walked through with Derek—but only the young and middle-aged guys bothered to check her out. Some of them acted like schoolboys and some just curious. Tania had seen only one woman who worked on the floor, and she had the same scarred, oil-stained hands as the men. The other women at Coville Machine worked upstairs and she'd only caught a glimpse of them.

Tania didn't want to watch the news. She knew in her heart that what she and Derek had seen was only a glimpse of the real horror out there.

And here were these guys shuffling past, some of them gawking at her. She wished she could believe they were just checking her out for her body, disgusting as that would be given that some of them were old enough to be her father. Seventeen she might be, but she knew the control she had over guys. God and the gym had been kind where her body was concerned, and the tank top and low-rise jeans she wore didn't leave much to the imagination.

But it wasn't that.

The dead were rising from their graves and these guys were starstruck by the presence of the little girl from Nickelodeon who'd grown tits and launched a singing career. They should be terrified. Hell, they should all have left by now, gone and tracked down the people they cared about the way some of the Coville employees already had.

The Italian quality control guy checked her out again, saw her watching the door, and spun in his chair. As he did, one of the workers appeared again, a fortyish guy with a paunch and thinning hair, framed in the doorway.

"Marco, go back to work," the quality control guy said.

But the paunchy worker ignored him, studying Tania.

"You're that girl from that show," Marco said. "That kids' show. You sing."

Tania forced herself to smile politely and lifted her right hand in what could have been a wave or an acknowledgment, like the guy was taking roll call and she'd just announced she was present.

"I mean, you're her, right? My daughter loves you."

"I'm her, yeah. Nice to meet you. How old's your daughter?"

"Nine. Can I ask you something?"

"Shoot."

"That girl you kissed, the one they showed the pictures of on TV. She your girlfriend?"

Tania froze. The two quality control guys did not so much as flinch, kept staring at their computer screens. Out beyond the open door one of the other workers said "Oh, shit" in a tone that indicated he couldn't believe the paunchy, middle-aged Marco had dared pop the question.

But his gaze didn't hold any of the mockery or twisted sex-fetish leer that she would have expected. Tania felt keenly aware of the presence of the QC guys and their computers. Either one of them could log onto the internet and in less than a minute, blog about this conversation. Today it would not spread as quickly as it would have on any other day, but it *would* spread.

She shifted in her chair, sat back, and crossed her legs, suddenly finding great comfort in the question that only hours ago had terrified her.

"Yeah. She was. For a long time."

Marco blinked, perhaps surprised by the truth. "You two break up?"

"She dumped me."

A genuine sadness touched his eyes and Tania found herself softening toward him. Maybe he had suddenly seen her for what she was—a girl not that much older than his daughter.

"I'm real sorry to hear that. Gotta be hard."

"It was. Doesn't seem that important today, though."

Marco's expression went dark. "Not much does. Listen, I'm sorry I bothered you."

"I'm not."

He brightened a little, then turned to go.

"Marco?"

"Yeah?"

"What about your daughter? Where's she?"

He hung his head a moment. The other workers out on the floor had fallen silent. Marco looked up, grief in his eyes, and Tania thought the daughter must be dead.

"Manhattan," Marco said, practically choking on the word. He shrugged. "Went down with her mother. Girls' day shopping in the city. They stayed overnight last night. I talked to my wife this morning on her cell phone. She and Becca are still in the hotel. They're staying put. I tried calling again, but you can't get through anymore. I woulda gone down there, but she told me not to try, figured I'd get killed on the way. On the news they were saying if we just locked up tight, stayed indoors, it would all be over soon."

He looked down again. "I got a feeling it ain't gonna be that simple."

"Me too," Tania said.

"They'll be all right, shut up tight in a big hotel, don't you think?" Marco asked.

She wanted to tell him the truth, that she didn't know, that she figured his wife and daughter had about the same chance as anybody did—as they did, stuck inside Coville Machine—but it was clear that guilt had started taking Marco apart brick by brick and he just needed her to lie to him.

"You'll see them again," Tania said.

She'd never been religious, but the way things were going, she had faith in those words now. One way or another, Marco would see his family again.

He paused and studied her eyes like he knew just what she was thinking. Their shared fear connected them and a bond of common dread formed. They understood each other.

Out on the work floor someone shouted. Then came a shattering of glass and a loud banging, pounding on metal.

Tania shot from her chair. "Tell me that's one of your machines."

But the look in Marco's eyes told her it was not. The quality control guys started swearing. The olive-skinned one shoved her out of the way and pushed past Marco. He turned left outside the door and was gone, his coworker following a step behind.

"What is it?" Tania asked.

Marco held out a hand to her. "Come on, kid. Can't stay here. Only one way out of this room, and we may need other options."

Tania took his hand. They fled together from the room. Her sandals clacked on the concrete floor of the workshop and she wished for sneakers. Hard-eyed men weaved among the machines, all of them wielding lengths of pipe, wrenches, metal bars, and even a fire extinguisher. Their amusement with her presence had been forgotten. Tania herself had been forgotten by all but Marco and a couple of young guys, no more than twenty, who fell in with them as though they were her personal guards.

"You'll be all right, Tania," one of them, a thin Latino kid, said.

She wondered if he had chivalry on his mind, or if sticking with her, trying to protect the TV star, let him imagine it all to be some kind of freaky dream. Even in the midst of chaos, she couldn't really escape the world she'd made.

"Derek!" she shouted.

Marco tried to pull her toward the glass doors that led from the workshop out to the main entrance. From the rear of the shop floor came screams and sounds that made her stomach churn, made her rational mind huddle down in the corner of her head in denial. No one should ever have to hear those sounds. Ever.

Tania pulled loose from Marco. He and the two young guys paused and looked at her like she might be insane.

"Die!" someone cried at the rear of the workshop. "Jesus, why won't you die?"

"Watch it, Tommy, there are more of them!"

There were other voices as well, low, rasping tones that whispered off of the rafters and could not have belonged to anything living.

The screams and the sounds of metal on flesh and breaking bone and the other, wet noises that she dared not identify all joined together in an infernal chorus. To Tania, it sounded like the suffering in the pits of hell, and that symphony was growing closer.

How could she blame the two young guys when they ran?

She looked at Marco. "Go with them. Get out of here."

Marco hesitated.

"Thank you," she said.

Without a backward glance Tania ran for the metal stairs that led up to the executive offices. Muffled shouting came from there as well. Before she could even start up the steps a body slammed against the door up there, the outline of someone's head visible through the tiny window set into the door.

It shook on its frame, then swung wide, partially driven by the weight of a thickly built guy with a buzz cut. Derek stepped through after him, wrapped one huge hand around the guy's throat, and slammed his head against the door.

"Touch me again and I'll end you!"

Buzz Cut held up his hands. "What're you waiting for? You want to go get eaten, have fun with that."

Derek shook his head in frustration and backed off, hurrying down the stairs. Above, Buzz Cut slammed the door behind him.

"We're out of here," Derek said. "Fools want to lock themselves up tight with no way out, that's their problem. Long as they don't try keeping me from you."

"D, are you sure? Maybe we should—"

At the bottom of the stairs, Derek put an arm around her waist and hustled her toward the far end of the workshop where three loading bay doors loomed.

"You kidding me? Those people are good as dead."

Running between the front wall and the first row of machines, Tania heard grunting off to the left. As they raced past a huge, oil-stinking metal contraption, she looked along the next row and saw the Latino boy who'd wanted to be her bodyguard, who'd told her she'd be all right. He had fallen to his knees, his eyes wide with shock, mouth open in a drooping O. Then he fell forward, face slamming into the concrete, revealing a bloody hole in the back of his skull and a little dead girl who'd been hidden behind him, her mouth smeared with bright red.

"I'm looking for Papi," she said. "Have you seen him?"

Breath hitching, Tania ran on. The little girl hissed, a moist gurgling in her throat, and sprinted after them. Something broke inside Tania, the last tether holding her to her old life, eradicating truths she had never before questioned.

They passed the glass partition that separated the workshop from the front door. The small windows in those metal doors had been shattered and hands were thrust through, clawing at the air and the inside of the doors. The bottom of the door had been bent inward by something stronger than she could imagine and it shook as the dead tried to force it open further.

The little girl's feet were bare. They slapped the concrete, coming closer.

Derek fell to one knee. Tania spun, worried he'd had a heart attack or something. The girl ran, a pout on her lips, arms out as though for a hug. Derek snatched something from his ankle, turned on one knee, and shot the little girl through the left eye with a little gun Tania had never known he carried.

Once, she might have cried.

Now she only dragged him to his feet. This time, it was Tania who sped Derek along, kept him running. The loading bay doors were ahead. Two terrible thoughts invaded her mind. What if the dead had surrounded the building? There hadn't been many away from the main road, so that seemed unlikely. But there was no way to know. And the other thought—if they opened one of these huge garage-type doors, the people inside Coville Machine wouldn't have a chance.

"Derek."

He looked at her and she saw that he'd already considered these things. His eyes were grim.

"We'll die if we stay here."

And the unspoken truth. Anyone else who stayed here would be dead soon anyway.

Tania bent down, grabbed the handle on the first loading bay door, and twisted, unlocking the door. Teeth gritted, she used both hands and raised it. The door rattled in its frame. A cool breeze brushed past her. The parking lot held cars and trucks and a big semi trailer with no cab. Beyond that there were only trees. To the right the paved drive led up to the road.

Something shuffled on concrete behind them.

"Go," Tania said, grabbing Derek by the arm.

Together they jumped from the loading dock to the parking lot and set off at a run up the drive toward the street. She heard other things drop from the dock behind them and glanced back.

"They're coming," she said.

Derek kept quiet. Strong as he was, at his size, running was an effort. Sweat beaded on his head, shining in the noonday sun. He still clutched the tiny gun in his huge paw of a hand. Tania wondered how many bullets it carried.

"Which way?" he asked when they reached the road.

Tania blinked, hating that the tables had turned, that suddenly their survival had ceased being his job. But all the old rules were erased. He didn't work for her anymore. They were just friends now, trying to stay alive.

"Back to the Merritt," she said, staring in that direction.

"But you saw how many of them wandered that way."

"And you saw how many of them were in that town before, never mind here. We need a car, D. And it's too late to go back and try to steal one from the parking lot."

They both glanced at Coville Machine one last time. At least a dozen of the dead were after them, some shuffling and some sprinting.

"Run," Derek said, pushing her ahead of him.

Tania heard his heavy tread as he jogged along behind her, heard his ragged breathing. And she knew they were never going to make it to the highway in time. Not together.

She reached back, grabbed his hand, and tugged him so hard that he seemed to be careening forward out of control instead of running.

"Come on!" she screamed.

And hated the look in his eyes, which had dimmed with dark acceptance.

"Don't do this to me, D! Move your ass!"

He nodded, keeping pace with her, moving as fast as he could. Gravel crunched under her sandals.

Tania didn't look back again.

9

The Merritt Parkway, Connecticut

The Jeep felt light, as though it might be flying just above the pavement. Matt stared out his window at the trees blurring past, letting his vision go out of focus, not wanting to glimpse the houses and neighborhoods that could sometimes be seen just off the Merritt. A couple of times, zombies had rushed out into the road like frightened deer, right in front of the Jeep. Noah's driving had saved them both times. Fortunately, most of the dead ignored speeding vehicles, preferring either to walk purposefully alongside the parkway or to prey on those trapped in the northbound traffic.

Matt tried not to look over at the northbound side.

"There are so many more of them," Amanda said from the backseat, sounding more like a little girl than a college professor.

Matt thought the woman was crumbling inside, and wondered if a time would come when she'd fall apart entirely. He also wondered what he would do if that happened. He had a lot of respect for Amanda, and he wanted her to survive, but if it came down to choosing to help her or getting to his family . . .

"Where are they all coming from?" Amanda went on.

"People die every day," Noah said brusquely. "And today, there's more dying than ever. The ones who don't get completely eaten are going to get up again, kill some more, and it spreads. If it goes on long enough, there'll be more people wandering around dead than—"

"Noah."

He turned to meet Matt's gaze, seeming oblivious to the grim picture he'd been painting. Amanda had started to fall apart, and Noah's pragmatism didn't help.

"We need gas," Matt said.

Noah knitted his brows, staring at him a moment before he turned his attention back to the road. Matt glanced at the gas gauge. They had maybe an eighth of a tank.

"You're not getting to Scarsdale on that."

Noah nodded. "I'm on it."

"You mean we have to stop?" Amanda asked, voice cracking.

In the front seat, Matt and Noah exchanged a look. Under pressure, Matt had discovered that when politics stopped mattering, he and Noah might be more alike than he ever would have guessed. The thought disturbed him. He told himself their basic beliefs were still different, that Noah believed in taking care of number one—and screw everyone else. But Matt wondered how well his own philosophy would hold up. To the core of his being, he believed that people had to look out for one another. And he'd help strangers when he could, certainly. But family came first.

He glanced back at Amanda again, not wanting to do or say anything that might tilt her over the edge upon which she teetered.

Then he looked at Noah. *How different are we, really?* Matt thought. He hoped he never had to find out.

"You can stay in the car," Noah told Amanda, speaking as though she were a child. "Matt'll pump and I'll stand guard. We've got guns now, Amanda. I know what I'm doing. We'll be okay."

Matt shivered. The idea that guns would solve all of their problems didn't sit well with him. But from Noah it came as no surprise.

Distracted, he found himself looking at the northbound side of the Merritt. The rain had begun to let up and now the figures that moved among the slowly rolling cars were more than just silhouettes. Some were people, abandoning the traffic to make a run for the illusion of safety. But dotted in among the flow of cars he saw the dead, clinging to vehicles that moved along at ten miles an hour.

Cars streamed off of the parkway at every exit, but the torrent from the south continued. The two lanes directed north had expanded to three or four in some places, where enough room existed on the grassy shoulder for vehicles to get by. But the landscape around the Merritt was unpredictable, narrowing at times down to nothing, forcing drivers to merge back into the two lanes, crashing into one another. Worse yet, abandoned cars and SUVs had become more and more common the further south they drove, snarling traffic even worse, forcing the exodus to navigate around them.

Noah drove as close to the southbound shoulder as he could. Dozens of cars had passed them going north on the wrong side of the Merritt, and there would certainly be more. The threat of a head-on collision seemed far easier to face than the death the zombies would give them.

Even now, Noah swerved onto the grass to avoid two SUVs and a minivan traveling in a kind of convoy, speeding north on the southbound side. In the Jeep, none of them even swore at this recklessness anymore. They had all agreed that they would do the same if they were headed north.

Matt looked over to the northbound lanes again. As he watched, a woman driving a Volvo station wagon swerved out of her lane to run down one of the dead. The thing tried to grab hold of the grille as it went down. The Volvo bumped over it, tires crushing bones and pulping dead flesh.

Silently he cheered her on.

Still, even on that side of the road, most of the dead seemed more intent on traveling to wherever their instincts led them than trying to attack people who were locked up in their cars.

For now.

Matt held the shotgun across his lap and focused on the road ahead. "We getting gas?"

The Jeep sailed down the road at eighty miles per hour. Noah shot him another look. "Next exit."

"Could you . . . could you turn up the radio a bit?" Amanda asked. "They just said something about the White House. I want to hear. Somebody's got to be doing something about all this."

Noah turned the volume up. Matt's stomach gave a twist. The shit had hit the fan just a few hours ago, maybe a little earlier in New York. After Hurricane Katrina, how Amanda could expect the government to get their act together in just a few hours astonished him. They hadn't seen a police or military vehicle for miles. Nobody would be solving this anytime soon.

If ever, a voice whispered in his head. Matt didn't listen.

" . . . center of the dead zone is obviously Manhattan," a young female voice said on the radio. "Look at a map and watch the news reports. It isn't hard to figure out."

"Officials haven't confirmed any locus, never mind a source—" the radio host said.

"You really need them to confirm it?" the caller said. "Make a circle on any map. If this was some kind of terrorist attack, a biological weapon or something, then Manhattan's ground zero. But I don't think it's any of those things."

"So what do you think is causing the uprising?" the host asked, voice edged with sarcasm.

An exit sign loomed up on the right. Noah braked quickly, Matt and Amanda rocking forward in their seats.

"Dude, log onto the internet once in a while. I just watched a time-coded video from that show *Sunrise* from this morning."

Noah pulled the Jeep off the parkway and followed the curving road up to an overpass, then paused for a second to decide before turning left.

"You're talking about the three mediums who tried to put on a mass séance—"

"Exactly. Things got freaky in there, then they all went, like, totally catatonic. A couple of minutes later, the first 911 calls started coming in from people driving past cemeteries. They're on their cell phones screaming about zombies. What do *you* think triggered all this? Sunspots?"

"There's no evidence that—"

"How much evidence do you need, Howie? Seriously. Have you tried calling over to the network? They won't say what happened to those three mediums, but I'm willing to bet they're still comatose or catatonic or whatever. They called up all these spirits and something happened, they got their candles blown out. If they were up and around, we'd have heard about it by now."

"Thanks for your thoughts, caller," the radio host said, obviously cutting her off. "Next we go to Arthur in Sag Harbor. What do you think about all this, Arthur? Where did it start and where's it going to end?"

But Arthur didn't speak. The only sound on the radio was a hiss of static. Arthur's phone might still be off the hook, but he'd apparently lost interest in the radio conversation, or been drawn away from it.

Matt couldn't escape the feeling that Arthur wouldn't be coming back.

"All right. Let's move on. Dave in Philly, you're on the air."

Dave started talking. Matt wasn't listening anymore. The two-lane rural road seemed devoid of any civilization other than telephone poles. They needed a gas station and he'd been the one to pressure Noah to get off and find one, but now he worried they'd made the wrong choice.

On the side of the road, a limousine had broken down.

"What the hell's that doing out here?" Noah said.

Matt tore his gaze from the limo and looked farther along the road. As they came around a bend, through a curtain of rain and the metronome swipe of the windshield wipers, he saw people running along the roadside toward them. A dark-haired white girl had the lead, a massive guy slightly behind her with the girl holding his hand, pulling him onward. As the Jeep ate up the road between them, Matt saw the horde of dead things pursuing them.

"Stop the car."

Noah glanced at him, speeding up. "Not a chance."

Matt cocked the shotgun. "Noah. Stop the goddamned car."

TANIA SPOTTED THE JEEP and started waving her free hand, hanging on to Derek with the other. He still clutched the small gun he'd pulled from the strap on his ankle but hadn't fired it again. Desperate, she led him out into the road.

"Watch it, girl, he's gonna run you down," Derek rasped.

"No he won't."

But the Jeep didn't even slow down. If anything, the guy sped up as he swerved around them and kept going. Tania slowed but Derek plowed into her from behind and started her running again.

"That guy just left us here to die," she said.

"Every man for himself now, darlin'. You got to remember that from here on."

Derek could barely speak with the effort of running. Tania knew it was no use now. Only six or seven of the dead were fast enough to keep up with them, but the zombies didn't tire. Any second might be the last. Running away seemed pointless now.

"D, how many bullets—" she started to ask.

Then she heard the squeal of tires and glanced over her shoulder to see the Jeep Cherokee turning around.

"They're coming back!"

Derek let out a grunt of pain as his right leg buckled. He let go of her hand and went down hard, sprawling on the road. In a heartbeat, Tania saw what had happened. When he'd turned to look for the Jeep, he'd stepped into a pothole and twisted his ankle. She screamed his name and stopped, taking a step back toward him.

"That's right, girly. Wait for us. We're empty. Sooo empty," a dead man in a John Deere cap called, a wet laugh bubbling in his throat.

They were more verbal now. Like they were waking up.

They surged toward her, fifteen feet away. Twelve. Eight.

"Derek, get up!" she screamed.

He tried, struggling to rise, pain in his eyes. But the first of the dead, the fastest, leaped through the air and slammed into him from behind.

Tania screamed. The Jeep's horn blared.

Derek shot the zombie in the face and it went still, but the others were only feet from him now. He put his little pistol under his chin, muzzle snug against his throat. "Run, darlin'. Don't look back."

"D!"

"Run!" he shouted, the word drowned out by the triumphant moan of the dead as they reached him, one woman moving past him to get to Tania.

A thunderclap filled the air and the dead woman spun around, her right shoulder turning to pulp. A young black guy hung out the passenger window of the Jeep as it came alongside and held a shotgun steady across the roof. He fired again and one of the zombies lunging for Derek flew backward, tumbling across the road.

"Come on!" the driver of the Jeep shouted.

Tania took one last look at Derek. She couldn't do as he said and just run, leaving him there. The zombies were all over him, teeth ripping at him. He pulled his right arm free and snugged the gun under his chin again. His eyes met hers as he pulled the trigger. The gun was small, but it did the job. Tania watched the lights go out in Derek's eyes.

Then the dead dragged him down and piled on top of him.

The Jeep kept going. Some of the things went past the feeding frenzy in the road and raced after her. Tania turned, one sandal slipping on the rain-slicked pavement, but she kept on her feet and started to run.

"Come on, come on!" a woman called from the back of the Jeep.

She pushed open the rear door. It hung wide. Tania felt fingers brush her back, and despite the burn in her chest and legs she found the strength to go faster. Rain pelted her face.

"Slow down!" she screamed to the people in the Jeep.

The driver stuck a gun out the window, pointed right at her face.

"Get in!" he shouted, and the Jeep slowed to a crawl.

Tania dove into the backseat. The driver fired, the echo of the gunshot loud in the Jeep. Then he floored it, tires spinning on the wet road before finding traction. The door swung halfway closed with the acceleration and Tania reached out and slammed it shut.

They sped away. Derek had told her not to look back. She'd made the mistake of not listening the first time. Now she did as he'd asked.

Until the driver slowed and began to turn around.

"What are you doing?" she asked.

"We need gas," said the woman in the backseat with her. "You all right?"

Tania shook her head. Of course she wasn't all right. Tania looked out at the road as they passed the limousine where she and Derek had abandoned it a little more than an hour ago. But then she caught sight of the frenzy of the dead on the road and could not look. The driver gunned the engine, tearing past them, but Tania buried her face in her hands and lowered her head. Derek had been one of the only people in the world she trusted. The others were all thousands of miles away, in L.A.

When the Jeep slowed and pulled over, she looked up at last to find they were at a Shell station.

"Thank God for self-serve," the driver said as he opened his door.

"Hey," Tania said.

The driver frowned and looked at her.

"Thank you."

He smiled. "Don't thank me. I'd have left you there."

He shut the door and went to the gas pump. Tania looked at the woman and the other guy, who sat in front still holding the shotgun he'd used to save her life.

"Well, thanks to you two, then."

"Civilization's on vacation," the guy said. "But that doesn't mean it's dead. We did what you would've done."

Tania hoped that was true.

"I didn't recognize you before," the guy went on. "In the rain and all, and then you had your head down. But now . . . my little sister used to watch your show all the time."

The woman looked at Tania strangely.

Tania shook her head. "Sorry. People mistake me for Tania all the time. Wish I was her. Probably wouldn't be in this mess if I was famous or whatever. I'm Lori. Lori Bennett."

"Amanda Littrell," the woman said. They shook hands, which felt strangely formal under the circumstances, but wonderful in a way as well to have that bit of civilized behavior. Or it would have been, if the woman didn't seem totally out of it. She was either drugged or traumatized or both.

The guy in the front looked at her oddly. Maybe he didn't believe her. But he ought to. Tania didn't want to be Tania anymore. She had an aunt named Lorraine Bennett back in Louisiana. If her old life was giving way to an existence of survival, she'd just be plain Lori Bennett from now on, free of the way the guys back at Coville Machine had looked at her.

For her, the end of the world was a new beginning.

"Our driver's Noah Eisen. I'm Matt Gaines. Glad we could help," the guy said, and got out of the Jeep, shotgun in hand.

He stood guard while Noah finished gassing up. Then Noah took a turn watching for an attack while Matt went into the station convenience store and came out with a case of water and a couple of plastic bags full of snacks.

"I left a note with my phone number," he said as he got back into the car. "If anyone's left to pay when this is all over, I'll send 'em the money."

Tania took a water gratefully and drained half the bottle.

"Don't be greedy," Noah told her as he turned the Jeep around and headed back toward the Merritt. "Unless you're in a rush to pee on the side of the road while we stand around with guns."

Tania put the cap back on the bottle.

Manhattan, New York City

THE RAIN SEEMED LIKE it might never stop.

Phoenix sat in the corner of a small office near the Green Room, just outside the studio set of *Sunrise.* She had felt guilty leaving her father alone, but his condition seemed stable, and Ray Creedon had agreed to watch out for him, make sure nobody went near him. She'd seen Peyton—who she'd stopped thinking of as Stubble Boy because the nickname had a kind of cute, amused quality to it, and nothing about him amused her anymore—talking quietly to some of the staff and crew who came in and out of the studio, and glancing at her from time to time. He gave her the creeps.

They had no way of knowing if separating the mediums and the TV hosts would stop the dead from walking. Logic didn't even necessarily suggest it. Ray had likened what was happening to a forest fire—it was spreading, and just putting out the original match wouldn't stop it from burning.

Maybe to deal with his own fear, or maybe because he really believed it would end things, Peyton wouldn't let it drop. And all his whispering with others in the studio worried her.

How far would a guy like that go—how far would any of them go—if they could be sure it would end things? The five unconscious people around that table couldn't be separated. But Peyton had tried to put that letter opener between her father and Steve Bell's hands. What would he try next?

The thought made her shudder. And those fears were only compounded by more fundamental ones. If he would just wake up—*Wake up, Dad!*—the whispering would stop, and she wouldn't have to worry about him anymore. Peyton and the others would have their answer.

She hated not knowing how long he might remain this way, or if he would ever wake from his catatonic state.

The producer, John Volk, had managed to get Katie or one of his other staffers to go down to the café on the third floor and scrounge up some food. Most of the café staff had left, but an assistant manager had given the people still in the building the run of the kitchen. Apparently the guy had decided that if someone wanted to fire him for helping others in a crisis, that would be fine.

Phoenix's chicken wrap lay half eaten on a desk beside her, lettuce spilled out onto the paper it had come in.

"Hey," a voice said.

She turned. Ray Creedon stood in the doorway, a bottled water in each hand. He offered a lopsided smile, tentative but kind.

"What are you doing in here?" she said, rising to her feet. "You were supposed to—"

"He's fine," Ray interrupted, raising a hand to calm her. "I've been talking to that web reporter, Leah, and to Jim, and they're keeping an eye on your dad and the others. They're not going to let anything happen. I just . . ." He shrugged, looking a little embarrassed. "I wanted to check on you."

"Jim, as in the medic, Jim? He was helping Peyton before," Phoenix said.

"No, he's okay, actually. Yeah, he thinks we need to try harder to separate them. And maybe he's right. But he's not going to let anyone hurt them. He's freaked out—he's got a girlfriend in Brooklyn—but his job is to keep people healthy and alive, you know? He's cool."

Phoenix hesitated. She didn't know who to trust. But Ray seemed sure, and hopeful, and she had to admit to herself that she did feel better just having him there with her.

"Thank you," she said, thinking about what he'd said. *I wanted to check on you.* Had he blushed a little when he'd said that, and glanced away? Quirky and eccentric he might be, but Ray had a combination of sweetness and self-confidence that she could not ignore. Fear filled her completely—for her father, for herself, for her mother, and for the world. But somehow, this guy could take a lot of that fear away, at least for a few moments, and give her a chance to exhale.

It didn't hurt that he was cute. His hair had been a mess before the world had gone to hell and it was worse now, but she found it endearing.

Now wasn't the time for thinking about cute guys, but she found herself feeling very grateful to have Ray there with her, and on her side.

"It's still raining," she said.

"Yeah. Thanks for keeping track of that. It's hard to tell from all the other windows," he said, giving her that disarming smile again. He crossed the office and held out a bottle. "You want one?"

Phoenix took it. "I wouldn't make much of a meteorologist, huh?"

"Something tells me you're not actually watching the rain."

"No. I'd say I was just thinking, but that's not really true either. Not much thinking going on. Just waiting, I guess."

Ray leaned against the desk. "For what?"

"For my dad to wake up. Or for whatever comes next." She uncapped the water and took a drink.

"You didn't eat much."

"Not having much luck getting it down. It feels like my stomach shrank. Nerves, I guess."

Ray sipped at his own water and gave her a sheepish look. "It's having sort of the opposite effect on me. I eat when I'm nervous."

Phoenix studied him a second, smirking. "Are you saying you want the rest of my lunch?"

"Well, since you're offering."

Ray dragged a chair over as Phoenix slid the wrap across the desk. He took a huge bite, then had to wipe a bit of lettuce from his chin.

"So, you know all about this medium stuff, right? I mean you're, like, a fanboy. The ghostbuster equivalent to a Trekkie."

He frowned. "That's not exactly how I'd put it."

"But it's pretty much true."

Ray swallowed. "Pretty much."

"You've studied my father and the others, read my dad's book. Your website covers stories about mediums and séances and ghost hunters and all of that crap. And you've never heard of anything like this before?"

He had just taken another large bite. Now Ray covered his mouth as he chewed.

"Heard of it?" he said at last. "Nothing like this has *ever* happened before."

"And you're really sure the séance caused it?"

Ray sat back, the wrap forgotten. "There's no way to be sure. It's all uncharted territory. But it's hard to deny the sequence of events. I mean, you saw what happened in the studio. The last thing Annelise said was something about how they'd made 'a terrible mistake.' Damn, I mean, we heard the voices of the dead. Their souls have gone on—all that's good and pure in them—but their spirits are still here. I don't claim to really understand what's happening, but I have some ideas."

Phoenix frowned, then threw up her hands. "Well? Spill."

"Spirits haunt people and places because they want life. Now they're in these dead bodies, some of them kind of withered away. There's no life to them, and not a lot of substance. Seems to me they must be trying to get substance, to get life. But they're also going home or to people they left behind because that's the other instinct driving them. One instinct for the body and one for the spirit."

Ray fidgeted under her scrutiny, then glanced away. "It's only a theory."

"No, I get it. It sounds better than any of the stupid things I was thinking about. What I don't get, though, is how they can walk around. From the glimpses I saw online, some of them are incredibly decayed."

"You've got to stop thinking muscle and blood and stuff," Ray told her, leaning forward, his gaze intense. "There are a million stories about poltergeists moving things around, right? Doors slamming, furniture floating, whatever. Now your father and the others have given them a kind of focus they've never had before. They were just ectoplasm, but now that ectoplasm is bonded to their physical remains, and lifting it up and making it walk around is no different from a puppeteer working the strings on a marionette. The strings control the puppet."

Phoenix winced at the image, gooseflesh rising on her skin.

"Wow. You've put a lot of thought into this," she said.

"How could I think about anything else?"

"I think you're wrong about one thing, though."

Ray frowned. "What's that?"

"It's happened before."

"How do you figure?"

Phoenix looked out the window into the storm and the driving rain. "All the stories. Zombies rising from the dead, eating people. Destroy their brains and you stop them—I'm guessing that means destroying the brain cuts off the connection between the spirit and the body. Anyway, point is, stories like that have been around forever. Now it turns out they aren't just stories? It must have happened before, a long time ago, and stories about it spread and turned into myth or whatever."

Ray didn't reply. Phoenix turned from the rain-slicked window and found him staring at her.

"What?" she said.

He smiled. "Nothing. I'm just pissed I didn't think of that."

"What did my father and Annelise and Eric do that was so different? I mean, how come this doesn't happen all the time?"

Ray's expression grew serious. "Your father isn't just some random medium. Not only is he the real deal, but all of the authorities on the subject believe he and Annelise have two of the clearest and most powerful conduits to the afterlife ever recorded. It's confluence of things, really. Three powerful mediums, three powerful spirit guides, all of them focused together as the spirit guides get the attention of the dead. If you're right, and this has happened before, it's never been on this scale."

Phoenix's stomach gave a little flip. She had to force herself to utter her next question.

"So, if the séance really did start this, do you think separating them will end it?"

"Like I said before, we can't be sure."

Phoenix reached up and touched his hand, and he glanced down at her fingers, then back at her eyes.

"I can't tell you what it means to have someone trying to help right now. Everything's all turned around, falling apart, and much as I hate it, I understand why people get selfish, stop caring about anyone but themselves. I don't want to be one of them, but . . ."

"You're not. You're just looking out for your dad," Ray assured her.

Phoenix squeezed his hand in hers. "I wish that was true. But I am. It's selfish. But I can't help it. He's my father."

"You don't have to make excuses."

"I'm just saying I'm really glad to have a friend right now, Ray. But you have to tell me the truth. I know it's possible Peyton's right. And it's possible he's not. I want you to tell me what you think. With all you've studied about this stuff, do you think it would stop the dead from coming back if we forced them apart?"

Ray dropped his eyes, reaching up to scratch at the back of his head. "I really can't be sure. But my opinion? The medic is probably right. We might not have tried hard enough yet. And I don't want to be wondering later if we could have done something and didn't. I don't know if I could live with that."

Phoenix felt emotion welling up in her throat and a tight knot in her stomach, but she nodded. "Yeah. I don't know if I could, either." Pulse racing, she rose and looked at him. "Let's give it a shot."

"Are you sure?" Ray asked as he stood to walk with her.

Phoenix reached out and took his hand. "No. But if we can end this . . . my dad would want me to try. Let's just try to do it quietly. I don't want anyone else involved. They might not be all that concerned about hurting the people at that table."

Slowly, Ray nodded.

Phoenix squeezed his hand again. She liked the warmth of his touch and only reluctantly withdrew her fingers from his. Then she led the way out of the office, down the corridor, and into the studio. Her father, Annelise, Eric, and the two hosts of *Sunrise* were still arranged unconscious around the table on the faux dining room set. The scene struck her as grotesque, like some killer had taken their lives and then arranged them in a cozy family tableau.

Several people looked at them, but fortunately, Peyton and the guys from the crew he'd been talking to before weren't in the studio. Leah and Jim the medic were chatting quietly near the faux dining room set. They looked up curiously as Phoenix and Ray walked over.

"What's going on?" Jim asked.

Phoenix hesitated, glancing from Ray to Leah and Jim. But she didn't want to waste time.

"We want to give it another shot, quick and quiet. Can you help?"

Jim nodded. "Yeah. Of course."

"What if it doesn't work?" Leah asked.

Ray shot her a dark look. "We just think if someone's going to try, it should be someone who cares about not hurting these people. There's still no good reason to think it will stop what's going on, but we're also thinking that separating them might be the key to waking them up."

"That's reason enough to try," Leah agreed.

Phoenix went up onto the raised platform of the set and took the chair she'd been sitting in earlier. Ray stood behind Amy Tjan, whose head lay on the table as though she'd fallen asleep there. If only it were that simple.

Leah continued to stand guard without appearing to be doing so. Jim crouched beside the table, where Amy and Professor Cormier's hands met.

For a few seconds Phoenix just sat and held her father's arm as though taking comfort or trying to give it. She'd sat with him earlier, so no one in the studio would be surprised to see her there. If they wondered what Ray and Jim might be doing with her, no one came over to ask, though a few glanced over curiously before turning away. Most of them had focused their attention elsewhere, either on televisions or laptops or on their own thoughts.

Phoenix felt her heart pounding in her chest. Her skin felt flushed. What if they succeeded in separating the mediums, but her father never woke from his catatonic state? Worse, what if that happened and it didn't help, if the dead kept rising?

You could think about what-ifs all day, she thought at last.

"Just do it," she whispered.

"Me?" Ray said, confused.

"I was talking to myself. But yeah. You, too. Let's do it."

Ray knelt down, his body and Jim's stance interfering with any view of what they were up to. With his right hand, Ray started pulling at Amy Tjan's forearm as Jim tried to peel her fingers away. Phoenix followed suit, pulling at her father's arm and fingers, trying to separate them.

"We tried this already," Jim said.

"Just try to get their fingers apart. We have to break their contact," Phoenix said.

"It's not working," Ray whispered.

"No way this is going to happen without someone getting hurt," Jim replied, voice low, glancing at Phoenix.

And she knew what he was thinking. *What's it worth to you? A torn muscle? A broken bone? Bruises?*

She couldn't do it, couldn't hurt her father. But she gazed at Ray's eyes and then at Jim's, and a terrible knowledge came to her.

"Screw it. Pull harder."

"You sure?" Ray asked.

Phoenix felt her face flush, but she refused to cry. She nodded. "Someone's going to try to force this. I'd rather it be me."

Grim-faced, Ray nodded.

Phoenix wrapped both hands around her father's wrist and Ray did the same with Amy Tjan's. On a silent nod from him, they started pulling again, putting their weight into it. Jim tried digging his fingers in between the clasped hands and fingers.

Phoenix gritted her teeth. She could see the worry in Ray's eyes but then he knitted his brows and pulled harder. It seemed impossible that their grip could withstand such force, that their fingers would not unlace. But then she thought of what Ray had said about strings of ectoplasm and wondered if there wasn't more holding them together now than merely a firm grasp.

"Come on, Dad," she whispered.

Closing her eyes, tightening her grip on Professor Cormier's wrist, she pulled with all of her strength, feet braced on the floor, hauling backward.

She felt his wrist give way even as she heard the bones snap.

Phoenix let out a cry and pushed away, knocking the chair over and sprawling on the floor. She stared at her father's broken wrist and then at her hands and stood, wiping her palms on her shirt.

"Oh my God," she said, and she began to shake. "That's enough."

Ray Creedon took her in his arms and she let him. Phoenix knew people would be looking at them now, wondering what happened.

Jim and Leah came over to them.

"There's just no way," Jim said quietly. "Nothing short of surgery's going to separate them."

Phoenix felt the blood run out of her face, sickened by the thought. She could not reply as she sank into Ray's embrace.

But in the back of her mind, she could still hear the sound of her father's wrist snapping. The memory of how it felt to break his bones, knowing it had been her doing, lingered in her hands.

10

Dobbs Ferry, New York

The Mustang's engine purred. Jack peered through the windshield, both hands on the wheel, his breathing slow and even. Kelli's father had a condo on the second floor of a complex called Windsor Heights, and the dead had already found the place. Some of the sliding glass doors on the first floor had been shattered. A toddler's stroller lay on its side on the walkway to the rear entrance, spattered with blood. It had to be fresh, or the rain would have already washed it away.

"Jack, please?" Kelli said.

He took a breath, studying the place. So far he'd counted seven zombies outside, huddled against the building or calling up in their reedy voices to condos on the second or third floor like Romeo summoning Juliet to her balcony. They'd come home, looking for family—for their wives or husbands or children or lovers. Some had already gotten inside and others would find a way in soon enough.

The third balcony from the left on the second floor belonged to Kelli's father. Nothing moved in front of the sliding glass door. The curtain didn't so much as rustle. The lights were on, though. Somebody was home.

"All right," he said. "You ready?"

He'd taken one look at the situation and decided there were only two ways to go in—slow and stealthy or quick and ugly. The third option would be not going in at all, but he'd already promised Kelli, so that was out. Jack didn't think either attack plan stood them a better chance of getting out alive, so he went for quick and ugly. He wanted it over fast.

"I'm ready," she said.

"We get your old man and we're out of there. No packing a bag or taking his photo albums or any shit like that."

"I know. You already said."

Jack gave the steering wheel a squeeze. His knuckles were white and he forced himself to relax. He reached into the backseat and got the pack that Big Boy had given him that morning. Five thousand dollars, a jacket, and some cigarettes. Not a lot of good any of that would do him right now.

He started to unzip the bag.

"Those tattoos," Kelli said, looking at his forearm. "Do they mean something?"

Jack pushed his long hair away from his face and studied the dragon tattoo that ran up his right wrist and the Hangul characters etched there. The Smoke Dragons had turned their backs on him, cut him loose. Running had been Jack's only choice, but in his heart he would always be one of them.

"They mean everything," he said.

He took the pistol from the backpack, checked the safety and the clip, made sure there was a round in the chamber, then slipped it into the rear waistband of his jeans. He took a backup clip and held it in his fist like brass knuckles.

When he looked up, he found Kelli staring at him. She looked as scared of him as she did of the dead.

"It's all right," he said, all smiles gone. "I know how to use it."

"Are you dangerous?" she asked, looking away as if she was embarrassed to have spoken the question aloud.

"Not to you. You ready?"

"Yes."

He dropped the Mustang into drive and floored it. Tires screeched on pavement, laying black stripes, and the car shot across the parking lot. He swerved around a row of parked cars and gunned it. A pair of old dead women standing in front of the rear entrance to the place turned to look as Jack steered the Mustang right up onto the grass beside the building. He ran them down, dragged the zombies a dozen feet, and parked right on top of them.

"Go!"

On Jack's command, he and Kelli opened their doors, stepped out of the Mustang, and slammed them hard. He slipped the spare clip into his pocket. Something snagged the leg of his jeans and he tore his foot away, then stomped down hard on the skeletal fingers reaching out from under the car.

Kelli scrambled onto the hood, eyes glassed over with dread. "Oh my God, I can't believe we're doing this."

Jack jumped up beside her but kept his mouth shut. He couldn't believe it, either. *Dumb son of a bitch. The damsel in distress'll get you every time.*

The story of his life.

"Watch your step." He jumped up onto the roof of the Mustang, wincing at the way the metal crimped under his weight. Taking Kelli's hand, he helped her up next to him, then looked around. One of the dead things under the car tried to crawl out, but one of its legs seemed pinned under a tire. A withered cadaver in a faded black suit limped toward them. Two others stepped out of a shattered sliding glass door and started in their direction.

"No place like home," one of them said.

Kelli cast him a desperate look.

"No going back now," Jack said.

She nodded, crouched, and leaped up, grabbing the second-floor balcony railing. Her foot slipped and she swung hard against the bars. Something scraped the Mustang's hood but Jack ignored it. He reached out and grabbed Kelli's leg, giving her something to push against. She dragged herself up and over the railing and landed on the balcony next to a round wrought-iron table and a couple of plastic deck chairs.

Jack leaped, snagged the railing, and climbed easily onto the balcony. He wondered if the dead would follow, if they could manage it. But it was too late for such concerns.

Kelli tried the sliding glass door but found it locked.

"Step aside." Jack picked up the wrought-iron table and tossed it through the glass, turning to shield his face. The slider shattered.

She started ahead of him, but Jack pulled her back. He pulled the gun from his waistband and stepped through onto carpet and shattered glass. The condo could have been a sales model, so bereft was it of any real personality. He'd seen it before in places he'd creeped as a kid. Some people got to be a certain age and wanted cleanliness and order more than anything. The family photos hung in a cluster on one wall. A framed art print, something fluid and European, hung above the sofa. Everything was dusted and vacuumed and polished. Jack knew all he needed to know about Kelli's father then. He'd been an older man already when his daughter came along, and when her mother had passed away he'd let other people make a home for him based on pictures torn out of decorating magazines. He'd have a gold watch and maybe some cash in his underwear drawer. On the bookshelf in the living room sat a small, clear plastic box containing a baseball signed by Derek Jeter of the Yankees. A glimmer of the man he'd once been.

Once the guy had probably had a home somewhere, had raised his daughter there. But this wasn't home. It was just a place to live.

"Daddy?" Kelli called as she stepped inside, heels crunching on glass.

Jack waved her in, then held up a hand to indicate she should stop. Gun barrel pointed toward the ceiling, he moved through the living room and into the small kitchen. Also empty.

"Dad?" Kelli said, out in the other room. "Are you home?"

On the kitchen counter a plastic jug of orange juice lay on its side beside a small glass. The juice had spilled out around the jug, spread across the counter, and poured off the edge to pool on the kitchen floor.

Jack held his breath, listening for any sound in the condo. Elsewhere in the building he heard a scream. But in the old man's place, only the drip of juice onto the floor.

He bolted from the kitchen. Kelli was not in the living room. Adrenaline surged through him and he rushed into the small dining room, finding it empty. He backtracked, keeping silent, and moved into the hall. That left two bedrooms and a bathroom.

He nearly collided with Kelli as she came out into the hall. She squeaked in alarm. Jack gave her a hard look but her expression was defiant. Taking a breath, calming himself, he pointed the gun at the ceiling again. Together they turned to look at the last door in the short hallway. It stood ajar. Something bumped the floor in there. Clothing rustled. Jack heard a kind of snuffling, like a dog rooting for grubs.

Kelli's eyes went wide and she seemed to shrink in on herself.

Jack tapped her, nodded his head back toward the living room. "We should go," he said, mostly mouthing the words, barely a whisper.

She seemed glued to the spot, staring now at her father's bedroom door. "Dad?"

"Where's your mother buried?" Jack whispered.

"What?" She frowned, unwilling to understand.

He repeated the question.

"South Carolina," Kelli said, her voice so small.

Jack stared at her until she lowered her gaze.

"My grandparents are buried here," she said, relenting. "Not far away."

He would've corrected her, said *were buried,* but the truth already pained her and he wasn't cruel enough to drive that knife in any deeper.

Jack held up a hand, warning her to stay back. Steadying his nerves, he banged through the bedroom door, gun raised. Her father's ravaged body lay on his bed, the floral spread soaked through with blood. In an easy chair by the window, her dead grandmother sat cradling Kelli's father's head in the crook of her arm and cooing to it like a baby, rocking back and forth.

Jack would never be able to close his eyes again without seeing that image.

He whispered a prayer in Korean.

The woman's corpse looked up at him, still humming a lullaby.

Jack shot her through the forehead.

Kelli shrieked, a cry not of fear but utter horror. Jack backed out of the room, pulling the door closed, trying to block her view as much as possible. Only when he began to turn did he realize the tone of her scream had changed.

Spinning, he raised the gun, but too late. He could see the withered form, the desiccated face of Kelli's grandfather as the dead thing reached out from the bathroom, clamped both hands on her skull, and dragged her off her feet into the room.

Kelli's cries cut off abruptly.

Jack went into the bathroom with the gun in front of him. The zombie's jaws were open, biting into the flesh of Kelli's arm. Jack didn't understand why she'd stopped screaming until he saw the angle at which her neck had bent and the dull glaze of her eyes.

He put three bullets into her grandfather's corpse, obliterating its head almost entirely.

Then he stood over Kelli, staring at her pretty face, remembering the way she'd smiled at him in the restaurant that morning.

"Should've come to Canada with me," he said, hating the sound of his own voice. Because Kelli had done the right thing. Jack had wanted to grab a boat and head north on the Hudson River, save his own ass. If Kelli had listened to him, they might both be alive now. But she'd have left her father behind, and she couldn't have lived with that.

She'd have been dead either way.

"Damn it. Goddamn it!" he fumed, hating himself for not saving her, for being too slow or too stupid, for not checking every room first.

Your time's not far off, he thought. *There's no surviving this.*

He didn't want to believe that, but hopelessness gripped him tightly. Kelli hadn't run away from death. She'd had courage that seemed foolish on the surface, but now Jack couldn't escape the feeling that his own instincts had been cowardly. He'd been running away even before the graveyards started to empty. So he'd wanted to keep running. And maybe that had made sense when it was the Smoke Dragons and D-Kings he was running from and the rest of his people weren't in danger.

But his parents lived in the Bronx. His little cousin Kim and her mother. The Smoke Dragons had turned on him, so they were on their own. But Big Boy had gambled his own life, helping Jack this morning.

And he'd wanted to head for Canada. Told Kelli he had no one back home he was willing to die for. Now he stared at her body, her head hanging awkwardly, neck broken and twisted, and he felt ashamed.

"I'm sorry."

Jack took careful aim and shot her in the head. It was the only way to keep her from coming back, and he couldn't bear to think of her like that—a zombie. That fate frightened him far more than death. He couldn't keep her alive, so he figured the least he could do was keep her dead.

Hurrying back through the condo, he stepped out onto the balcony. A woman only recently dead stood on the roof of the Mustang, reaching up toward the balcony with a plaintive moan, mouth opening and closing like a baby bird waiting for Mommy to come back with a worm. Jack had four rounds left in the clip and he used one on the baby bird, getting her off his car.

"No scratching the paint," he said.

But tough words didn't make him feel any less numb inside.

Four other dead things were gathered around the car, plus the one that still scrabbled at the pavement, stuck under the tires. From the balcony it was as simple as target practice. The moment the last one fell, twitching, not quite destroyed but at least out of range, he went over the balcony, down onto the roof of his car, and then dropped to the pavement.

As he unlocked the Mustang, slid behind the wheel, and fired up the engine, others started to appear from within the shattered remnants of Windsor Heights condominium. Jack peeled out of the lot, leaving them behind.

He drove out to Broadway, the very same street that ran all the way down into the heart of Manhattan, and he turned south, toward home. Toward his parents. He prayed he wouldn't be too late, that he'd still have a chance to protect them.

No more running away.

Scarsdale, New York

Once over the New York border, they'd gotten off the Merritt and started making their way west toward Scarsdale. Now Matt had taken the wheel, with Noah literally riding shotgun in the passenger seat. The side streets would make the going slower and with so many houses and so many cemeteries, they would have to be on guard at every turn. Matt had never been to Aubrey University before, but Noah navigated for him while watching the trees and the spaces between buildings. In the backseat, Amanda and the new girl, Lori—who looked so much like that actress from kids' TV, Tania, that it was scary—kept their eyes peeled as well.

The rain had diminished to little more than a drizzle.

"Take a left here," Noah said.

Matt turned, speeding up around the corner when he spotted a figure staggering out from an open garage door.

"There's a stone wall down there," Lori said, tapping her window as she pointed along a side street. "Some black metal fencing, too. I can't tell from here, but it looks like a cemetery."

"It is," Noah replied.

"That's not good," Matt said.

"No. It's not. Keep driving."

Three blocks later, Matt heard Amanda whispering in the backseat. At first he thought she would be talking privately to Lori, but when he looked in the rearview mirror, he realized she whispered only to herself.

"What's going on, Amanda?" he said.

Noah glanced back at her and then at Matt, who offered a tiny shrug.

"Amanda?" Matt said. "Professor Littrell? You all right?"

"They're everywhere," she said. "How can there be so many?"

"Everybody dies," Noah said, gazing out the window, shotgun held firmly in his hands, ready to fight.

You're not helping, Matt wanted to say. But Amanda's nerves were so frayed, he didn't want to stress her any further.

She was right, though. As Matt drove he saw dead things moving between houses, some of them wandering on the road. More than once a living person hung out an upper-story window when they passed and tried shouting to them for help. The first time, Matt had started to slow, but Noah urged him on, reminding him there wasn't any more room in the Jeep. Once they picked up his girlfriend, Mara, they'd be jammed together as it was.

He hated driving past, ignoring those cries for help. But there would be dozens of cries for help along their route today, hundreds maybe, and where could they draw the line?

Two college girls sat on the roof of a house where they apparently rented an apartment. They shouted as the Jeep went by, pleading and crying. One of them fell, slid down the shingles, and barely caught herself before going over the edge.

Matt's fingers tightened on the wheel. He reached up and ran the back of one hand over the bristly stubble of his goatee, trying to combat the emotions roiling inside of him.

"I can't do this, man. We've got to help them."

Noah shot him a hard look. "Yeah? And while you're playing hero, what'll your father and your sister be doing? Let's take care of our own first, and then you can save the world, all right?"

Hate flared in Matt's heart, not for Noah, but for everything he believed. But the worst part, he thought, with a combination of sorrow and shame, was that the bastard was right.

"How can you see this and not care?" Matt asked through gritted teeth.

"I care. But I'm not God, and neither are you. We can only move forward, and do what we can do. You stay alive, and help when you can, that's a win."

Matt scowled, gripping the steering wheel. "There aren't going to be any winners. This isn't war. It's just death."

"No doubt. But when you're up against death, I'll call living a victory," Noah said. "Take this right."

Matt turned and drove on without another word.

The street led right into the heart of the campus. Aubrey University was a beautiful sprawl of academia, much more attractive than Matt was used to at UMass. Many of the buildings had the flair of the nineteenth century; others had come later but been built to complement the original campus. Paved paths wound through gorgeous grounds full of shade trees and small gardens.

The dead meandered around the campus as though they were lost, unable to remember what class they had next or what dorm they lived in.

"Oh my God," Lori whispered.

Matt kept on, right through the center of the campus, passing a bookstore and a brick campus center. One of the buildings was a language arts center. They were coming to an intersection and Matt didn't want to stop.

"Which way is her dorm?" he asked.

Noah had his face turned toward the window, his grip on the shotgun relaxed. After a moment he rested his forehead on the glass.

"Hey, man, which way?"

"Keep going. Head for Pelham," Noah said, voice flat.

"What? Why?" Amanda asked.

Matt blew the stop sign and went right through the intersection. "What about Mara?"

Noah looked at him. "I just saw her. Walking."

"You saw her?" Lori said. "Why didn't you say something? We could have—"

Matt shot her a glance that silenced her. She seemed to deflate and sink into the seat.

"Oh no."

"Noah . . ." Matt began.

"Just drive."

Matt kept his hands on the wheel and drove. As sorry as he was for Noah, his mind had already skipped ahead to what they would find when they reached Pelham—when he got home. He tried to tell himself that Sara and his father would be all right, that his dad would have gotten her out of there or found a way to barricade them into the house, keep them safe.

But Noah's words echoed in his mind. *Everyone dies.*

Matt drove.

Pelham, New York

SARA AND ZACK SAT together at the bottom of the stairs. She leaned against him, grateful for his arm around her. The power remained on, but she worried that it wouldn't last. Where did the electricity come from? Obviously the power lines, yeah, but where did it originate? Sara didn't know and when she'd asked Zack, all he'd said was "the power station." Duh. Neither of them had a clue where the power station might be or what kind of security measures they would have. She figured that after 9/11 there would be fences and guards and stuff. Or so she hoped. 'Cause with all the windows boarded up, if the power went out it would be really dark inside. They could go upstairs, but after nightfall . . .

She couldn't even think about it. Not the dark, and not about going upstairs. On the second floor, she'd be drawn to the windows. It would be impossible to avoid looking outside and then she'd see the car with its door open and she'd stare at the shadowy place underneath where the old dead woman had dragged her father.

A tiny sound escaped her lips, a small sob, but she didn't cry. Sara couldn't cry anymore. Her eyes burned, but she was all out of tears.

Something thumped on the door. She and Zack flinched at the same time and Sara's upper lip pulled back in disgust. She knew what had made the sound.

Mrs. Goldschmidt.

"I've seen you, little bitch!" the dead woman shrieked. "Stealing the apples from my tree! You and that boy who follows you like a puppy, eating my apples."

The old woman had been calling to them through the door for

a while now. At first it had been more of the same. *Empty,* she would say, begging Sara to come out. Sometimes the dead thing would say she was hungry, but it meant the same thing. Hungry. Empty. When she'd said those things it was difficult for Sara not to picture her father's eyes, wide with despair as the old woman had pulled him under the car. Sara forced herself not to make the intuitive connection. She couldn't allow her mind to go there.

"Come out, damn you!" the dead woman yelled. "Or I'll come in!"

I'll huff and I'll puff and I'll blow your house in. Sara shuddered at the thought. Zack pulled her closer and she let him, grateful for the strength she felt in his arms.

"Maybe we should go upstairs," he said, sorrow filling his blue eyes. "We could go into your . . . into the back of the house. Shut the door. Maybe we wouldn't hear her from there."

"You ate my apples, girl! You owe me. Apple for apple, eye for an eye, tit for tat."

Sara's face went slack and she stared at the door. What the hell was Mrs. Goldschmidt saying, that because Sara ate her apples she ought to let the old woman eat *her*?

"I'm in a nightmare," she whispered.

"*We* are," Zack said. "Together. And we'll get through it."

The door and the bookcase blocking it shook under a sudden assault. The blows slowed after a few moments but did not stop, settling into a steady pounding. Sara began to flinch in time with the rhythm.

"Maybe," she said. "Maybe not. I think they're getting smarter."

"What makes you say that?"

"You saw the news. First they were just attacking and wandering around, then they started traveling, going home or wherever. Whatever brought them back makes them hungry. But they're not totally mindless. They're starting to know who they are, remembering things. Mrs. Goldschmidt's talking more, and she's more, I don't know, herself . . ."

"She never said stuff like this before."

Sara separated herself from him, huddling down inside her UMass sweatshirt. "I know. But maybe she thought it. And maybe she's so hungry now that she's just really pissed, really nasty. She'll say anything."

The pounding ceased.

The two of them fell silent. Sara held her breath, wondering what it meant. Could the dead woman really get in, as she'd threatened? There was no tree to climb that stood close enough to the house for her to reach the second floor. Surely if she could break through the boarded windows, she'd have done it already.

"What do you think—" Zack started to ask.

Sara held up a hand and shushed him. She'd heard another voice outside. Her heart thrummed in her chest and her temple throbbed. She dared not hope, but still couldn't help the tiniest spark from igniting in her. She knew that voice.

"Baby girl?" he called from the other side of the door.

She froze. "Daddy?"

Zack began to speak but again she quieted him.

"I took care of her, Sara. Let me in, baby."

"Oh my God, Daddy." She jumped and rushed to the door, grabbing hold of the bookcase and trying to slide the heavy piece out of the way. She began to cry, tears of relief this time. Apparently there were always more tears.

"Open the door!" her father called.

The bookcase screeched on the wood floor, too heavy for her. She spun toward Zack.

"Help me!" she said.

He had come up behind her. Now he grabbed hold of the other side of the bookcase, but instead of helping her move it out of the way, he put his weight behind it and forced it back the few inches she'd managed.

"What are you doing?"

Zack stared at her. "He's dead."

Sara shook her head. "You heard him! Does he sound like—"

"What were you *just* saying? They're getting smarter. Remembering more of who they are."

"Open the door, honey. Janice is gonna get me."

Sara hesitated, confused. Her father had just said he'd taken care of Mrs. Goldschmidt. How could the dead old woman get him?

"Daddy?"

"You'd better open up, girl. This is your father talking."

Pieces of her broke off deep inside. Sara surprised herself by not crumbling to the floor. She leaned on the bookcase as grief rushed in anew and hope sputtered out. He sounded angry now. Not like himself at all.

"Sara?"

"I can't, Daddy," she said, so quietly she was sure he wouldn't hear.

Outside the door, he screamed. Fists hammered the wood, shaking the door on its hinges. A couple of books spilled off the shelf. There were two of them out there now, pounding on the door. Two dead things.

"Open up this door, you little slut!" her father's corpse sneered, enraged.

Sara hugged herself and backed away. Zack tried to reach for her but she flinched from him and pressed herself against the wall, shaking her head.

"I read your journal, Sara. Found it by accident. I couldn't help reading it, then I wanted to dig the words right out of my head. I know what you are! Sixteen years old and already you screwed two different boys? And that party where you kissed Janie Gibbs! A girl! How could you sit there in church every Sunday? The Lord should have struck you down! I read every word, you goddamned drunken whore! Now you've got to pay. You've got to be punished. Open this door!"

Shaking, flushed with humiliation, she slid to the floor.

The pounding continued and so did the words, turning into a torrent of filth. When Sara managed to become aware of her surroundings again, she realized that Zack had not changed position at all. He still stood a few feet away and when she looked up, she saw him staring at her.

The disappointment in his face forced her to lower her gaze again.

"That's all true?" His voice sounded flat.

Sara didn't reply, which was answer enough.

"You're my best friend," Zack said. "All that stuff, and you never told me?"

Her mind spun. With the pounding on the door and her father's shouts, she couldn't focus on anything other than the knowledge that he was dead.

"I know how you feel about me," Sara said, at the end of despair. "Maybe I didn't tell you because I didn't want to hurt you."

Zack made a disgusted noise. "Or maybe you were just ashamed of yourself."

The words rocked her. A tremor went through Sara and she brought her hands up to cover her face.

"Wait, I didn't mean . . . that came out all wrong," Zack started.

He reached down and touched her hand and she slapped him away.

"What's wrong with you?" Sara screamed, rising to her feet. "Now? Right now? You don't have the right, Zack. I never pretended with you. And now's not the time!"

Hands raised, he nodded. "I know. I'm sorry."

Sara pursed her lips, wishing she could hit him and knowing she only wanted to hit *something*. Someone she knew would never hurt her.

"Your parents are in Canada," she said. "They're safe."

The pain in his eyes made her blink.

Outside, her father continued to shout and to beat on the door.

"He's not your dad," Zack said. "That's not Hal Gaines out there. He's gone, Sara. That thing's just what he left behind."

"Then how does he know all that stuff? Why did he call me baby girl, the way my dad does?"

Defeated, Zack looked away. "I don't know. But I know they're dead. They're zombies. Your father loved you, Sara. He was a sweet guy. If that's him out there, where's that part of him?"

Sara buried her face in her hands, surrendering to despair. A strangled sob welled up from deep inside her. Anguish wracked her body, and she had no one to hold her.

11

The Bronx, New York

Jack weaved the Mustang around an abandoned Chevy, grip tight on the steering wheel. He'd been listening to the radio, and while the details kept getting worse, the story always started the same way—with those psychics having their séance on TV, broadcasting from Times Square.

"Asked for an update on the condition of the mediums, Joseph Cormier, Eric Honen, and Annelise Hirsch—and the show's hosts, Steve Bell and Amy Tjan—the producers of *Sunrise* replied only with a hasty 'no comment,' and the subsequent network broadcasts have not mentioned their status. A plea for information has been posted on Honen's website by his parents, but it has gone unanswered."

The news went on like that, back and forth between recaps and updates about where the Uprising had spread. Jack left it on, but it all became a drone to him.

He wondered about those mediums, though. Could it be a coincidence that all hell broke loose at the same instant they promised to let everyone talk to the ghosts of their dearly departed?

That didn't seem likely.

Which made him really curious about what had happened to those three. Were they alive or dead? Had they even woken up after? Were they trying to stop this?

Someone better do something soon, he thought. *The military sure isn't doing shit.* Jack had seen almost zero military or police presence in his travels. From what he could tell from the radio, they were mostly trying to keep the dead contained.

Like that was going to work. If the effect kept spreading, more of them would just climb out of graves behind whatever cordons were set up, hemming them in with zombies on every side.

Frustrated, he tapped buttons on the radio, at last finding a station still playing music.

His gaze shifted right and left, watching the alleys between buildings and the corners of every cross street. The dead staggered through parking lots and stood inside shattered windows and doors. The rain had ceased but the skies still hung low and gray, threatening more. For a time he'd driven with the window open, but he'd closed it tightly. Jack told himself he didn't want to take the chance he'd be attacked if he slowed down, but in truth he couldn't stand to hear the cries for help. People were on their roofs, tossing potted plants and other debris down at his car as he drove by, trying to get his attention.

But Jack couldn't help them. He didn't even slow down when he heard voices crying out from upstairs windows and he could see the dead had broken in through the front of the building. His only concern was for his family; Jack wouldn't stop for anything else. The gun sat on the passenger seat, a comforting presence. They were going home.

He gunned the engine, the Mustang leaping forward, leaving the Chevy behind. An old woman staggered into the road ahead and Jack hesitated a second before edging the car to the right, racing past her. The way she walked she might be injured and slow, or she might be dead. He didn't even look back to figure out which one.

His parents' place wasn't far now. Bang a left at the Harlem River and he was practically there. Just ahead, the sun broke through the clouds and he squinted against the abrupt reappearance of that pure light, glaring on his windshield. He loosened his grip on the wheel—his fingers hurt from holding on—then tightened it again. Soundgarden screamed from the speakers of the Mustang, music a little older than Jack himself, but it pounded in rhythm with his pulse.

He lowered his visor to cut the glare of the sun and caught a glimpse of the bridge ahead, and the sign on the corner of 225th Street. On instinct, he clicked the indicator to signal a left turn, then felt stupid. All the rules had been suspended, maybe even eliminated. They had no purpose anymore.

Jack blinked, narrowed his eyes, tried to focus on the street in front of him. It looked as though someone had scattered diamonds across the road. But they weren't diamonds at all. Jack swore and started to hit the brakes but it was too late. He swerved on instinct, crossing the road, driver's door scraping against several parked cars. Front and rear tires on the passenger side blew as he drove over the fat shards of shattered glass that had been spread across the road. He cut the wheel hard left to keep the Mustang from drifting right, then hit the brake, slowing down.

The dead came from nowhere. They sprang from between cars and out the doors of buildings, ran out from behind bushes in front of a building on the left, and rushed from the shadowy stairs that led down into the Marble Hill train station. Jack had two seconds to realize the broken glass had been spread on the street to stop passing cars, to recognize the half dozen vehicles ahead as the result, and to wonder how dead things could be smart enough to set a trap and lie in wait. But they *were* smart, and getting smarter by the hour.

Then the first zombie, a Latino woman, landed on the hood of his car. The Mustang had been limping along on two ruined tires. The shock of the dead woman hitting the hood snapped him out of his shock and he hit the accelerator again. The whole car dipped to the right, rubber flapping and tearing. Dead fingers scrabbled at the doors but Jack floored it, to hell with the car. The metal of the rims hit the pavement and the sound made him wince but he kept going, scraping the road.

He wouldn't get far. The dead thing on his hood held on. Its face, gray and pitted with rot, meat putrefying, twitched into a smile.

Jack drove right past 225th Street. Turning would slow him down—even more with two blown tires. They'd have him then. He kept his foot on the gas, running up onto the sidewalk to go around the abandoned, mashed-up cars of those who'd already fallen into this trap. The dead burrowed in those cars like pigs rooting in filth. He aimed the Mustang's nose at the old, rusted bridge ahead that spanned the Harlem River. He could see New York Presbyterian Hospital on the other side.

But then he spotted the figures milling about on the other side of the bridge and the wreckage of cars that had made it that far, and he knew he wasn't going any farther. Twenty feet onto the bridge, sparks flying from the rims of the right-side tires, he slammed on the brakes and threw the car into park.

Jack threw himself across the seat, popped the glove compartment, and took out the box of ammo, which rattled in his grasp, half empty. He snatched the gun from the seat just as the zombie from the hood jumped down and hammered on Jack's window. The glass splintered, but he didn't wait. He rammed the door open, knocking the dead woman backward, then stepped out and pulled the trigger, blowing the back of her head apart.

Crumpling the ammo box around the remaining bullets, he shoved it into his pocket and ran for the side of the bridge. If he'd driven halfway across he could have jumped down into the river, but the drop was intimidating and he had no idea how the gun would function if it was wet. Maybe in action movies that kind of shit wasn't a problem, but he couldn't bet his life on things he'd learned in a movie theater.

The ground sloped down toward the river, a bunch of scrub brush and garbage, tossed-out tires and supermarket carriages, and a pile of old gravel. He wished the gravel was close enough to land on, but that would've meant luck was with him.

Luck isn't with anyone today.

The dead rushed him, closing in, old women in gray dresses and punks in beater shirts and droopy jeans, a few kids, and one old man in a porkpie hat. Jack had no choice. He could stand there and waste bullets or take the jump.

He went off the side of the bridge, arms pinwheeling as he fell. As he hit the ground, he let his knees buckle into a roll that turned into an out-of-control sprawl down the hill. The barrel of the gun whacked him in the cheek and hot pain stabbed at the spot.

Finally he got his legs out, caught himself, and wondered what kind of dumb-ass hits himself in the face with his own gun. He'd been fortunate not to accidentally shoot himself.

At the bottom of the slope there were railroad tracks, and not a dead man in sight. Jack started to stand and sucked air in between his teeth. He'd done something to his right ankle. Panic flared as he glanced back up at the bridge and at the top of the slope, but none of the zombies seemed to be following him. Too much work, maybe. Gingerly, he tested the ankle and found the pain was abating. He might've twisted it when he landed, but it wasn't broken. Might not even be sprained.

Jack hobbled to the bottom of the hill. The river rushed by, brown and ugly, strong and deep. He turned east and started walking off the pain in his ankle, glad he hadn't ended up jumping into the water.

Soon he was walking almost normally, and his mind started running in circles again. He'd been fortunate to get out of that trap alive. Just in the past few hours he'd seen the evolution of the dead. The ones that had been in the ground a while weren't going to get much smarter, or if they were, they wouldn't be able to do much with those brains because they couldn't move very fast. Some of them were going home, looking for the people they had loved while they were alive. But others . . . they were just hungry. Maybe the people they left behind weren't home, or didn't live around here, or maybe they just didn't have anybody they loved.

Not that it mattered. The only thing Jack cared about—the thing that scared the shit out of him—was that they were getting so much smarter. They were like lions, hunting their prey in the jungle of the Bronx. But lions didn't lay booby traps.

He tried not to think about what it might mean for his family, but couldn't get it out of his mind. Several times, walking along the train tracks, he thought about putting the gun in his waistband, tired of carrying it. But no way was Jack going to let his guard down. Not when he was so close. He'd grown up on 204th, just off Grand Concourse, a neighborhood with plenty of Koreans, but two years back his family had moved a short way south, to a duplex on Valentine Avenue. The Saw Mill and the Major Deegan had been so snarled with abandoned vehicles and people still trying to escape the city that he'd just come down Broadway from Dobbs Ferry. Now he was less than a mile from the house his parents shared with his aunt Kathy and his six-year-old cousin, Kim.

No. Don't think about Kim.

The dead children on the bridge haunted him. Jack took a breath and shook off the last of the tightness in his ankle. After he'd gone another couple hundred yards, the railroad tracks ran parallel to the Major Deegan Expressway, and Jack left the train tracks. In a crouch, he ran into the darkness underneath the highway and crossed into the neighborhoods to the east. He went up Sedgwick to West Kingsbridge, sticking close to the front of buildings and whatever other cover he could find. One man, having seen him passing, opened his door. Jack spun, gun leveled at the man's face, and the door closed again instantly. Whether the guy had been about to offer him sanctuary or ask for his help, Jack would never know.

The dead were not quite so plentiful here, and he managed to avoid most of the ones he saw. Some did not bother with him, focused entirely on whatever loved one they sought, hammering on doors and calling out names in their ragged, wispy voices. But others were clearly predatory. Hungry. Empty, as some of them moaned. A well-dressed corpse climbed out of the broken sunroof of a BMW and leaped at him, and Jack had to shoot that one. He ran then, hoping most of them were not smart enough to know a gunshot probably meant fresh meat.

When at last he came to the duplex on Valentine Avenue, he found the place locked up tight. He saw only a single broken window, but no sign anyone had gotten in that way. None of the cars on the street looked familiar and a cold kind of certainly entered his heart.

Jack used his key to open the door, stepped inside, and locked it behind him. The house was quiet. His father would have been at work when the shit hit the fan. His mom would have been babysitting Kim while Aunt Kathy did nails down at the salon. There were no keys hung on the hook by the door. He hurried through the house, checking every room. In his parents' bedroom, the closet door hung wide and several drawers had not been closed properly. Clean clothes were strewn on the bed and a small shoulder bag had been left behind.

Nobody home.

They'd left in a hurry, but they had left, not been dragged out of here by the dead. Right now they might be in Connecticut or Massachusetts, or they might be stuck in traffic on Route 95, trapped in their car, waiting for monsters to pull them from their car and eat them alive. Hell, they could be dead already. Jack had no way of knowing. All he could be certain of was that they had gotten out of the house. Ever since 9/11, his father had had an escape plan to get away from New York City when the next thing happened, "when the other shoe drops," he'd say in his thick Korean accent. So they'd gone, and they'd had a plan.

"All right," Jack said to himself, nodding. "All right."

He tried the phone, but got no dial tone. Things were breaking down. Power and gas would run for a while on computers, but eventually, it would all go wrong. The phones were already out. He'd lost his cell phone, but his parents would have theirs, or Aunt Kathy. If he could find another cell, maybe he could reach them, but earlier all the lines had been tied up, so that didn't seem promising.

Jack let out a breath and fell back on his parents' bed, trying to figure out what to do next. He'd meant to go to Canada, but after what happened to Kelli, he'd just wanted to do the right thing. He owed his family that. But now he couldn't help wishing he'd gone to Canada after all.

"Not even a note," he said out loud. But of course his parents hadn't left him a note, or any indication where he might meet or catch up with them. They would never have imagined he would come back for them.

The realization made him sick.

What had he allowed his life to become?

The only other person he cared about, the only member of the Smoke Dragons who hadn't betrayed him, was Big Boy. But Jack realized what a fool he'd been to think his family would be sitting around waiting for a rescue. He could try to make it to Big Boy's place, but no way was the guy just hanging out at home. If he was still alive, he'd be trying to get the hell out of New York. And here was Jack, trying to get back in.

He laughed softly at himself. "Dumb-ass."

Boosting a car would be easy enough. He'd done it before. Set a Smoke Dragons record. But getting out of New York—just getting out of the Bronx—was not going to be easy now. The idea of a boat still appealed to him, but this time he'd head east, just keep trawling the coast until he found something.

What Jack needed now was information. He clicked on the television. Footage from the set of *Sunrise* came up, while some talking head narrated over the video, talking about the moment all the chaos began. The "trigger," the reporter called it.

The word made Jack flinch.

Eastchester, New York

TANIA STARED OUT THE window. The rain had let up and shafts of sunlight had broken through the clouds, but she wished the rain would come back. She wished it would pour hard enough to obscure her view of the northbound lanes, and all the cars jammed together there. An engine revved and she saw an SUV moving north on the far side of the road, running along the shoulder and up a hill, around a stand of trees. A little girl pressed her face against a window in the backseat and Tania wondered how far they would get.

"Where are we?" she asked.

Noah drove into the breakdown lane, then onto the hard ground, to get around the scene of an accident. There were at least six cars and a camper, but Tania didn't look too closely. She didn't want to see what might still be in the wreckage.

"Hutchinson River Parkway," Matt said. He held the shotgun on his lap firmly, like he was afraid it might try to escape. "Pelham's not far."

"Yeah?" Tania said. "And then what?"

Neither of them had a reply for that. And the college professor—Amanda—wasn't saying anything, either. The woman had fallen asleep not long after they'd pulled away from the college campus where Noah had seen his girlfriend walking around, dead. Tania tried to catch his gaze in the rearview mirror, but Noah didn't even look up. She felt badly for him, and for deceiving all of them. But she was Lori now. She needed to be Lori, to leave behind the life that had made her Tania. Singing and dancing wasn't going to get her very far in the world. Not anymore.

The parkway curved. As Noah followed the road, the sleeping professor slumped toward Tania, leaning against her. Tania cast a sidelong glance at Amanda, uncomfortable with the closeness. She barely knew this woman and now they were cuddled up in the backseat of Noah's Jeep.

"God," she whispered.

"What's wrong?" Matt asked.

"Nothing, if you like middle-aged women snoring in your face," Tania said softly, smiling to take the sting from her words.

Matt turned in his seat to look back at her, grinning. In the same moment, Tania frowned, feeling something was out of place. Amanda lay slumped heavily against her, the depth of her slumber almost remarkable under the circumstances. In spite of what Tania had said, however, she wasn't snoring.

She wasn't even breathing.

"Lori?" Matt began, staring at Amanda. "Are you sure she's—"

"Oh my God!" Tania cried, pulling away, jamming herself as far against her door as she could.

Amanda slumped forward, swaying in the harness of her seat belt. Her left hand slipped from her lap, fingers splaying open, and a plastic bottle rolled out. It fell to the carpet underfoot, along with three or four white pills. But only three or four. She had apparently taken the rest of them.

Noah started slowing down. "What the hell's the matter with you?"

"Me?" Tania cried.

"Pull over, Noah," Matt said, voice flat, eyes dull.

"Why?"

"Damn it, pull over!"

Noah glared at him, but pulled to the side of the parkway. "What's going on?"

"It's Amanda. She's dead."

The Jeep skidded to a halt. Tania pressed herself against her door, and the instant the car halted, she rammed her door open and stepped out. She looked around to make sure none of the dead were close, and then allowed herself a moment to shudder, rubbing at the place on her shoulder where Amanda had leaned against her.

Noah and Matt had gotten out and were talking quietly in front of the Jeep. She only caught a few sentences, but it was obvious they were debating what to do with the body.

"I'm almost home, man," Matt said.

"We take the time to bury her, they'll be on top of us," Noah muttered.

For the first time, they'd agreed on something. Their college professor had committed suicide in the backseat of Noah's Jeep, and they weren't going to bury her body. The world had changed—the rules had changed—that much.

Tania shook her head. It was just wrong. The woman had lost all hope. Whatever those pills were, she'd swallowed enough to end her life. Tania would never commit suicide, but she understood that hopelessness now, here on the road with these strangers, so far from safety and from anyone she loved.

She looked through the open door at the dead woman, still suspended by her seat belt. The pill bottle lay on the carpeted floor in the backseat. Curious, she went to the door and poked her head into the Jeep.

"Lori?"

Tania didn't respond at first. The name was only borrowed, and she didn't recognize it as her own. Then Matt called to her again and she looked over the top of the door at him.

"What are you doing?" he asked.

"Just wondering what she took. I never even noticed her taking them."

Noah nodded. "I was wondering the same thing."

Tania hesitated only a moment, then crawled into the backseat of the Jeep. Careful not to touch the body—the idea creeped her out—she picked up the pill bottle.

"It's a prescription for lithium," she said. "Her prescription. Guess she was bipolar."

Matt whistled. "Wow. Never would have guessed that."

"Me either," Noah said. "Apparently the pills were working. Now let's get her out of the car. I'm not chauffeuring a corpse around. Speaking of which, Lori, get out of there. We don't know if they all come back, or how long it takes, but no sense taking chances."

Tania cursed her own stupidity. She hadn't given it a thought. The pill bottle clutched in her hand, she scooted backward toward her door. She heard the rustling of cloth and the seat shook under her, and she knew she was in trouble even before the hand grabbed a fistful of her hair, fingers twining there and dragging her back into the car.

She screamed, lifting her head, reaching up to try to break the grip Amanda's corpse had on her hair. Tania locked eyes with the dead woman and saw the terrible sadness in her gaze, not very different from the look she'd had before her suicide. Then the corpse's nostrils flared and she seemed to grin.

Only it wasn't a grin at all. Amanda opened her mouth, bared her teeth, and thrust her head toward the hands with which Tania was trying to break her grip. Amanda bit Tania's left wrist, but the seat belt caught her like a dog on a chain and she had barely snapped her jaws closed when Tania pulled away. Blood flowed, and pain flared, but Tania reached up and yanked Amanda's fingers out of her hair, snapping bones.

She scrambled backward out of the Jeep, still screaming. In the backseat, Amanda ran her tongue over her lips, unsmiling, eyes full of sorrow, and unsnapped her seat belt. The dead professor crawled across the seat toward the open door.

"Oh Jesus! Oh shit!" Matt shouted, over and over like a mantra.

"Amanda, no," Noah said softly, and Tania almost giggled because it sounded like he was chiding some house pet.

The dead woman spilled out of the Jeep's backseat and began to climb to her feet.

"Shoot her, Matt! Come on, man! Shoot her!"

Matt looked down at the shotgun in his hands as though he'd forgotten he was holding it. He raised it to his shoulder abruptly, sighted down the barrel, and then hesitated.

Tania clutched her bleeding wrist and stared at him. "What are you waiting for? Shoot her!"

The barrel shifted. Matt shot at her leg, obliterating her knee. The dead woman fell onto the grass beside the breakdown lane, but was barely slowed by having to drag the ragged remnant of her leg behind her.

"Just get in the car," Matt snapped. "Let's go."

"Bullshit," Noah said. He ran to Matt and snatched the shotgun from his hands, then pumped another round into the chamber. "She was a good person, Matt. Maybe not a friend, but close enough. I'm not leaving her like this."

Tania looked away just in time to avoid the sight of the dead woman taking a shotgun blast to the face. The noise hurt her ears and then she heard the wet slump of the body hitting the ground.

"Get in," Noah said, tossing the shotgun back to Matt. "And reload this, just in case you ever feel like using it."

The guys went to the Jeep and started to get in. Tania only stood and stared, first at Amanda's corpse and then at the bite marks on her wrist.

"Hey, Lori, let's go," Matt said kindly. He stood just inside the front passenger door, watching her. "I know how freaked you are. We all are. But we've gotta keep moving."

"She bit me," Tania said quietly.

"So?"

"In the movies, if they bite you, that means you're infected." She felt so cold inside. Already the bleeding had almost stopped and she stared again at the bite marks in her wrist. "I'm going to die."

Tania didn't look up until she realized Matt was standing right next to her. He took her hand, his skin so beautifully dark and smooth against the blood smeared on her pale flesh.

"This isn't the movies," he said, voice low and strong. "This wasn't started by some meteor, and you're not going to die just because you got bitten."

"How do you know?" she asked, meeting his eyes.

Matt's gaze only wavered for a second, but it was enough to tell her that he didn't know, that he wasn't sure. Not at all. Still, the tone sunk in. They had no way of knowing what had happened to the dead, if there was some kind of virus that she might contract from having been bitten. But other than a bunch of B movies, she had no reason to think such a thing was even possible.

"Come on," Matt said, leading her toward the Jeep. "Get that wrapped in something and when we get to my house, you can clean it up, put some alcohol on it or something."

Or something? Matt might be a sweet guy. He might be a cute guy. And he was damn sure a brave guy. But he wasn't much of an action hero. Of course he wasn't, because this really wasn't a movie.

Somehow, Matt's ordinariness made her feel better.

Tania got into the Jeep, found a shirt, and tore a strip off to bind her wrist. As Noah pulled back onto the Hutchinson River Parkway—leaving Amanda's twice-dead corpse behind—she took a look around and counted at least seven of the dead coming from all different angles, moving toward the place they had been stopped.

If they'd been stopped any longer, they would have been outnumbered. With a shiver, she wondered about the ratio of dead to alive. Were the living already outnumbered? If not, they soon would be.

12

Manhattan, New York City

Only one elevator had been left in service, and even that only after building security had confirmed that although the glass front doors at street level had been shattered, the metal grates—rolling grillwork often used in front of shops when they closed up for the night—were still in place, preventing anyone from getting into the lobby, dead or alive. As soon as the reality of the situation had set in, building security had gone into lockdown. Those who had left beforehand were on their own. Those who remained in the building were now inside for the duration.

Even with the grates locked in place, Phoenix had been hesitant about using the elevator, both because she felt guilty leaving her father's side—even for a few minutes—and because the thought of moving any closer to the wandering dead made her sick with fear.

But Jim, the medic, had once again promised not to let anyone mess with her father, and she had come to trust him. Ray thought she needed to get out of the studio for a few minutes, just to be moving, and had suggested that they go down to the café on the third floor to get something to eat. Phoenix hadn't felt hungry at all, but her stomach had started to feel tight and hollow, and she at last surrendered to the idea that she should put some food in it, keep her energy up. The little bit she'd eaten of the chicken sandwich Katie Phelan had brought her earlier hadn't done much to fill her, and there was no telling when they'd eat again.

Now she rode down in the elevator with Ray, so anxious she felt like she might crawl out of her skin. She bit at the nail on her right index finger before forcing herself to stop. It was a terrible habit and she'd mostly conquered it. Biting her nails in front of Ray would just be gross.

The numbers lit up as they descended. She stared up, watching them tick by. No thirteenth floor in this building, a pretty old-fashioned bit of superstition. But that kind of thing lingered in New York. As American cities went, Manhattan was old; it had plenty of ghosts.

"Hey." Ray tapped her arm.

Phoenix looked at him, nodding at nothing.

"Jim won't let anything happen to him."

She shrugged. "I still feel guilty. He's just sitting there and nobody knows what to do and it's not like we're going to get a team of specialists to come in and figure it all out right now. Not today. Maybe never."

"If he was in a coma in some hospital, you wouldn't sit by the bed 24/7. You'd get food, take a bathroom break, whatever. This is just that. Besides, the guy's a medic."

Phoenix nodded. He was right, but still she hated to be away from her father.

The elevator slowed at the third floor. With a ding, the doors slid open. Phoenix reached out and jabbed the L button for the lobby. Ray glanced curiously at her, and she knew why. She'd been afraid to even get into the elevator, and now she wanted to go all the way down to the lobby?

"I need to see," she said.

"Haven't we seen enough on the news?" he asked.

"I need to try to understand."

As surprised as Ray seemed, he couldn't have been more surprised than Phoenix herself. But now that she was in motion, and so close, she felt compelled to see for herself the horror unfolding downstairs. John Volk and a security guy named Garth had insisted that the lobby was perfectly safe at the moment—the network wouldn't have allowed camera crews down there otherwise.

Despite her fear, she wanted to see. Coffee and sandwiches could wait.

Ray opened his hands in acceptance as the elevator doors slid closed. The elevator rocked a little as it dropped the last two floors and then opened again. Phoenix had expected quiet, but such noise rushed into the elevator that she almost did not get off. Then Ray stepped out, breaking the spell that had held her there, and she followed him onto the marble floor of the lobby.

People called to one another. Footfalls echoed off of marble columns and the cathedral ceiling. Phoenix and Ray emerged from the elevator alcove and then halted, both staring. Three separate camera crews were set up in the lobby, all manner of cables snaking from their equipment. Two had on-air reporters standing by, preparing to record or broadcast some kind of piece, but the third just had the camera rolling, taking in the phenomenon in the lobby.

The wide marble chamber was not actually at street level, but built as a kind of mezzanine, accessed by two gently curving staircases on either side of the reception desk. The north stairs led down to the corner of Broadway and Forty-fifth Street, the south stairs to Broadway and Forty-fourth. Each street entrance had a row of glass doors. According to Garth in security, all of them had been shattered.

But Garth had been right. Nothing was getting into the lobby mezzanine from those stairs. After-hours, building security lowered heavy metal grates that blocked access to the stairs from the lobby and locked them into place. The grates were down now. The street-level doors might be shattered, and the staircases open to anything that staggered in from outside, but the mezzanine was protected.

Beyond the grates the restless dead mingled, some in clusters and some idly shuffling on their own.

Ray made a small sound in his throat, and Phoenix glanced over to see that he'd covered his mouth with one hand, not like he was going to throw up but in an entirely unconscious reaction, as though he held in a scream.

"There aren't many of them," Phoenix said.

Ray looked at her. "One is more than I'd like."

Phoenix counted maybe twenty on the stairs at the north grate, and nine at the south. Some were rotting things that must have dug themselves out of their graves and made their way into Manhattan, seeking out the people they had left behind. Others were freshly dead, victims of the zombies who'd risen before them. Phoenix found them even more disturbing than the desiccated cadavers, because they would have looked alive if not for the pallor of their skin and the torn, bloody flesh where they'd been ripped and gnawed at. One homeless-looking woman had had her throat torn out and kept trying to speak. A handsome, older black guy with a goatee was so untouched from the neck up that he still had his glasses on, but his right arm had been chewed off below the elbow and his shirt and stomach had been ripped open.

Some of them moaned, low in their throats, but others were talking in raspy, desperate voices.

"Frank. Look at me, Frank. I'm right here. Why won't you let me in?" a dead woman called, voice filled with sadness the likes of which Phoenix had never heard. The woman had been dead long enough that she might have been any age, her hair thin and her skin dry and papery, but her features were mostly intact. Her eyes were sunken pits, possibly empty orbits, but she looked around as though she could see perfectly fine.

"Frank!" she cried.

Ray put his hands over his ears for a second, then self-consciously lowered them. "Who the hell is Frank?" he said, loud enough that half of the news staffers and camera operators turned to look at him.

A guy moving a lighting rig to shine more brightly on the dead beyond those grates turned to stare at Ray.

"I'm Frank," he said.

Phoenix shuddered, a pit of ice forming in her stomach. She stared at the dead woman—at all of the corpses walking and shambling or just standing patiently out there—and then at Frank.

"Who's she?"

The man looked pale, like he might be sick. "She used to work here. Her name was Paige. We were . . . we had . . ."

Frank shook his head, unable to continue, and instead went back to adjusting the light.

Ray took Phoenix's hand. "I don't know about you, but I've seen enough."

"Yeah. Me, too."

They walked back to the elevator and hit the button. The doors slid open immediately. Nobody else had called it in the meantime. Most people were barricaded inside their offices. Ray pressed the button for the third floor and when the doors opened, they stepped off in silence.

Phoenix didn't know if she could eat after what she'd just seen. Earlier, she hadn't even been able to finish her chicken wrap. She'd really only come down to be doing something, sick of feeling helpless in the studio. She had to eat something eventually, but not just yet. Whatever she picked up at the café, she'd put it aside and eat later, when the images from the lobby weren't so fresh in her mind.

The café had all its lights on, maybe to fight the grayness of the stormy day, or just for comfort. They walked in and Phoenix tightened her grip on Ray's hand as she took in the mess that had been made in the place. Coffee cups lay on the ground, contents spilled. Someone had dropped fruit from the displays onto the floor. Napkins were scattered around. Half a dozen people sat at tables, some talking and others just sharing solemn silence.

Behind the counter, the assistant manager stood waiting, as though nothing out of the ordinary had happened.

"Damn," Ray said, "is there anything left?"

"Plenty," the diminutive Middle Eastern man replied. "Anyone can have anything they like. No charge today. What would be the point? But it is all refrigerated here, and there are stoves. I only let people take what they need for now."

He spread his hands in a welcoming gesture. "So, what can I get for you?"

Ray laughed softly. Phoenix shook her head in amazement at the man's calm demeanor. They got iced coffees, plastic containers of pasta salad and hummus, some crackers, and a piece of carrot cake. A strange banquet, but the word *strange* had such little meaning now.

They rode the elevator back up with their hands full. What they'd seen in the lobby contrasted so completely with the amiable assistant manager that it felt surreal. Phoenix could not escape the grim ugliness of the whole thing, but her heart had stopped racing.

The doors from the reception area—normally guarded fiercely—had been propped open. Ray led the way and Phoenix followed, lost in thought, as they wended their path through the offices and then into the studio. The television screens flickered with news reports, images of the Uprising, of the dead and the chaos they were causing. Last time she had checked, the effect had spread as far south as Virginia. Phoenix didn't bother reading the crawl at the bottom of the screens and she tried not to listen; she wished they would just shut the damn things off.

"No, damn it! You're not doing anything, Peyton! Back the hell off, right now!"

Phoenix snapped into focus. Ray set his coffee and plastic bag of food down and moved quickly. All of the people remaining in the studio were in the midst of some kind of argument down on the set, right in front of the faux dining room area where Phoenix's father, the other mediums, and the two morning show hosts were still locked, hand in hand, in their catatonia.

"Katie, get out of the way. We gotta put a stop to this."

The producer, John Volk, and Katie—one of the associate producers, who'd been so nice to Phoenix—stood with their hands up, blocking access to the area around the dining room table. And they weren't alone. Leah, the reporter who'd been part of the audience that morning, stood warily by them, along with nine or ten people, most of whom were staff.

"Peyton, you're losing your mind. This isn't *Lord of the Flies* or something," Katie snapped. "Keep it together."

Peyton had been a nervous, kind of pushy kid that morning. Now he looked a few seconds away from shattering.

"Keep it—Are you shitting me?" Peyton shouted, face reddening.

He looked at the three others who seemed to be on his side, a heavyset guy about his age, an older man, and a gorgeous girl who was either on-air talent or hoped to be.

Jim, the medic, stood watching from a few feet away, doing nothing to help. Phoenix felt sick looking at him. He'd promised her he wouldn't let anything happen, and now he had just stepped aside and let it all go to hell.

"Are you even paying attention?" Peyton went on, jittery, like he might need a regular dose of caffeine or drugs that he hadn't gotten in a while. "The dead are rising. It's *Apocalypse Now* out there."

John Volk held up a hand. "Look, Peyton, if this is a religious thing—"

Peyton snorted laughter. "Who's talking about religion? This isn't about heaven or hell, dude. This is about right here and now. Western civilization has been living a dream of what we thought the world should be, and now the alarm's gone off, and we're waking up to *this!* We thought it'd be global warming or dirty bombs that'd knock the legs out from under civilization, but instead it's this. Messed-up shit, yeah, but if we're about to take a bullet, does it matter what kind of gun fired it? I don't think so.

"Nine-to-five jobs, soccer moms, and table manners are yesterday, John. Now I'm telling you there's maybe one way to stop it, and you're pandering to me like you're Mr. Religious Tolerance. Open your eyes!"

Katie slapped him.

Peyton blinked and stepped back, staring at her, touching his face.

"You sound like a lunatic. Maybe you're the one who needs to wake up," she said.

Trembling with anger, he looked around again, his gaze sweeping over those who stood with him and those who stood against him. Ray Creedon slipped over to stand beside Leah, helping form a barrier between Peyton and his cronies on one side and the unconscious participants in the séance slumped at the dining room table on the other.

Phoenix took a step toward them, and then another, stepping over some of the electrical cables that snaked along the floor. They paid her no notice. Jim saw her and glanced away, ashamed of himself.

"Look, we all saw it," Peyton said. He pointed emphatically toward the mediums and the two TV hosts. "We saw them. We were here when it started. I heard those voices. I never believed in ghosts, but we *all* heard those voices. The five of them linking up, the séance, that started it all. We've got to separate them, no matter what the cost!"

He started forward, trying to push his way between Volk and Katie, but they wouldn't give way. As furious as Phoenix was at Jim's betrayal, Volk's behavior gave her hope. He wanted the five catatonic people separated as much as she did, as much as they all did, but he wasn't going to let Peyton hurt anyone.

They grappled with Peyton and shoved him back, where the others caught him. With a cry of frustration and disgust he turned to face them.

Leah was looking at one of the huge television screens, at the horror unfolding there.

"You know," she said, "he may have a point."

Volk and Katie and a few of the others looked at her, offended by the mere suggestion.

Ray moved away from her. "You can't really condone—"

"There's only one way to end this, and you all know it," Peyton said. "Now get out of the way. We're gonna break that circle if I have to cut off one of their hands to do it."

Again he started to push through, and the other three joined him. Katie and John Volk argued loudly with them, holding Peyton and his cohorts back with the help of the other staffers.

Phoenix felt all the blood drain from her face. She dropped her coffee and her plastic bag from the café, and then she was running. Ray's mouth moved and he might have said her name, but she couldn't hear anything except the curses spilling out of her own mouth.

Peyton heard them, too. He turned and had just enough time to register surprise before she slammed into him. The others jumped aside as she drove him to the ground. His head hit the carpet of the faux dining room set, a few feet from her father's chair. Her fist rose and fell. Peyton tried to defend himself but she slapped his hands away and kept hitting him. Blood spurted from his nose.

Hands pulled her off him. When she tore herself loose, she saw it was Jim who'd gotten hold of her.

"You son of a bitch!" Phoenix shouted at the medic. "Do something! You promised!"

Ashamed, he held up both hands. "I'm out of this. Something's gotta be done, but I can't be the one to do it."

"Coward," she spat, turning away.

Furious, breath coming in ragged gasps, she glared at Peyton as he climbed to his feet.

"Psycho bitch," he muttered.

Phoenix jabbed a finger toward him. Peyton flinched.

"You will *not* touch my father, or any of the others. They've done nothing wrong. None of this is their fault, and you want to cut off somebody's hand? Who'd keep them from bleeding to death, you moron? Jim can't even keep a promise. You can bet your ass he's not gonna be able to perform surgery."

The mere suggestion made them all turn to look at Jim.

Angry now, maybe at himself and at all of them, he shook his head. His face flushed a hateful red. "No. I'm not in this. I'm not a surgeon and I'm not going to be responsible for how this ends. You can go to hell, the lot of you."

With that, he turned and stalked from the studio. The door swung shut behind him, and Phoenix had no doubt he was gone for good.

No one said anything for several infinitely long seconds.

Then Peyton shook his head in revulsion. "You know it needs to be done. You know they started all of this, otherwise how do you explain the timing? Explain why they're unconscious, and why we can't break them apart."

Phoenix glanced at her father, his head lolled to one side. "I can't explain it. Not yet. But I'll tell you this . . . I look at the dead people on the news reports and then I look at you, all ready to become a butcher, maybe a murderer, because there are questions you can't get answers for, and I can't say I'm surprised." She pointed to the nearest big screen. "When the good parts of us are taken away, that's what we become. And so will you."

Peyton wiped the blood from his nose with the back of his hand, staring at her. Then he looked at John Volk. As he was the producer of the show, they all seemed to still consider him the one in charge.

"What if I'm right? We do this, and we can end it all," Peyton said. "You were with me on this, John."

Volk stared at him, unblinking. "I was. Before you decided you were willing to maim, maybe kill someone to test a theory. If you're right, and we do nothing, then we'll have to live with that for the rest of our lives. But if we just stood aside and let you do this, and you were wrong, that I couldn't live with."

The kid didn't have a reply to that. He shot a final look at Phoenix and then strode from the studio, his three cronies in tow. When the door swung closed behind them, the whole room seemed to breathe a sigh of relief.

Phoenix caught Ray giving Leah a dirty look. The woman rolled her eyes and went back up to sit in the auditorium seats overlooking the set.

Phoenix said quiet thank-yous to Volk and Katie and a few of the others, passing through them on the way to the table. She crouched beside her father and leaned her head against his shoulder, listening to him breathe.

Ray sat on the floor next to her and leaned against Amy Tjan's chair.

"That's not going to be the end of it," he said.

Phoenix didn't look at him, instead burying her face in the fabric of her father's jacket, biting her lip, hiding her tears. Without lifting her head, she reached out blindly for Ray, and when he took her hand, she let out a shuddery breath and felt a little stronger. How she wished she could have met him another time, on a different day, before the world had begun to tear itself apart.

Pelham, New York

Sara Gaines felt like a dead girl. She lay on the bed in her father's room at the back of the house, on her side with her knees drawn up to her chest, and stared at the crystal lamp on the bedside table. Her back was to the window. She didn't want to see outside—didn't want to see anything. A hank of her thick brown hair lay across her face and she could not summon the will to reach up and move it. But the linen pillowcase felt cool against her cheek, and now that the rain had stopped, she missed the sound of its patter against the window. Her eyes were open but she did not so much as twitch, barely even drew a breath.

It would have been easier if she was dead. Then she wouldn't have the pictures in her mind of her father being pulled under his car, wouldn't hear the echoes of the things he had said to her, the things he had called her.

It's not him. Zack had told her that. She knew he was right, but it still hurt so much. His death, and those words, had carved out her insides. Maybe being dead just meant you didn't have to pretend anymore, and you said what you really thought without worrying about who you hurt. Maybe her father had believed those things.

Numbness blanketed Sara. She couldn't even cry anymore.

From the front of the house, Zack called her name. Sara closed her eyes and pretended not to hear him.

"Sara, c'mere!" he called. Then she heard him swear, followed by rapid footfalls in the hallway. "Sara!"

Her eyes snapped open. He stood in the open doorway, one hand on the frame. The gel he'd used in his hair that morning had mostly worn off, so instead of spiking, it only looked wilted.

"I hear a car. Someone's coming."

She blinked once, and then launched herself off the bed. Zack turned and sprinted back down the corridor to her bedroom, Sara right on his heels.

"Push out the screen," she said. It was the newer kind, all one piece, so there was nothing to slide up or open. Just the screen, blocking the way.

She looked around frantically for some way to signal whoever was coming. Nothing on her dresser would help—a hand mirror, a music box, her hairbrush, a ton of pictures and hair clips—but in the corner she spotted her softball glove. The ball it held was gray and rough with age. She snatched it up and turned just as Zack shoved the screen outward, letting it fall. From the noise, she figured it had struck her father's car below, but by then she was focused on the growing sound of a car engine.

No, not a car.

As she went to the window, nudging Zack out of the way, she saw the Jeep Cherokee coming down the street, rolling slowly, like the driver was looking for something, or maybe just taking the time to study the houses, watchful for threats.

She cocked her arm, ready to throw the softball, praying her aim would be true. Sara had always been the athletic one, thick-bodied for a girl her age, and formidable on the field. If she could hit the Jeep, let the driver know they were up here, maybe they could get help.

But Sara didn't need to throw the softball. The Jeep pulled to the curb right in front of the house, engine idling. The rain had stopped but the sky was still gray and she couldn't get a decent look through the passenger window.

"Who is it?" Zack asked.

She shook her head, staring at the car. And then she frowned. Other than that engine, the neighborhood was quiet.

"Where are they, Zack?" Sara said. "Mrs. Goldschmidt and . . . and my dad? Where did they go?"

They both leaned out the window, searching. Sara peered at the bushes over in Mrs. Goldschmidt's yard, wondering if what she saw was a person—a dead person—or just a part of the shrubbery.

"The car," Zack said.

Sara looked down. He was right. Mrs. Goldschmidt had probably gone back under her father's car. But more troubling was the figure slumped over the steering wheel, unmoving.

Dad.

The zombies had heard the Jeep's engine, too. And now they were playing dead, and waiting.

The Jeep's passenger door opened and Sara glanced up to see her brother, Matt, climbing out. He was a strange sight; he'd grown a goatee and was dressed in gray pants and a cream shirt, like he'd been on his way to a job interview. But if that had been the case, he wouldn't have been carrying a shotgun.

THE SHOTGUN FELT HEAVY in Matt's hands. Noah had reloaded it but they were quickly running out of shells. He didn't bother shutting the Jeep's door. His father's car was parked at an angle on the lawn, front end mashed against the house, door hanging open. He couldn't see if there was anyone inside.

"Watch your ass," Noah said.

No shit, Matt thought. In the backseat, Lori remained silent.

He spotted his little sister and her best friend hanging out her bedroom window at the same moment that Sara screamed his name. A wave of relief swept through him and Matt felt himself smile.

Her terror, her words, barely registered. In the space of those few heartbeats, all that mattered was that she was alive. After what had happened with Noah's girlfriend, he had feared the worst.

Her hair was a little wild, and she looked like she had been crying—her face always got puffy when she cried—but she was still his beautiful little sis, with her high cheekbones and striking features. She wore the UMass hoodie he'd given her, and seeing her in it, he realized how much he'd missed her, and just how frightened of losing her he'd been.

"Hey, baby girl!" he called, using the nickname his father had always called her.

Sara shouted something about their father, but Noah was talking behind him, so all he made out at first was "Daddy!"

Matt nodded. He'd seen the car. Much as he didn't want to accept it, something had happened to his father. Either the old man had gotten inside and was wounded, or whatever had caused him to crash his car had caught him before he had gotten to the house.

He glanced at the car again, then scanned the yards around him. Far down the street a dead thing shambled across the Cardiffs' lawn, but headed in the other direction. Noah started talking to him through the open Jeep door. Sara kept shouting. From upstairs, Zack began calling down to him as well, something about his father.

"He's dead!" Zack shouted.

Then he understood Sara, and the fear etched into her face. "They got him!"

The happiness he'd felt at seeing his sister crumbled. Matt swore under his breath, wishing he could deny what they were saying. The dead had gotten to his father. Whatever happened, he wouldn't have his dad to depend on. Sara's survival was his responsibility.

Noah killed the engine and opened his door, getting out even though they'd agreed he and Lori would stay in the Jeep.

"Wait!" Matt snapped, starting toward the house.

Sara kept talking. "In the car, Matt! Daddy's in the car."

Matt hesitated, studying the car more closely, and saw the figure slumped over the steering wheel. A tremor of dread passed through him and his grip tightened on the shotgun.

One of the Jeep's doors slammed.

"Get away from the car, man," Noah called.

Matt frowned, staring at his father. He was close enough now to see the body collapsed on the steering wheel.

From the car, Lori joined in, shouting at him to back away. At least she'd started talking again, he thought. A nonsense thing to be thinking right now, but he couldn't help it. Matt found himself shaking his head. This wasn't the way things were supposed to happen.

Behind the wheel, his father twitched. A glimmer of hope rose in him. Maybe Sara was wrong. If he crashed here, maybe he was just hurt. Matt took another step toward the open car door.

"No!" his sister screamed.

Her fear halted him. Something moved down along the ground. Matt jumped back as a hand grabbed for his legs. He still had the shotgun in his hands, but he held it like he was in a marching band. He recognized how useless that was and stopped retreating.

They were all shouting at him now, but Matt wasn't listening.

When the dead thing dragged itself out from under the car—moving fast, like an animal—and started to rise, he leveled the shotgun at it. Only then did he frown, recognizing Mrs. Goldschmidt.

He pulled the trigger, obliterating her face. The blast knocked her off her feet. The corpse struck the car and began to slide toward the grass, but already the bald-headed figure behind the steering wheel had started to move, climbing from the car.

"What is wrong with you, son?" his father asked, staggering toward him, brown skin gone a weird gray. Most of the lower half of Hal Gaines's left leg had been removed, leaving bone and red sinew behind. "Have you got rocks where your brains should be, Matthew?"

Matt raised the shotgun but couldn't focus enough to aim. Something had crumbled inside of him. All along he had told himself that the world might fall apart, but his family would make it through, the three of them would be okay.

"You always were a stupid little bastard," the dead thing said with his father's voice.

Matt's lips quivered, and then curled into a sneer as he took aim.

Two quick pops echoed across the yard, one bullet passing through the dead man's throat and the other through the side of his head, blowing out his left temple. The zombie fell.

Matt followed its collapse with the barrel of the shotgun, but he hadn't had a chance to pull the trigger. He kept the weapon trained on his father's corpse, hands shaking, convinced it would get up again, try to get hold of him.

Noah came to stand between the two dead things, pistol hanging at his side.

"I couldn't . . ." Matt tried to explain.

Noah put a hand on his wrist, gently pushed his arms down, forcing him to lower the shotgun. Matt locked eyes with him.

"I get it. He was your father," Noah said.

Matt shook his head. "No. Not that thing."

Zack called to him from the window. "Watch out, you guys. There could be others. Sara's coming down to open the door."

Right, Matt thought. *Sara. Got to look out for her now. Nobody else to do it. There's just us.*

His insides flooded with ice. He let himself grow cold, welcomed it. Lifting the shotgun again, he swung it around, scanning for other dead. They would be coming, he felt certain of that. Eventually, more would wander over this way.

"Get Lori."

"What for?" Noah said. "Let's get these kids and get the hell out of here."

Matt shook his head. "No." He gestured toward the house with the barrel of the shotgun. "Look at the windows. They boarded the place up good. We need food and rest. Supplies and information. All this time I just wanted to get here. Well, now we're here, and that means we need to figure out what's next. Make a plan. Where do we go from here, and how do we get there?"

Noah hesitated. Matt could see him weighing it in his mind. Then he shrugged.

"I could eat," Noah said. He ran a hand through his short blond hair—spiky now from getting wet in the rain and then drying several times over—and then went to get Lori from the car.

Matt jogged up to the front door, heard the dead bolt sliding back, and when Sara opened it, he propped the shotgun against the frame and swept her into his arms. They stood on the threshold, hugging so hard it hurt. Sara tried to talk but couldn't manage it through her tears. She sobbed so hard it shook them both.

"Hush, baby girl," Matt said. "We'll be all right now."

Sara stiffened and stepped back from him. "No," she said, wiping at her tears. "Don't call me that. *Please* don't call me that."

Matt almost let the grief overwhelm him then. Baby girl had been their father's name for her, and now it had died with him.

"All right. Now let's get inside."

Sara moved back to let him pass. Matt picked up the shotgun and stepped inside, but when he glanced at Sara again he saw that his sister had frozen, staring back out the door. He spun, thinking something had happened, but she was only watching Noah and Lori come across the front lawn. They were talking, faces grim, and Lori had the baseball bat over her shoulder like she was about to step up to the plate. As they entered the house, Sara did not move out of their way.

Noah looked nervously out the door, looking for more of the dead. "What's wrong with her?" he asked.

Matt didn't know.

Sara pressed the heel of her hand against her temple, like she had a headache, and then looked pointedly at Lori.

"This is crazy," she said. "You're Tania."

Lori gave a nervous laugh. "Sorry, hon. Happens all the time, but actually, my name is Lori."

Sara knitted her eyebrows and thrust out one hip, looked Lori up and down, and cocked her head.

"Uh-huh. Lori? Okay, girl." She nodded. "Okay."

Zack came down the stairs, an exasperated look on his face. "Jesus, somebody shut the door."

Noah shut it hard and locked it. Matt saw that they'd used the big bookcase to barricade the door, and went to help Noah move it back into place.

"Sara?" Zack said, staring at Lori. "Tania is in your house."

"I know. Weird, right?"

NOAH'S MOTHER HAD TAUGHT him how to cook. She'd been dead two and a half years and he had thought it would feel good to be in a kitchen, that cooking would give him that familiar warmth, like he still shared something with her even though she'd been gone so long.

It didn't.

All he'd done was boil a bunch of pasta, fry some ground chicken, and mix it in a casserole dish with chopped-up ham and cheese from the fridge and a can of baby peas. But instead of making him feel close to his mother, the act of cooking made him feel entirely separate from her. Where he'd always felt her with him, now he felt nothing but a gaping void.

He wondered where she was now, if she had managed to dig her way up and out, if she was walking around. He wondered if Suzette Eisen's corpse was at that very moment trying to find its way home. He'd promised himself he wouldn't think about it, buried that fear deep in his mind, but like the dead, it kept rising.

"Hey."

Noah turned to see a nervous-looking Lori standing in the entrance to the kitchen. "Hey."

"Anything I can help with in here?"

"You can set the table if you want."

Lori came over to the granite-topped island in the middle of the kitchen. She'd tied her hair back in a ponytail and scrubbed off her makeup, and she looked even younger than she was. "You think they're going to leave the living room? They're all glued to the TV."

"They're just trying to figure out what to do next."

"What *are* we going to do next?" she asked.

"We'll talk about it over dinner," Noah said. "Are they doing all right in there?"

Lori rubbed at the bandage on her arm. They'd cleaned her bite wound with antiseptic and wrapped it in gauze.

"As all right as any of us, I guess," she said, looking up at him. "I'm sorry about your girlfriend."

Noah leaned against the counter. "Thanks. I hope yours fares better."

Lori blinked. "My girlfriend?"

He smiled. "Yeah. You're her. I get that you're trying not to be, and if you want us to keep calling you Lori, that's fine. What's in a name, right? We're, like, seven hours into a new world, so we're making it up as we go. You can be anyone you want. All I'm saying is, I hope that girl you were involved with is okay."

She looked at her feet for a second, gave a sad kind of laugh, and then looked like she might cry.

"Hey, hey," Noah said. "I'm sorry. I didn't mean—"

"No, it's fine," she said, looking up quickly. "And thank you. That's sweet."

The oven beeped. Noah went to grab a pot holder and glanced at her. "Are you going to set the table?"

"On it." She looked around until she found dishes in the corner cabinet and started pulling plates out. "And Noah?"

"Yeah?"

"My name is Tania. But famous doesn't mean much anymore. I'm just somebody trying to stay alive, like everyone else."

Noah slid the casserole dish out of the oven and set it on top of the pot holder on the counter. As he closed the oven, he looked at her.

"Nice to meet you."

As Tania set the table, Noah got out some bowls and fished around in the fridge again, throwing together a salad. While he was slicing tomatoes, Matt came into the kitchen.

"Guys."

"Hey," Tania said. "How's your sister?"

Matt nodded. "She's all right, I guess."

"What's up?" Noah asked.

"I've been watching the news. They keep running down the facts—at least what they know—and it seems pretty obvious this thing started with those psychics or mediums or whatever. They did that séance, and they all passed out, right?"

Noah and Tania looked at each other.

"Yeah?" Noah said.

"They were on *Sunrise,*" Tania said. "I've been on that set. Actually, I was supposed to do the show tomorrow."

Matt gave her a curious look, but then went on. "I saw a report from that building. They're not doing any live broadcasting from the show's studio, but this one reporter said none of them—not the hosts of the show or any of the psychics—have regained consciousness. They're in some kind of coma. She interviewed a member of the *Sunrise* stage crew, and the guy said they haven't been able to separate them."

"What?" Noah said.

Tania leaned on the back of a kitchen chair. "Are you serious? They were holding hands for this séance, and now nobody can pull them apart?"

"That's what this guy was saying."

Noah felt a twist of nausea in his stomach, but it quickly turned to dark anger. He looked at the others.

"You two are with me on this, right?" Noah said. "I mean, that's not a coincidence, that this started at the same moment their little séance went all to hell. And now they can't be woken up and they're, like, fused together? What does that tell you?"

"That if them starting this séance was the beginning of all of this, finishing the séance might put an end to it," Matt said.

Tania scoffed. "Come on. You think if you separate these people, this is all just going to stop? The dead people are going to apologize and crawl back to their graves?"

"No," Noah said. "But maybe they'll be dead again."

"We've got to go to Manhattan," Matt said.

Tania stared at him, eyes wide. "Are you kidding me? If that's ground zero, we've got to get as far away from there as possible. Besides, you just said nobody's been able to separate them."

Noah turned to her. "Maybe somebody needs to try harder."

13

The Bronx, New York City

Sara stood on the street corner, watching for anyone who might interrupt them—police would be bad, a horde of the dead worse. She glanced up and down the road. Look both ways before you cross the street. A giddiness built in her chest but she forced herself not to laugh. Her father had died twice today, and laughter would feel obscene.

She waved to Zack, who signaled from the far corner. All clear on his end as well. He looked out of place in his tight orange T-shirt and crisp blue jeans, like he'd gotten lost. Zack Through the Looking Glass.

"Go!" Noah shouted from behind the wheel of the Jeep.

Matt and Tania grabbed the tow chain Noah had hooked to the back of the Jeep and ran to the door of the gun shop. The place was called Gunsmith's, and iron bars blocked the windows and front door. Tania hauled on the chain to get enough slack while Matt slid the end through the bars on the door grate and hooked it.

"Come on!" Noah called. Sara watched him, thinking how much he reminded her of Matt Damon in *Saving Private Ryan,* the short blond hair, the eyes, the grim sense of purpose.

Matt held up his hands. "Done!"

Her brother shared that grim quality now, and it saddened Sara. She wasn't used to seeing him like this, but everything had changed now, for both of them. Even his look was severe, with his hair clipped so close to the scalp and that sculpted goatee.

Tania pulled her own hands away just as Noah dropped the Jeep into drive. Sara stared, heart hammering in her chest, as the chain went taut. The Jeep's engine growled and she heard a popping noise and a screech of metal. Matt and Tania hurried away from the front of the store just as the metal grate tore away from the door with such force that it hit the back of the Jeep, smashing a taillight.

"I can't believe we're doing this!" Sara called to her brother.

Matt shot her a glance full of regret, but he didn't have to put words to that look. They both knew it had to be done. There were three choices: give up and die, try to survive, or try to survive *and* do something about the situation. The versions that didn't involve dying required them to protect themselves.

Tania heaved a brick through the glass door. And how freakin' weird was that? Sara never imagined she'd commit a crime in her life, but here she was breaking into a gun shop with a girl whose TV show she'd been singing and dancing along with for years. Or she had until recently. She was too old for that stuff now. But she wouldn't tell Tania that.

All of it seemed slightly surreal, until she thought of her father. Then reality crushed her again, stabbed her, destroyed her.

The alarm went off, echoing off the faces of buildings up and down the street. They were in the Bronx, in a rough neighborhood that would've made Sara nervous on her best day.

"Oh, fantastic!" Zack called from the opposite corner.

Noah unhooked his chain from the door grate and started gathering it up. "It doesn't matter," he said. "Nobody's coming. Just move your asses and we'll be fine."

Sara looked at the buildings around them, up and down the streets that intersected at her corner. Noah was right. Some curtains moved, gray faces peering out from behind them and then vanishing. But no doors opened, no one came to try to stop them. Nobody dared to come outside. She wondered if that was a hint they just weren't taking. Why were *they* the ones taking chances?

Something had to be done, of course, but why were they the ones who had to do it? Surely there must be other people who had figured out that the way to stop the dead from rising was to break up the connection the mediums had established? Hundreds of people, probably. Maybe thousands.

But when her brother had explained to Sara what they planned to do, she'd agreed immediately. Sitting in her house with her father's twice-dead corpse outside would tear her apart. If someone had to stand up and do the hard job, then she and Matt were willing. Their father had raised them that way.

Even so, when she saw the two dead girls coming down the street, she started to scream.

Over the wailing of Gunsmith's alarm, only Tania heard her. Matt had already gone inside and Noah was opening up the rear of the Jeep. On the other corner, standing sentinel on the lookout, Zack had his back to them.

Tania ran over. Sara still hadn't recovered from the surreal nature of her presence, but right now she was more concerned with the two dead girls. Tania had left her baseball bat propped against the front of the gun shop and she retrieved it as she rushed over.

"What is it?" she asked.

Sara pointed to the two dead girls, though her eyes strayed to the bloodstained gauze wrapped around Tania's wrist. She'd been bitten. One of Matt and Noah's professors had committed suicide right next to her. She'd seen a friend eaten by dead people this morning. All of this Sara had learned in the past hour. She wondered how Tania could still run around, fighting back, after all of that.

But then, they'd all been through hell today, and here they all were.

"Noah!" Tania shouted.

Sara caught a glimpse of Noah running into the gun shop. Matt had been in there a minute or so and not come out yet. Noah looked worried.

The two dead girls were still a block away, not quite running, but these weren't shuffling cadavers. They were freshly dead. They'd be quick and hungry. Tania brought the baseball bat up onto her shoulder, like she was waiting for a pitch.

"What are you doing?" Sara asked.

"Defending myself. What the hell are you doing?" the girl snapped.

Sara grinned. "Um, not fighting zombies with a piece of wood, that's for sure. Not with a roomful of guns right freakin' here!"

For a second, perhaps two steps for the dead girls, Sara and Tania just looked at each other. Then, as one, they bolted for the Jeep and the gun shop. Matt walked out the door with a box in his arms.

"Incoming!" Sara cried.

The alarm wailed. Matt might not have made out what she'd

said, but he saw the look on her face and that said it all. He dropped the box into the back of the Jeep.

"What's wrong?"

"We've got company," Tania said.

"Dead or alive?" Matt asked, looking toward the corner where they'd been standing seconds before.

Sara didn't have to answer. At that moment, the dead girls came around the corner. Matt swore, started shouting for Noah, and ran to the passenger door of the Jeep. Whatever guns they were stealing, he hadn't loaded any of them yet. He opened the door and grabbed the shotgun from the front seat, pumped a round into the chamber as he turned, and then ran back to the girls.

He waited until the dead girls—they couldn't have been more than thirteen—got within perhaps ten feet, and then he shot the nearer of the two. The major advantage of a shotgun appeared to be that no experience was necessary. The blast spread enough that it was basically a point-and-shoot weapon.

Matt pumped the shotgun and dropped the other girl with a second round. The shotgun blasts echoed off the buildings, loud even over the blaring of the alarm.

Sara stared at her brother. His expression remained grim. Shooting the two dead girls had not troubled him very much. Maybe it would be impossible to disturb him any more than he'd already been disturbed by all of this, but watching him now, she felt cold inside. It might not really be killing, but it *felt* like it. Sara didn't like the idea that anyone could get used to shooting people, especially Matt.

Noah rushed out the door carrying several rifles, another shotgun, and funky, boxy-looking things Sara knew had to be assault weapons. He had them piled in his arms like firewood.

He took in the two dead girls, glanced at Matt, and then piled the guns into the back of the Jeep.

"Hurry. Just ammo, and we're good," he said to Matt. Then he glanced at Sara. "Back to the corner."

Zack shouted something from down the street. Sara waved to let him know everything was all right and he nodded. Matt started to follow Noah back into the gun shop, but Sara grabbed him by the arm.

"Hey."

Matt looked at her. For a moment, his expression remained frozen. Then he smiled and ruffled her hair. "Hey."

"You're not gonna get all trigger-happy on me, are you?" she asked, trying to keep her tone light.

He looked surprised, started to shake his head to reassure her. And then he stopped and his expression turned grim. "We're still alive. We've gotta stay that way. We may have to do a lot of things we never thought we'd do, but—"

"Okay," she said, squeezing his hand. "I get it. I just want to make sure you're still you when it's all over."

Matt smiled. "Don't worry. I'll tease you more than ever."

"Good."

He vanished into the shop. She caught a glimpse of Noah stacking boxes of ammunition on a counter. Then Tania pulled her by the hand and the two girls went together to what had been Sara's corner. That made her feel better, not being alone there.

Down the street, a couple of oldish guys had come out, drawn by the sound of gunfire, their curiosity getting the better of them. They stared but did not approach, and after a minute or two, they went back inside.

Then Noah was slamming the back of the Jeep and Matt

shouted for them all to get in, and their first major crime of the day had concluded. They all piled in and Noah pulled away from Gunsmith's, beginning to lecture them on firearm safety and etiquette.

"How can this be happening?" Zack said, looking around at them, face pale. "We're thieves now. We're going to shoot people."

"It's gotta be done," Tania said.

"And they're dead people," Matt added.

Zack didn't look like he took much comfort in that.

"The world's off its axis," Noah said, his eyes on the road. "Someone's got to tilt it back."

"One of these days it's going to go off balance and that'll be the end of things," Tania said, hugging herself in the backseat, between Zack and Sara. "And nobody's going to be able to fix it. That'll be it. Last call. Put the chairs up on the tables, turn out the lights, and lock up the doors forever. Things keep happening that people think will be the end of the world, and every time it's worse. One time, it really will be the end."

"But not this time," Sara said.

"How do you know?" Tania asked.

The Jeep was silent except for the hum of the engine.

THE BAD NEWS BECAME a drone on the radio, but Jack kept it on, just to have the companionship of human voices. Up in his parents' neighborhood he'd had his pick of cars to steal. People had either fled the city or were holed up tight in their apartments, hiding out until things improved, or until dead things dragged them out into the street for a feast. Compared to getting eaten alive, a little thing like getting their car stolen wasn't enough to worry anyone. Glass shattering, engines starting up—even if someone had looked out the window and seen their car getting jacked, they weren't gonna come outside and try to stop him.

If he'd looked long enough, he probably could have found a car with the keys still in it. People were in that kind of hurry. But on foot and alone in a city of the dead, Jack didn't have time to waste. He had scanned the street, picked the car he wanted, and had it hot-wired and purring in about ninety seconds. He'd picked an old Volvo station wagon, mainly because of the steel frame. If things got bad and he had to do something crazy with the car, the Volvo gave him the best chance of surviving.

"The president, vice president, and many key government figures have been moved to an undisclosed location," a voice on the radio informed him. The woman sounded like she was gritting her teeth as she said it, like she wanted to scream at someone. But she kept on in that clipped tone. "A spokesman for the White House said this is the usual protocol in the case of a national crisis. Should the authorities not be able to keep Washington, D.C., safe, the president will be in a position to continue to lead our country."

The reporter actually scoffed at that before continuing.

Jack gripped the wheel, knuckles white. What the hell did he think he was doing, driving right into the heart of this thing when the president was hidden away in some bunker?

Doing the job, he thought. *You're doing the job, because they haven't figured it out yet.*

As he drove south, entering Manhattan, he was surprised not to encounter any roadblocks. He heard sirens in the distance, and along the way he spotted police and military vehicles, ambulances, and fire engines all rushing to some tragedy or another, but he didn't bother trying to flag any of them down. There'd be no point. Obviously, nobody had figured out how to put a stop to this situation yet, or it would've been done already. Jack could've told them, but he knew they wouldn't listen to him. He was a tattooed gangbanger from the Bronx.

No, there'd be no help. And as long as nobody got in the way, that was fine with Jack. He'd never killed anyone before, but this was a day for firsts, and a time for desperate measures.

He was close now. Fifty blocks north of Times Square. And the gun sat heavily on the seat beside him. The Volvo wagon had a car seat in the back and kids' toys and loose Cheerios and coloring books scattered all over. The gun was an intruder. But soon enough, he and the gun would be gone, and the Volvo could go back to being the car of some mom and her baby daughter. Jack told himself they were still alive, somewhere.

A new voice took over from the woman on the radio—a man this time—and though he had a more polished delivery, he, too, sounded anxious. The National Guard and state police had set up quarantine lines to the south and west, but reports were coming in from all areas that the quarantine zones could not be maintained. They had to keep moving the lines because the affected area kept growing. The authorities would establish roadblocks and medical stations and military positions; it would be all right for a little while. Then the phenomenon would go past them, the dead beginning to rise in towns outside the quarantine zone, and they'd have to move back.

The effect was spreading, with no end in sight.

Already the lines had been moved as far south as Virginia and as far west as Columbus, Ohio. The Canadians were supposedly coordinating with the U.S. government, but Jack had a feeling that, like everyone else, they were doing more freaking out and shooting dead guys than coordinating anything. Despite all the assurances that the radio served up in tiny sound bites, it was easy enough to read between the lines. Unless some scientist had a brainstorm, nobody had a clue how to stop the dead from walking. Somehow, the effect was contagious, and the contagion was spreading.

Meanwhile, Jack drove south on Broadway, right into the heart of the city. He saw people on rooftops in the distance, watching the city below like they expected the Macy's Thanksgiving Day Parade to go by. Eventually he let the radio voices sift into the back of his head again, not paying attention, and he just started watching the street signs as he drove past.

Eighty-first Street.

Eightieth Street.

Seventy-ninth Street.

A countdown, ticking toward murder.

Manhattan, New York City

From a distance, the FDR Drive looked like a parking lot. The cars weren't moving. If Noah had to lay bets, he'd put money on most of the people who'd tried getting out of the city that way already having abandoned their cars. By now, either they'd been evacuated, they were holed up in the buildings near the highway, or they were dead. Chances were that some brave fools might still be locked up in their cars, afraid to get out, thinking the whole thing would blow over if they just waited long enough. And maybe they were right.

Maybe.

Noah drove the Jeep south on Second Avenue. Tania sat silently beside him, but something had changed in her over the past couple of hours. She'd been on the verge of some kind of breakdown when they'd picked her up. In shock, maybe. Now she wore a look of determination that made him glad to have her along. Whoever she'd been before the world went to hell, there was no trace of the diva about her now.

A couple of times she glanced over and smiled thinly at him, then reached out to pat him on the leg or squeeze his arm. He knew there was nothing flirtatious in it. Tania didn't like guys. Even so, the warmth he felt toward her for the comfort her presence offered made him feel guilty.

In his mind's eye, he could still see Mara, walking along the side of the road on her college campus. The others hadn't known her, wouldn't have recognized her. So only Noah had seen her corpse, one arm torn away, wounds at her throat and abdomen, shirt hanging open so that she was half naked. He'd seen her first from behind, and known her instantly from the cut of her blond hair and the curve of her back. As they'd driven by, he'd had to force himself to glance back for just a moment, to make sure, to see those green eyes. But even without that glance, he'd have known her.

He bit his lip at the memory, funneling his grief into anger, keeping his emotions in check. It hurt so badly, carved him up inside. Her death had hit him hard, but to see her like that, bloody and exposed, had made it so much worse. She had been so modest. If any of her soul remained, he knew it tormented her to see her flesh so violated.

"Noah!" Tania shouted.

A dead man in a dark suit staggered off the curb right in front of them. Instinctively, Noah hit the brake and swerved around him, and they kept rolling down Second Avenue.

"Damn!" Matt said from the backseat. "Keep your eyes on the road, man."

Noah gripped the wheel. "You worry about your sister. I'll worry about the road."

"Asshole," Matt muttered.

"Maybe. But this asshole's been keeping you alive."

An icy chill settled on the passengers in the car. Noah flexed his fingers on the steering wheel.

"Jesus, you guys," Zack said. "Don't we have enough crap to deal with?"

Noah glanced at Tania, saw the sadness in her eyes, and let out a breath. He thought of Mara. "Yeah. Yeah, we do."

But he didn't apologize. When he'd woken up that morning, he'd had a healthy dislike for Matt Gaines. Turned out Matt wasn't a bad guy. He had balls, and a spine, and Noah had been glad to have him along on the road today. Even so, the frisson of hostility between them hadn't gone away. Trying to survive together might make them allies, even give them a grudging respect for each other, but it wouldn't make them friends.

Still, he had to hand it to the guy. Noah had lost the person that meant everything in the world to him today. But Matt had been attacked by his father's corpse, and had to deal with not only his death but seeing him taken out by gunfire. And Sara . . .

Noah looked in the rearview mirror, shifting his head to get a glimpse of the girl. Matt had an arm around her and she leaned into him. Maybe that was it; the two of them could get through this because they took strength from each other. Even so, the things that Sara had gone through made him feel sick. Sara hadn't told any of them what her dead father had said, and Zack wasn't talking. The kid obviously loved her, though Sara didn't seem to feel the same way. Whatever it was that Hal Gaines had said to his daughter, it must have been horrible.

It made Noah wonder. He hadn't talked to his father or sister in months, and he doubted if his dad even cared if he was alive or dead. And his mother . . . he couldn't stop himself from wondering what she would say to him if she rose from the dead with the kind of malice and savagery that these things had. What hateful venom would she spit at him, but more important, how much of it would be true? How much would he deserve?

They weren't comfortable thoughts.

At Forty-fifth Street, he turned right. There were abandoned cars everywhere now, and he had to weave around them, going up on the curb in some places. Other than a few muted exclamations from Zack and Tania, no one spoke. There where shattered windows everywhere. The dead were far more scarce in Manhattan than they'd been in the Bronx—likely because there were far fewer graves—but still they could be seen wandering in hotel lobbies and along streets. One sat in a crouch at the top of the stairs leading down to the subway, as though waiting to pounce.

At Fifth Avenue, he had to turn the Jeep south one block to avoid a pair of police cars that sat in the middle of the intersection with their light bars flashing, doors hanging open. Something moved in the darkness beneath one of the cars, but Noah didn't look too closely to see what it might be. He thought he knew.

He continued west on Forty-fourth Street, right into Times Square, and then he stopped, engine purring. "Which building is it?"

Tania pointed diagonally across the street. The network building was a tower of glass and steel. Noah could see logos and cameras through windows on the third floor, one of their sets overlooking Times Square. As he studied the front of the building, he felt the world rumble around him and heard the roar of an engine.

"That's hideous," Zack said right behind Noah.

Sara made a noise of disgust. The rest of them just watched as a massive snow plow, unleashed from some city department garage, lumbered up Broadway and passed within ten feet of the Jeep's nose.

The plow's blade hung inches off the pavement as it rumbled by, and bits and pieces of dead people clung to the yellow paint, stuck there with smears of blood and gore.

Noah closed his eyes against the nightmare, but he knew it would return to him in dreams. That image, so surreal, would haunt him always. He didn't open his eyes again until the roar of the plow's engine had nearly vanished.

There were more of the dead in Times Square than they'd seen in other places. According to radio reports, a lot of the walking dead were returning home, whatever part of their mind that remained—memories, spirit, whatever—guiding them back to people they left behind, even as their hunger made them attack. But in America in the twenty-first century—especially in New York City—a lot of people were more at home in their offices than in their living rooms. So among the dead in the city, many had returned to their workplace.

A handful of the dead wandered the intersection. But as Noah tapped the gas and the Jeep rolled across Times Square, he studied the front of the network building and knew why they hadn't seen even more of them in Manhattan. They were inside already, or milling about in the lobbies, riding elevators and walking stairwells.

The glass and steel tower from which *Sunrise* was broadcast every weekday morning had drawn more than its fair share. The glass doors—even the revolving doors—had been shattered, and the frames buckled. The dead had pushed their way in.

"How are we going to do this?" Matt asked, bending forward to peer through the windshield.

"Let's see." Noah pulled the Jeep up onto the curb, as close to the shattered doors as he could.

The dead had gathered on the steps leading up to the mezzanine-level lobby, but over their heads he could see the top of a metal grating like the one that had blocked the front of the gun shop. The grates up there were keeping the dead from getting beyond the top of the stairs. The corpses shuffled together on the steps like cattle in a boxcar. There were two main entrances to the building, and he imagined the other had been similarly overrun.

"You ever heard the expression 'shooting fish in a barrel'?" Noah asked.

"I have," Zack replied. "But the fish don't eat you."

Noah shot him a dark look, then glanced around at the others. "We go in, all of us armed."

"Not Sara," Matt said.

Sara punched him in the arm. "Uh-huh, dumb-ass. You think I'm going out there without a gun, with all those things around?"

Before Matt could argue, Tania leaned into the backseat and touched them each on the leg.

"Noah's right," she said. "I don't think Zack and Sara should use their guns. Honestly, I don't think I should be firing a gun, either. But we all need to protect ourselves, even more than we need to get into that building."

Noah didn't agree with her. Getting into the building was top priority, no matter what the cost. But he wasn't about to say that out loud. It would be too difficult for them to accept, even though they all had to know it inside.

One by one, they all chose not to argue and looked at Noah.

"So, we go in?" Matt said. "And we just start shooting, cutting them down, until we get inside?"

Noah gave a small shrug. "I left all my *Mission: Impossible* gear in my other pants."

Matt held up a hand. "I'm not arguing. I just think we all need to be prepared for what that means: a lot of dead bodies, and a lot of blood."

Tania nodded. "After the day we've all had, I don't think anyone's going to hold back."

Already a couple of the dead who had been wandering aimlessly had turned toward the Jeep, sensing or smelling the living flesh inside. One of them looked to have been dead for quite some time, but the other seemed fresher, still wearing the suit he'd been buried in. Noah noticed that the man in the suit wore no shoes—only dark socks—and wondered if people were always buried with no shoes, if perhaps they couldn't fit properly in the casket.

"Are we going?" Matt asked.

Noah turned off the Jeep and tugged out the keys. "Yeah. We're going."

Matt and Zack reached into the rear of the vehicle and began distributing guns. The two sixteen-year-olds got handguns only, while Matt took both a pistol—which he stuffed into the rear of his waistband—and a fresh shotgun. There were a couple of mesh bags he'd grabbed from the gun shop, and Matt took one while handing Noah the other. They filled those with ammunition. Zack and Sara took extra clips for their guns. Noah took a pair of assault rifles and he and Tania went to work loading clips for those guns. He'd been pretty happy with the selection at the gun shop. The HK G36 assault rifles were serious business, and they'd snagged plenty of ammo as well.

Tania took the longest to decide. Eventually she agreed to carry a pair of handguns and to wear a long-range rifle over her shoulder for Noah, in case he needed it. He'd done well in sharpshooter training for ROTC. The shotgun was good for Matt because it was an up-close weapon, just like the pistols. But the assault rifles required control, and the rifle accuracy. Those weapons would be as useful as wooden clubs to any of the others.

"Take a breath," he said.

In the moment before he threw the door open, they all froze. But then he did it, the driver's door swinging wide, and they all followed suit, piling out of the Jeep.

"Matt, to your left!" Tania called.

Noah heard the shotgun blast but was too busy shooting to pay attention. He took down a zombie that had been lurking around the hood of the Jeep. A couple of others had come in close. He shot one, and Tania the other.

He blinked in surprise and turned to her.

"Lucky shot," she said.

"You've fired a gun before."

"At a range. I had my first stalker when I was thirteen. My mother thought I should know how to protect myself."

Twisted as it felt under the circumstances, Noah smiled. "Diva's full of surprises."

"Don't call me that," Tania snapped.

Noah's smile faded. A sore spot. "Sorry."

"I just don't want to have to shoot you," she said.

Tania laughed at his expression and then she and Matt started working their way toward the shattered doors on the southeast corner of the building. Sara and Zack followed, watching for other zombies who might surprise them out on the streets. Right now, though, they needed to focus on the ones inside.

"Hey!" Noah called. "That's not funny."

Tania waved to him to hurry. Noah ran to catch up and they hustled for the shattered glass doors, weighted down with guns and ammunition.

They were fifteen feet from the doors when the engine roared, tires squealed, and a car bumped up onto the curb and skidded to a halt a dozen yards away. As one, the five of them turned toward the car, guns up and ready. Noah's first thought was that the police had come, and from the stricken looks on Tania's and Zack's faces, he knew he wasn't alone.

But unless NYPD had started using battered old Volvo station wagons, it wasn't a cop at all.

The Asian guy who stepped out of the car—gun muzzle pointed toward the sky to indicate he meant them no harm—might've been in his late teens or early twenties. The tattoos on his arms gave him away as a gangbanger, either present or former, and his demeanor sealed the impression.

"Guess you guys beat me to it," he said, striding forward, gun still in the air.

"That's far enough," Matt said, sighting along the barrel of the shotgun.

The newcomer stopped. "Pointing that thing the wrong direction, man. If you're here with all that ordnance, I figure you came to put a stop to this. So did I. If you want to play action hero and have some kind of standoff, do it with your friends. Me? I'm going inside."

Noah hesitated, a twist in his stomach. But he studied the guy's eyes and played back the tone of his voice in his head.

"What's your name?" Noah asked.

"Gaesomun Kim. But everybody calls me Jack."

Noah held up one of the HKs and nodded toward the Jeep. "Plenty more where this came from, Jack. Grab what you want and come on."

"Don't mind if I do."

It took less than thirty seconds for Jack to arm himself. He trotted over to join them with an assault rifle slung over his shoulder and a pair of nine-millimeter pistols jutting from his belt.

And then they were six, moving toward the doors again. As quietly as possible they stepped in through the frames of broken doors, shattered glass crunching underfoot. Noah figured at least twenty-five of the dead spread out on the stairs above them. Only a few noticed their arrival. The other zombies were rattling against the grate, trying to get it open so they could get inside, return to the place where their lives meant something.

From beyond the grate, Noah heard noises.

"Voices," he said to Tania. "I hear people talking up there, past the grate."

Matt and the others all heard him.

"Hey!" Sara called. "Hey, up there in the lobby! Get away from the grate! There's going to be shooting."

At the sound of her shouts, the dead seemed to pause in a moment's contemplation. And then they started to turn, drawn by her voice. Some of them laughed, and some began to speak, to say dreadful things. But Noah didn't want to listen.

He pulled the trigger, spraying the stairwell with bullets so quickly that the echoes off the marble walls drowned out any other sounds. The others might be shooting as well, but he heard only his own gun, his own bullets, and he watched the dead begin to fall in masses of blood and torn flesh.

Dust to dust, and to dust again.

14

The rain had started up again, a drizzle that gathered like condensation on the windows. Phoenix stood in a small room that John Volk used as his office. His job might be more interesting than most, but the television producer's office had the same clutter as anyone else's.

Volk had been kind enough to offer her a few minutes alone in here, so that she could try yet again to phone her mother. Volk and Katie and Ray Creedon had all agreed to sit by her father and to come get her if anything should happen—especially if Peyton came back. The kid had half lost his mind, but that wasn't what frightened Phoenix the most. What scared her was the other half of Peyton's thoughts, his logic. She understood his thinking. Breaking the séance circle might create even greater problems—hell, it might make the current situation permanent—or it might make no difference at all. But she recognized the rationale behind Peyton's efforts, and she knew everyone else did, too.

How long before they decided it was worth drawing blood, maybe even taking lives?

Drastic action was called for. But Phoenix couldn't allow that action to put her father's life in jeopardy. No matter what. She'd spent so many years not knowing him, barely seeing him. During all that time, she'd seen him through the eyes of a hurt little girl, who couldn't understand why her father loved work more than he loved her. The truth still hurt, even though she was eighteen now, but she'd made an effort—they both had—to create a new relationship. They were really just learning each other, laying groundwork for the future. They'd created an opportunity together, and now it was slipping away.

Stretching out in Volk's chair, she felt the muscles in her neck pop. How easy it would be to just stay in here and let events outside this room unfold without her. But Phoenix couldn't leave her father. And Ray had stood up for her. She owed him for that.

Phoenix leaned forward and picked up Volk's phone. The intercompany phone service seemed to be working, but when she tried to get an outside line, all she got was dull silence, yet again. God, how she wished she could talk to her mother.

She stood and went to the window. For half a minute, she stared down through the gray drizzle at Times Square, watching the blue lights flicker from the tops of two abandoned police cars. The lights seemed to move slowly, almost lazily, as though they—like the world—had begun to wind down.

Phoenix pulled away from the window and left the office. Down to the right, she heard voices. One of them might have belonged to Peyton. He'd started spreading his message like a prophet, a fanatic with a lust for murder. She wondered how many people would listen to him.

She turned left, headed back into the studio. From behind, she heard a cheer. What the hell were they cheering for? She picked up her pace, but even before she got to the studio door, Katie Phelan rushed through, eyes alighting on Phoenix immediately.

"Hey! I was looking for you. Get in here; you've got to see this."

Phoenix followed her back to find that everyone in the studio had gathered around yet again to watch the row of television screens on the wall of the *Sunrise* set. Even Ray stood there, having abandoned his post near her father. Phoenix glanced over at the faux dining room set where her father, Annelise, Eric, and the two hosts, Amy Tjan and Steve Bell, still slumped unconscious in their chairs.

They look dead, she thought.

But she didn't have time to focus on that chilling observation. The people clustered in the studio talked excitedly and her gaze was drawn to the video monitors that had so entranced them.

"Someone turn up the sound," John Volk said.

But no one moved, and that was all right. They could hear enough, and certainly there was no mistaking the events unfolding. The central screen showed a live feed from the lobby of the building, coming from one of the camera crews the network had put in place down there. Even for Phoenix, who'd never been inside the building before this morning, it would have been impossible to mistake the lobby design, including the patterned tile floors. And a small box in the upper left-hand corner of the screen read: LIVE.

The image showed the dead, dull-eyed and muttering, some biting at the air, pressing up against the metal grate that blocked them from entering the lobby. But the *pop-pop* noise of gunshots came through the speakers in the studio, and as Phoenix watched, several of the dead dropped to the ground like marionettes with their strings cut. One of them, face pressed between two of the bars in the grate, stiffened as its head exploded. The thunder of bullets echoed off the marble.

Behind the dead, impossible to make out through the camera feed, people continued to attack.

"It's . . ." Ray began.

"Gotta be the military, sweeping the city. Taking back control," John Volk declared.

Katie hugged him, practically doing a victory dance. The others all started talking at once. Phoenix wasn't certain the time to celebrate had arrived. Out the window of Volk's office, she'd seen no sign of the authorities except for those two abandoned police cars. But she couldn't stave off the hope that ignited within her.

Ray Creedon grabbed her, and she let herself be embraced, felt herself returning the hug, smiling. He kissed her once, for only a moment, nothing sexual about it, just a simple expression of happiness. Still, it startled her, and she found herself backing tentatively away.

He noticed. Ray was a sweet, smart guy. He frowned and looked at her, searching for something.

"Hey. I'm sorry," he said. "I'm just . . . it's like the end of a war or something."

"It's not over yet."

"I know that. I'm just happy to have help. I didn't want to die; can you blame me?"

She managed a smile. He deserved that. "No. And I'm sorry. It's not that I minded. You just surprised me, is all. And maybe now's not the best time."

Ray arched an eyebrow. "So maybe another time?"

Phoenix reached out to take his hand and they turned to watch the monitor together. Shouts and more gunfire came out of the speakers. Phoenix tried to get a better look beyond the grate and the dead, to see who it was coming to their rescue. She caught a glimpse of a boy, maybe fourteen or fifteen years old, and confusion gripped her. This wasn't the army or the cops.

"Who the hell are they?" she said aloud.

By now others had noticed, too. Some of the happy chatter died down.

Ray tugged her hand. "Let's go find out."

"No," she said, drawing her hand away. "I'll go. Me and John. I need you to stay here and watch out for my dad, in case those pricks come back."

He started to argue.

"I need you to do this," she said.

In Ray's eyes, she saw the question forming. Why him? Why wasn't Phoenix the one sitting by her father, watching over him? Even if she could have found a simple way to put the answer into words, she wouldn't have spoken them in front of the others. How to explain that she had a terrible feeling about these newcomers, their so-called saviors, without admitting that Peyton might be right?

"Please?" She lowered her voice. "I don't *trust* anybody else."

Ray glanced over at the unconscious figure of Professor Joe Cormier. He nodded. "All right."

The others in the studio were all so focused on the monitor that they'd paid no attention to her exchange with Ray. Now Phoenix went over and pulled Volk aside.

"I'm going downstairs. You coming?"

He hesitated. "I don't know. Stray bullets."

Leah overheard them and stepped over to speak with her, voice low.

"I'll go. I want to know what's happening outside. I'd like to get out of here and back to my place if it's safe."

Volk stared at her. "Safe outside? Are you nuts?"

Leah smiled. "I have a cat at home. She'll be starving and probably terrified. They sense it when things change, like storms. You'd be surprised."

"This isn't a storm," Phoenix said.

"Isn't it?"

Volk sighed. "All right. The three of us, then. I wouldn't mind knowing who these people are. They're obviously not military."

He nodded toward the monitor. A couple of the newcomers—a young black guy and a teenage white girl—could be seen stepping over the fallen dead, firing at the others.

"You've gotta be shitting me," Leah said.

"What?" Volk asked.

She shook her head. "Nothing. That blond girl, with the ponytail—for a second she looked just like that tweeny pop star, what's her name?"

Phoenix didn't know what she was talking about and neither did Volk.

"I didn't get a look at her," he said.

Volk shared a quiet word with Katie and then the three of them were rushing for the elevator. It took a while to arrive, but once they were on board, they descended swiftly.

Several floors above the lobby, Phoenix could already hear the muffled report of gunfire. When the car came to a halt and the doors slid open, a white-haired man and a thirtyish guy with black-rimmed glasses were waiting. The younger guy had his hand clamped over his left shoulder, where blood soaked through his shirt, and the gruff-looking older man was helping him.

For a second, they all stared at one another.

"Christ's sake," the white-haired guy said. "Out of the way. Trust me, you don't want to go out there."

Volk started to step back to let them in, but Phoenix and Leah moved forward, out into the marble corridor that served as a foyer for the elevators. Volk followed.

"Are you going to be all right?" Leah asked the younger man.

"Hell if I know. Never been shot before."

On that, the elevator doors whispered shut.

For a moment, they just took in the scene. Dots and dashes of bright red blood spattered the marble floor, like some gruesome Morse code. At the end of the foyer, a man and a woman huddled just within the mouth of the corridor. Another burst of gunfire startled them, and Leah pressed herself up against the wall and began, carefully, to inch her way along it. Without taking time to consider the wisdom of this course, Phoenix followed suit. Volk hurried after them.

"This may well be the stupidest thing I've ever done," he said.

No one replied.

At the corner, they could see the reception desk between the two metal grates, as well as two of the camera setups. One camera lay on the floor, abandoned, but the other stood on a tripod, still capturing the unfolding events. Several people had taken refuge behind the reception desk.

"Where's everyone else?" Volk asked the two people hiding in the elevator foyer with them.

The woman looked up. "In the café, mostly. My sound guy, Vernon, took a bullet, but I think he's okay."

"Who the hell are they?" Phoenix asked.

"No idea," said the man with her. "But they're killing these things, maybe cutting us a way out of here."

"To go where?" Phoenix asked.

Shifting her position, she could see that the grate on the left was still totally overrun with the dead, possibly even more than it had been before. But the other—where the gunfire originated—revealed only a few.

In a minute, the last of the gunshots came, and she could hear voices.

"Hey!" Phoenix called. "Are they all gone?"

"This batch," a male voice replied. "There'll be more, I'm sure. Come and let us in."

Phoenix stared around at her companions. "Is he kidding?"

"Do they seem like they're kidding?" Leah whispered.

After a moment's hesitation, Phoenix stepped into the lobby. Volk reached out to try to pull her back, but she was too quick. She saw faces at the south-side grate, including that of a black girl a few years younger than Phoenix herself, and it lifted her spirits to see people actively doing something, fighting back. Then she remembered that their idea of fighting back had brought them here, and she grew wary again.

"What do you want?" she asked, moving closer to the massive grate.

"What the hell do you think we want? Let us in. More of them are bound to be along any minute." This from a severe-looking, twentyish guy with a military haircut and some kind of automatic rifle in his hands.

The sight of the weapon made Phoenix freeze. She stared at his hands on the gun, then at his grim gray eyes. Scattered on the stairs and the landing around them were the now unmoving remains of dozens of dead people. Blood spattered walls and stairs, dripped from the grate, and stained his clothes. With him were the handsome, stylish black guy she'd seen before—it had to have been his voice she'd heard moments ago—and three teenagers, a boy and girl who might have been sophomores or juniors in high school, and another girl who carried herself much older. At the back, beyond them all, an Asian guy covered the shattered glass entry doors with another automatic weapon. They all carried guns, even the two young ones, who had pistols in their hands.

Not exactly the cavalry.

Volk stepped out from the elevator foyer. "Who are you?"

Several members of the camera crews came out of hiding now, and Leah emerged as well.

"Are you nuts?" the Asian guy said, coming up the stairs, glancing back and forth between the street-level doors and the grate. His clothes and the tattoos on his arms gave him the look of a gang member. "Let us in. Look, we've figured out how to put a stop to this thing. Give us five minutes, and all the dead things will drop in their tracks."

As if in answer, the dead who crowded against the grate at the north-side entrance began to moan, some to call out. Others spoke the names of those they had come looking for, whispered terrible things about them. Phoenix closed her ears to them, refused to hear.

"You think you've got the answer?" she asked.

"We know we do," said the older girl, drawing their attention.

"Jesus, it *is* her," Leah said. "What the hell is going on?"

Phoenix glanced from Volk to Leah, and then back at the teenaged girl. Leah might have recognized her, but Phoenix didn't.

"I know you," Volk said. "You've been on the show. You were booked to sing tomorrow. Tania."

The girl, Tania, laughed. It was a sad, desperate sort of laugh. "Here I am. Hope you don't mind me being early."

The younger girl, whose chocolate skin and strong, elegant features made her resemble the black guy enough that Phoenix thought they must be family, stepped up to the grate and wrapped her fingers around it. She stared at Phoenix.

"Please, just listen," she said, and then turned to the others. "Everyone shut up a minute. They're afraid. Don't you get it? We're all afraid."

The black guy—maybe her brother—put a hand on her shoulder. "It's all right, Sara."

"No, Matt. It's not. You'd be afraid if you were on the other side, too."

"On the other side?" the blond white guy with the crew cut said. "What about out here?"

"Shut up, Noah," Sara said.

Phoenix felt some of the tension leaving her.

"Yeah," one of the camera crew yelled. "Shut up, Noah. Whoever the hell you are. You shot at least two people in here. One of 'em's a friend of mine, and he's bleeding all over the place. I don't think he's gonna make it. If you didn't have those guns—"

"We didn't mean for any of that to happen," the skinny boy called, his expression wracked with guilt. He held on to his pistol so loosely it looked like he might drop it. "We're just trying to help."

Phoenix went up to the grate.

"Careful," Volk said.

She ignored him, walking up to Matt and gripping the grate. "What. Do. You. Want?"

Matt's soft eyes searched her face and she saw him flinch with understanding. "I think you know." He shook his head. "Of course you guys know. We're smart, but we're not that smart. The radio, the TV, even your own network have been talking about the psychic shit that happened here this morning. That was the trigger. The lady medium even said it when the shit hit the fan. 'I think we made a terrible mistake.' Something like that. So unless you tell me those people have all woken up, we're here to wake them."

"You don't think we've tried?" Phoenix asked, hating the shrill panic in her voice.

"Screw waking them up," the guy they'd called Noah said. "Just separate them."

"We've been trying for hours," Leah said, coming closer to the grate, just over Phoenix's shoulder.

"Look, there's no proof that separating them will solve anything," Volk said. "We're all terrified, but it will all be contained eventually. And then we'll figure out—"

"Bullshit," snapped the Asian guy. "This is spreading so fast, there won't be anyone left to figure it out if something isn't done soon. And if we're wrong, so what? Another couple of corpses among thousands. A drop in the bucket."

Phoenix froze. Icy fear rippled through her and she backed up two steps from the grate, staring at them all, at the anger and desperation and fear in them.

Now, though, Tania turned from the grate to stare at him. "Hold on. We're not killing anybody. We'll separate them, whatever it takes. But I'm not murdering someone."

"Nobody said *you* had to do it," Noah said.

Phoenix stared. So the crew-cut guy was on board with murder as well. How many others?

Sara looked at the black guy. "Matt?"

He held a shotgun, but now he clutched it in one hand and reached out to comfort her with the other. "That's not why we're here."

"It's not?" Noah said. "I'm sorry, haven't we been talking about this for hours?"

"We talked about separating them," said the teenaged boy, coming up to stand with Matt and Sara. "Not about murder."

"Can we debate this inside?" Tania asked.

A moan came from the shattered glass doors. They all turned at once to see two of the dead, one of them in a police uniform, coming into the building. The one they'd called Jack turned and strafed the dead with bullets. He shot one in the head, and it crumpled to the ground. The other staggered up the first few steps with half a dozen bullets in its torso, until Jack walked down to meet it, raised the automatic rifle, and shot it point-blank in the face, obliterating the head.

He turned to look up the stairs at them. All eyes were on him. "We're coming inside. Now."

Phoenix glanced around and saw her own fear reflected back from those around her. Leah and Volk and the members of the camera crews . . . whatever their feelings about what lengths they might go to in order to stop the dead from walking, they were united in this, at least.

"No way are we letting you in," Phoenix said.

Noah swung the barrel of his weapon toward her. "We're past the point of asking politely. We're coming in."

RAY CREEDON WATCHED THE studio monitor, hands clenched into fists. He stood by the table where Professor Cormier and the others still sat slumped and unresponsive. He'd promised Phoenix he'd stay with her father, but all hell was breaking loose downstairs and she had gone down there in the midst of it. There were gunshots and shouting, but he couldn't make out half of what transpired; the images were jerky and blurred.

Torn, he glanced again at the five people arranged around the séance table. He'd been following Professor Cormier's career and his writings for years. It had been Cormier whose exploits had persuaded him at last that the spirit world was real. Others either were charlatans or had used their abilities to become showmen, so that it was difficult to tell the difference between true mediums and hustlers. Professor Cormier had been the real thing. In becoming an avid supporter of the man's work, Ray had discovered Annelise, and certainly her reputation was beyond reproach. The kid, Eric, was another story. Like teenaged tent revival preachers, he had embraced the performance element so thoroughly that it no longer mattered if it contained any real spirituality. And then there were the two TV hosts. Ray didn't know them. They meant nothing to him. But they hadn't asked for this.

He looked again at the studio monitor. The same cluster of people stood there staring at it. Nobody had bothered to look out the window in minutes, entranced by what unfolded in their own lobby. Hell, no one had stepped away even to go to the bathroom in a while.

"Katie," he said, raising his voice just enough to get her attention, not enough to alarm anyone.

The associate producer of *Sunrise* tore her gaze from the screen. She looked harried, much older than she'd first seemed to him. But then he figured they all must share that look by now, haunted, burdened with dread.

Ray gestured for her to approach. Katie hesitated, but then walked over to him.

"Someone's got to go down there. Whatever's happening—"

She looked at him like he'd lost his mind. "Don't even think about me going. I can't believe Phoenix got John to go with her.

There are enough people down there already, and if you hadn't noticed, there are bullets." Katie scowled. "No way."

Ray stared at her, but he couldn't argue. Had he not promised Phoenix, he'd be riding the elevator down right now. But that was stupid boy heroics, thinking he could rescue the cute girl with the green eyes. Dumb-ass stuff. There were plenty of people down there in the line of fire already and if he called the elevator up, that might just delay them being able to escape. What could he do for Phoenix that she couldn't do for herself? The answer was nothing, and he hated that.

Katie had not gone back to the monitor. She watched him closely.

Uncomfortable, Ray shot her a look. "What?"

She blanched and shook her head. "Nothing." A sad smile touched her lips and she gave him an apologetic look. "It's just that I'm so far from my family. My mother and my sisters all live in Jersey, and I haven't been able to reach them. I know they must be afraid for me, like I am for them, and I hate the idea that . . ." Her voice cracked and she took a breath, then went on. "I hate the idea that I'm going to die surrounded by strangers."

Ray felt like she'd knocked the wind out of him. He knew he ought to say something, to come up with some way to comfort her, but nothing came to mind. Instead, he reached out and took her hand, and together they turned to watch the monitors again.

The cluster of people watching the big screens had grown. Ray frowned, studying the group, and then realized what had set off the alarm bells in his head. Peyton, the kid who'd caused such trouble earlier, had returned, along with the others who'd agreed with him, who wanted to separate the quintet at the séance table no matter how they had to do it.

As he stared at them, Peyton turned to look at him, slow and deliberate, almost like he'd known Ray was watching him. Or like he'd been paying attention to Ray, only feigning interest in what unfolded on the screen.

"Ray . . ." Katie said.

The warning in her voice made him blink. And then he saw what she'd already noticed. Down by his side, Peyton held a metal pipe—part of a tripod or a boom mic.

Ray glanced around for something with which to defend himself, but there was nothing. Peyton stepped away from the crowd around the monitor, and then five others followed suit, most of them armed with bits of things from around the studio. One had a long, silver adjustable wrench.

Katie moved to separate them from the séance table, putting herself between the group and Ray.

"Don't be an ass, Peyton," she said, holding up both hands. "This isn't going to accomplish anything."

Wordless, they rushed her. Katie grabbed Peyton. He fought to get past her. As they struggled, the man with the wrench brought it down on her head, the sound the most sickening thing Ray had ever heard. She collapsed, bleeding, maybe dying. Among strangers.

At last those mesmerized by the studio monitor seemed to come out of their trance. Some of them shouted, others rushed to help Katie, or to interfere with these men and women bent on violence.

"It's got to be done," Peyton said, raising that metal bar. "Out of the way."

Ray Creedon had never been in a fight in his life, not even in the school yard. But Katie lay bleeding, or worse. And he'd made a promise to Phoenix. Not that any of that mattered. Peyton only gave him half a second to decide, and then he lunged.

Ray put up one arm on instinct and the bar hit his forearm, pain singing along the bone. Then he stepped in close and reached for Peyton's throat, not wanting him to get another chance with that metal bar. They went down, gouging and punching and grunting with a savagery Ray never could have foreseen in himself. He would do whatever it took to survive. Anything so that he would not have to die among strangers.

SARA COULDN'T BELIEVE WHAT she was hearing. Everyone else stared through the grate at the people on the other side, but Sara couldn't tear her eyes from Noah. This guy Jack was talking about killing people, and Noah seemed totally on board with that. She blinked and looked at her brother. He'd brought Noah—and Tania—home with him, but maybe that didn't mean they were friends. Matt couldn't possibly agree with them. Maybe killing one of those psychics would stop all of this, and maybe it wouldn't, but there had to be another way to separate them. Matt would make them find another way.

Wouldn't he?

Her brother seemed to feel the intensity of her focus on him and glanced back at her. Sara asked the question with her eyes and he gave a quick nod, a silent communication between them.

Then his gaze tracked past her. At the same moment, Sara heard the crunching of glass underfoot and a low groan.

"They're coming in!" Zack shouted.

Sara turned to look. She'd forgotten all about Zack for a moment, the way she always did. Not fair to him. Never fair. He stood a few steps below her, his face etched with fear. A handsome enough face, but more important, Zack's face, so familiar that it was ingrained in her mind, as much a part of her life as her father had been, as her brother was, almost as much as her own face in the mirror.

A dead man in a bloody T-shirt and jeans ran up the steps toward Zack.

Sara screamed his name, understanding suddenly what she was about to lose. Her best friend. Her boy next door.

Noah and Jack screamed at Zack to get out of the way; they wanted to shoot. Matt and Tania started down toward him, to help. Despite the pistol's weight, Sara remembered it in her hand too late.

But Zack had his own gun. He raised it just as the dead man grabbed him, drove him down on the steps. Zack cried out as the hard granite edges of the stairs dug into his back, and he pulled the trigger. The bullet went through the zombie's chest and out its back, spraying blood. The thing jerked backward, perhaps on instinct, but that wouldn't kill it.

Sara raised the pistol and aimed at its head. She couldn't pull the trigger. She'd never fired a gun in her life; how could she risk hitting Zack?

Something changed in Zack's face then. He reached up with his left hand, grabbed the corpse's throat and shoved it backward, then raised the pistol in his right and shot it point-blank in the face. As it fell dead upon him he had to shift to topple it aside. He rose, spattered with its blood. Once upon a time, the boy she knew would have cried. Zack looked sick, but he shed no tears.

Sara went to him. "I'm sorry. I was afraid I would hit you by mistake."

Zack didn't say anything, but he held her very tightly. She thought he might kiss her on the head. Even though she'd always made it clear they were only friends, it was something he did often enough. But there were no kisses from him today. Sara felt content with that. Having him hold her, still alive, all in one piece, was enough. Whatever else might be in her heart she would have to sort out later. If they earned themselves a later.

"Matt," Tania said, "we can't just stay here."

Sara looked at her, still finding her presence so surreal. Tania being there made it all seem like maybe it could be a dream after all, just a nightmare. It was dream logic, surviving among the dead with this girl she'd watched on TV.

But Zack took her hand, and his touch was real. No, there'd never been any question about the reality of this day. Not really. She thought of her father again, and then put him out of her mind. Just for now. Just until they were all safe.

Matt had looked back only at Tania, but now he glanced at Noah and Jack.

He pumped the shotgun and stepped up to the grate. "We're coming in," he told the petite brown-haired girl who'd been arguing with them. "Anyone who doesn't want to get shot, get out of the way."

For a second, no one moved. It was like everyone left alive in the world had held their breath. Then the girl swore and started running back toward the little foyer where the elevators were. The older bald guy and a bunch of other people followed.

"Matt?" Sara said, unsure what he meant to do.

"Do it," Jack said. "Let's just get it done."

His voice had a terrible weariness, and for the first time Sara felt sorry for him. He seemed ready to kill, if that meant putting the dead back in their graves, and he had an air of real danger around him, like he was no stranger to violence. But whatever Jack might be, she didn't think it was something he'd ever wanted to become.

Matt hesitated. His chest rose and fell as he took a deep breath.

Then he aimed the shotgun at the round lock set into the bottom of the grate and pulled the trigger. Sara flinched and the sound echoed off of the stairwell, hurting her ears. Noah, Jack, and Tania tried raising the grate, but it was still held in place.

"Again," Noah said.

Matt pumped and fired, tearing metal, and this time the twisted barrel of the cylinder lock popped out the other side, landing heavily on the marble floor.

"We're in," Jack said as he and Noah started raising the grate.

They lifted it only high enough to get under. Matt and Tania held it as Jack, Sara, and Zack went through. But when they tried to haul it back down again, it wouldn't go. Sara tried to imagine how it worked: some kind of chain or gear or something, like the metal gates castles had in old movies. But this would be mechanized, usually lifted electronically. Whatever they'd done, it was jammed.

Fearful, she glanced back down at the shattered doors to the street. Several silhouettes moved in the gray afternoon light. Many of the dead were just shambling husks, but some were very smart. They'd already seen that.

"They're going to come in," Zack said. His eyes were blue and wide with dread. "Some of them watched us drive up. They know we're here."

The brown-haired girl came out from the elevator foyer. "What the hell have you done? Pull it down. You have to pull it down."

Others emerged as well. There were cameras set up there, cables on the ground, and Sara realized most of them must be network employees. They were all talking at once now, yelling at Matt and Noah, though most steered clear of Jack.

"Forget it," Noah said. "Shut down the elevators. The stairwell doors will be locked down here. They're not getting up that way. We only need a few minutes, and it'll all be over."

"You don't *know* that!" the girl screamed, and she rushed at Noah.

"Phoenix, don't," the bald guy said, obviously somebody's boss. Used to being in charge. He looked around at the other employees, hands raised. "Everyone just take a breath. We'll figure something out."

She didn't take her eyes off Noah as she replied. "They're not touching my father."

Sara blinked, staring at her. "Your father?"

The bald guy looked at her. "He's one of the mediums your friends are talking about killing."

Her stomach gave a sick twist. Sara went to her brother and pulled on his arm. "Her *father,* Matt. You can't let them do this."

Matt shot a hard look at Noah. "Nobody's killing anyone." He held the shotgun up in one hand, barrel up, almost like a peace offering, and he looked at Phoenix. "We'll find another way."

But the girl still looked pale and afraid. She studied him a second, glanced at Noah, and then back at Matt again. "I'm not so sure that's gonna be up to you."

Zack grabbed Sara's wrist. "More at the door!"

Jack turned and pulled the trigger, bullets cutting down the dead teenaged girl who'd come in so quietly while they were talking. She'd made it a quarter of the way up the stairs.

He gave a humorless laugh and started forward. "You guys are wasting time talking about this. Let's go up."

The bald guy stepped in front of him, put his hands on Jack's chest to stop him. Without even breaking stride, Jack swung the butt of his gun into the guy's temple, dropping him to the floor so fast the guy only managed a low grunt of pain.

"John!" a woman cried. She glared at Jack and then Noah as she dropped to the ground beside the bald man.

Jack kept walking. They were all moving toward the elevator then, as if on some silent signal. The grate couldn't be brought down, which meant there would be dead in the lobby soon. Nobody wanted to stay downstairs, but nobody else was going to try to stop Jack and the others. Sara looked around at the men and women in the elevator foyer and saw fear in their eyes. They should have been afraid of the dead—and they were, she knew—but right then they were more afraid of her brother and his friends and their guns.

Jack pressed a button and an elevator slid open. A couple of men tried to get on, and he leveled the barrel of his weapon at them.

"Uh-uh. You can take the next one."

They debated that silently for a moment and then stepped back. But as Sara and Zack followed Noah, Tania, and Matt onto the elevator, the girl, Phoenix, moved with them.

"I don't think so," Jack said, aiming at her chest.

The girl met his gaze with one even grimmer than his own. "Shoot me."

For a moment, Sara thought he might just do it. But then Jack raised an eyebrow and stepped back, allowing her to board, and Sara found herself right next to Phoenix on the elevator. She glanced at the other girl.

"No one wants to hurt your father."

Phoenix stared at her like she'd lost her mind.

The doors slid closed, and the elevator began to rise.

15

No one spoke on the elevator.

Jack kept a solid grip on his gun and stared at the numbers as they ascended, watching as they lit up and faded, one after the other. The air-conditioning must have been turned up high in the building, he thought, because he'd never been so cold. It felt as though something had lodged in his throat.

In his time with the Smoke Dragons, Jack had hurt a lot of people. He'd broken bones, drawn blood, even sent a couple of guys to the hospital. Somehow, though, he'd managed to avoid killing anyone. Some gangs, that was how you earned your way in. But the Smoke Dragons were a neighborhood gang, mainly about protecting turf and collecting a tax on drug sales.

The elevator rattled as it passed the fifth floor. He flinched.

His skin prickled and he told himself, again, that it was the air-conditioning. Not fear, that was certain. Jack

Kim had never been afraid of anything in his life, except for being alone. That, he couldn't survive. That's what the Smoke Dragons had meant to him. He wondered where his family had run to, and if they were safe. He thought about Big Boy, who'd put his own life on the line for Jack that very morning, given him cash and a gun and a way out of New York.

A tiny smile touched his lips. How could Big Boy not understand that Jack would never have stayed away? He might have lost himself in a series of girls for a while—Jack had the charm when he wanted it; girls always wanted to tame him—but he would have come back to the Bronx eventually. Without the Smoke Dragons, and separated from his family, he might as well have been dead.

Canada? You were fooling yourself.

And he had done a good job, telling himself that he didn't love anyone, that he didn't have anyone to come back for. If he'd never met the waitress, Kelli, in Dobbs Ferry, he might have gotten all the way to Canada before he realized how good he'd gotten at lying to himself.

The elevator jittered again, and he closed his eyes. A mistake. The moment he did, images rushed into his mind, a grotesque parade of horrors he'd seen that day. Worst of all had been Kelli's father, and the way Kelli had died.

Inhaling sharply, Jack opened his eyes.

He wouldn't close them again. He didn't want to see any more.

In his time with the Smoke Dragons, he'd managed to avoid murder. But if becoming a killer was the price of putting an end to the spread of this hell on Earth, then Jack would pull the trigger and think himself a hero.

He had nowhere else to go.

•

PHOENIX HUGGED HER ARMS tightly around herself, staring at the numbers as the elevator rose. She didn't want to touch any of these people. Sara seemed to want to help, but she still had a gun in her hand. Fifteen, maybe sixteen years old, and she held that pistol as easily as if it had been her cell phone. Was that the world now?

Exhaustion dragged at her. God, when had she ever felt so weary? Her breath came in short, tiny sips, and her body trembled. A terrible numbness enveloped her and for a few precious seconds she imagined herself one of the dead, a zombie, walking around with her flesh cold and unfeeling. *Shock,* she thought. And maybe it was. The world had fallen apart today, and just when she thought it could unravel no further, that she had no more naïveté or innocence to scour away, it had come to this: riding in an elevator full of gun-toting teenagers intent upon killing her father.

Phoenix might be eighteen years old, but just then, she wished for her mother with a fervor she hadn't felt since kindergarten.

With a ding, the elevator slowed, stopped, and the doors slid open.

"Let's go," the one called Noah said, ushering her out.

Phoenix stepped off with the rest of them, skin prickling with the intensity of her awareness of these people around her, and their guns. The quiet kid with Sara only had eyes for her. Matt seemed charged with frenetic energy, and Phoenix hardly knew what to make of Tania's presence. But it was the other two—blond-haired Noah and the Asian guy, Jack—who worried her. They carried assault rifles, along with other guns, and they both held them with a frighteningly easy familiarity.

Staring at Jack, she spared a moment's worry for John Volk and the others she'd left downstairs. But then her thoughts returned to the present, and she had no room to worry for anyone but her father.

"If you want to kill my dad, you'll have to kill me first," she said to all of them, but mostly to Jack.

He gave her a curt nod, but she couldn't be sure if he was acknowledging her statement or agreeing.

"Can we stop talking about killing, just for a couple of minutes?" Tania asked. "You, what was your name, Phoenix? Lead the way."

Phoenix hesitated. The doors were propped open on either side of the receptionist's area, though no one was at the desk. Through the door on the left, she saw empty cubicles and people standing in front of glass offices. A group had been watching monitors there, but now they were staring into the reception area—staring at the newcomers and their guns.

One woman screamed. Several people scattered to hide behind cubicle walls. Two men broke off from the others and strode toward the reception area.

Noah swung the barrel of his gun toward them, and the menace and swagger in the men evaporated. They faltered.

"Don't do anything stupid," Noah told them. "We're here to end this thing."

Confusion reigned on their features. One of them glanced over and seemed to recognize Tania, and that made him even more confused. He tapped the other guy, whispered something to him, but the guy shook his head, clearly having never seen Tania before.

"Which way is the studio?" Zack asked, strangely polite given the guns they all carried. "The one where they had that séance."

They both pointed through the reception area, away from their section of the network offices. Phoenix stiffened.

Noah glanced at her. "You really think we wouldn't find it, or are you just trying to delay things?"

Phoenix said nothing. It wasn't the sort of question that required an answer. Noah gave her a little shove and she shot him a grim look, then started walking. They went to the right, and she led them out of the reception area and back through the corridors where just that morning she'd waited in the Green Room for her father to start his interview. A green light burned over the doors that led into the studio. Several people stood in the doorway, backs to them, crowded around like paparazzi.

"What's going on?" Sara asked.

Phoenix caught her breath. "No idea," she said. But it didn't bode well.

"Coming through," Jack said.

One guy glanced at them, but the others didn't even budge.

Matt racked a round into the shotgun's chamber and the sound made the people gathered at the door spin around, eyes wide. They saw only the guns. No one even looked at Phoenix.

"Move," Noah said.

They backed up, bumping one another, one woman knocking into the door. Beyond them, from the studio, Phoenix heard shouting and she recognized Ray Creedon's voice. A terrible certainty filled her. She pushed between Matt and Tania and ran through the door.

Noah shouted after her. Phoenix barely heard him.

At least two dozen people were in the studio, most of them in the midst of a brawl. Punches were thrown, people swore and grunted and fell down. Two men crashed into a lighting setup and knocked it over, shattering glass and clanging metal. Four people stood watching fearfully, older employees who seemed to want to help but knew better. The fighting spread across the edge of the platform upon which sat the faux dining room set. Like corpses, the five unconscious people at the table sat in their chairs, totally oblivious to the violence erupting around them.

A woman slipped and fell, and an older man—Phoenix thought he was a cameraman—tripped over her. But her focus was not on the tangle of their limbs, it was on the pool of redness upon which the woman had slipped.

Blood.

And Phoenix saw its source. Katie lay on the ground, either dead or bleeding to death.

"Ray!" she called.

He didn't reply. But then an opening formed in the midst of the melee, and she saw him, curled into a fetal position on the floor. Peyton—who'd seemed like such a joke to her this morning, a stereotypical clipboard jockey—stood above Ray, kicking him.

Phoenix flew across the room. All sense of reason left her. Darting through the brawlers, she made a path, leaped up onto the set, and hurtled toward Peyton.

"Bastard!" she shouted as she slammed into him, dragging him off of Ray.

Surprise gave her the edge. Peyton tried to throw her off, but Phoenix grabbed him by the hair and slammed his head against the floor. She made a fist and punched him. Pain shot through her hand but she hit him again, and again, filled with hatred and funneling all of it into this little weasel who wanted to hurt her father.

He tried to grab her arm but she batted his hands away, raised her fist to hit him again and stopped. Her stomach convulsed with nausea and she pushed away from him, standing and staggering back against the table, bumping her father's hand, where it clasped Amy Tjan's.

Phoenix stared at Peyton, who rose, wiping blood from his

mouth and nose across the back of his hand, glaring at her. But in that moment, all of her fear and disgust was reserved for herself. Wasn't anyone immune to this? To what the day had unleashed? Was this the way all people were, just under the surface, ready to throw away all civility the moment the order of things broke down?

Gunfire erupted in the room, shattering ceiling panels and lights.

Everyone froze and turned to look at the new arrivals, at their guns. Noah had his weapon aimed at the ceiling. He'd been the one to fire. Phoenix was not at all surprised.

Tania still had the rifle slung over her shoulder and a pistol stuffed in the rear of her waistband. She had the other pistol in her right hand but kept it aimed at an angle toward the ceiling. People were scared enough by the guys with their machine guns, or whatever, not to mention Matt's shotgun. They weren't even going to notice a pistol or two right now. Not that she would have bothered with a pistol in each hand. As cool as that crap looked on TV, she wouldn't be able to aim with her left hand any better than she could write with it.

Noah and Jack moved toward the people, herding them away from the set at gunpoint. Matt kept the shotgun aimed at the face of the guy that Phoenix chick had just been pounding on.

"Go over there with the others," Matt said.

The guy, who needed a shave and a better attitude, kept his hands up like he was being robbed and hurried away from the set, merging with the other people who'd been in the midst of the fight.

"All of you, sit your asses down," Jack said, sweeping the gun to indicate the whole group.

They took their seats as though they were the audience and the morning edition of *Sunrise* was about to start. Tania caught several people looking at her, frowning, recognizing her. One woman nudged another.

"Yeah," Tania said, staring at them. "My interview's not until tomorrow. I'm early. So shoot me."

They stared, and now that she'd drawn their attention, so did other members of the morning show's staff. Sara had said several times how surreal it was for her to be with Tania during all of this, to deal with fame and celebrity in a world that should be so far beyond such things. What Tania hadn't told Sara was how much more surreal it felt to her.

And maybe that was the curse of the modern world. The more things happened that people had never believed could actually happen, the more divorced they became from reality. Tragedy and horror were make-believe, and only celebrity was real enough to matter.

One woman lay on the floor, bleeding and unmoving. Tania knelt and searched for a pulse, but found none. She wasn't a nurse or anything, but she knew how to look for a heartbeat.

"Is she dead?"

Tania looked up and saw that Phoenix had asked the question. The girl knelt on the ground beside the good-looking young guy who'd been taking a serious kicking when they'd come in. He sat up now, nursing the bruises on his bloody face.

"Is she?" Phoenix prodded.

Tania nodded, and the girl shook her head, sickened. Phoenix shot a look of utter contempt at the stubble-faced guy she'd attacked, and then she helped her friend to stand. They stayed by the table, which had been arranged with a bunch of chairs on the set of *Sunrise* to look like somebody's dining room. Of the five people passed out around the table, Tania recognized the show's two anchors, Steve Bell and Amy Tjan. The other three had to be the mediums.

"Is that your father?" Sara asked, pointing to a gray-bearded man slumped in one of the chairs.

Matt stood next to the table, studying the five unmoving figures. Tania wondered if he was capable of killing someone. She doubted it, but she'd learned, even in her short life, that people were often capable of far more—and far worse—than she ever imagined.

Phoenix touched the man's shoulder. "Yeah. His name's Joe Cormier. He's a college professor."

Tania felt a sudden chill. She understood what Phoenix was doing, trying to make them connect with her father as a person, not a problem to be solved. It was working.

She forced herself to look away, and caught sight of someone pointing at the monitors hanging above the set and on the far wall. Many of the images were news reports from various networks, but two of the screens showed scenes that could only be live feeds from the camera that still stood down in the lobby.

"Matt," Tania said.

Sara and Zack looked up first. Zack swore.

Still focused on keeping the staff under control, Noah and Jack only glanced up. But Matt stepped away from the set, shotgun hanging at his side, and together he and Tania walked over to stare at the monitors.

The dead poured underneath the metal grate they had left jammed open. Tania saw no sign of the people they'd left downstairs, but she hoped they'd all made it to the elevator.

"Where did they all come from?" Phoenix asked, still standing with her father.

Sara's voice, when she replied, sounded dreamy, like she was talking in her sleep. "They saw us come in. Some of them must have spread the word."

"What word?" Phoenix said.

Zack gave a hideous chuckle. "Fresh meat."

Tania watched the images flashing on the screens, the dead rushing past the camera, some of them close enough to blur. One of them slammed into the camera and it fell. There came a terrible screaming from the speakers as the camera was kicked. The spinning image provided a glimpse of the dead trying to break down the door to the fire stairs.

As the camera's whirling slowed, Tania caught sight of the elevator foyer. One of the elevators stood open and people were jamming themselves into it, the dead reaching in, grabbing at them. The staff tried to fight them off so the doors could close. The dead dragged a screaming man back out and pulled him to the marble floor, the mic on the camera picking up sounds of tearing and snapping. Wet sounds.

The doors of the elevator closed.

"They made it," Sara said, somehow able to hold on to some hope, even in the midst of all of this.

"Bullshit," Jack said, turning to look at her. "Some of the zombies got on with them. Nobody's getting out of that box alive."

"It's your fault," Phoenix shouted at them. "Those people are dying because of you! They're coming up here—they're going to get in here—because of you!"

"Damn it!" Matt shouted, but not at Phoenix. He wasn't arguing with her. How could he?

Tania strode over to him, grabbed his arm, and forced him to focus on her face. "Get it together. We've got to do this." She scanned the people seated in the studio audience. "Who has a blade? A knife? Anything!"

Noah nodded to Jack, who went over to the guy who'd been attacking Phoenix's friend.

"What's your name?" Jack asked him.

The stubbled guy—maybe twenty-four—tried for tough but only looked pathetic. "Peyton."

Tania hated him on sight. He looked like a total weasel.

"Looked to me like you worked things out the same way we did, Peyton," Jack said, "like you were maybe trying to get to the psychic hotline trio yourself. We want to end this. We need something sharp."

Peyton nodded, got up, and ran for the door. He'd barely left the room before he returned, carrying a heavy square of black metal.

"We got it from the art department just a few minutes ago, but didn't bring it in at first. We didn't want anyone panicking at the wrong moment."

Tania frowned, staring at the object as it was carried toward the dining room table up on the *Sunrise* set. Even with the obviousness of the metal chopping arm along one side, it took her a moment before she flashed back to junior high school and recognized that eighteen-inch square for what it was—an old-fashioned paper cutter.

She knew it would be sharp. A finger of unease went up the back of her neck, but Tania ignored it. Sharp was good. Sharp would be necessary.

16

Matt held his breath when he saw the paper cutter. Then the guy Phoenix had been standing by the table with—Matt thought he heard her call him Ray—started toward him. "Are you shitting me? We just fought to stop these assholes from killing people who can't protect themselves, and you're all best friends now?"

Phoenix grabbed his arm. "Ray. Guns."

Ray shook his head, pulled away from her, and stared at Matt. "Screw that. Someone wants to shoot me, go ahead! These guys killed someone already. You see that woman on the ground? Her name was Katie."

At that, Jack looked up. "She's dead? I thought she was just hurt."

"You're not real bright, are you?" Ray snapped.

Jack marched over to the dead woman, pulled one of the pistols he'd jammed into his belt, and shot the corpse through the head. "We're lucky she hadn't already turned."

"You son of a bitch!" Ray screamed as he rushed at Jack, who swung the pistol up to aim it at Ray's nose. The guy stopped short, seething with hatred.

Matt heard his name softly spoken, and he turned to find Sara and Zack beside him.

"*Do* something," his sister whispered, eyes imploring.

He didn't hesitate. While Noah and Jack were still willing to hold off killing anyone, someone had to act before the dead swarmed in and finished them all.

"Jack," Matt snapped. "Get to the elevator. They're probably already here. Kill as many as you can. Zack, you go with him."

Sara started to protest, but Matt cut her off with a look. Zack nodded. He looked scared but said nothing. He understood what had to be done, and that getting Jack away from the argument was a good idea. *Brave kid,* Matt thought.

Jack glared at Matt. The Korean guy was good-looking, kind of a pretty boy for a gangbanger. But right now he just looked mean. Clearly, Jack didn't like taking orders.

"Tick-tick-tick," Matt said. "We're wasting time."

With a glance at Noah, who nodded—like they were new buddies, comrades in trigger-happiness—Jack ran for the door with Zack following him.

"The rest of you, stay put," Noah told his captive audience.

Matt handed his shotgun to Tania and walked over to take the paper cutter out of the hands of the weasel, Peyton. It was even heavier than it looked. He carried it up to the table, unnerved by his first close-up look at the five unconscious people. They didn't seem to be sleeping but drugged, or brain-damaged or something.

Phoenix and Ray blocked his way.

Matt focused on her, meeting her gaze. "I'm sorry, but this is going to happen. I won't hurt your father, but someone's going to lose a hand and it's got to be now. Before we're all dead. Otherwise instead of protecting your father, you'll be eating his damn brains."

She paled and swallowed hard.

"Look, I'll choose at random if I have to," Matt said.

Sara came up next to Matt. "You can't hurt that old lady."

"Well, I'm not going to choose," Phoenix said. "I can't."

Tania stood closer to Noah, but she called to Matt. "Not Amy, okay? I kind of know her."

Matt turned to look at her, and she shrugged.

"She's interviewed me before. She's really nice."

He shrugged and pointed to the other TV host. "Process of elimination, then. It's this guy."

"His name is Steve Bell," Peyton announced.

"Please tell me he's a prick," Matt said.

"Actually, he's a pretty decent guy," Peyton replied.

Matt glared at him. "Great."

He put the paper cutter on the table in front of Steve Bell, hurrying now.

"Hold up," Noah said.

Everyone looked at him. For the first time in hours, he looked unsure, blue eyes half lidded as his gaze shifted to take in each of the catatonic people around the table in turn.

"That guy's one of the hosts, right?"

The crazy-haired, college-looking guy, Ray, was the first to respond. "His name's Steve Bell."

Noah nodded. "Yeah. He's one of the hosts."

"They're part of the circuit," Matt said, still bent over the paper cutter, staring up at Noah. "What difference does it make?"

Ray ran both hands through that wild hair. "No, he could be right. I mean, if there's any logic to this—"

"Ray!" Phoenix said.

The guy faltered, as though just realizing what he'd been saying, and looked about as apologetic as Matt had ever seen anyone.

Tania held her gun down by her side and went to Phoenix. The green-eyed girl refused to look at her first.

"Hey," Tania said quietly. "This is gonna happen. And Noah has a point. If we do it on one of the hosts, and it doesn't work, we still won't be sure it wouldn't have worked if we'd done one of the mediums instead. Then we'll have to maim somebody else. This is hard enough. I don't want to have to do it twice."

"Exactly," Noah said. He pointed to Professor Cormier. "So if that guy is Phoenix's father, and Sara says no way to the lady"—he gestured to the fiftysomething woman with the red-dyed hair—"then that leaves the kid."

"His name's Eric," Phoenix said softly. "He's only eighteen."

Noah gave her a dark look. "It's going to be one of them."

Phoenix looked away. Ray slid an arm around her and she melted against him.

With a sick feeling twisting in his gut, Matt moved the paper cutter to Steve Bell's other side, where his hand was locked with the teenaged psychic's.

They all watched Matt in silence, maybe praying, maybe sickly fascinated, maybe just wondering if it would work. He picked up the kid medium's arm and lay it across the base of the cutter with the blade up like a guillotine, positioning it so that the blade wouldn't touch Bell's hand. He'd thought about splitting the difference, trying to cut only fingers, right down the middle, but the angle was all wrong. They'd both end up losing half a hand. It had been hard enough for him to think about cutting off Bell's hand, but the hand of a kid even younger than he was?

He hesitated.

"What are you doing?" Noah asked.

Matt shot him a withering glance. "What's it look like?"

Noah rolled his eyes. "Too slow. It's not art, Matt. Get over here and cover these people."

A wave of relief swept through Matt. Someone needed to take charge, and he'd done so, but if he'd brought that blade down, he never would have forgiven himself.

Let Noah carry the blood on his hands.

GUNFIRE ERUPTED OUTSIDE THE studio, echoing down the halls from the reception area. Noah took that as his cue. He ignored the people he'd previously held at gunpoint. Their fight had finished and none of them knew what to do now. If they wanted to run, he wouldn't stop them.

"There's going to be blood," he said, striding toward the set. "Something to soak it up would be good. But I need something for a tourniquet. A shirt would do, but a belt would be better."

He glanced at Tania. "Right now."

The girl might have been a diva before today, but she moved, hurrying toward their no-longer-captive audience. "Come on, guys. A belt."

Matt stepped away from the table. "What about something to cauterize the wound?"

Noah scowled. "You seriously think we have time?"

More gunfire came from out in the studio offices.

Matt turned to the rest of them. "Is there a lunchroom? A microwave nearby?"

Several of them started talking at once, but it was Phoenix who answered. "In the Green Room. It's close."

Noah saw where Matt was going and shook his head. "I'm not waiting."

"No time, I get it," Matt said, turning to the employees. "Anyone who doesn't want to see this guy bleed to death, go bring me that microwave and a pot or a pan. Right now!"

Despite the obvious danger of leaving the studio, Peyton and two women stood up immediately and hurried for the door.

"Guess somebody wants a raise," Tania said.

Sara gave a small laugh, and that made Noah feel good for a second. A teenaged girl laughing—that was ordinary, normal-world stuff. But then he looked at her and saw that her eyes were wide and she had put one hand over her mouth. Her laugh had been one of disbelief. Matt's little sister was on the verge of hysteria.

Noah couldn't blame her. He felt the same. He'd fired guns plenty of times in ROTC and the military was definitely part of his future. Hell, he had a sharpshooter's eye like nobody else his instructors had seen. But he'd never mutilated a man before. People would call him a savage, say he'd been brutal, but if this worked, none of that would trouble him. If he survived, all he wanted was to know that he had done what he could, especially when no one else would.

Matt had put Eric's arm across the paper cutter and raised the blade. Noah put pressure on the unconscious kid's forearm, holding it firm to the surface of the cutter, and gripped the handle of the blade with his free hand.

"Jesus, don't!" Phoenix shouted.

Noah looked at her, saw tears in her eyes. Sara stared at him as well, and he knew she thought him a monster.

"It's got to be done," he said, his voice quiet. "It's this, or we have to kill someone."

The two girls stared at him, imploring, and finally Noah had to look away. He took a breath.

The doors banged open and Zack came in, looking pale, bleeding from a gash on his face. Noah held his breath, thinking the zombies would be two steps behind him, that they were all going to die now, but then Jack came through the doors right behind Zack. All business, Jack slammed a new magazine of ammunition into the HK G36 that Noah had stolen from the gun shop. Noah figured it had to be his last and wondered how soon they'd have no bullets left at all.

"Better hurry before the ones on the stairs get up here," Jack said.

Tania swore.

Zack twisted to one side and puked.

Noah glanced at Sara, then at Matt. He forced himself not to look at the teenaged medium, or any of the other unconscious people around the table. He gripped Eric by the arm, swallowed hard, and then slammed the blade of the paper cutter down on the guy's wrist. It sliced through muscle and tendon and Noah leaned on it, put all of his weight into it. Blood sprayed his face and shirt and pumped out onto the paper cutter and the table. The blade was sharp as hell, but still it didn't go all the way through. He had to rise up and practically drop his weight onto the blade, and with a crunch it finished the job. The hand—still tightly clutched in Steve Bell's—flopped to the table.

Forgive me, Noah thought.

He took a step back, and even as he did, Matt moved in with a belt and wrapped it around the kid's arm, cinching it tightly. Tania started mopping up some of the blood with T-shirts and sweatshirts she'd gotten from employees as Matt readjusted the tourniquet, trying to get the belt as tight as he possibly could.

Noah glanced around but saw no sign of the people that had gone off to get the microwave. Most of them were staring at Eric's bloody stump of a wrist, but some of their eyes were on Noah himself, and he turned away. Not that he expected to really be able to cauterize the wound with a hot metal pot anyway. It'd probably spark and cause the microwave to explode.

"Pull them apart," he told Matt as he moved around behind Eric's chair. He dragged the chair back, away from the table. The woman medium, the redhead, slid sideways in her chair and would have fallen to the floor if not for the grip the gorgeous female TV host had on her other arm.

Matt dragged Steve Bell's chair in the opposite direction, opening up the circle, separating them.

Phoenix's friend Ray stepped up to the table and stared at them. "The circle's broken."

Noah scowled. The guy had a gift for stating the obvious.

"Check the monitors," Tania snapped, throwing the bloody clothes onto the table and going around it to jump down from the elevated set into the audience. She stared up at the TV screens that hung from the walls.

Sara and Zack held hands, standing close together. Phoenix crouched by her catatonic father, close by, as though she could protect him. Ray had a hand on her shoulder. Matt and Noah just looked at each other, and Noah didn't like what he saw in Matt's eyes.

Doubt.

Jack held his HK ready for war and walked over to stand with Tania.

"Well?" Noah asked.

"The camera in the lobby's gone dark," Tania said. "But there's CNN, FOX, and every other news channel on up here. If it worked, we'll know pretty quickly."

"Maybe it'll take a while to spread," Zack suggested.

The studio fell into utter silence, save for the grim voices coming from the TV monitors.

The studio doors banged open again. They all turned to see Peyton and the two women who'd gone with him. One of them carried the microwave, and Peyton had a metal coffee mug in one hand. But they were in a hurry.

"Barricade the doors!" the second woman said.

"No, it's okay," Sara said, so sweetly. "Noah did it. It's over."

"Over?" Peyton laughed. "They came up the stairs. They're pounding on the door, and it's going to give."

SARA STOOD FROZEN AT the edge of the raised set platform, holding Zack's hand. She could smell vomit and blood.

Almost as one, people scrambled from their seats and rushed toward the studio doors, talking fast, shouting at one another. The doors locked, so that was good. They started dragging heavy equipment over to barricade the entrance. Matt picked up his shotgun, and Sara stared at the doors, waiting.

At her father's side, Phoenix sobbed quietly, holding on to him. Her friend Ray stood by her, glaring at Noah.

"So now what, huh?" Ray demanded.

Noah had bright crimson splashes of blood in his blond hair. He glanced over at the puddle of scarlet on the table, at the paper cutter, at the hand that Steve Bell now held. The one that had been attached to an eighteen-year-old just a minute ago.

"Now we go to Plan B," he said.

"No choice," Jack agreed. "And no time."

"You can't!" Sara said, letting go of Zack and putting herself between them and the table. "We still don't know what's causing this. You could be wrong."

"I don't want to kill anyone," Tania said, "but they could be right."

"Exactly," Noah said. "The circuit's still there. Separating them didn't do the job. That doesn't make us wrong about this."

Jack started toward the table, staring at Sara. "Now all we have to do is decide who's going to die."

Sara's breath came in quick gasps. She shook her head, meeting his gaze. Scared as she was, she wouldn't move out of the way.

From behind the table, Matt lifted the shotgun and aimed it at Jack's chest. "Get away from my sister."

It happened so quickly then.

Noah swung the barrel of his automatic rifle toward Matt.

Tania pointed a pistol at Jack.

Shaking, Sara and Zack both aimed their handguns at Noah.

"You people are crazy!" Noah shouted. "We have to *do* something!"

Phoenix rose to her feet. Ray tried to hold her back, but she tore free of him, green eyes alight with fury. "Do what? Murder people? You're *guessing,* you asshole. Just hoping. You don't even know if this can be stopped. Maybe it's too late. Maybe the whole world just tipped over the edge. It's bound to happen sometime. Nukes and terrorism and ecological suicide. The human race has been trying to destroy itself for a long time, pretending that everything's fine so we don't have to change our behavior. And you think, what? One more murder is going to fix it all?"

Jack aimed his gun at her. Nobody else moved. "No, you crazy bitch. But it might fix *this*. If you knew for sure that we were right, would you still stand in the way? One life, or the apocalypse? You choose. I'll wait. We've got loads of time."

He said this last with dripping sarcasm, but he didn't need to bother. The shouts and action of the employees barricading the doors were interrupted by screams and the shattering of glass. Something scraped on the floor, metal shifting as the dead reached the outer doors of the studio, trying to force their way in. Sara thought about all of those people out there in the network offices, and she knew they must be dead now. Some of them would be among the zombies, hungry, trying to get in.

Not a single gun barrel wavered.

Jack turned on Matt. "Listen to me. They're here, man. We've gotta do this. I'm going to do this right now. Tell your sister to get out of the way, or she's going to get hurt."

Matt raised the shotgun barrel slightly, aiming now at Jack's face. He came around the table as he spoke. "There are a million sources of fresh meat in this city, so there can't be that many of the dead already here. We can kill this wave like you did the ones from the elevator. Go down and seal off the stairs. We calm down, and we make a rational decision."

Noah actually laughed. "Bleeding heart to the end, Matt. It's way too late for a rational decision."

Matt hesitated. Sara could see in her brother's eyes that he didn't want any of this. But that hesitation cost him. Jack swung the barrel of his weapon away from Phoenix.

"I don't want to kill you, Matt," Jack said.

The words made them all relax, just a bit. Exhale.

Jack aimed low and pulled the trigger, and bullets tore into

Matt's legs. Sara screamed in unison with her brother. Matt fell, clutching at his legs, dropping the shotgun.

Sara pointed her gun at Jack and fired. The gun leaped in her hand and she missed him. Jack twisted, aimed the assault rifle at her.

"Put down the gun," he told her.

Noah and Tania shouted at Jack, their words getting tangled together, but the message was clear. Enough. Back off. No more bullets.

Zack fired twice, both bullets hitting Jack in the chest.

Jack staggered back, then went down hard and didn't move.

Zack let the gun fall from his hand. Sara's heart ached as she stared into the hollowness of his eyes, but she could not go to him. She ran to Matt, dropping to kneel beside him, staring at the bloody holes in the legs of his pants, at the agony etched on his face as he tried to hold his hands over his wounds.

Noah and Tania came over and looked down at them. Tania wiped away a tear, her hand shaking. Noah seemed full of regret. He might not have liked Matt, but Sara didn't think he'd wanted this.

Ray went to check Jack's pulse. "This guy's dead."

"Oh my God," Zack said, his voice so small.

People screamed over by the doors. The dead were talking to them. Sara could hear their voices, moaning, hungry, and cruel. She remembered the things her father had said to her and shut out the sounds.

Noah looked at Tania. "It's got to be the one already missing a hand. He's still bleeding. He might die anyway."

Phoenix laughed, eyes wide. "Genius plan. And if *that* doesn't work?"

Tania looked at her, biting her lip, tears sliding down her face. Sara knew what she was going to say to Phoenix, silently pleaded with her not to speak the words.

But Tania said them.

"If that doesn't work, we might have to kill them all."

Phoenix shook her head. "You'll have to kill me, too."

"Six, then," Noah said.

Sara blinked in surprise. But then, beside her, Matt moved. Grunting in pain, he sprawled across the floor, leaving a trail of blood behind. In one move he reached out, grabbed the shotgun he'd dropped, and raised the barrel to aim it at Noah and Tania.

"Don't," Matt said, sweat beaded on his forehead from the pain.

For a second, they were at a standoff. Then someone shouted that the dead were coming through. Sara looked to the doors to see zombies crawling in through broken windows, hauling themselves up over lighting and metal ladders and other equipment.

Then Ray shouted Phoenix's name.

They all turned to see Jack staggering to his feet, blood dribbling down the front of his pants from the wounds in his chest. His flesh had taken on a gray pallor and his mouth was twisted up in hatred.

"Empty," he whispered. "I'm empty."

Dead but risen, Jack rushed at Tania. She screamed but couldn't get her pistol up fast enough. Matt fired the shotgun but only tore off part of Jack's shoulder before he drove Tania down to the floor. She fell hard, the rifle across her back, but she fought against him, trying to keep his jaws away from her. Screaming.

Sara started to rise, to help, but Matt grabbed her by the leg. She spun and saw him glaring at her.

"Don't," he said, afraid to lose her.

Tania and dead Jack scuffled on the floor. Employees screamed as the barricade fell apart, metal scraping as it was shoved out of the way.

Out of the corner of her eye, Sara saw movement.

Phoenix picked up the pistol Zack had dropped, walked toward the table with a strange calm, almost as if she was in a trance. She put the barrel to Eric's forehead and pulled the trigger. The kid's body jerked and then went slack in the chair like a discarded doll.

Jack went still. Tania tossed his corpse off of her.

The dead fell all over the barricade and inside the studio, dropping to the ground. Sara couldn't help staring at them, waiting for a twitch, for some sign that they would start moving again.

Nothing.

Sobbing, still clutching the gun, Phoenix went to her father. Professor Cormier, the lady medium, and the two TV hosts began to stir. They let go of one another. Eric's hand fell from Bell's, flopping wetly to the floor.

Phoenix knelt by her father, pressed her face into his chest. "I'm so sorry. But I couldn't let them . . . couldn't let them kill you."

A terrible smile stretched across the professor's face, but his eyes were still closed.

"Spoiled it all. Spoiled our fun," Cormier said, in the voice of a very old woman.

And then his features went slack and his eyelids fluttered, and he began to wake.

"Phoenix, sweetie?" he asked, in a voice that must have been his own.

Who or what that other voice had belonged to, Sara hoped never to learn.

Zack came to sit next to her and Matt.

Ray moved around the table, checking on the other sleepers who had awakened.

Noah looked at Tania, but she turned away from him, no one to comfort either of them.

"It's over," Matt said, speaking through his pain.

"Yeah," Zack agreed. "But what's next?"

Sara had been feeling a rush of relief. Matt would survive. They would get him help. Things would be terrible for a while, but in time they would return to normal. Hope had risen within her. But Zack's words sent an icy shiver up her back.

"What do you mean?" Sara asked.

He glanced at her, but then looked down, staring at the hand in which he'd held the gun that had killed Jack.

"There's always something that's next," Zack said. "Something uglier than the last time. We mess with things without thinking, screw with the natural order of the world. Disaster hits. Then we clean it up and keep going. People don't learn."

Sara reached out and held his hand, squeezed it, forced him to look at her.

"Then we'll have to teach them."

EPILOGUE

Five Weeks Later, Pelham, New York

A forest of black umbrellas surrounded the grave of Hal Gaines. Matt and Sara stood at the head of their father's simple coffin without any shelter from the rain. Umbrellas had been offered and refused. Both of them wanted the rain on them. Matt didn't ask, but he suspected Sara's reason mirrored his own. It had rained that day, the skies heavy with dark menace, so this only seemed an appropriate farewell. But more than that, it all felt like one long storm to Matt, and when it ended, and the sky cleared, and the sun shone, they would all have a new beginning.

Five weeks just to bury their dad—it seemed unbelievable. It seemed wrong. But the entire northeast quadrant of the United States and some areas of southeastern Canada were recovering from the most catastrophic event in either nation's history. The federal, state, and local governments, the military, and private organizations had been first responders in the aftermath, and more had come from across both countries and around the world. With the difficulty telling the newly dead from those who had risen from the grave, the task of tallying the loss of life seemed impossible, but estimates ranged from eighty thousand to over a quarter of a million.

Identifying those people—if the dead had left enough of them to be identified—would take years. Some would simply never be found; their families would never know what had happened to them. Matt didn't know what would be worse, knowing the grisly details or holding out hope forever.

If identifying the newly dead seemed a monumental task, finding a way to ID the risen presented an even more insurmountable problem. They had dug themselves out and wandered far from where they had been buried. With some it would be simple, since they had visited the homes of those they loved and even identified themselves. But with others—and the *New York Times* had quoted a White House source as estimating the number of displaced corpses at north of a million—it would take DNA testing. Decades would pass. Samples would be taken, remains tagged, and then they'd be put in storage or buried en masse to be exhumed later if DNA matches came through.

America would never be the same.

The world—knowing what it did now, that spirits existed, that ghosts were real, that in some way human beings continued after death—would never be the same. It was too early to know what new shape the world would take, but change rippled through the human race.

Sara took Matt's hand.

Matt glanced at his sister, saw the little rivulets running down her face, her tears merging with the rain, and he put an arm around her and they stood close together. He told himself they were fortunate and tried not to choke on the bitterness of it. As they'd entered the cemetery, they had both stared out the car windows. Most of the graves were disturbed, damp piles of dirt or little towers of upturned soil like giant anthills in front of headstones, showing where the dead had dug themselves up from below. Some headstones were cracked or knocked over. Many of those graves would remain empty for quite some time, waiting for their inhabitants to be returned, reinterred.

With so many dead, so much demand for funeral and burial services, it had taken five weeks to arrange for Hal Gaines to be buried. Matt knew other people who were still waiting; he knew they were lucky, but the word made him feel sick. They'd gotten the only casket they could find, a showroom model, and the flowers that decorated it now, as the rain fell and pattered a rhythm on top of the black umbrellas, had been stolen from Mrs. Goldschmidt's garden. If she'd been alive, she'd have yelled at them for going into her backyard. But she was beyond caring, and Sara couldn't say good-bye to their father without flowers. It meant something to her, so Matt made it happen.

Sara would be his responsibility now. They would stay together. They had already agreed to sell the house. Neither of them slept well under that roof anymore. Finishing college would wait. Matt had thought vaguely about night classes, but he had to take care of Sara, make sure she finished high school and got into college herself. He had to be the man his father had raised him to become.

Rain streaked his face and ran down the back of his neck from his freshly cut hair. He'd shaved the goatee as well. Too much work, and looking in the mirror one day, he'd realized it didn't make him look older or more mature. It just made him look like he was trying to be someone new, his own man instead of just Hal Gaines's boy from Pelham.

Now he couldn't think of anything he wanted more than for people to know him as Hal Gaines's boy. His father had always been proud of him. Matt intended to make sure he always would be.

He and Sara stood in the rain and listened to the pastor talk about life after death, about the soul, and about how their father had gone to his eternal rest. But the words sounded strangely hollow now. If Professor Cormier's theories were correct—and a lot of people now believed they were—then the souls of the dead, the pure goodness in them, went on to that eternity or nirvana that religions around the world promised. But their spirits, maybe the selfish, petty parts of them, were left behind as ghosts. And they were never at rest.

The pastor concluded and everyone began to gather around. Someone began to sing an old hymn, a song about owing their hearts to God. Matt only mouthed the words as he and Sara went to the casket. He kissed his fingers and touched them to the cold, rain-slicked metal. Sara sobbed and bent, putting both hands against the casket, and Matt helped her to stand, pulled her away.

"He's all right now," Matt whispered in her ear. "The best of him is gone, somewhere safe. We have to look after each other now, baby girl. That's what he'd want."

Sara nodded and clung to him, not even chiding him for using their father's old nickname for her.

Matt and Sara went past the pastor, around to the other side, and started toward the waiting car. Other mourners followed, still raising their voices in song as, one by one, they said their good-byes to Hal Gaines.

Black umbrellas appeared from behind them, shielding them

from the rain. Matt shivered, realizing for the first time just how completely drenched he and Sara were. He looked around and saw Zack holding an umbrella over Sara. The kid's father was doing the same for Matt, while his mother held her own. Zack had stayed with Matt and Sara for days before regular phone service was restored and his parents were finally able to get through. They had been up in Canada for a romantic getaway when the crisis had struck, and the border had been closed. But then they'd come home and been reunited, and Zack had his parents again.

Matt had been happy for him and jealous at the same time. Sara had admitted feeling the same. But they were good neighbors, and Zack had been her best friend forever, so they were almost like family.

And now Matt thought that maybe Sara and Zack were going to be more than just friends. As the kid shared his umbrella with her, Sara gazed up into his eyes, and then she clung to him, sharing the shelter from the rain, and Zack kissed the top of her head.

Once upon a time, as her older brother, Matt would have been concerned. But Zack had done the unthinkable for her. He'd confessed to Sara—and she had then told Matt—that he'd had nightmares about pulling the trigger every night for the first few weeks, when he could manage to sleep. He still had trouble sleeping, but the nightmares didn't come so often.

Zack had a lot of courage, and he loved Sara. Matt was happy to have him around.

At the car, they thanked Zack's parents, who started walking back to their own car.

"I'll see you at home," Sara said, and she kissed Zack on the lips.

When the kid saw Matt watching them, he blushed a little. Matt liked him even more for that.

"Here, take my umbrella," Zack said, handing it to Sara.

"Thanks, man," Matt said, as he opened the passenger door for his sister.

But Sara's gaze was elsewhere. She looked past Zack and her brother, back toward the grave site. A ripple of dread filled Matt as he turned, and then he saw the two girls coming toward them and found himself smiling in surprise.

"Hey. I'm sorry. I didn't even know you were coming."

Tania had cut her blond hair to shoulder length. It made her look older, much less like the child star she'd once been. The girl with her had short, stylishly severe black hair. They'd been walking hand in hand, but now Tania released her and stepped close to hug Matt.

"How could I not come? I'd be dead if not for you guys."

Matt felt such gratitude. Part of him hadn't ever wanted to see any of the people he met on that horrible day ever again. And yet there was something about being in the company of people who had been through it with him, a kind of comfort and understanding that no one else could share.

"Thank you so much," he said. "It means a lot."

Tania broke the embrace and turned to the girl with her. "Matt, this is Emma. Emma, Matt."

As Matt shook Emma's hand, Tania moved on to hug Sara and Zack. Any awe they'd once felt at her fame had vanished in the *Sunrise* studio that day in August, but they were both as glad to see her as Matt was.

"Nice to meet you," Matt said to Tania's girlfriend.

"And you," Emma replied, her smile sad. "I'm just sorry it isn't under better circumstances."

"Me, too."

"So I have you to thank for keeping her alive, huh?"

Matt smiled. "Tania did just fine on her own."

"Okay, so wait," Sara said, one hand on her hip, the other clutching Zack's umbrella, leaving him to get rained on. "I thought you guys broke up. Wasn't that the whole big deal?"

Emma stared at Sara for a second, taken aback by the question. Then she shook her head, smiling, eyes alight with mischief, and Matt saw what Tania must have seen in her.

"When something like this happens, you realize what really matters. I . . ." Her smile vanished. "All that day, I thought Tania was dead. And now, well, everything's different, isn't it? It's like a new age. A time for second chances."

Tania reached for her hand and Emma took it. "We both made mistakes. I put my career first. I won't be doing that again."

"I'm happy for you both," Matt said.

"Thanks," Tania said, and he noticed that she squeezed Emma's hand a little tighter, as though she wished she would never have to let go again.

"You're staying in L.A., though?" Zack asked.

"For now," Emma said. "It's home."

Tania looked at Matt. "Have you heard from Noah?"

"Not a word," he replied.

"And we don't want to," Sara snapped.

Matt held up a hand. "Hey. Whatever else he did, we might not be alive without him."

"I heard from him," Tania said. "Talked to him last week."

"Is he back at school?"

"No," Tania replied. "He has an older sister in Pennsylvania. Did you know he was from there?"

Matt shook his head. "I never asked."

"I guess his mother died when he was in high school, and he never got along with his father. But he stayed with his sister for a while, and now he's joining the army."

"What a surprise," Zack said, voice thick with sarcasm.

But Matt couldn't share Zack and Sara's disdain. How had he never known these things about Noah? They'd lived on the same floor, debated a hundred times in the halls and common areas, and spent the worst day in the history of the nation keeping each other alive. Matt and Noah had had nothing in common except their dislike for each other, or so he'd thought. But Noah's mother had died, just as Matt's had. His family consisted of him, his father, and his sister. They weren't the same, not at all. But they had more in common than they'd known, and the knowledge made Matt feel an odd regret he didn't think he would ever understand.

"It's too bad he's not going back to school," Matt said. "He's a smart guy. Probably would have been a good engineer."

Tania cocked her head. "He'll go back eventually, I think. He said after all he'd seen, he wanted to help. There's so much work that needs to be done that he wanted to serve." She smiled. "But he said from now on, he just wants to take orders, let someone else make the decisions."

Matt laughed. "Are you sure we're talking about the same guy?"

"Hey," Sara said, "why are we all standing in the rain? You guys should come back to the house."

"Oh, I don't think . . ." Tania started, glancing at Emma.

"No, Sara's right. Come visit with us. I'm sure we could all use something hot to drink right now," Matt said.

Again, Tania looked at her girlfriend.

Emma lifted their twined hands, joined so tightly, and kissed Tania's fingers. Then she looked at Matt, and at Sara and Zack. "If you're sure it's no trouble, we'd love to."

Alexandria, Virginia

PHOENIX LAY IN BED with the shades drawn, headphones on, listening to music to drown out the sound of the rain on the windows. The room smelled stuffy and musty, and she knew part of that smell came from her. She'd been wearing the same oversized purple T-shirt and blue plaid flannel pajama pants since the day before yesterday. A plate with two barely touched pieces of pizza sat on the desk by her closet. Clothes were hung and piled everywhere.

Today she would get up. She had decided. For the past five weeks she had gone through huge mood swings, cycles of mania and depression that she was aware of but which she could not control. As though trapped inside her body, looking out through her eyes, all Phoenix could do was try to hold on tight and go for the ride.

"Get up," she said aloud.

Her body didn't respond. *Just a few more minutes,* she thought, closing her eyes, listening to the music.

When the smell of the room became too much for her, her nose wrinkling in disgust, she opened her eyes. According to the clock on her nightstand, nearly another hour had passed.

With a sigh, she forced herself to sit up, then flopped onto her pillow again and remained there, watching ten more minutes tick away before she sat up again. This time she threw back the covers and slid her legs off the mattress.

"God, it stinks in here," she said to herself.

Phoenix had always muttered to herself, a habit she'd picked up from her mother. She wondered if she'd been doing it more lately.

Pulling the headphones off, she dropped them on the bed and went over to the windows. She opened the shades, squinting against the daylight, and saw with some surprise that the rain had stopped. The sky had begun to clear, patches of blue visible in the gray.

Some people might have taken that as a good omen. To Phoenix, it was just the weather.

She opened both windows, letting in the fresh, chilly, early autumn air. Immediately she felt more awake, and some of the unpleasant odor of her bedroom diminished.

Shoving down her pajama pants, she stepped out of them and started for her bedroom door. Before she reached it, there came a knock. Without waiting for an invitation, her mother opened the door.

"Hey, you're up!" Mary Cormier said brightly. Then she frowned and looked around. "Wow, it stinks in here."

"Gee, thanks," Phoenix said. Her left calf itched, and she scratched at it with the heel of her right foot, feeling the stubble there and realizing how badly she needed to shave her legs.

"No, seriously," her mother said. "It smells like a men's locker room."

Phoenix laughed, hooked a dirty pair of underwear off the floor with her toes, and flicked it at her mother.

"Hey!" her mom said.

"When have you ever been in a men's locker room?" Phoenix asked.

Mary put her hands on her hips. "I've been a lot of places you don't know about."

"Eeew," Phoenix said, smiling. She could never resist her mom's humor. Besides, the woman deserved points for trying.

"So, you're up. Does that mean you're going to have lunch with your father today, after all?"

She studied her mother's face. In high school, all of Phoenix's guy friends had teased her about how beautiful her mother was, like making inappropriate comments about her mom was some kind of sport. Mary Cormier had always been beautiful, and she admitted to being sassy, which Phoenix had informed her many times often meant she was a flirt. The woman had come out of a marriage to a man who had stopped noticing her, and she'd spent all the time since regaining her confidence.

Phoenix was proud of her mother. It was herself she was ashamed of, herself that she couldn't live with.

"I just want to take a shower and clean up in here. If I don't strip the sheets and put in a load of laundry—"

"I'll do that for you," her mom said. "You go. You need to get out of here, and you need to see your father. Also, Ray called again this morning."

Phoenix took a breath and let it out slowly. Her father had quickly become one of the most famous people in the country, maybe the world. Every news program and talk show wanted him on, every magazine wanted an interview, and the heads of governments and churches wanted private meetings. The publisher couldn't print copies of his book fast enough to keep up with demand. Everybody wanted a piece of Professor Joe Cormier. He'd been to the White House twice since the Uprising. Lots of people hated him, and blamed him and Annelise—who'd gone into seclusion—for what had happened. But most people ignored their part in it in the beginning and just wanted to know more about how it was possible, what it all meant, and how they could be sure it wouldn't happen again.

Reporters wanted to talk to Phoenix, too. They wanted to talk about how it had all ended, and if she was afraid of what would become of her now. The police in New York were still investigating, and no decision had yet been made as to whether they would charge her with murder in the killing of Eric Honen. A spokesman for the White House had already indicated that the president would issue a pardon for any charges that might be brought against her.

She'd been the one to stop it, after all.

But Phoenix wished they would charge her with something. Eric was dead, and she had pulled the trigger, and it didn't seem right that she should be free to sleep all day, hiding out from the press, while his parents were burying him.

Except that they had forgiven her, and that only made it worse. They'd come to visit, and they'd hugged her and forgiven her. Everyone who'd been in the studio, and nearly all of the news reports afterward that mentioned her, had declared that what she'd done had stopped the Uprising. Jim, the medic who had so betrayed her, had come back into the studio when the dead had all collapsed and had been the first to examine Eric, and he'd told Mr. and Mrs. Honen—and any reporter who asked—that the boy would have bled to death from having his arm amputated without proper care. He'd left out certain details, like how he'd abandoned them all, and that if he'd stayed, he might have been able to stanch the bleeding. But in trying to avoid any blame himself, he deflected a lot of it from Phoenix as well.

The only one who didn't seem ready to forgive her was the girl she saw when she looked in the mirror, those green eyes so accusatory.

Zack had killed someone, too—pulled the trigger—but he'd done it in self-defense. He hadn't murdered anyone. The girl in the mirror, though . . .

"Phee," her mother said.

"I know."

Mary Cormier put two fingers under her daughter's chin and lifted her head, forcing Phoenix to meet her eyes.

"You should call Ray back. You like him, don't you?"

Phoenix nodded. "A lot. I'm just not sure I'm ready."

"Fine. Later, then. But at least go and see your father. No book signings, no cameras. Just you and him."

"Why are you his biggest fan all of a sudden?"

Her mother sighed, shaking her head. "I'm not. But I've never hated the man. You know that. I loved him once, and if not for him, I wouldn't have you. You finally started being father and daughter, and I'd hate to see you let that slip away now."

Phoenix knew she was right.

"We've still got a lot of lost time to make up for, right?" Phoenix said. "All those weekends he forgot he had a daughter? But maybe now he'd like to forget all over again."

Mary Cormier gave a little gasp, and the shock on her face looked entirely genuine. "Don't ever say that. You protected him, Phoenix. You watched over him when others would have let him die. You probably saved his life, and you know that what you did saved *thousands* of lives."

Phoenix's eyes burned with tears. She felt her lip quiver and hated it. "But what I *did* . . ."

Her mother slid her arms around her and Phoenix slumped gratefully into her embrace.

"What you did was horrible. A terrible thing," she whispered. "But you did what you had to. For the rest of your life, you'll have to live with it."

"How do I do that?" Phoenix asked.

"You just do. You go on. Just like we all have to go on now. But I've been thinking about this, honey . . ." Her mother stepped back, holding her at arm's length.

"About what?" Phoenix asked.

"You always talk about your relationship with your father in terms of making up for lost time. But lost time is just that. It's lost. It's the past, sweetie. Whatever he did before, and whatever you did that day, none of it matters today. And it won't matter tomorrow. You can't change anything that's gone before, but if you spend your time trying to make up for what you did, or expecting your dad to make up for the past . . . well, that's a lot of weight to carry around. You've just got to forgive him and start over."

Phoenix looked at her. "Just like that?"

"Just like that. And you've got to forgive yourself, too."

Phoenix wanted to scream. All of her anger and shame rose up and she wanted to direct it at her mother, but she held her tongue. Her mom didn't deserve any of that.

"You say that like it's easy."

Mary Cormier laughed softly, without humor. But her eyes were hopeful. "I know it isn't easy, Phee. But you're strong enough to do the hard things. And you need to do this. The whole world's waking up now, to the realization that there are no guarantees. Forgiveness can't wait. Love can't wait. The only day we can count on is today, and there isn't time for fear or regret. No time for hiding from your life. Just for living."

Phoenix smiled, knowing that when her mother got all inspirational there was no room for argument. She stepped in close for another hug and then broke the embrace.

"No time for sitting around being stinky. My shower can't wait."

Her mom sighed, then reached up and stroked her face, looking at her with such love that Phoenix had to look away. "Will you at least try to take this all to heart?"

Phoenix nodded. "I already have. And I'll keep working on it."

"That's all I can ask," her mother said.

As Phoenix left the room, her mother started to strip the dirty sheets off of her bed.

In the bathroom, she ran the water for the shower, waiting for it to get hot. As steam began to fill the room, her mother's words resonated in her head. *No time for hiding from your life. Just for living.*

She stepped into the shower, the water almost too hot, and she could feel the stink and sweat of the past couple of days sloughing off of her. When she started shampooing her hair, the scent of fruit and flowers mixed with the steam.

Maybe she would call Ray later, after she had lunch with her father. A new start sounded so good, and her mother did make it sound simple, but Phoenix knew it just wasn't that easy.

You could *try, though,* she thought. *A new start. And today is day one.*

She turned her face into the spray of the shower and had a tiny epiphany. In that moment, she thought she really understood what her mother had been telling her.

It wasn't just today.

Every day is day one.